DISINTEGRATION

by j. d. neill

ISBN (print): 978-1-7339739-0-8
ISBN (e-book): 978-1-7339739-1-5

Published by:
Lanni LV, LLC
1000 S. Green Valley Parkway,
Suite 440–269
Henderson, NV 89074

Title: Disintegration
Printed in the United States of America

Cover design by Tim Durning
Typeset by Scribe Inc., Philadelphia, Pennsylvania.

This is a work of fiction. While places and many of the incidents are based upon real events and the author's experiences; individuals described in this book are composites or the product of the author's imagination. Names and characters are used fictitiously, any resemblance to actual individuals, living or dead, is coincidental.

UK Copyright Service 2019
4 Tavistock Avenue,
Didcot, Oxfordshire.
OX11 8NA, United Kingdom.

I dedicate this book to the men who never hurt me:

Jack Hayward Broom,
my grandfather.

Dean Hayward Neill,
my brother.

Stephen Hayward Silberkraus,
my son,

Sawyer Hayward Silberkraus,
his son.

And to the best of husbands,
my dearest,
Tom.

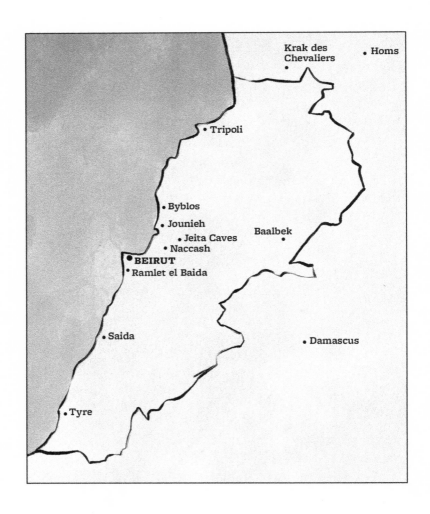

Krak des
Chevaliers

Homs

Tripoli

Byblos

Jounieh

Jeita Caves

Baalbek

Naccash

BEIRUT

Ramlet el Baida

Saida

Damascus

Tyre

Character List:

in order of appearance:

Genie	Main character
Rob	Genie's husband
Nashad	Rob's coworker
Adnan	Rob's coworker, Abbad's fixer
Shana	Adnan's Irish wife
Abbad	Rob's Boss 'Little Boss'
Stuart	Friend studying Arabic in Beirut
Noura	Maid
Mark Langdon	Rob's coworker
Kat	Mark's wife
Colonel	Rob's friend
James	Mark & Kat Langdon's child
Karam	Genie and Rob's Syrian friend
Doreen	Genie's mom
Kourk	Landlord and friend
Rubina	Kourk's wife
Victor	Neighbor
Nabil	Neighbor and doctor
Mary	Nabil's Irish wife
David	Teacher/ friend
Jacqui	Genie's friend—a teacher
Roslyn	Genie's friend—a teacher
Khalil	Roslyn's Lebanese husband
Keith	Rob and Genie's New Zealand friend
Margaret	Keith's Canadian girlfriend
Michel	Head gunman at Genie's birthday party

Political Entities:

Camille Chamoun	Lebanese Politician, Maronite Christian, Former President
Pierre Gemayel	Lebanese Politician, Maronite Christian, Founder Right wing Phalangist/Ktaeb Party
Kamal Jumblatt	Lebanese Politician Leader Druze, Left wing Militia Leader
Maarouf Saad	Pro Palestinian, Assassinated Politician
Hafez Al-Assad	Syrian President
Yasir Arafat	Palestinian leader (PLO)

Political Groups:

ISF Gendarmerie	Lebanese National police and security force
Lebanese National Movement (LNM)	leftist militias
Phalangists/Ktaeb	Maronite Christian militias
PLO	Palestine Liberation Organization
People's Liberation Army (PLA)	Druze leftist
Mourabitoun	leftist Independent Nasserite Movement

Orange blossoms and Blood.

Bartering and bombs.

Smiles and knives.

That was my Lebanon.

1

ENGLAND, 1972

SINCE HE LEFT THEY HAVEN'T spoken—not once. Genie has received communiques from company lawyers in London, and a single long telegram from Rob:

'Miss you, love you, you'll love Beirut, ticket
following. Georgina, this is more than I ever
imagined. I'm just 27 and running major manufacturing for the entire Middle East: Baghdad,
Tehran, Amman, and Beirut. Will explain all when
you get here.'

The bulb overhead is harsh. *How different it looks now the furniture has gone.* But it is long gone, on a ship, hopefully on its way to Beirut.

Briefly, she wonders if she'll ever see her belongings again and switches off the light, the moon is sufficient, she doesn't want to look around, it no longer resembles their home. They were happy here, but already it is of the past.

She goes through the motions to prepare for the night, decides to stay clothed, less vulnerable than undressed. The single remaining bed is comfortable, the charity shop will collect it before she leaves, but sleep won't come.

Her boss's voice in her head is insistent.

"Why do you have to go?"

Thinking back to that day, the day when everything changed, she wonders the same thing, forces herself to face what's ahead, and tries to stem the concern which has threatened to suck her in since Rob first mentioned leaving.

She faintly regrets the lack of courage which prevented her from refusing to go, but she was raised to believe she couldn't make it alone, needed someone to complete her; and from the first Rob had seemed to be the one.

He challenged her to stand up, question her views and offered a promise of something better. She wanted that. Something better. Something more. More freedom, more money, and no violence, to forget her childhood struggles, the darned socks and the constant lack of everything.

"Let's get married?" Voilà. Three words and two birds with one stone, the decision was made. Rob's proposal came at precisely the right time, ended the years of daily fear of her father's volatile temper.

Marriage equaled escape and security, and it had turned out well. She grew closer to Rob and made extraordinary progress with her career.

My career! So much for that. A deep sigh floats upward. *For one whole day, I was on top of the world.*

Now Rob has been gone for over a month, and she wonders if at any time she could have slowed the process, altered anything, she doubts it. But tonight she is reflective, and her mind floats her back just a few short weeks . . .

The large group of stern grey faces watches her, not one smile. No indication they are softening. She hasn't shown any fear, but inside she's quaking. This is extremely important and not just to her, the livelihoods of hundreds depend on the outcome of what she is trying to achieve today.

In for a penny, she thinks, and she continues:

". . . You, Gentlemen, are in the unique position to help put the Great back in Great Britain and at the same time to singlehandedly affect, for the better, the lives of hundreds of men, women, and children. Hardworking people who ask for nothing more than to provide a solid days work in return for the chance to feed their families and keep a roof over their heads."

Genie glances around the room. Impossible to read. She thuds her hand on the table.

"We must stop buying inferior imports at the expense of our own industries. Look around at what's happening across this country." She sweeps her arm around the room. "You have the power to start turning the tide, begin to make a difference." After a pause to let the idea sink in, she continues. "Sign a five-year contract with us. That's all it will take. We can then contract competitively for raw materials, you get the absolute best product available at a good price—and we're all winners."

Frowns from her group. Her staff thinks she's come on too strong, these hard-headed men aren't accustomed to dealing with a woman. In England, in 1972 the 'fair sex' is supposed to be secretaries, shop assistants, teachers or housewives, not pushy businesswomen. But she figured she had nothing to lose. Hoped the long hair, long legs and gentle south of England accent would soften them a little.

Anyway, without this contract, the mill would probably close its doors, the biggest and last mill in England. Imports from Asia were killing everything, and she had built an affinity with the hardworking men and women whose families for generations had built up sweat equity in the outcome of the aged mill. She cared about what happened to them.

It worked. The contract was signed. The mill was safe, for five years at least. And they made her a director.

A director. She could hardly believe it as she touched the shiny new sign on her door and left to go home, dying to share her news with Rob.

Word had spread like the flood and when she walked out the sound of foot stomping and applause fought and overpowered the click and clack of the machinery, made her feel six feet tall.

What a fantastic day. She smiled and waved, had never been happier, not imagining how soon that would all begin to unravel.

Full of excitement from the promotion she rushed home to prepare a romantic dinner by candlelight.

Rob's look of stress when he walked in, his new almost permanent look, disappeared and his dark eyes crinkled in surprise when she popped a cork from a not bad bottle of champagne.

He raised an eyebrow, looked at her tummy.

"No," she said. "But I do have news, great news actually. Peter made me a director."

"Wow." A long minute passes.

"I thought you'd be proud of me? What's the matter?"

"I am—proud of you, Georgina. It's just the timing. I got news today, too. Coincidentally it might seem. I've been offered a kind of promotion."

"That's unbelievable!"

And then it came:

"It's not so simple, The thing is, well, it's overseas, in Beirut."

"Beirut, are you mad, Rob? We've finally settled down here, why in God's name would we want to go there?"

"Maybe we should talk about this later."

"No, Let's do it now."

And they did.

At first it is hard for him to get the words out, he doesn't want a fight tonight. In reality, he never wants a fight. But this is out of his hands. He takes a gulp of the champagne and plows in.

"If I don't go I'm out of a job in six months, they're downsizing. In Beirut, we'd have an apartment overlooking the ocean, staff, short hours, great money, travel." He runs out of steam, rubs his hands through his short, black hair. "Anyway, we don't have to accept. It's up to you."

Genie looks out of the window at the dark, craggy hills toward Pendle, where witches once lived. As if on cue a series of lightning flashes light the room adding a biblical dimension. Almost choreographed bursts of thunder follow. They stare out of the French doors at the rocky outcroppings of the Lancashire moors beyond.

"Up to me?" A hard lump forms in her throat, it's difficult to breathe. "Will you forgive me if you lose this opportunity because I don't want it?" She senses she's caught in a trap from which no-one will win, but she's not giving up yet, not without a fight.

"I thought this was to be our forever home, you brought me up here, told me to make a life for myself. Well, I've made

a life—found something I'm good at. What am I supposed
to say?"

Unlike Georgina, who is ready to do battle, much of his
energy evaporates. He slides deeper into his comfortable leather
armchair, and he looks at her angry face. How quickly the joy of
a few moments ago has disappeared, now she looks at him like
he's a stranger.

"You knew our life wouldn't be nine to five. You had a
horror of being like our parents . . ."

She cuts him off.

"A horror of repeating their failures. I wanted a HOME
Rob, that no-one could take away. I wanted to sleep with someone who loves me and who would still be there in the morning,
no matter what."

She gets up, paces the room which suddenly feels too small
to contain both of them. The clock strikes the hour, and she
turns to glare at it. Why did she ever buy that stupid thing? It's
ten o'clock, and she'd expected to be snuggled up in his arms
by now, instead, here they are pouring ashes on the last of her
splendid day.

"For God's sake Georgina, grow up. You sound like a
romantic teenager! Be honest. You want things. A house, holidays, cars, travel, these things have a price."

Outside, the thunder grows louder. The drumbeat of hailstones clatters from the top of the car parked close by. God, she
hopes it rains forever, harder and harder, so they never have to
leave.

"And where is it written that I'm the one who has to pay?
I have a career now, too. This is our life, I'm not merely a bit
player. Everything I want is here."

But she knows that she will lose this argument when he says, "Oh. Genie, come on. Can you deny how bad it's become here? England isn't what it once was. Power outages, unemployment, the IRA bombs, and now strikes and rationing. Did you ever imagine they'd cut off the electricity every other day?"

He stops, and in a quieter tone, he tells her. "Candlelight is no longer romantic. On alternate days if we want to take a bath or eat a hot meal, we have to go to a friend's house. How can we go on like this?"

She breathes in deeply as she comprehends the depth of his frustration. Why hasn't she realized how hard this has been for him?

"It's not a civilized way to live, the government calls for constant states of emergency, four already, and there's no sign of it ending. People stand in line in the rain for hours for petrol, that's on the days they're even allowed to buy it." He glances at her. "I waited for two hours yesterday, and people physically fought at the pumps over who was first or who was entitled."

His voice holds neither his earlier conviction nor any enthusiasm, but he feels the need to get it all out, to make her see. He leans his head against the soft leather back of the chair. God if he could just close his eyes and go to sleep, wake up tomorrow and have all this be over.

"Anyway, I have no choice. If you stop for a minute and think, you'll see it's an opportunity for us both. You get your security, your better life and we can build a home and family of our own together—just not here," he stops, exhausted from his dilemma.

"But . . . what about me?"

With a tremendous effort, he pulls himself up and takes her into his arms before he answers. He feels her resistance, knows this is an enormous ask. In spite of all the daily challenges she loves life here, she has the gift of breezing through and making the best of things, an ability that he has never possessed.

"Don't you see this could be great for us both, we'd never achieve anything like this here. The biggest adventure of our lives."

A last flash of lightning, a long pause and a distant roll of thunder signals the energy of the storm has gone, leaving in its wake just a patter of rain against the floor to ceiling windows. Like the storm, Rob is spent.

The flashes outside remind Georgina that this wild, beautiful part of Northern England which has finally become her home will also be left behind, and she will need to embrace yet another new life, new job, new friends.

He takes her face in his hands and delivers his promise. "If you're unhappy after you've given it a fair try, we'll come home."

She relaxes against him.

And that was that. She can't pinpoint why, with so little argument, she has given in, resigned, and now is prepared to follow Rob into the unknown.

The pale light of dawn creeps across the ceiling, and she glances out to the purple and pink Lancastrian hills. Morning has arrived and time has run its race. What is the point in continuing to wonder about his promises or if this new job will be the start of an upscale new life, the comfortable, stable life she yearns for? It's time.

She had severe reservations about going to live up north a couple of years ago, and that worked out, so the move to Beirut has to be an opportunity, she thinks, doesn't it? Her life is ahead of her, and anyway, in a few hours she leaves this house, and a few days later, when she has taken care of a personal matter, she'll board a plane, so it's moot.

Beirut is known as a pearl in the desert. She'll soon see for herself if the reputation is deserved and how Rob's promises pan out.

2
BEIRUT, SPRING 1972

"FASTEN YOUR SEAT BELTS FOR landing in Beirut."

She grasps the glass as gravity beckons it toward the floor. The stewardess slips it firmly from her hand.

The Middle East Airlines plane banks, circles from the center of the country, the rugged mountains, the fertile plains of the Bekaa Valley and Damascus, the ancient capital of Syria, beyond.

Genie peers out of the small window. Through the clouds, the water sparkles below. The plane has begun its descent.

Belatedly the seatbelt sign comes on, and the glamorous hostesses fall into their seats.

She is nervous. At twenty-four this is the first time she has traveled by plane, and it's the farthest from home. She could happily get used to flying. Once she had considered becoming a stewardess, but now she realizes she is more suited to being a passenger and letting others spoil her.

The ground rushes to meet them, and she closes her eyes. *Please don't let this all be one gigantic mistake.*

Along the jeweled Mediterranean, Lebanon is uncomfortably straddled by Israel to the south and the mighty Syrian nation to the north. The homeland of intrepid Phoenicians, who once traded to the far ends of the planet, tinier than Puerto Rico, it is nevertheless the gem of the vast Pan Arabian world.

The plane is only half full, and within a few minutes, she is propelled forward by a surge of eager travelers, across the tarmac toward a long white terminal building with a tall flight tower at one end. She lifts her hand to shield her eyes from the bright sun high in the sky, half searching. She doesn't see him.

Her hair clings stickily to her neck, she brushes it back as the overwhelming humidity, heat, and dust settle on her. In the distance, unfamiliar, disconcerting sounds echo, a seductive wail, as invisible minarets send out the afternoon call to prayer.

She pauses to listen.

Under the building and inside the terminal a few men fall to their knees and begin the age-old ritual motion of bowing to Mecca, a line of shoes discarded behind them as they pray. Fascinated yet frightened by this exotic and entirely new experience, she quickly reminds herself not to stare.

The airport is a hive of activity, the heat and the babble approach chaos, a mixture of foreign languages which assails her on all sides and she looks around, eager for Rob to welcome her after their weeks apart.

Most of the people who hug and greet around her are dressed in western clothing, but there is no familiar face for Genie. Strange, fragmented sentences surround her, switching between French and Arabic, peppered with vast amounts of gesticulation and a few other tongues she doesn't recognize.

A pair of pretty, expensively dressed young Arab girls wearing the latest high-end European fashions; Hermes scarves, Gucci handbags, and Ferragamo footwear, almost bump into her. They step back, apologize and run into the Ladies restroom full of giggles. Genie smiles and listens carefully but cannot distinguish what they say.

The cacophony of unfamiliar tongues reverberate in her head, and a wave of dizziness envelops her, threatens to engulf her. She reaches out, grabs onto a tall white column and rests her forehead against it as the mass of people swirl by. Its cool, smooth surface calms her.

In less than three minutes two small women draped head to toe in floating black emerge from the bathroom, still giggling they wave to her. She notices the elegant Ferragamo shoes on their feet and small Gucci purses on their arms as they head for the Saudia Airline desk. Their transformation complete they can now head home to the heart of Arabia.

She smiles to herself as she tries to imagine such a disjointed way of living.

Across the room, a man, dressed in white with sandaled feet and black toenails, busily works "worry beads" through his fingers and quietly watches through hooded eyes which constantly scour left and right, like an angry cat's tail. He is static, only his fingers and his eyes move.

Startled by a blaring sound, a number of bags appear on a moving carousel behind her. Several of them pass before she recognizes the small four-leafed clover emblems tied to two cases and she successfully retrieves them. They are heavy but she relaxes a little now she's reunited with something familiar.

The "Exit" signs are not far but she hesitates, scans faces for a glimpse of Rob. *Where in heaven's name is he?* she wonders.

People swirl past, unselfconscious and animated, she inhales an occasional whiff of garlic as they bump her.

A few snap fingers at hired help who struggle to keep up while carrying their employer's bags; others travel with goats, pots, pans, and disregard traditional suitcases in favor of cloth and paper parcels clutched close to their breasts.

Minutes pass and no-one comes. The area is clear now, quieter, just a few bags remain on the carousel. She sits on her suitcase and searches in her purse. No local currency, no phone number except the London office of Rob's firm.

Should she make a reversed charge call? What would they think?

She shoves everything back and snaps the lock shut, notices for the first time her ordinary English handbag, nothing like the designer ones being carried by many of the wealthy travelers in the airport and she becomes conscious of the curious looks of passing strangers.

She brushes uselessly at the creases in her summer dress, it was white when she started, now she feels grubby and out of place, like a scruffy country cousin.

Don't panic, be patient. It's only been half an hour after all. Anything could have delayed him. He could have gotten the time wrong, even the day? Oh, God. What if he got the day wrong?

She'd have to stay at the airport—where could she go? She doesn't know anyone here. Maybe her family was right, she should have stayed home.

The man with black fingernails materializes, smooth as a serpent. "Bonjour, Ahlan, may I be of service? You seem lost."

Genie is startled, on the verge of tears, she glances around, then back at the man. "Uh. My husband is supposed to be meeting me . . ."

He slowly examines her, his fingers constantly work his worry beads. "He is Lebanese?"

"No he's English—he works here."

"Maalesh, no matter." He snaps his fingers at a porter who lifts her bags, he reaches for Genie's elbow and guides her against her will. She protests but finds herself propelled along, swept outside and along to a row of waiting MBZ taxis. She attempts resistance, but her English manners prevent any real opposition.

Confused and a little overwhelmed she doesn't immediately notice a meticulously dressed young man appear and walk rapidly toward them. Her helper towers over the new arrival but the man holding her elbow bends his head in obeisance as the two men exchange heated words in Arabic. He rapidly scuttles away intimidated, tapping his bent hand against his forehead he continues to apologize as he disappears back into the bowels of the airport.

The taxi driver mutters, deposits the bags on the kerb and moves along to a new fare.

Polite and good looking the new stranger turns to Genie with a slight bow of the head.

"Hello, I am Nashad. I work with Rob. He called and asked me to collect you, so here I am."

Taken aback, she is unable to gather her thoughts and glances at her belongings which have been dumped at her feet then back to Nashad, dumbfounded.

"He called?"

He faces her eye to eye. "You should not speak to strangers."

Genie steps back. "But I . . . Where is Rob, why isn't he here?"

Nashad opens his hands, he has beautiful dark eyes with enviable eyelashes and when he briefly smiles his teeth are perfect. He signals another porter to handle her bags and turns to

Genie, his shoulders raised and palms outstretched toward the sky. "Our boss had plans for him."

"Boss—plans?" *Why does she keep parroting his words? She must sound like a moron.*

"The big boss," he walks on, leads her to a waiting car. She follows.

The heat has already gone from the sun and inside the car is cool. Nashad is extremely polite as he settles her inside the back seat, but he seems shy and although articulate with a near-perfect command of English, he drives silently as Genie peers out at alien back streets, headed blindly to who knows where or what?

Makeshift light bulbs dangle from yards of cable as they pass myriad shops, wares cascade from crates on the cracked and desiccated sidewalks outside. Pepsi Cola signs and rusted fridges abound. So different from the wide open moors she left behind.

Small, brown-skinned, tousle-headed people crouch over stoves and brew coffee in long-handled blue pots. Occasionally she catches the fragrance of roast lamb from cone-shaped meats, spit roasting in cafes along the way.

The car turns frequently through streets which are grubby and foreign, so narrow she feels like Gulliver trapped in Lilliput. Genie wraps her arms around herself and sighs deeply.

"What have we done?" she whispers to no-one. She closes her eyes and dozes.

The car stops and Genie pulls herself from her reverie. They are parked outside a lone three-story building in the corner of a large cul-de-sac. Gleamingly white and new, it sits on several pillars with extensive gardens underneath, surrounded on the coast side by orange groves which cascade down the hill all the way to the Mediterranean Sea far below.

Nashad turns off the engine and climbs out. "It's at the top," he indicates upward and grabs Genie's bags from the trunk.

The fragrance from the orange blossom is heady, delicious and envelops her. She pauses for a moment, eyes closed she breathes it in. Nashad watches her enjoyment and smiles, then quickly looks away.

Above her head sunlight filters through olive trees which deepen into a thick grove climbing upward, it covers the hillside above them on the far side of the crescent-shaped driveway. She looks hopefully at the building in front of her as Nashad ushers her in.

"Is Rob here?"

"Later," he replies. He notices her expression and reassures her. "Soon."

They walk together into the building and climb the extra wide marble staircase. Nashad insists on carrying her luggage and, although he is diminutive, he is clearly strong and too much of a gentleman to allow a woman to carry her own bags. A light goes on as they reach each floor, still only a faint glow in the afternoon light.

The walls and high ceilings of the building are white and inside it feels cool after the heat of the day. At the top Nashad takes out a key and opens a large, imposing double wooden door, he switches on lights and carries Genie's bags into the hallway.

Ahead through a wide set of open double glass doors, she sees an impressive, long, open plan lounge dining room and beyond sizable terraces which overlook the ocean below. Beirut shimmers on a seemingly distant peninsula.

"How far are we from the city?" she asks.

"Less than a 10-minute drive once you get out of the hills."

The spacious, hardly furnished penthouse occupies the entire top floor. It is fresh and new, never before occupied, rather grand with high ceilings, pale marble floors and French windows which open to the long terrace.

Genie walks cautiously into the room. Nashad does not follow. She looks around and thinks of their small house left behind in England. Certainly, it loses some luster in comparison to this space, but it was their first house, they bought it together, and for months in each spare moment she had sewn curtains and cushions, sanded floors and painted walls to transform it into a home.

All the economies we made to be able to furnish it and now it's gone, sold to a stranger who will probably change it all, she thinks. *And all of our personal possessions have been packed away on a ship, on the way to who knows where?*

"Maghel saleme, Madame Rob," a voice calls out. "Bye,"

Startled from her reverie she turns, but Nashad has already gone.

She walks quickly to the front door and stares out but the landing is empty and his back disappears down the stairway. With a sigh, she closes the apartment door and turns into the adjacent kitchen, an immaculate marvel of hand-painted tiles spanning the end of the building.

In the fridge, she finds bottles of water, wine, a salami, a hunk of cheese, some crackers and a bowl of pears. *Bachelor life!* Her tummy growls, reminds her she hasn't eaten for hours, she takes a pear and hungrily bites into the ripe fruit. Juice runs down her chin and she wipes it away with the back of her hand.

Munching the pear she drags a suitcase along the long cool corridor in search of the master bedroom. More French windows line the passageway to her left, each with its own small balcony and opposite, through open bedroom doors the red and gold of the sunset floods the space with warm light, coloring the marble beneath her feet.

At the far end, she discovers a large pale aqua bathroom beside a larger barely furnished large white room. She dumps her bags and walks outside onto a generous balcony and throws the remains of the pear into the orange groves below her as the sun sinks into the embrace of the Mediterranean and the light quickly fades to blackness.

It is beautiful, she thinks. *But so foreign and so far away.*

The railings support her as she gives in to her fears and the awful sense of loneliness and despair that has been poised to encompass her for weeks. Below and in the distance, lights come on and through misty eyes, Beirut sparkles into life.

With the fading of the sun the air has cooled dramatically, she shivers and goes inside, there is nothing to comfort her here. She rummages through her bag, extracts a framed wedding photo but finds little reassurance in the faces who stare out, blind to a future they could not have foreseen. She embraces them and curls with the picture onto the unmade bed, two single, metal framed creations which have been carelessly pulled together.

The flight and the stress of the day prove exhausting, impossible to resist. She grabs her sweater around her, closes her eyes and falls into a fitful sleep filled with dreams.

A red convertible MGB piled with suitcases snakes across the Lancashire moors, a "Just Married" sign on the back, an attractive young couple hold hands and laugh as The Box Tops blare out:

"Gimme a ticket for an airplane,
Ain't got time to take a fast train
Lonely days are gone, I'm a-goin home."

A gust of wind catches Genie's red scarf, it slips through her fingers and she grabs at it. Rob swerves as Genie clambers recklessly over the back of her seat, almost dislodges the carefully piled bags to catch it. Like a slow-motion butterfly, it floats into the sky above and away. She shields her eyes against the sun, pulls a face and twists her wavy auburn hair into a coil on her neck.

"We'll never get it back."

"You're crazy. Let it go . . ." Rob has the look and quirky smile of a young Jack Nicholson. The same dark 'I know a secret' eyes. His thick, dark brown hair blows in the breeze and he fumbles in the glove compartment for his very expensive Italian designer sunglasses to keep hair out of his eyes, an unusual indulgence. His strong hands grip the wheel and he straightens the car, puts his foot down and speeds on.

She turns in her sleep and whimpers. Her head turns back and forth on the mattress and another fragmented dream engulfs her.

Candlelight—the pop of a champagne cork.

"I'm a director."

Why does he look so uncomfortable about such good news? she wonders.

"This is more than I imagined I could achieve, Genie.— We'll have kids—I'll be the breadwinner—It makes sense."

Rob walks into the quiet house and finds her asleep on the bed nursing their photo, he smiles and drops a small overnight bag on the floor. God, he feels bad that he couldn't make it to the airport. For a few minutes he watches her sleep then reaches out carefully to touch her hair.

The movement disturbs her and she opens her eyes, glances around tries to situate herself and pulls her tired frame into a seated position. Still confused, she sucks in her breath.

He switches on the bedside light and smiles at her.

"You scared me," she says.

He remains still, searches her face. "I've missed you, my love. I'm so sorry I couldn't meet you," he pulls her to him.

She watches quietly. He looks exhausted she notices, as she wrestles with her earlier annoyance.

He sees she is upset and rightly so. *How must she have felt landing in a foreign country with no-one there to meet her?* He shudders to think about it.

"I didn't understand how this would be, Genie, I promise. They pay extravagantly but expect complete dedication, immediate attention. It's a Feudal system if you're not the boss you have no voice!" He looks into her face and can see she wants to understand.

"They sent me to California," he explains.

"California?" she is astonished. "You were in California?"

He nods. "I was at the US partners' factory—I met the people there, looked at their operation—I was supposed to be back two days ago, but there was a delay, I couldn't get back till now," he indicates his bag on the floor. "I didn't know how to reach you. It was last minute, I called your mother but she said you'd already said your goodbyes and left."

It was true, she hadn't told anyone about her last days in England. She had been to visit her father without a word to anyone. He was persona non grata with the family, locked away, but she couldn't leave without a goodbye.

Rob extricates a jewelry box from his bag. "But I come bearing gifts with my deepest, deepest apologies."

He opens the box and takes out a magnificent necklace.

He is tanned but tired after his weeks in the sun and this whirlwind trip. Faint lines have appeared around his eyes and the creases in his cheek were not there two months ago. There's a subtle change in posture she can't yet fathom.

Genie lifts her hair and he fastens the clasp around her neck. She resists the urge to ask more questions, she's too tired to fight right now. She lifts her hand, touches the necklace.

"I guess we'll both have to adjust."

Half expecting another embrace she gets up from the bed, but instead, Rob steps back to look at her.

"Gorgeous." He waves his hand in the air. "What do you think of this place?"

He pulls her through the apartment, seems excited at the home he has found for them. "I know it's almost empty now, but we have a sizable furnishing budget and look at that view! Think you can turn it into a real home for us?"

She nods her head, smiles at him and feels him visibly relax. Finally, he puts his arms around her and sweeps her into him. He sighs. *It's going to be alright.*

She hugs him tightly and heads back to their bedroom.

So what if he couldn't collect me? We're here now in a gorgeous, or potentially gorgeous, penthouse and we'll be living on the Mediterranean earning lots of money! We're adults, away from our childhoods and past lives, able to plot our own future.

She sits on the end of the bed, smiles and pulls him close. "Maybe I could create a nursery now I'm unemployed?" she teases. "Why don't we start the process right away?" She pulls him toward her and brushes her lips on his, gently.

"Kiss my eyelids," he says.

She does. And with a small intake of his breath, the reconnection is immediate. They make love cautiously at first. It seems like forever since they were together. But with every move, the weeks slip farther away.

It's still sweet between them, thank God, she thinks, as Rob falls into a deep, exhausted sleep.

She should be tired but her mind won't let her rest. Not yet. She watches him sleep, the black eyes she loves, so dramatic and unusual in a European face, now hidden under pale eyelids and long dark lashes.

The fragrance from the orange groves below washes over her and she turns at the sound of night creatures outside the window. But as she dozes, a voice in her head begins: *You've left behind friends, family, a promising career, given it all up to follow his dream. You may be poised for adventure, but can you make this work? Will love be enough?*

He turns, reaches out an arm and cradles her to him. She pushes the voice away and drifts into sleep.

3

BEIRUT, 1972

Magical!

THE EARLY WEEKS ARE MAGICAL and Lebanon, she discovers, is a magical place.

She loves the foreignness, even the sound of the names on her tongue. Places which beckon, she recites them aloud, feeling her tongue move in unfamiliar ways: Ashrafieh, Antelias, Byblos, Faraya, Jounieh, Tripoli. And locally the soft whisper of Bourj Hammoud, with its Armenian influences from earlier refugees who, almost a century before, fled Turkey to Beirut.

Genie touches tinkling jewelry, lets silky fabrics slip through her fingers as she browses wide-eyed through the Souks. Their soft sound and labyrinthine alleyways tempt with glittering goods. Rob slips on a long black leather coat which instantly transforms him.

"You look fantastic," she says "It'll be wonderful for winters when we go home."

"But we've just arrived," he laughs. "And I hope this will become home!" But he buys the coat.

Somewhere deep inside the alleyways a transistor radio echoes haunting strains of Arabic music and the distinctive voice of Fairuz sings out, epic yet strangely seductive.

Awareness hits Genie. Rob's right, this is not a holiday it's their life now, together in a far away land.

The freshly familiar fragrance of roasting lamb floats along the narrow aisles and hunger nibbles at her. "God, that smells so good."

"It does, but let's head to Hamra for food, maybe we'll bump into some friends."

Surprisingly no less foreign, the westernized area and modern buildings around Hamra Street pay homage to France but incorporates a decidedly un-European mix of lifestyles.

She has quickly fallen in love with this multicultural part of the city, a trove of fantastic shops and cafes.

Arab and foreign intellectuals sip tea, and everywhere, everyone encourages free thought and speech. Palestinian thinkers in Beirut since 1948, soon after the war and the creation of Israel, share coffee and conversation with foreign diplomats, businessmen, and bankers.

Jeannie and Rob find a seat at the Horseshoe café, unsurprisingly shaped like a horseshoe. A haven for artists, avant guarde thinkers and a host of conspiracy theorists. It is seductive, at once secretive and conspiratorial, but somehow conveying a sense of absolute freedom. They settle in to watch the passing parade.

Several beautiful, slender girls with dramatic, kohl-ringed eyes sashay by followed by equally gorgeous young men, arms around one another, they flirt and tease. One boy slides a hand down and openly squeezes his friend's derriere.

Genie glances at Rob, such public displays are rare in England.

"It's the custom, it signifies nothing here, they are totally unselfconscious," he tells her. "The men even prefer to dance together, you'll see when we go to parties."

Genie laughs and relaxes. "It's like a second honeymoon, but better, I couldn't have imagined it would be like this." She reaches over to Rob and nibbles his ear.

"You do realize when the lab is finished we won't have so much free time?"

"I know."

But he wonders if she has grasped the change about to take place, hopes she will grow to embrace it here and forget the job she loved and all their friends back in England.

She sees his thoughtful look. "Not to worry, while we do have the time can we explore more of the country?"

"Of course."

Maseratis, Alpha Romeos and their designer-clad drivers cruise past them in a constant mechanical promenade of wealth and privilege, seeing and being seen.

She watches old and new Lebanon jostle for a place. Alongside the Italian machines, lined and sunburnt villagers, aged well beyond their years, are swathed in yards of dusty fabric hanging loosely between their legs. They swish sticks against the rumps of loudly braying donkeys, who precariously transport goods tied to their backs and attempt to avoid the fumes, praying not to be squashed by the expensive sports cars.

He sees her watching. "Such a contrast in lifestyles."

"Yes," she nods. "And brash, expensive modernity looks to be the winner."

He takes a bite of the three-tiered burger and sips his milkshake. "Uh, I should have mentioned it before, we've been summoned," he says.

"Summoned?"

"They call it an invitation, but actually we can't refuse. Lunch at my boss's home tomorrow."

"Be wary of admiring anything," Rob instructs her as they park and enter the lobby. "It's their custom if admired they must offer it as a gift. Also, it's impolite to refuse what's offered, it'd be construed as an insult."

God. How will I remember it all? She wonders. Nevertheless, she follows him, determined to try.

The home of Rob's boss is a large residence in Ras Beirut, an upscale neighborhood of Druze, Muslims, Christians, and Jews. Lunch is being served around a long heavily laden table in a high ceilinged room that could easily be part of a splendid French Chateau. A dozen and a half guests and family members chatter loudly in a seamless blend of Arabic, French, and English.

Genie is introduced to the 'little boss,' Abbad. He is far from small, but as a nephew, he is junior in all things. Oozing charm and entitlement he smiles and takes her hand. "Marhaba," he says. "Welcome."

His smile doesn't reach his eyes, Genie notices, and she has a visceral reaction to him, hopes they won't sit next to each other.

She doesn't have long to worry as she is soon directed to a seat next to Adnan, Rob's co-worker. *He could be a film star with those smoldering looks and that engaging smile,* she thinks, and she relaxes.

Adnan seems utterly at home here. His smile widens, and he introduces his wife, a sweet, Irish Catholic girl. Her sparkling but watchful blue eyes crinkle and almost disappear when she smiles. Shana has cropped, shiny black hair and a delicate face with perfect, pale skin. She appears understated, almost submissive, but she doesn't miss a thing and has a habit of bending forward into a conversation in a conspiratorial way.

"You're going to love it here," she promises.

They talk and consume large portions of the delicious Beluga caviar which is spread in delicate bowls along the length of the table.

"It was brought in fresh from the Caspian today, on our trucks returning from the factory in Tehran," Adnan says.

"You seem really at home here," Genie observes.

"Well, Adnan has known the family for a long time. He was working for them when we met in Benghazi," Shana says, in her lovely Irish lilt. "I was a midwife there, and he ran their trucking company."

On Genie's other side the family doctor smiles and nods. Someone applauds as waiters carry around two large silver serving platters, displaying a celebrated local dish of Kibbeh Nayyeh, raw minced meat.

Bearing in mind in this country one should never refuse Genie accepts a small serving. Surprised, she watches her companion decline. She pauses as she lifts the fork to her mouth and the doctor whispers in her ear.

"When you have finished eating I will tell you why I refused."

In panic, her throat constricts, and the food on her fork becomes instantly unappetizing. Bile rises in her throat.

"Tell me now," she whispers.

"Non, bon appetit. Enjoy." He smiles, turns to the man on his other side and converses loudly in a mix of Arabic and French.

Across the table, an elegant, older Frenchman nods and smiles sympathetically. He addresses her. "It doesn't seem possible only sixty years ago this wasn't a country, only a part of the Ottoman Empire, does it?"

Anything to delay eating this offensive lump of food, she thinks, *maybe they'll come and take it away if I keep talking.*

"I hear it's called the Switzerland of the Middle East," she replies.

"In 1926 we joined together the Christian community around Mount Lebanon with Beirut and the surrounding areas," he says proudly, as though he personally drafted the agreement. "France provided the political framework for proportional representation." He drops his voice, leans close, glances around the table. "Now ambitious leaders have begun fomenting division. The influx of Palestinians from Israel and Jordan has changed the balance and tension has increased, I can feel it."

As a close school friend of their host from their early days, he is free to offer these ideas, but Genie fears she's getting in over her head. She smiles politely and turns to eat.

Swallowing the soft, spicy stuff is like consuming lumps of highly spiced, chewy earth. The smell of meat and mint engulfs her, and she fights not to wretch at the thought of what each mouthful might contain. If only she could hold her nose and close her eyes. But the others tuck in and savor it.

Across the table Shana has noticed Genie's discomfort, she smiles and raises her shoulders, an indication that there is nothing to be done but to accept and get through it.

Genie pushes the remains around her plate in an attempt to make it disappear, but the doctor notices her pathetic attempts and smiles.

"Worms," he whispers. "Worms." He warms to his thesis. "It's raw! Notorious for giving worms in the intestines. They curl around and can grow to twenty or more feet."

She can barely handle the next two hours.

As they say goodbye Shana hugs her and says, "I'm nearby if you need anything. Come over sometime with Rob, we live at the factory compound."

All the way home Genie holds her stomach and complains; imagines the creature that may be growing inside her, devouring her from within.

"Don't be silly, he was teasing you," Rob laughs, entirely unsympathetic.

At home, she heads straight to the bathroom and tries to throw up. When she finally comes to bed, she is red-eyed and distressed.

"Honestly, sweetheart. He was trying to get a rise out of you. You'll be fine." Rob pats her hand. "No more exotic food for a while. How about a change of scene, to Palmyra?"

But as the end of the week arrives Rob would far rather stay and supervise the completion of his new lab, he struggles with his decision but when he comes home on Thursday evening, the clothing she has chosen for the weekend is spread across the bed, and he reluctantly keeps his promise.

Across the fertile Bekaa Valley, they pass the still beautifully intact Roman Acropolis at Baalbek and Genie begs Rob to stop.

She jumps from the car and breathes in, the palpable sense of history engulfs her. It is an ancient site, and not one whisper echoes through gigantic pillars which have stood sentinel for centuries. Captivated by the place, she notices Rob seems distracted, going through the motions.

"Isn't it fabulous?" she says, but he is silent. "Did you hear me?" Her voice startles him.

"Yes," he replies. "There are concerts here sometimes. We'll come back." He whisks her back to the car and drives on through the Bekaa Valley, mile after mile of Lebanon's food basket.

The Syrian border guards puff away and joke with each other.

"What do they think we're here for?" he mutters.

The men have no apparent interest in the drivers who sit in a dusty line waiting to cross into their land. Engine fumes and cigarette smoke float back into the stationary car.

"It's been an hour!" She is hot, hungry and irritated at Rob's earlier impatience.

"If we hadn't taken so long at Baalbek we'd be there by now."

She opens her mouth to protest, but before she can respond, he hits his palm against his head.

"Dolt!" he says and takes a handful of Lebanese notes from his wallet. "Of course, Baksheesh."

Baksheesh sounds like a Greek pastry to Genie, but it is the regional lubricant that makes things function. Doors open and so do border crossings. The guards smile, pocket the cash and with a burst of activity and lots of noise, they wave them to the head of the line, past annoyed drivers who scowl and continue to wait, presumably without the funds to grease palms.

"I've had enough, let's call it a day," he says and drives directly to the center of Damascus, trying hard to avoid potholes, animals and crazy drivers.

She looks around at the city as he drives. She'd hoped to be in Palmyra tonight, but she doesn't argue.

It's hard to follow the road signs which are in French as well as Arabic. Damascus is older than Beirut, both more ancient in terms of history and less modern in its construction.

"It's so dry and dusty. Is that because it's far from the ocean?" she asks. "It feels like we're in a third world country, one that has seen better days."

"Yeah, for all its shortcomings Beirut has thrown its arms around the twentieth century," he replies.

"Here we are." He points to the hotel. "We'll head on to Palmyra in the morning and come back to explore Damascus another time. It's only a day trip," he reminds her as he pulls up outside the Semi Ramis Hotel, a large, solid, perhaps seven-story building.

Inside, pale walls are inlaid with tiles, the marble archways house hidden, secret chambers and muted chandeliers boast of past grandeur. She smiles as she spots an outdoor patio overlooking the river,.

The employees are pleasant, most speak French, this land too was part of the French Mandate, and after a small mezze supper, they head to their room.

Hoping to remove some of the day's dust Rob jumps in the shower.

"I hope they're better at antiquities than modernity," she calls, holding an electric socket which has fallen from the wall into her hands. It's not a good introduction to Syria, but she laughs.

"Don't worry about anything, let's try to relax a little," Rob calls back and smiles as she steps in to join him, grabs a bar of soap and begins to lather his shoulders, he turns and embraces her.

Still wet she lets herself be pulled to the bed, for the first time today she feels they are connected and she curls into him. But later, before sleep captures her, she wonders anew if it is possible this massive change in their lives can work for both of them.

They wake in the morning to the hypnotic sound of the call to prayer, she slips out of his embrace and grabs a croissant and Cafe Americain from the room service tray. Pouring hot milk and coffee into an enormous cup, French style, she stirs in sugar and carries it to him in the bed.

Far away from work he is the old Rob and now has one thing on his mind, he reaches for her, pulls her down and as they explore one another, the coffee grows cold.

The drive to Palmyra is uneventful, and the desert road is quiet but as they near the town they pass a yellow Porsche which drives slowly.

"Haven't we passed that car before?" Rob asks.

She nods. "We have, that's bizarre. I didn't see it overtake us."

"Look, there it is again, it's going back in the opposite direction, what a crazy bugger," he says.

Genie settles back, but after two minutes, as if by magic, the yellow car is in front of them again, this time driving like a bat out of hades toward Palmyra.

"Crazy, I wonder what on earth he's up to?" Rob says.

Driving in, they notice the town is grubby and has little to recommend it except for the proximate, inspirational ruins of the past, a former caravan oasis at the heart of trade routes between China, India, and Persia. Palmyra was once the meeting place of civilizations and one of the most significant cultures on earth.

They park in town, and Rob chuckles as he sees a line of six yellow cars lined up alongside a film crew.

"See that?" he points.

As they get out one of the drivers grins and walks over to them.

"Had you wondering if you imagined us, did we not?" he asks. He tells them they are filming a commercial of a German Automobile racing across the desert. "But we are not staying."

He emphasizes 'we' and 'staying' and indicates the poor accommodation with a laugh as he sees their bags and the look on Genie's face.

They join the men for coffee, then head out to wander slowly through the ancient ruins, magnificent, gigantic columns which glow pink and gold in the sunlight. As always Genie admires the remaining sense of Rome's power and domination.

"It's awe-inspiring," she says. "But I'm disappointed at the lack of care and the sense of abandonment. All these vast colonnades, monuments and temples show what civilizations are capable of. How can they spend such enormous sums on the military yet have little concern for their treasures?" she asks.

It is a profound shock to realize that this mighty nation has such disregard for its past glories.

In cloak and dagger style, villagers from the town, which now encroaches upon the site, follow them around and clandestinely offer an array of illicit antiquities.

"Haqiqiun fi suria." One of them says. Others take up the chant.

"I think he's saying it's genuine," Rob tells her.

The short, burnt skinned men hold small statues, pieces of glass and myriad other goodies.

They have begun to collect artwork and mementos on their travels, but these they refuse.

"It's not right," she whispers to Rob.

"Agreed, they're probably fake."

"I mean it's not right that all this history is left to crumble away."

In front of them, an immense graveyard filled with sculptures echoing ancient cultures now rests under tended. Partial skeletons poke out from some of the graves, and the weeds seem to have reached an agreement to be left undisturbed.

"Shhh," he says. "Quietly."

She looks over her shoulder. Nearby the men who have been unsuccessful in selling to them watch and glare. It feels vaguely menacing and, although it is still warm, she shivers and wonders if it was worth the long drive.

"The ancient city is impressive, but a night in this mediocre and shabby 'modern' accommodation is decidedly unappealing. I can't wait until we get back," she says.

How she's changed from when they met three years ago on a blind date, he thinks. That naive girl now has firm opinions of right, wrong and how things should be as well as the taste for an upscale life.

He laughs and reaches for her. "This is the last exploration for a while, when we get back I'll have to knuckle down," he says.

4

BEIRUT, 1972

California Dreams

THE FOLLOWING WEEKS CONSUME ROB.

"There's no time for anything anymore, my whole focus is on the business," he tells her as he collapses into a seat at their "local"; The Rose and Crown pub. He takes a gulp of cold lager.

It is a career move for him and failure, an ignominious return to the U. K., out of work and unemployable, terrifies him, she knows.

He hands her a couple of letters from home.

"They're filled with negative news from England, more strikes, unemployment and constant rationing of basic amenities," he says and lifts his glass to his lips. "By the way, we've been invited to a party, tonight."

"Really?" Her face lights up. "It could be good, we could meet new people."

Rob groans inwardly, noting her pleasure, he doesn't mention that he feels mentally and emotionally exhausted, in no mood to talk much less party, but he hasn't the heart to disappoint her when she is trying to adjust and spends so much time alone.

They take the stairs to the third floor of a modern block in Ras Beirut, home of a locally based UK journalist. Inside it's highly decorated, a European's idea of an Arab tent, fabric draped from the ceilings and dotted with embroidered cushions, a few hookahs stand around.

The apartment is overfilled, and the party extends into the corridor and spills onto the small balcony where a light rain has begun to fall. Arabic music reverberates through the various rooms and people lounge on ornate cushions, deep in heated discussions.

The mix of westerners and well-dressed Beirutis is eclectic; representing the varied faces of Beirut.

"It's great to be out together after so long." She squeezes his hand. In truth Genie prefers smaller gatherings of close friends, is more at home when the faces are familiar, but she accepts that will never happen unless they go out in the word and make friends.

In the corner, a couple of young men smoke from the hookahs, "Hubble bubbles," and gesticulate wildly in apparent disagreement over something. Genie's eyes move quickly left and right scanning the room, she spots the group and watches cautiously, but the disagreement turns to laughter, and she lets herself relax.

Joining a group of dancers she performs her loose-western version of a belly dance, a scarf yashmak-like to her face. With a newly acquired veneer of sophistication, her hair is longer, eyebrows plucked into an arch, she sways her hips in an exaggerated, overtly sexy fashion and laughs as a photographer from the Daily Star takes her picture. She enjoys seeing herself in the "society" pages of the newspaper the morning after.

There are more males than females, maybe two to one. For the most part, they are young and single, posted to the region for brief periods on the first steps of their career ladders. Teachers, reporters and some who are here to promote products from international companies to the Arab world.

She stops dancing and accepts a drink which Rob has somehow procured, he points to a friend who waves from a recess across the room, and they head over to him.

Stuart is surrounded by a group of clean, innocent-faced trainee diplomats who all happily eat and enjoy themselves. He stands out, has a sense of controlled energy in his movements and his high cheek boned, intelligent, face speaks of future ambassadorial material.

Dispatched here they live in Lebanese homes and immerse themselves in the language and culture as part of their Arabic studies at the Middle East Center for Arabic Studies, (MECAS); now and forever the Spy School, since the famed spy Kim Philby put it on the map a decade earlier.

"Looking lovely as always," Stuart tells her and bends to whisper in her ear. "You're always at the center, aren't you? You must think the world revolves around you."

Taken aback she glances at Stuart then at Rob, but he is engrossed in conversation with another of the guys and hasn't heard the interaction.

Genie looks back at Stuart warily, her feelings bruised. *Was that a criticism? It certainly sounded like it. What's she done to upset him?*

She summons a smile and moves away to talk with a girl she met in her Arabic class, but Stuart's comment has lodged, and she cannot shake it for the rest of the evening. She plans to steer clear of him if she can.

———※———※———※———※———

"The bosses have both gone to Baghdad, and they want us to host the US partners who are in town, en route to Israel," Rob tells her.

His black eyes are shining, and she can sense his eagerness for the opportunity to entertain them and maybe forge a stronger connection.

"I really hope when my contract ends we can have a future in America." He fluffs up a cushion and Genie watches, astonished. This is not a man who notices fripperies. "The company intimated as much when I was in California, so tonight is another step in that direction," he says.

Rob has a host of suggestions, "Make your sherry trifle, they'll love that, and maybe that great Beef Wellington. Do we have good champagne?"

She smiles and nods.

"Do we have enough?" His excitement about the night is contagious, and she's excited too.

Our first dinner party in Beirut, a chance to show off all my efforts and our newly furnished home.

It has been a labor of love, and she is proud of the results. Elegantly modern, yet faintly exotic, in tribute to the middle east, which she is growing to love.

She kisses Rob on the cheek and pushes him toward the door. "It'll be fine," she tells him. "Stop worrying, trust me."

"I do." With a last look around, he leaves.

A small brown skinned girl dressed in peasant style garments runs barefoot back and forth placing footed silver bowls piled high with tropical fruit around a Persian samovar inlaid with silver, it sits on an intricately carved, wooden sideboard.

Noura hums softly as she works. She comes most mornings, but today she will stay on to help with preparations for the evening. She carefully carries in sweet delicacies and waits as Genie holds up a hand to put an Arabic coaster on the new table before taking bowls of nuts and crudités from the girl.

She wonders what on earth her mistress finds so special. A table is a table after all, and this is not even large, it will seat only ten. Noura turns, still humming softly she returns to the kitchen.

Furnishing has been a challenge. After combing the city for weeks Genie discovered Lebanon has few furniture showrooms, the custom is to select from designer catalogs and each item is painstakingly and faithfully handcrafted by local artisans. She imagined long delays, but instead, the finished pieces arrived on time, uncannily authentic copies.

Noura places flowers in the center of the dining table, a locally crafted Roche Bobois imitation, already set for eight guests.

"These are very beautiful," she says.

Genie pauses, she vaguely wishes she had some of their own belongings here, but after shipment, none of it has ever been heard of again. *Not to worry*

"You're right, Noura, it does look beautiful."

There's a lightness and sense of space, a sparkle on the marble floor.

She gives a final unnecessary plump to the soft, Cerulean cushions relaxing on a long white settee which sweeps around one corner of the room. *Why on earth did I get such an enormous piece?* She wonders, but she already knows the answer, she couldn't resist.

She tries to see the place through the eyes of a stranger, looks at the handmade side tables, thickly decorated in silver inlaid with Arabic calligraphy, imagines hours of painstaking work tap, tapping the silver filigree into place; like adding a veil to a beautiful woman, creating an air of mystery and beauty. She hardly believes she owns them. In Europe, they would have fetched at least ten times what she paid. She would have happily given the full asking price, but stallholders hate if foreigners pay what they ask, they feel cheated, think they could have asked for more. So suppressing her guilt, she bartered twenty percent off the price, and he was happy.

Rob seems to like everything she's done, but in truth, if he can sit on it, eat off it or sleep in it, he's happy. *He is the least demanding of men, always appreciative and encouraging, unlike other husbands he doesn't interfere in the running or decorating of our home. I'm lucky,* she thinks.

The air is delicious, faintly perfumed from the lush and fragrant Magnolia plant in the corridor combined with the ever-present orange blossoms from the groves below.

They have a beautiful home in an exciting country, and she tries to push aside her feeling that apart from tonight's party, she has no purpose, is merely passing time.

Controlling her thoughts she reviews the erstwhile bar, pewter, and copper-trimmed it is a marvel near the French windows, it is well stocked, she should have known.

Rob has recently taken to collecting wines and some exotic spirits, he has shrouded one of the bedrooms in gloom, erected extensive shelving, creating a would be "cellar." The stock is growing. When friends leave or are posted elsewhere, they donate what they didn't drink, and Rob is always happy to accept.

The fronds of tall potted plants dangle and move in the soft breeze and give the apartment a peaceful, colonial feel. Genie leans over the coffee table, adjusts a retractable overhead light, pulls it low as Noura sets down the coffee service.

She hopes Rob's guests will love it, California is supposed to be quite something but who could resist the pull of these ancient lands, at once mysterious yet somehow familiar from the Biblical stories told in Sunday school and the tales of Aladdin.

As an afterthought, she puts out after dinner chocolates and selects music, a little Vivaldi.

Genie relaxes, a last look around and she smiles, satisfied.

If success is judged by the hour of the guests' departure, the party is a triumph.

In addition to the four American visitors, Rob also invited his colleague Mark Langdon with his slender wife Kat, whose posture is so perfect Genie imagines she too was forced to practice in school with a stack of books on her head.

Although British Mark has lived almost his entire life overseas, the child of a military man. After his University days, he was never drawn back to the cold shores of England. Now he is the General Manager at the Beirut branch of Rob's company, and Beirut has been his home for almost two decades. He is handsome, erudite, a consummate charmer and the drooling American wives lap him up, love his accent, his dry humor and his English manners.

It was an excellent decision to invite Mark, Rob thinks.

The group is scheduled to leave the next day to Israel, by way of Cyprus. Genie notices the kitchen clock through the gap in the door. *If they don't say goodbye soon we'll be taking them directly to the airport,* she thinks.

But the Americans love every minute of their evening. They eat well, seem to judge how good the food is by the size of the portions and there is not a morsel left of the Beef Wellington. In their world it seems, bigger is better, and they polish off probably two kilos of the puff pastry encased filet mignon. Of the sherry trifle, only traces of cream are left around the edge of the crystal bowl, and each of the chocolates on the dish is gone.

I guess they liked it, she decides, as she catches Rob's smile of pride over the table.

"More coffee?" she asks.

Shakes of the head, mutters of. "So full," until Rob offers brandy and the men all accept. He grabs four snifters and pours liberal nightcaps. No-one seems in the least tired nor moves to leave, but unnoticed Genie pinches herself to keep herself awake.

At two thirty in the morning, the owner of the company takes Rob aside in a paternal gesture and reaffirms he'll happily sponsor the young couple to come to the United States when his term is complete. "We'll talk more on the next trip," he says, and they leave.

They've barely closed the door when Rob spins around. "Did you hear him?"

Genie carries plates from the table to the kitchen, he follows her in, opens his arms, lifts her and swings her into the air as she laughingly balances the plates.

"California here we come, right back where we started from," he sings. "He said he'll sponsor us, offer a job and help us get started over there."

She laughs, too. *How great to see Rob this happy.* She hadn't realized how much this meant to him.

He sets her down, she extinguishes candles, turns off the remaining lights and follows him along the corridor. She pauses at their nursery door. The full moon throws a beam across an empty white crib in the center of the room and a breeze tickles the delicate mobile, the small jungle creatures move with a brief tinkle, the hint of a lullaby. She smothers her sigh. *It's only been a short while*, she reminds herself. *When the crib is occupied, maybe I'll be singing, too.*

"Oh, say can you see, by the dawn's early light, what so proudly we hail, at the twilight's last gleaming . . ."

Rob's deep voice moves on to a verse of the Star Spangled Banner, and she is back in the moment.

For days Rob is over the moon, as he dreams away their next four years.

———✳︎——✳︎——✳︎——✳︎———

The decorating and the shopping is done, Genie has run out of things to do and for the first time in her life has no function. *Four years, that's forty-eight months, she calculates quickly. Two hundred and eight weeks. God, it seems like forever.*

Their decision not to get two cars, not to put in a television or a telephone at home now proves isolating. She agreed, with no friends they would have little use for a phone, in an emergency they can be reached via their neighbor. But now, without a vehicle, she feels dependent, she must drop Rob off at the crack of dawn if she wants the car, or rely on the public taxi shuttle service, which passes by the end of their cul de sac hourly.

Nevertheless, she makes the best of it and spends time, too much time, in the reinvention of herself. As spring passes into summer, she takes taxis to Arabic classes where she finds a handful of vaguely familiar faces, girls who are here as teachers.

"You should sign up to study TEFL. You'd be a great teacher of foreign languages," one encourages, and she mentally files it away under "possibilities."

"Maybe, but for now I want to learn a handful of Arabic sentences, so I feel confident walking about town."

"Your schoolgirl French not working?" the girl asks.

"I get by, but I sense that in the Souks and more ancient parts of the city Arabic is the lingua franca."

'Learn Exotic Dancing' the sign in the window reads, and in July she signs up. Thrilled at her mastery of the movement, she gains awareness of her body, of its sensuality, and feels powerful, a new and un-English sensation. She casts aside English dresses, slips on floating, silky pants, long diaphanous skirts, and she achieves a new sense of self.

Rob smiles as they prepare to go out for lunch. "You look fantastic. I like having a new wife."

Rob watches as she wraps her hair in a soft silk, hand painted scarf, twists it around her head, a flamboyant knots fall over her shoulders and holds her hair hostage.

"To combat the constant humidity," she explains. "Not even my friends would recognize me anymore."

He is relieved that she is occupied and he can concentrate on his own frustrations, growing by the day, and she doesn't tell him shopping and dressing, parties and dancing offer no challenge, don't occupy her imagination, her time or her mind.

She tries chatting a little with their maid, Noura. The girl's family history before they relocated from the mountains is a fascinating one; full of revolution and honor, a proud ancestry.

Genie is fond of her, but the different language and life experiences make for limited conversation. She is increasingly lonely.

And now summer has gone.

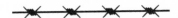

On the terrace, a long dining table can seat ten, but this morning, as on most mornings, Genie relaxes in one of the two bentwood, rocking chair lounges.

Sipping fresh orange juice from a decorative glass, she picks at a croissant on the small table beside her and scrutinizes the local newspaper, distractedly clipping photos from the social section with an oversized pair of scissors as her own face peers back at her, captured at a local event, she slides the severed pieces into an album.

Indulged, surrounded by beautiful things and with little to do, she has begun to feel like a penthouse pet.

"Could you turn up the radio?" she calls to Rob.

Frequent horn blasts grow louder and closer, an old MBZ taxi stops at the end of the street. Genie peers through the long clear glass of the terrace as a passenger squeezes into the almost full vehicle, holding tightly to an enormous bag of oranges. One falls to the ground, but the taxi is already in motion, the woman yells at him and closes the door,

One arm in his jacket, Rob finishes a croissant and gulps his cup of coffee. He looks invigorated. Work finally seems to be going well, and he believes the challenges which frustrated him in the construction phase, will soon be a thing of the past.

"That must be the nine o'clock taxi, I'm late. Gotta go."

She lowers her paper. "Always in a rush. I, on the other hand, have nothing to hurry for." She lifts her brown sandaled feet onto the chair abandoned by Rob, watches him finish putting on his jacket and lift his briefcase.

He knows she is watching him and he sighs, wonders what to do about her. *Maybe it was unfair to take her away from the job she loved.* But by now he'd hoped she'd find a way to feel fulfilled out here as she had in England. *It's a great home, we see friends from work, she has money to spend, all she could ask for, almost.*

She waits as he gets ready. *He looks good with a tan. Excitement bursts from his eyes and affects the way he walks these days,* she notices. His new suit is pale and lightweight, fits in all the right places. *He's grown into a sense of himself.* She wishes they had more time to play like before, but she's happy for him.

He lightly kisses her bare shoulder. He may be sexy and appealing, but since he's always preoccupied, it doesn't help her or change the fact she's bored out of her mind.

The doorbell rings, and he turns to leave. "Georgina, I told you from the beginning, you need to make a life for yourself. I can't be responsible for your sense of fulfillment," he tells her sharply.

Georgina! She's startled. *That's serious, he hasn't called me that in a while.*

He softens, bends to kiss her on the lips. "Remember, your Mother arrives today, that'll keep you busy, and the rental car will give you the chance to get around and explore."

He opens the front door and lets in Noura, she smiles, waves to Genie, heads to the kitchen where she deposits a cloth covered parcel.

The door closes.

In the kitchen Noura takes out a dish piled high with stuffed vine leaves, dark green and glistening in a bed of olive oil, she carefully arranges a few on a plate with wedges of lemon and Arabic bread and carries them out on a tray.

"My sister and I have maked these for you," she proudly rests them beside Genie who immediately bites into one. Noura smiles, her teeth are small and white, her eyes dark and probing in a young prematurely lined face. She turns quickly without waiting for a thank you.

"These are delicious," Genie calls to her. Noura turns

"I show you how they are made if you will like," she offers. Her accent is strong, but her voice is sexy; deep and throaty, surprising from such a tiny frame, the sound of a singer.

Loud explosions in the distance stop the conversation. Bombs cascade from the air. They turn together as Genie jumps up and rushes to the handrail, she grabs tightly, leaning as far forward as she can, but it is far away, and although she can see smoke billowing into the sky near the airport there is nothing else visible.

Rob's factory is adjacent to the runways of the International Airport, she thinks, *but surely he can't be there already?*

Noura sees her concern and echoes Genie's thoughts. "Mr. Rob cannot be there yet, Madame. You should not fear. He will be well."

"Really?" she asks.

"It is too far, he is not yet halfway," she says.

Genie smiles at the small girl who hurries to the kitchen and prepares a pot of coffee.

When she returns, Genie pulls herself away from the balustrade and takes the cup offered to her. "Join me," she says to the girl, but she giggles shakes her head and runs back to her domain.

The Al Sultan Brahim restaurant, a little way along the coast, outside Beirut, is the most popular and upscale fish restaurant in the region. At this hour it is filled with loud laughter and the clatter of plates as people tuck into freshly harvested produce, newly caught fish and warm, straight from the oven, Arabic bread.

Rob and a large group of friends look in amazement at the typical Mediterranean style Mezze set out across the table. The dozens of vibrantly colored dishes are a still-life painter's dream.

"There's nowhere else on earth you would find such a spread," Stuart says, and Rob agrees.

Golden roasted pine nuts nestle in a glistening pool of oil topping creamy hummus, shiny, green tabouleh, a combination of mint, parsley, tomatoes, and onion; smooth lightly smokey baba ghannoush, a blend of eggplant and tahini sesame seed paste used in many middle eastern dishes.

The table almost groans under it all. The men order drinks and tuck into stuffed vine leaves, olives, nuts.

Stuart has brought along a military looking friend, complete with handlebar mustache. He introduces the Colonel who is completely flabbergasted by the spread. "Just look at the colors and shapes," he says, pointing to the slices of pale green cucumber, purple pickles. orange carrots, calamari, and octopus salad.

"And the fish hasn't even arrived yet," Rob laughs.

Frazzled, Genie scans the dining area, spots Rob among the group of European men against a far window. She recognizes some of them, nods to the Maitre d' and makes her way across the restaurant. She kisses Rob's cheek and sits beside him.

"Mumma's plane was redirected because of the dogfight over the airport today. She could be in Athens, Baghdad or Timbuktu for all they know or care!"

Rob nods but makes no comment. He puts an arm around her shoulders and introduces her to the man next to her. "Genie meet the Colonel. Colonel, my wife, Genie."

She offers her hand to the Colonel. He is slightly rounded, in his early 40's, distinguished by his mustache, harking back to some earlier time. He takes her hand, raises it to his lips and kisses. She is surprised by the gesture, *Rather formal,* she thinks, but her attention has drifted, redirected over his shoulder to a man at the bar who watches them with a cat got the cream smile. Slim, blond and sexy. The Colonel also notices, turns and nods toward the stranger.

"Bright guy. Brilliant chess player. Word is he's with Syrian Intelligence."

"Why would he work for Syria?"

His mouth full of food the Colonel turns away, scrapes a rather large helping of octopus and chats to a tall, slim, ex-pat who sits on his other side. Genie recognizes Stuart. He winks his sparkling blue eyes and offers an easy smile, but she sucks in her breath, she hasn't forgotten his recent dig about her need to be the center of attention, and she greets him coolly.

Like a few others seated around the table, he is with the for-eign office, at the Middle East Center for Arabic Studies, but several guys are from competing major tobacco and leading automotive companies, sprinkled with a couple of news photographers and reporters who cover events in the area from this preferred base.

But tonight politics are not on the menu, surprising in this land where conspiracy theories are served at every coffee shop and cafe.

They relax, eat with their fingers, scoop food with Arabic bread, laugh and fall into easy conversation. Most of the group are young and male, in their late twenties or early thirties. But Genie can't relax or be conversational, she picks at her food and tries to get Rob's attention.

"I'm concerned about my mother," she tells him "No-one knows what happened to the plane after it left Zurich."

Half-heartedly he squeezes her hand. "Let's enjoy dinner and talk later. Have a drink."

But wine doesn't lift her mood. For the past two hours, she questioned airline staff at Beirut airport to no avail. They tell her when the airport closes planes can't land and are redirected, and this particular plane has disappeared.

"I can't sit here while she's who knows where she'll be so scared." Genie stops, realizes she's talking to herself, Rob has turned to chat animatedly to his friends.

She sighs. *I've tried hard to settle. It's a beautiful and extraordinary land of contrasts, and we live a good life, but it still doesn't feel like home.*

Almost a year, and for the most part, Genie has remained isolated. They meet with Rob's colleagues, go to the handful of local pubs frequented by ex-pats, most are noddingly familiar to them. Despite parties, movie nights at fantastic high-end local cinemas and dinners in fabulous locations, something is absent. She occasionally meets Adnan's Irish wife Shana, but she has two small children who occupy her and serve as a reminder to Genie of their continued status as a two-person family.

She turns back to watch Rob, he seems happy here, although she knows he dreams of a future one day in America.

There is a movement across the room, the blonde man at the bar helps a well dressed blind man tap his way out of the restaurant. She looks over as he opens the door, shakes his hand and bends to pet the guide dog, it slobbers his hand.

Sensing her distress Rob finally turns, "Genie, we can't do anything right now. Try to relax, and after dinner, we'll stop by the airport to see what we can find out, alright?"

She takes a deep breath, excuses herself and heads to the ladies room where she splashes water onto her flushed face. She pats it dry and is startled. Reflected in the mirror covering the length of the wall is the man from the bar nearby washing his hands. She looks at his reflection, annoyed.

"What, may I ask, are you doing in the ladies bathroom?"

"As you see, I am washing my hands, removing traces of an eager dog," he indicates the sign above the doorway. "They are actually unisex basins, but I apologize if I have made you uncomfortable." He turns quickly to leave, shakes the water from his hands without stopping to dry them.

She reads the notice, grabs a paper towel and hurries after him. "I'm sorry—I was rude."

He stops. They make eye contact. He has beautiful, probing green eyes which hold her gaze, tunnel right into her. Her breath catches, she breaks eye contact, blushes and stutters.

"Forgive me." She holds out the paper towel. "Please won't you join us for a drink? It'll make me feel less awful."

He's extremely well mannered and engaging, but she notices he doesn't actually smile, he pats his hands dry and escorts her back to the table. Rob stands as they approach.

"Karam Sulman." He extends his hand.

"Karam?" Genie is surprised. "So you're from here? It's hard to believe. Your English is perfect, and you look like a Viking."

"I'm from Aleppo," he acknowledges. "A throwback to the Crusaders, I imagine. They left behind a castle, Krak des Chevaliers, which still stands not so far from my home."

She imagines an ancient far removed grandsire with Karam's looks, dressed in Crusader's chain mail, a large red cross on his front. A seed planted centuries ago carrying through the ages to this young Muslim man with green eyes and fair coloring, an act of the past reaching on into the future.

Rob watches her face and sees them interact easily with each other. *She seems to have forgotten the missing plane,* he thinks and turns back to the group.

5

SEPTEMBER 1972

Planes and Helicopters

GENIE PUTS ON HER ONE and only Vivaldi record and turns to greet their Armenian landlord Kourk and his wife Rubina, up from their Regency styled home on the floor below. His curly hair and mustache are grey, but he always wears a youthful smile and is invariably clad in shorts, tee shirt, and flip flops. Twenty years younger Rubina shares the features of her Armenian ancestors. She's quiet in company, but it's clear she has a strong say in how their world runs.

Half a dozen neighbors spill onto the terrace and Victor, a darkly handsome man, holds a protective arm around a beautiful young woman while he playfully flirts with Genie's mother Doreen, who has at last arrived.

A decade older than Rob, Genie finds Victor's secretiveness mysterious, rather exciting. He never takes a public political viewpoint, and she can't remember how they met. His wife flicks aside folds of shining hair and gazes in adoration at her husband through large, kohl circled eyes.

"She could almost be my daughter, don't you think?" He displays her with pride.

Doreen laughs, sips suspiciously at her cup of dark, sweet Arabic coffee and nibbles honey soaked slices of filo pastry, which hold chunks of chopped nuts hostage, a Levantine favorite.

Nabil Haddad holds out a gift, a brightly colored wrap and a bag of Lebanese nuts tied with a red ribbon. He places it in Doreen's hands, adjusts his glasses and introduces his wife Mary, another Irish girl. They have lived just down the hill since they married and Mary is a remarkable fount of information. She is tiny but tough. An efficient former airline stewardess.

"Thank you, so much," Doreen smiles at Nabil, tall, slender he is a modest man and a remarkable doctor. He kisses her cheek.

"He's just been named the top Oral and Maxillofacial Surgeon in the country," Mary boasts.

Doreen has no idea what that is and hesitates to ask. Slim, attractive and blonde she is in her early forties, with alert, wide blue eyes and a tiny space between each of her perfect teeth. After a harrowing three days trying to get out of Baghdad, she arrived in Beirut, now she recounts her adventure but stops abruptly as the door opens.

"Sorry, I'm late. Hell of a day," Rob announces and hurries in. All eyes turn to him as he mops his forehead, drops his briefcase by the bar and joins them.

Noura offers a cup and saucer as he joins the group. He smiles at her but declines,

"I have a better idea. It's almost six who's for champagne?"

"I'll have to take a raincheck," Nabil puts down his cup and stands. "I'm needed at the hospital in an hour, and I walked up from home." He indicates their house a few hundred yards down the hill. "Mary will stay if someone sees she gets back safely." He kisses cheeks and leaves.

Noura closes the door behind Nabil and heads to the kitchen. She noisily fills a bucket with ice, brings it to Rob who has popped the cork and shared the contents of one bottle, he nestles a fresh one into the bed of ice. Noura keeps her eyes averted does an odd half curtsey, glances furtively at Victor and scurries off.

Genie glances across at Rob, he lifts an eyebrow but turns away as Victor tells them, "Your mother was telling us of the delays in her trip."

Doreen smiles. "Yes. We stopped in Zurich, and the plane was surrounded by the military with machine guns. I've never seen that before. I guess it's a reaction to the Munich killings."

"Munich killings?" Rob interrupts.

"Yes, At the Olympic Games four days ago." She stops and looks at him, surprised. "Eleven Israeli athletes were murdered. It's been all over the news. The whole world is stunned."

"Are you sure? We've heard nothing about it."

Mary watches Rob reach into his briefcase and pull out a newspaper. Large sections have been blacked out.

"I guess this is why."

Genie takes the paper and examines it. "So we're being censored? Is this unusual?"

Kourk and Rubina share a look but remain silent. They know better than to question or voice dissent outside their own Armenian community.

But Mary looks around, believes herself among friends and replies candidly with her quiet Irish lilt. "I actually don't think it's new. Listen to the BBC. It's the only way to get news." She turns to Doreen. "I'll bet that's why the airport closed and why you were delayed. After the massacre, Israeli planes must've bombed Palestinian bases here and in Syria. Retaliation, no doubt. The airport always closes when there's a bombing." She delivers the news as if bombings are par for the course.

Victor deftly switches back to Doreen, quietly sophisticated he commands attention when he speaks.

"Now, tell us of your adventure in Baghdad." He takes her arm and coaxes her into the center of the group. "Mesopotamia is magical, is it not? An historic center of learning along the Tigris river."

It was hardly magical, Doreen remembers. After the initial surprise at not landing in Beirut, the entire trip was a challenge.

"Well, it was interesting, but I would happily forego a repeat," she says. "I imagined myself as Scheherazade in one of her tales from One Thousand and One Nights, beside the Tigris river I could almost see Ali Baba and Aladdin. But the bus veered off away from the river lined with sparkling hotels and turned down dark alleys to a grubby fourth rate hotel. I was afraid to sleep. The toilet was public—a ceramic lined hole in the ground," she shudders.

"Two days with little food, no news, and the interminable waiting. Waiting for information. Waiting for a plane. Finally, they found an old, quasi-abandoned machine and rounded up an ex-war pilot. But the piece-de-resistance was our ride to the airport." Her voice drops for some reason. "There were decapitated heads, strung on poles—a warning. I tried not to look, said to myself it's make-believe, not real." She takes in a deep breath and exhales. "It was barbaric, like the middle ages. I was never so happy to leave anywhere."

"Ah, well not to worry," Victor says. "You're in Lebanon now, the wonderful Paris of the East. The most civilized and sane part of the Arab world."

Doreen smiles but doesn't respond. After the past few days, she already suspects that sanity may be a veneer and that lunatics threaten to run the asylum.

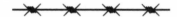

With her mother in town to share lazy days at the beach club, shop in the souks, laugh and share hugs, Genie's recent boredom has disappeared.

Barely eighteen when Genie was born, they are like sisters and Genie fears that four weeks will fly fast.

"A month's stay is too short," she says. "England is too far away."

Doreen nods and squeezes her arm but skillfully avoids the subject, she turns back to the stall in front of her. "Look how beautiful." She holds up a piece of locally made jewelry.

"Don't let them see you love it, you'll never get a bargain."

"I can't argue about the price," Doreen says. But she watches Genie negotiate, and within minutes she learns to bargain and over the coming days she polishes and perfects the art.

"Shall we drive out of town to a beach for a change? Some solitude, just the two of us." Genie suggests.

At a long, almost deserted beach dozens of tiny crabs scurry across the sand. It's private and remote, they feel free. Free from the constant gossip, the conspiracy theories and most of all free to be themselves.

In a red bikini, close to the shore, Genie floats on her back and sings at the top of her voice; she is no competition for Carly Simon, but "Anticipation" has never been performed with such energy. Her voice carries across the beach, and Doreen looks up from lazily browsing her magazine and smiles.

The trip has been a good thing. When the plan to move out here had been mentioned, Doreen was worried. Now she has seen the affluent and relaxed life they've carved out and their group of bright, charming neighbors, she accepts this has been a positive move.

Genie plops down on a brightly colored towel beside her mother, breaks into her reverie.

"That was divine, it's lovely to be away from the crowds and chatter at the beach club. I've been bored lately, even with all of the experiences and entertainment I'm just not challenged. When you go home, I think I'll get more involved. Do something."

Before Doreen can reply a thunderous noise threatens to deafen them. A loud, insistent whir fills the air and vibrations shake their bodies as a black helicopter approaches in a direct line toward them, fast and low.

They have no time to process what is underway as the austere, unmarked machine slows and hovers. Sand whips up and around, painfully blasting their skin.

Genie turns her eyes away. "What on earth . . . ?" she begins, but quickly closes her mouth as it fills with airborne sand. She spits, wipes her mouth and raises her hand to shield her eyes which smart from the particles scratching her eyeballs.

Unable to see, she grasps for her mother's hand, and Doreen grabs hold, almost crushes her fingers with a grip of iron, fleeting evidence that her mother is terrified.

Will it pass by? Should they run?

The helicopter is enormous, almost low enough to touch. Genie raises her arms and lifts a towel over their heads, she pulls her mother to her and tries to shield their ears against the noise which threatens to overwhelm them. The continued blast of sharp, beige, grains stings like a hundred paper cuts, reddening

their skin. She sees the look of fear in her mother's face but realizes they are helpless.

She tries to reassure her. "I'm so sorry, Mumma."

Tears from the irritation in her eyes run down her cheeks.
Her mind races through all of the possible outcomes, but she
cannot fix her mind on what's happening or why.

Without warning the helicopter lifts and flies off, it travels
fast for a short distance, seconds later it turns and with deafening intent circles back. Slowly the tip of a machine gun pokes
from the side.

"No," Doreen screams.

In unison, they wordlessly grab their things.

Fear washes over her, and she clutches her mother, temples
pounding, Genie's heart is in revolt as she catches her breath.

"Run," she cries.

They carry what they can, stumble up the beach, throw
themselves behind the car and cling to each other. They realize it
offers no real protection.

The helicopter circles for a moment that goes on forever and
fires into the ocean. Doreen whimpers but the machine promptly
elevates and disappears over the water, the way it came.

They stare at each other in stunned silence, peer at the
ocean too shocked to move.

In an eerie foreshadowing of the future Genie feels afraid in
her new land, and her mother who has undergone so many challenges since she flew out of the UK, is understandably in shock.

They cling to each other without speaking for half an hour
then climb into the car covered in sand, calm enough to drive
home. The joy has gone from the day.

After a silent journey they walk into the apartment, wind-swept and forlorn, with no regard to the sand they spread across the marble floors they tiptoe to the terrace and flop down, not breaking the silence.

Unperturbed and without comment, Noura watches them trek in. She fills a bucket and throws water across the floor behind their gritty footsteps and sweeps it into the corner of the living room where discreetly placed drain holes swallow the days' accumulation of dust and dirt.

The floors dry quickly and sparkle in the warm sunlight, unlike the two disheveled women. Noura puts away her cleaning paraphernalia, calls goodbye and leaves, she passes Rob in the doorway as he returns home.

At first, he doesn't notice the frightened pair outside. He pours a drink, spots them through the window, waves and joins them. He embraces Genie, rubs her hair. "New hairdresser?"

"Don't be frivolous, Rob, you have no idea what we've been through." She reaches out and grabs onto him. It takes him by surprise, and she lets herself weep.

Doreen, also on the verge of tears, shakes her blonde head and tells Rob of their day.

"We were terrified, we didn't know who they were or what they might do to us. We felt so vulnerable, Rob."

He listens and pats Genie's head. "They were probably playing with you."

"Playing? What kind of fools play like that?" Doreen asks with no expectation of an answer. "I'm not thrilled about Genie here alone when this sort of thing can happen," she pauses "This is a beautiful country, I'll give you that, but these must be crazy people if they think its fun to terrify women, and who in God's name has a helicopter to play with?"

He shrugs, "These things happen but no lasting damage. Genie loves it here, don't you? Don't worry, it's perfectly safe here, virtually no crime."

And in the late summer of 1972, that's true. There is little petty crime in Beirut, it feels safe on the streets, particularly for a westerner.

But a few linear miles down the road in Israel, shock over the death of their athletes has left a pall over the country. And the consequences are inevitable.

The Israeli Prime Minister has created a committee to review response options.

The consensus—"a dramatic response is essential, not out of revenge but to deter future acts of violence against the State."

Public opinion demands all those involved should be assassinated and a list of planners and executors alike is in preparation—all are members of the Palestinian Liberation Organization and Black September. West Germany peremptorily released three of the killers, so there is no longer ambivalence about what must be done.

The Prime Minister writes: 'I want to share my plans. Not one of the people involved in any way will be walking on this earth for much longer.'

The Mossad intelligence agency discreetly goes into action, and word quickly spreads—some of the planners live in Beirut.

6

BEIRUT, 1972

The Ruling Class

A LOW THROATY HUM AND an Alfa Romeo passes a soft drink bottling plant on a small tributary road discreetly located in Schweifat, on the far side of Beirut airport. It turns into a narrow entrance secured by a barrier gate. The elderly gatekeeper hurries out to welcome the driver.

"Ahlaan wa Salaan."

Abbad, Rob's boss, waves dismissively and speeds past, his eyes hidden behind Cartier sunglasses, which cost more than his gatekeeper could earn in a year. The old man limps back to a small wooden hut, his daytime home.

The lines on his face are a map of his life, and he loves his job. It's a largely symbolic authority, he would be unable to resist any determined attempt at entry, but he has been trusted with the role of guard, and he values his place in the hierarchy. He recognizes the man in the fast car is at the top of that hierarchy.

The driveway winds down to a manufacturing plant nestled beside a long building which houses a laboratory. Above this, is a spacious flat covered in bougainvillea; home to Adnan, Shana, and their two children.

Deeper into the several acre compound, amid colorful, lushly planted gardens, a white Hacienda style villa, with a large sparkling pool is the longtime residence of Mark Langdon, Kat and their nine-year-old son, James. They've lived here and loved it for all of James' life. For all of those years, Mark has been General Manager of this factory, and they can't imagine a life anywhere else on the earth.

The sports car has driven far into the property, past groups of men who sit on the ground. As the sun rises high in the sky, the day grows warmer, and they work worry beads and brush away flies from their sandwiches.

Nashad, who met Genie at the airport, sits his five feet six-inch frame at the new white, spectrophotometer. It is designed to help them more accurately evaluate the colors they have to match in the laboratory. He thinks the human eye is the most accurate, but he's the chief lab technician and has to embrace the latest technology. Today the machine is switched off, there is no need for it or for his eyes. He looks over as Rob explodes.

"Ten of them stay home because a cow died! How can we run a factory and meet orders? I can't do my job like this. What shall I tell Abbad?"

Rob stops and turns to Mark who winks at Nashad and runs his hands through his close-cropped, dark hair. Rob sees them smile at each other.

"How have you lasted this long? What's it been, ten years?"

"Almost twelve, actually. I was twenty-seven when I came here, the same age as you."

This isn't their first setback, the immense effort to turn farm workers into factory help has become par for the course. In the corner Adnan quietly makes coffee, he takes the long handle of the large blue coffee pot and avoids eye contact, fills five cups.

Nashad takes two of them and walks out in search of Abbad. Mark offers one to Rob.

"What on earth did you expect? Ahlaan to la vie Libanese." Like a local, he seamlessly combines Arabic and French. "Welcome to Lebanese life." A dimple appears in the side of his angular face as he smiles. "If you think it's similar to working in the UK, you'll be frustrated every day of your tenure. You must've noticed by now, life is totally different here. Their values are not ours. You have to find common ground."

Rob takes the coffee and plops down on a stool. "You can laugh Mark, but it exhausts me, this struggle day after day. When we were in the construction phase I could understand delays, but it never gets any better, does it? Honestly, I don't know how to handle it."

A chemist by profession, Rob shoulders responsibility for the Laboratories, manufacturing and the quality of all the Master-batch produced in each of their four factories across the middle east. This concentrated colored product is added to natural plastics creating the myriad colored plastic items which are generated daily.

Outside, angry voices grow louder, Rob pokes his head out of the Lab window. Tin cans fly by, and he quickly pulls his head in, but not before one hits him—hard. He yells, and blood starts to pour down his face, a dark red stain forms on the front of his lab coat and a large lump blossoms on his cheek.

Adnan clicks his tongue and holds out a towel to mop Rob's face.

"Shit." With that loud curse, Rob follows Nashad who is at the door and, quick as a whippet, heads to the guard's hut.

Inside it is stacked high with cans, a mangy cat licks happily at piles of empties which litter the floor. Men shake the semi-toothless gatekeeper, wave their arms and yell incoherently. By the looks on their faces, the loud curses and frequent spitting on the ground, they are extremely upset.

"He has bought a cheap job-lot of canned food, and he cannot read, so he has used cat food to make their sandwiches, AND it is ten years out of date," Nashad explains "One of the men has read the cans, and now they are angry. It is not OK for Muslim's to eat cat food."

"Actually it's not OK for anyone to eat cat food, Nashad," Rob assures him, he presses the towel to his face and touches his tongue to the inside of his cheek, wonders if he has loosened a tooth. It hurts.

He takes fifty Lebanese pounds from his wallet, the cat circles around his feet, her tail captures his leg. "Please, will you go and buy them all a proper lunch." Rob shakes off the cat.

Mark watches from the doorway, still cool calm and at ease. He smiles and claps his hand on Rob's shoulder as he returns to wash away blood from his coat. Mark's smile fades as he sees the awful gash on Rob's cheek and above his eye.

"You know nothing much will happen here today, why not have Genie collect you? Go and tend to that bruise before it turns black."

"I saw Abbad arrive," Rob says. "He'll want some feedback." The project is Abbad's venture, but Rob's head has begun to throb, and he lets himself be convinced.

"Here's a thought for the day: Shway Shway—little by little. It'll all work out, Rob. Don't fret. I'll explain." Mark promises as Rob phones Genie.

By the time Genie and Doreen arrive Rob's face is swollen, and he climbs in the car without a word.

Abbad silkily approaches. He is beautifully groomed, and Genie can smell his expensive aftershave when he leans in, almost kissing her cheek. He smiles politely to her mother before he turns to speak to Rob.

"Next Thursday at seven?" he says, ignoring the wound on Rob's face.

"Absolutely, I'm looking forward to it. Wives, too?"

The delay is barely discernible. "Of course." He gets into his sports car and roars off, leaves them in his fumes.

"He's extremely handsome, isn't he? But there's something about him."

Rob's laugh turns to a grimace, it hurts to smile. "There's always something. You have an overdeveloped sixth sense. He's charming. You know, he was only a young boy when a fall from a horse killed his father. His uncle, the Big Boss, became his second father. This project is important to him."

Family ties are paramount here. Blood Ties. Lebanon is predominantly run by sixteen families, and theirs is one of them.

Nevertheless, Genie has a feeling about Abbad and, in spite of Rob making light of it, she is rarely wrong.

Doreen has forgotten the recent trauma and settled into a daily rhythm. When Rob called, she was excited at Genie's suggestion of an impromptu mid-week trip to the ancient Roman Hippodrome in Tyre, where two thousand years earlier chariots raced.

Now she smiles as Genie spreads her arms wide and breathes in deeply. "Isn't it amazing? It may sound weird, but I swear I feel the energy."

Doreen nods. "I do, too. I could stay here all day and imagine those who went before. So much history. Who wouldn't love it?"

"Can you believe Jesus came to Tyre to preach? It is often mentioned in the Bible, Nebuchadnezzar unsuccessfully laid siege for thirteen years, AND we are on the path once trodden by Alexander the Great!" she lowers the guide book and admires the ruins, tries to inhale it as Rob wanders away.

The sun is relentless, and he has spotted a drinks vendor who has waited eagerly for half an hour. There hasn't been much trade, he's almost given up and is about to go when Rob approaches.

Genie sits on the steps beside her mother whose eyes follow Rob.

"Is Rob OK? He seems to have lost some of his sparkle since you two came here." She stops as Rob returns with bottles of Sohat water.

"He offered me fourteen goats, three cows and two barrels of olives for you. Green eyes are at a premium, it seems," he says to Genie.

She glances at the man dressed in full Arabic garb. Several gold teeth glisten, he smiles and nods, puts his folded fingers to his mouth. "Mnihah!" he calls out.

She takes a bottle of water and walks away. "And you said?"

"I told him I wouldn't dream of taking such a deal." He sips the water, tosses a couple of painkillers down his throat. "I told him to keep the olives,"

He teases her until they find an incredible restaurant at the port where tall, dark, half-naked Nubians wave oversized feathered fans to cool them while they eat. Strutting peacocks present a brilliantly feathered fashion parade strolling among the tables, Doreen is captivated.

The fish is fresh, and they sip local wine.

Genie holds out the bottle "Chateaux Muser. From the Bekaa Valley. Maybe we could visit the vineyard?"

Rob shakes his head "I think it's unlikely we'll get to visit the vineyard or anywhere else in the near future," he says quietly. "Work has gone from an exciting challenge to a daily chore."

Genie reaches a hand across the table. "I'm so sorry, why didn't you say?"

In his weaker moments, he wonders if he's made the right choice. Rob likes the guys he works with, enjoys the travel and their impressive, comfortable home but he hardly gets to enjoy it, is always tired now. He pushes away the thoughts and vows to make it an enjoyable day for Genie and her mother.

"For three centuries this was the capital of Mount Lebanon," Genie tells her Mother as they pass Damour. Indulged and content they lazily drive up the coast.

"We can stop for coffee on the way home," Rob calls over his shoulder, "but let's press on, it's another hour's drive to Beit Eddine."

Doreen silently groans. So far her car sickness has remained under control, and she hopes she makes it up the hill, but Beit Eddine soon comes into view, and she gasps.

It was worth the drive. Nothing prepared Doreen for the architectural masterpiece, a palace redolent of the Alhambra in Granada built by the Moorish monarchs of Spain, and no less beautiful.

"This land continues to astound me," Doreen says. "It's almost too much to take in."

"They say the Emir who built these palaces asked every strong male to donate two days of labor when the palace was finished, legend says he cut off the architect's hands so he could never again create such beauty." Rob's head still throbs, and his cheek hurts like hell. "I need some shade, I'll catch you later." He wanders off toward courtyards and stables, which once housed six hundred horses.

Genie and her Mother slowly float through arches, bathhouses and harems, pause to listen to the bubble of marble fountains, touch intricate mosaic tiling and admire the fabulous marquetry.

"Penny for them," Doreen whispers in her ear.

"This is seductive, my favorite place in the world. I'd join the harem if the Emir was cute and I could live in such splendor," she declares.

"I'd better make lots of money, so you won't have to." Rob chuckles as he walks up behind her. "But somehow I don't think you have the temperament to share!"

"No, probably not," she agrees, and gently touches his cheek. "How are you feeling? It looks pretty bad."

"I'll survive. It's hard to imagine the talented people who could do this. I could use them now to help me!" he comments, only half in jest. The past few weeks Rob's frustration has grown and wormed its way into his psyche.

I wonder where they found the workers for the factory, she thinks. She knows his half dozen Lab staff are trained and educated, but the rough, grubbily clad men who spit and scratch and laze about the plant are plucked from a rural lifestyle and ill-suited for the demands of a production line. *If only he could be a step removed like Mark.*

But this is a massive promotion for Rob, and he experiences setbacks as personal failures. It worries her, hurts her to see his daily battle.

On the roof Noura struggles to collect the laundry, the wind is warm and strong and almost as soon as the final item is pegged up the clothes have dried. Above her head rain clouds gather and she's relieved when she hears the car return. She smiles as the rooftop door opens and Genie and Doreen appear with offers of help as the first drops fall.

"Just in time," she calls. Arms filled with sheets, they pull more from the line. "Aaah," Noura cries as one billows up and away. Air is sucked up, they struggle to hold the fabric as two black jets from nowhere streak by at supersonic speed, loud and extremely low,

"You can almost touch them." Genie pulls her hair away from her eyes.

The remaining sheets fly everywhere. Noura runs to gather some and heads for the door as Doreen raises her arms to protect her ears and trips, shrouded in a large white sheet like an Egyptian Mummy.

The jets scream into the distance and disappear, Noura creeps cautiously back from the doorway to help Genie unwrap her mother.

"You can't relax for more than a minute in this place," Doreen complains.

"Probably Israeli reconnaissance planes doing a check. It's not unusual, part of the excitement of living here."

Before Genie finishes speaking the planes, streak back overhead so fast, that apart from the blast of air it would seem a figment of the imagination. "I'll bet that was close to two thousand miles an hour. Amazing," Genie chuckles.

"It's not amazing or exciting, Genie. This stuff happens too much. It's a beautiful country, but it's also frenzied and schizoid. You can never relax, it doesn't feel safe. I'm leaving tomorrow, in my opinion, you should convince Rob to come home."

Noura turns away from the family discussion and quickly waddles off looking like a pregnant penguin, arms full of laundry which almost overwhelms her.

In the warm rain on the rooftop Genie wraps her arms around her mother and places moist kisses on her cheek.

"No, Mumma. There's nothing there for us anymore. We've put it behind us. You've seen how beautiful Lebanon is. Until I have babies, I'm going to teach, and when Rob finishes his contract maybe we'll move to the USA, the American partners have made suggestions about the future." She puts a final kiss on her mother's cheek. "He's my husband, this is our home, at least for the next few years, and you shouldn't worry. Believe it or not, it is pretty safe and secure."

Doreen accepts her daughter's decision but doesn't agree with her analysis. Unlike Genie, she is filled with foreboding, but she says a prayer and the following day she leaves.

A week later Genie commences her studies in TEFL. It is a new method, Teaching English as a Foreign Language, without translation. An articulate and interesting mixture of role play and language games added to the more traditional system.

David, her designated teacher, is inspirational and makes teaching seem simple. She grows fond of him, and his slender, live-in friend Marvin dresses like a schoolboy, is friendly and a jokester, but his hands can never reach deeply enough into his pockets when it's his turn to pay. He's legendary in his tightfistedness, and it's a challenge among the guys to find ways to force Marvin to foot a bill.

Within a short while, she gets her diploma, starts to teach, and her life takes on a sense of purpose. The young students who earnestly grapple with the challenge of a new language are a pleasure, she loves the light bulb moment when one of them grasps a concept she imparts. In large part it's theatre, and she feels like a drama coach as she plans, and acts out the words and phrases.

The novelty of being back at school is shared with another English girl. Long and lean, Jacqui belongs on a cat-walk. At less than thirty, the distinctive streak of white which runs straight back from her forehead through short black hair is striking. Born in Worthing, eight miles from Genie's home, her older French husband's work with United Nations Relief and Works Agency (UNRWA) takes them around the globe. When they're not on a posting, they call Cannes home.

Genie envies her self assuredness, a gracious way of being she would love to achieve.

For the first time since they arrived Genie feels alive, like a person with a life of her own.

Three months later Roslyn arrives. "Is this the right place to study as a TEFL teacher?" she asks.

When Genie turns, she is surprised to see a tall, voluptuous girl in designer clothes whose shoes probably cost two months salary. Why would she want to do this? Genie wonders. Lunches poolside at the St. Georges look more her style.

"I'm Roslyn," she holds out a hand. Her smile reveals enormous sweetness and warmth. "I've always wanted to teach, and I've waited so long for the chance," she admits.

Genie feels a moment of remorse. *I'm turning into a judgmental bitch,* she thinks. "I'll show you to the office, I enrolled a few months ago."

Roslyn is an open book. She tells Genie she met and married a successful Lebanese industrialist straight out of school in England, quickly bore two kids and has never needed to work. Now she wants a sense of accomplishment and before they've even reached the office seeds of friendship have been planted.

When Genie finishes classes and becomes a teacher, Roslyn stays behind each day to observe. She slips into the back of Genie's classroom, waves her fingers and watches, making copious notes with an oversized, purple pen on an artist's pad.

On Friday students surround Genie. One of them offers her a large box of beautifully wrapped Lebanese chocolates.

"I bought them for you, Mrs. Genie. You are the best teacher," a young man tells her. He is dedicated and determined to polish his English, he's in love with the Beatles, E-type Jaguars and longs to study in England. "The Lebanese make the best chocolates."

Genie hesitates.

"The best for the best," he adds.

Charmed by the notion she accepts them.

Roslyn comes to give her a hug "One day soon that'll be me. I've been feeling unfulfilled. I want to become a great teacher, maybe even the best?" she teases.

"I'm sure you will, now let's get out of here, do you have time for lunch and shopping!"

On Hamra Street, it is impossible to resist the bookshops, sidewalk cafes and elegant French boutiques, as well as a variety of small local shops. The AUB, American University, located nearby draws free thinkers and the intelligentsia to this vibrant area, and it throbs with life day and night.

After a couple of hours, they are shopped out and laden with packages.

"Let's stop for something at Movenpick," Roslyn suggests. They find a seat, review the long and glossy menu; colorful pictures of various, irresistible ice cream concoctions, at this, their favorite cafe.

"They look delicious, but very rich," Genie says.

"We only live once," Roslyn smiles and orders a half cantaloupe melon filled with ice cream, fresh fruit and topped with swirls of Chantilly cream.

"I'll have the same."

Sated, warmed by the sun and sleepy they head back to Genie's car.

The cafes successfully keep beggars at bay, but on the side streets thin, open hands and pleading eyes approach at each street corner. Since the recent skirmishes, there are so many more in the city, as their ramshackle homes have been destroyed.

A small, wide-eyed child approaches, "Baksheesh," he says. He is tiny and underfed. Genie gives him coins, a bar of chocolate, and an orange. He nibbles the chocolate and passes the remainder, along with the orange, to an even smaller boy, clearly his brother.

Moved, Genie hands him the entire bag, and like pirañhas who've scented blood, barefoot kids appear from nowhere, swarming them.

"Aah," one cries out and falls to the pavement, she lifts her foot, it bleeds copiously from shards of broken glass, her brother bends and gently pulls them out.

A shopkeeper hurries out and with a string of abuse shoos the children away, to him they're no more than cockroaches.

Genie turns to Roslyn. "Those children have no shoes," Roslyn stops and looks at her. "It's the least of their worries. Some have parents who break their bones. They rely on people's sympathy generating more money. You need thicker skin my sweet, or it'll break your heart."

"No, Roslyn, doing nothing will break my heart. I'll catch you later."

Without a goodbye, she takes off as Roslyn looks after her in astonishment.

At Spinneys supermarket Genie finds what she needs. In a few minutes, she is back, cruising up and down Hamra in search of the children.

Roslyn is nowhere to be seen, probably home by now.

Genie focuses on the task at hand and doesn't notice their Syrian "Crusader" friend Karam, who chats as he eats falafel in the doorway of his cousin's restaurant, nearby. He watches as she passes and minutes later he sees her drive back.

What on earth is she looking for? He wonders.

Eventually, she spots the children disappearing down a side street. She pulls over, grabs two large bags and jumps from the car.

Karam turns to watch as a tall, older beggar blocks her path. She walks around him. The children reach out, but he tears at the bag, it splits. Bars of chocolate and more than a dozen pairs of brightly colored plastic shoes and pairs of socks spill out. The children scramble for them. He shoves them aside, kicks one out of the way, raises a stick and turns on Genie as she tries to defend the children.

She starts to argue, but Karam scuttles across the street and quickly steps in. He takes the stick from the man's hand and pulls her firmly away.

"Genie, your heart is kind, but he is right. You cannot help these little ones. This is their fate."

She recoils from him. "Who are you?" She searches his face for empathy. "Our conduct determines their fate. We should try to help them," she says and pulls her arm away.

"Others have thought this. Yet here they are, still poor and helpless."

His words are drowned out, from nowhere planes scream by overhead and the quiet of the day is shattered.

Not again, she thinks as bombs fall nearby. Involuntarily Genie feels a scream come from her throat.

Bits of paper float, disconnected from time or gravity, one after another more and more bombs fall amid explosions which deafen. Dust, debris, fragments of metal fly about and the small children cry, reach for each other and run.

Black smoke fills the air, billows, fills her lungs. She chokes, pushes Karam aside, cries out and runs to the nearest wall, attempts to scale it without result. She scratches 'til blood runs from her fingers. A pointless waste of effort, but she scrapes and clings to the wall as if her life is at stake, almost crazy with fear.

Karam chases her, pulls her into his arms, pries her away from the building. She looks down at her bloody hands, at the street awash in shattered glass and she falls silent, conscious of the sirens as they approach, muffled sounds, as if through water.

From somewhere in the dust muted screams continue to fill the air. Genie holds tightly to Karam, her eyes frantically scan the deserted street.

"Where are the children? Were they hurt?"

He holds her and croons. "Shh. They have gone, they are alive, and you are safe. But the bombs hit a refugee camp, maybe more than one. We should check on Rob and get you out of here."

He finds a taxi and takes her to her husband.

Rob drives home slowly, he is quietly shocked at how this attack has affected her. He holds Genie's hand, feels the roughness of tape on her fingertips.

The beggar children, still barefoot, now sit on the pavement near the old man who seems to control them. They are dustier than earlier in the day, pieces of debris cling to their hair. At the man's feet, he now displays a pile of small shoes and socks for sale.

Still shaken from the earlier bombing, she looks out of the window.

"Maybe Karam was right after all. It is their fate."

"It's horrible, but overwhelming, a Caste system," Rob says. "Here, if you're born to this, you've almost no way out."

"Especially when those who could help have no plans to do so."

It has been days since the bombing and Genie marvels at how quickly things have returned to normal. They cruise along the coast with the windows open, a warm breeze blows her hair, she lifts a hand to push a strand out of her eyes.

The bracelets on her wrist jangle and she turns her tanned arm to appreciate them. She admired them in the Bazaar in Damascus when they'd taken her mother, and Rob secretly bought them for her. She loves the sound they make and feels feminine and faintly gypsy-like. *Wouldn't it be great to tell fortunes?* she thinks. The tiny scars on her fingertips are discreet, but they remind her of the dramas of this past year.

They swing into the semi-circle of the driveway at the Phoenicia hotel, tall palm trees sway in the slight evening breeze, and the setting sun has left a haunting, translucent quality to the light.

"I was uncomfortable last time. Are you certain I was invited?"

"Of course."

They stop, an attendant opens the door. she steps out of the car and the fragrance hits her. She breathes in. It's delicious and heady, like an expensive French perfume a reminder of the unique mix of ancient and modern in this fabulous city.

"Great place, isn't it?" Rob says. He puts an arm around her as they head toward Adnan who waits underneath an enormous chandelier at the top of an extraordinarily broad and impressive flight of stairs.

Adnan is all smiles as ever, but she notices in Abbad's face the slightest flicker of irritation when he sees her, for less than a second, and it immediately disappears, but it doesn't go unnoticed by Genie.

"I shouldn't be here," she whispers.

"Nonsense," Rob replies "You're too sensitive, you always imagine things."

But from the first moment, she realizes she should have known better. Rob assured her she should come, her dilemma was whether to risk offense by declining a sincere invitation or embarrassment by accepting one that was not intended.

Now she sees they should have KNOWN. Again Abbad spoke out of politeness, his upbringing didn't permit him to decline when presumably Rob asked, but it was understood, wasn't it?

What on earth was he thinking? She wonders.

She's miserable and unfortunately grows resentful, withdraws into herself. Rob is blithely unaware of the tension, but Adnan has noticed it increase, and as business discussions end Abbad has quickly lost his veneer of charm, the alcohol perhaps compounds this.

She watches as he freely orders French champagne, caviar and an abundance of seafood on ice. Oysters on the half shell, mussels, crab legs, lobster all regally displayed on a three-tiered, silver stand. She looks at the opulence, the surfeit of food and it fills her with sadness. She can't eat as she thinks of the dusty little children who need to beg for coins and oranges. It's unreasonable, not his fault, but she resents Abbad for his lack of awareness.

A dribble of champagne hits the table as a nervous waiter opens a second bottle and Abbad castigates the shy insecure boy whose hands shake as he mops away the liquid, apologizing profusely, but Abbad demands a replacement server. The charm he exudes to a few people has slipped, replaced by a cool arrogance as the evening proceeds.

Her head doesn't stop pounding until they get up to leave, but in the Lobby, an exchange in Arabic, which she doesn't understand, has now upset and insulted a man who attempts to grab Abbad.

Deftly Adnan takes the man aside, pulls an enormous wad of notes from his pocket and subtly pays him off, preventing an escalation.

It's so smoothly done it can't be the first time he has acted as Abbad's "fixer," Genie decides, and she glowers at Adnan for his participation in this scenario.

By now Rob has sensed her mood and fumbles for her wounded hand. "I'm sorry, it was a mess of a night," he says. "I guess you were right all along, you weren't supposed to be here. Nevertheless, you could have handled it more graciously."

She doesn't protest. Rob is right, she was petulant and moody and probably made the situation worse. It was an insight into the pecking order and the ability to behave atrociously and be pardoned if one is "someone" in this town.

They claim their car, and she rolls down the windows, the breeze feels good on her skin as they drive along the Corniche. Slowly her demons float out of the window.

"I'm sorry. I didn't handle things maturely. I don't do well when I feel embarrassed. If I sense I don't belong. It makes me feel small. But I wasn't wrong about Abbad, he's completely self-involved."

7

BEIRUT, APRIL 1973

Settling Scores

THE ISRAELI NATIONAL INTELLIGENCE AGENCY Mossad has obtained photos and the addresses of three planners of the Munich Olympic Games massacre, all live in neighboring apartments on Rue Verdun, not far from the center of Ras Beirut.

Aware of the heavily guarded location, Mossad has secretly formed 'Operation Spring of Youth' an offshoot of 'Wrath of God', which has successfully operated across Europe and eliminated many of the assassins.

Over the past twenty-four hours, Mossad agents have secretly entered Beirut with fake passports, they've rented vehicles, confirmed their locations and plans.

Among those charged with the removal of the planners and perpetrators of the massacre is future defense minister Ehud Barak.

The date they've chosen is tonight, April 9–10.

Israeli Navy missile boats wait offshore. Along the coast, under cover of night, manned Zodiac speedboats are lowered into the water. Heavily armed Commandos from Israel's Shayetet 13, Sayeret Matkal and Sayeret Tzanhanim slip silently ashore to be met by additional Mossad agents who have three cars, engines running, ready to take them to their targets.

"The American partners are passing through town again, I said we'd meet for dinner."

Genie sighs. "I'm so tired, why couldn't we just stay home?"

"They're only here overnight, they leave for LA tomorrow. It's our one chance for you to say hello. We'll kill a couple of hours at the Bristol. They'll be disappointed if we don't, and it's important to me, for our future."

In fact, it's very late when they eventually leave the Bristol Hotel on Madame Curie Street. Rob slips his arm around Genie.

"Well, the food and ambiance were good, but I could have happily gone home hours ago."

"They're really nice, but God they can talk, I thought they'd never stop. It's only an elevator ride for them up to their beds, but we still have that drive." She puts her shawl behind her head in the car. "I'm going to nap if you don't mind."

But she doesn't nap for long. Along the road, scores are being settled.

An ear-shattering explosion and the front door of an apartment is blown wide.

Inside Muhammed Abu Youssef—al-Najjar sleeps. In seconds agents storm the bedroom leaving him no time to grab the pistol he keeps nearby, not near enough as it turns out. In a selfless act, his wife throws herself over his body and is caught in the spray of bullets intended for him. They die together.

A member of Fatah's central committee, Palestinian Liberation Organization (PLO), Black September and also third in line to the Chairman, he is no more.

As Genie and Rob drive they are heading toward the battle.

On the second floor of an adjacent building, Kamal Adwan wakes as his guard is killed outside the door. He grabs a machine gun but is taken by surprise as men enter through the kitchen window. Bullets are shot into his head and neck before he's able to return fire.

Palestinian's Fatah central committee has lost one more member.

Meantime a third group flies up to the third floor, into the apartment of Kamal Nasser, Poet, PLO Executive Committee member and head of information. With a 6mm pistol he tries to resist, fires every round in his weapon until it runs out, but his opponents have superior firepower.

Each team exits the building.

And along Rue Verdun, Rob brakes hard, throwing Genie forward as the tires screech. She sits upright, alert and startled at the gunshots.

"What on earth's happening?"

Up ahead an action scene plays out, like a film set. A gun fires, a man falls to the ground. Their car slides to a halt.

Rob's grip on the wheels is so tight she can see his knuckles are white, the blood has fled to safety.

"Let's get out of here!" she cries over the gunfire which continues as a mixed group, with a couple of strangely dressed women, runs into waiting cars.

People have been caught in the crossfire and are slumped on the ground. With a squeal of tires, the cars speed away.

Genie grabs onto the overhead handle. "Turn around. Drive, drive."

"Give me a chance, I'm going," he spins the car around and takes off in the opposite direction.

Along the coast, a series of explosions shatter the night, but as they drive away, the danger has passed, for them at least.

Rob screeches to a halt outside their building and races upstairs two at a time. He grabs his camera with a telephoto lens and rushes out to the balcony, he scans the coast, and peers through the camera lens.

"Something is on fire down the coast," he tells her. "Jeez, it's like fireworks' night. It's big."

Leaning against the window Genie watches his excitement. "This isn't a movie. We could've been caught in the middle of whatever it was."

Just along the coast in Ramlet al Baida, unseen by anyone, ripples lap the shore. Without fuss, the commandos disappear into the Mediterranean blackness unhindered by the Lebanese beach patrol which, in a life-preserving decision, decides to turn a blind eye.

The next day the Lab is abuzz.

"Some say they made their way back to the beaches for extraction, others that the US Embassy offers them refuge. They've called it Operation Spring of Youth." Mark tells them as he walks in after lunch.

Adnan picks up an Arabic language newspaper and reads out occasional sentences. Each "b and p" sound is accompanied by small explosions of air.

"A six-story building, headquarters of a Palestinian organization, was attacked—strong resistance. Two attackers died, the building was destroyed." He sips his coffee before he continues. "Naval commandos and paratroopers also raided Palestinian fuel dumps and arms facilities. Up to 100 were killed—one Israeli wounded."

"I think we saw some of it when we left the Bristol last night," Rob says offhandedly.

They all stop and stare at him, speechless.

"Of course we didn't know what it was. It looked like a robbery, there were a couple of women, too. Later I saw explosions along the coast."

"That was them. Two of the Israelis dressed as women to avoid suspicion," Adnan says. "There are sure to be protests in town, Rob."

Mark examines a plastic sample with Nashad, he sets it aside and turns to Rob.

"Do you understand what he means, Rob? They believe the Israelis from the Verdun killings are being hidden by the American Embassy, doesn't Genie go that way to school?"

Adnan glances at Mark for support. "There are furious protests all across the Arab world. They could think she's an American."

Mark continues. "I tend to agree with Adnan it could be dangerous if she's in town teaching today. How does she usually get home?"

"She's there 'til six, and she'll grab a taxi, but she's obviously not American! There's no cause for alarm. She'll be fine." Rob walks back into the depths of the factory.

Mark shrugs to Adnan and rolls his eyes.

"A river in Egypt!" Mark says offhandedly. Adnan stares at him, perplexed.

"The Nile—Denial! It's meant to be a joke." They say no more, but there is an uncomfortable awkwardness at the end of the day as Rob collects his things and heads home without further discussion.

Adnan watches him go, stares at the lab clock for a while, then shakes his head, takes off his white coat and grabs a jacket.

On West Beirut's northern waterfront, walls and gates obscure part of the stone facade of the American Embassy.

Adnan drives slowly around the headland along the sparkling Corniche searching for Genie. There is a larger than usual crowd outside, but eventually, he catches sight of her as she approaches the chanting crowd.

He screeches to a halt, startles her. "Get in."

Surprised, Genie does not move.

People hear him shout in English and they turn. A man yells. "Damned Américain." He spits at her feet and moves toward her.

Shocked, she starts to protest.

Adnan screams at her. "Get in the bloody car, NOW."

She opens the door, but the man has covered the ground between them and grabs at her, drags her. She sees the fury in his face, doesn't understand why he hates her, but Adnan's voice screams out, and she kicks violently, her heel lands hard against the man's shin, he cries in pain, and she wrestles free, barely ahead of the angry crowd which circles them.

She jumps into the car and slams the door, shocked as fists rain down and hammer ferociously on the roof and windows.

She sits with her back pressed hard against the seat. Boots kick the door, and she flinches, faces full of rage press against the window, one woman spits, and it slides down the glass. Others rock the vehicle back and forth.

"My God. What do they want?" Her terrified eyes scan Adnan's. He reaches over, puts a hand in front of her, and she sees he looks frightened, too.

"Hold on," he yells. There is a smell of rubber as he accelerates, knocks people aside. Rocks crash into the car and pieces of ripe fruit splatter the windows as he speeds away, up the coast and out of town.

"What's going on and where is Rob?" she demands.

Adnan shrugs. "He sent me."

They drive in silence all the way to Naqqash. Genie thanks Adnan and heads into the apartment.

The sounds of Johnny Cash fill the corridors, Rob is in the bath rubbing a foamy loofah on his back while he sings loudly.

I keep a close watch on this heart of mine,
I keep my eyes wide open all the time,

Genie walks in. "You need a cowboy hat."

Rob lets out the water, climbs out of the bath and encompasses Genie in his towel, she stiffens.

"Why didn't you come for me today?" she asks calmly.

He looks confused. "What?"

"You sent Adnan to get me."

He makes a mental note to thank Adnan for covering his rear.

"Why didn't you come yourself?"

"I had problems at work. You've no idea." He is defensive.

"So tell me, Rob. What was more important than the safety of your wife?"

He holds his hands, palms out, in a dismissive gesture. "Nothing to tell. I simply thought Adnan exaggerated, and I know how competent you are."

"Well, surprise, surprise, he wasn't, and I don't think it's about competence," she says. She wriggles free from the towel. "I was terrified. We were almost caught by crazies who wanted to hurt us. It would've been nice to have my husband rescue me! This nonchalance of yours is no longer charming, it's becoming old hat. Do you not get it or don't you care?"

She goes to the mirror and unwraps the scarf from her head, her hair falls softly over her shoulders and down her back, and he watches her nightly ceremony as she slowly brushes out her long, wavy hair.

She sees him watch her. "If you do still care, about me and about this marriage—at all—you need to show it because honestly, I'm pretty sick of this."

8

OCTOBER 6~24, 1973

Yom Kippur War

THINGS SETTLE AGAIN, AND SO do they. Six more months have flown by and this is now indeed their home. She is busy with work and friends and continues to embrace the culture.

"Come up to the mountains with us tomorrow," Roslyn says after school. "The restaurant is ethnic, you'll love it, we laze around on cushions eat with our fingers and smoke hookahs."

That night Rob laughs when she tells him about it, but they accept, and the next day Roslyn's husband Khalil drives them to the mountains.

"It is good to do this now before the start of Ramadan, for that we stay in town with family for the evening meal," he says.

Genie has never grown close to Khalil. He is always polite and pleasant but slightly removed. Genie cannot understand what attracted Roslyn to this plump, self-indulgent man. *Perhaps he has changed over the years?* She has seen other Lebanese husbands who change when they marry after returning from their overseas studies.

The owner creates a fuss of Khalil and leads the group to a low table, apparently reserved for special guests. He snaps his fingers, and a young man puts a bottle of Arak and a jug of water in front of them.

"With my compliments," the man says as the young waiter loads the table with the usual nuts, olives, vegetables, and hummus.

No menus are presented, but soon several large platters are put before them. The restaurant owner beams and with a sweeping movement of his hands reveals the feast.

"Enjoy," he says and, walking backward, he retires.

"What on earth is that?" Genie exclaims as she looks down.

"Sheep's eyes," Khalil says. "They are interesting, a delicacy. Just think, each sheep has only two eyes, so they are prized."

Genie tries to hide her reaction. *Not again*, she thinks. This time she won't feel obliged to partake.

"They are spongy, taste a little like cream," he says and pops one into his mouth.

Rob looks at her out of the corner of his eye and tears off a piece of Arabic bread, he wraps it around one and eats it. She watches, but he avoids looking at her as he takes a long sip of Arak to wash it down.

"They specialize in these and sweetbreads, also testicles," Khalil says.

Roslyn has her head down, eating sweetbreads and salad, and Genie wonders if Khalil has deliberately invited them here to shock them. He laughs at her reaction.

"You British eat blood sausage, offal, and sweetbreads," he scoffs. "Why so squeamish?"

She ignores him, takes some salad and some of the chopped Tabouleh, a Lebanese salad she quite likes, and for tonight she decides to remain vegetarian.

"If you stand at the airport long enough, sooner or later everyone we know will pass through," Rob jokes.

There is some truth to his words. They often run into friends at airports around the Mediterranean. Like Genie and Rob, they're young and have been born into an age which allows them to explore their world freely.

Although Rob is cranky at times, the opportunities to travel to neighboring Syria, Egypt, Turkey, Tehran, Greece, and the islands make his challenges worthwhile, Beirut seems to be at the center of the world, and he enjoys that feeling.

But halfway through October 1973 whispers grow more frequent in cafes and pubs around Beirut about an Arab-Israeli War. For some reason, there are few broadcasts, and neither Genie nor Rob can discover how significant this may be.

Ramadan has arrived, the time for abstaining from food during the daylight hours and the guys in the factory are lacking in energy as they wait for sunset to enjoy the evening meal.

In the lab, Adnan is a little less strict, and he sips water and looks at the Arabic paper.

"An Arab coalition led by Egypt and Syria surprised Israel on their holiest day, Yom Kippur," he says.

Rob listens, hoping to learn something new.

"Egyptian forces have made gains into Israeli-held territory," Nashad adds.

"How come nothing is reported in the Daily Star?" Rob asks. But he knows the answer, only the positive gains are reported, he suspects there is probably more to the story.

"Fighting in the Sinai and the Golan Heights does not affect Beirut," Adnan tells him.

Little more is mentioned when the tide turns, and the coalition is pushed back to the pre-war cease-fire lines.

When Nashad says "The Israelis are shelling Damascus." Rob grows concerned.

He decides to hide it from Genie, there's nothing to be gained by worrying her, but he makes a dreadful poker player, and when he walks in he knows she knows something is up.

"What's going on?" she demands as he whistles and pours a drink.

His joviality is unusual these days and anyway it seems forced, she is suspicious, his expressive eyes are unguarded and give him away.

"Rob?"

He turns on his country music, and Johnny Cash sings:

I hear the train a comin'
It's rollin' round the bend,

He pulls her into a slow dance, nuzzles her neck.

And I ain't seen the sunshine
Since I don't know when

She laughs as he spins her around. "I know you. I can tell something is going on."

"OK, lay another place at the table. The Israelis could be here by dinnertime!" he says.

"What are you saying?" She pulls away from him, aghast.

"They're outside Damascus, a couple of hours drive from here, and I know where I'd rather be if I were them," he says.

"But we're an independent nation! Are you serious? Could we be actually caught up in this?"

"I'm kidding, sort of. But the Israelis are shelling Damascus."

The Israelis, of course, do not come, and a few days later when Genie passes their neighbor Mary on the hillside walking with her little daughter, she hears the story.

"The Israelis crossed the Suez Canal and surrounded the city of Suez," Mary says. "Amazing we only hear of the victories, never the defeats. Now the US and the Soviet Union have imposed a cease-fire, and the war has ended."

Genie breathes a sigh of relief and life goes on. Work, pool, parties, travel.

Months slide by with few crises. Slowly they find a rhythm of life which satisfies them both.

The dry, hot Hamsin wind buffets her with stinging sand blown from North Africa and her irritation mounts.

Uncomfortable and feeling hot, she waits for Rob and fights to stay upright on the corner of Bourj Hammoud. Her arms ache from holding a load of fresh vegetables for dinner, and she wishes for the umpteenth time Rob would treat her with more care, look out for her.

Where the hell is he? She wonders yet again. *This is the second time this week he has forgotten me.*

Her scarf blows across her face and brushing it aside she spots a series of clocks displayed in a jewelry store window, each a ticking reminder that Rob is almost half an hour late.

A car passes, toots its horn. *The fourth idiot so far,* she thinks. But she knows the driver probably believes she's for sale and she's embarrassed. Sooner or later the police will notice, and she'll be questioned. *This happens way too often,* she tells herself and secures the last seat in the local taxi.

She fumes all the way home into the hills.

"Where've you been, you're late?" Stuart laughs as she pushes open the front door. One of the bags splits, and she sucks in her anger, she'll save it for later. Stuart and his friend Keith stand as she walks in.

Their apartment is a stopping off place for many of the single guys, she's gained a reputation for feeding the 'homeless' as they call themselves, there's always a welcome 'chez Miller' when they're hungry or need to reconnect with their roots, and she really loves the constant stream of company.

"I have two husbands to answer to now?" she replies as they hurry to help. "Excellent. Maybe one of them will be able to remember to pick me up next time, as arranged."

She tries to sound light, gives Stuart a kiss on each cheek.

"Aahlan, welcome."

She deliberately avoids kissing Rob, but Stuart doesn't seem to notice, and she turns as Keith helps her with the bags. A consummate gentleman, he is polite, tanned and healthy, and Genie imagines him at home on a yacht back in Dunedin on the far side of the world; his sun bleached hair tossed by the wind. His gentle, warm and soft-spoken manner is perfect for the work he does with the UN relief organization which supports refugees.

He wouldn't forget his wife, she thinks.

Stuart takes his seat beside Rob and gives him a sidelong look. Rob recalls his promise and is full of apologies.

"I get so distracted, I don't remember what I am supposed to do half the time," he calls to her. "I'm sorry Genie, it's not personal."

"It feels pretty personal to me when the locals drive by and offer money for who knows what? Anyway, enough of that. Who's hungry?" she calls over her shoulder as she goes to join Keith unload the groceries in the kitchen.

Stuart's eyes light at the promise of food. "Let me help," he says.

She and Stuart have resolved their earlier coolness. He assured her he had almost no memory of the remark. "It was a throwaway comment with no great significance. I was probably trying to make an impression."

Good food, wine, and laughter lift the tension, but Genie still resents Rob's apparent indifference. *He seems less available these days, but I deserve some attention, for God's sake. How would he feel if I left him waiting and forgot all about him?*

Dinner over, Keith helps carry plates to the kitchen, and the two visitors grab their coats. "It's great that you take us all under your wing" he says. "It feels like we have a home here."

Rob has barely closed the door behind them before Genie confronts him.

"It's not ok, Rob. I'm sick of your indifference."

At first, he apologizes, but almost immediately he's had enough.

"I can't stand any more conflict." He storms out slamming the front door. She hears the car below as it drives off and with nowhere to put her fury it festers.

When he returns later, he doesn't come to bed and instead sleeps on the couch.

In the early dawn light, she walks into the lounge. He wakes, and the row which erupts is the strongest they've ever had.

"I'm so angry at you and your attitude. We hardly make love, you're always tired. Frankly, I wonder who you are and what you've done with the man I married. I don't want you, I want him!"

We could be happy, but Rob refuses to make an effort, she thinks, and her resentment increases.

Gradually a chasm has opened, and it threatens to widen.

Rob calls Genie to meet him at the Rose and Crown, she's been on edge for days, and he hopes that meeting with friends it will dissipate.

The pub is full, Keith and Stuart are at the bar chatting with Rob and Karam, their charming Syrian friend, now a fixture in the ex-pat community, who sits nearby along the semi-circular bar.

"We're to be guides, fixers, and aides de camp for a documentary film crew, in the upcoming 1974 Liban-Syrie Desert Rally," Stuart says. "Through Lebanon, Damascus, Palmyra, Aleppo and so on. Three days and three thousand kilometers."

"Supposed to be tougher than the Moroccan Desert Rally and the East African Safari," Karam says. "Drivers compete from Europe, Kuwait, and Lebanon."

"Lots of sand—thirsty work," Rob laughs taking a long swig.

"There's a Champagne celebration at the St. Georges when it ends," Stuart grins.

Karam lifts his head as Genie arrives and nods a greeting. But before she reaches the bar, he has been waylaid and book-ended by two girls in shorts and University sweatshirts who unsuccessfully attempt to engage him.

What is it about men who are disinterested that make them catnip to women? Genie wonders. She waves and walks over to Rob. She is filled with excitement at her news.

"I've been offered the chance of an expenses paid trip to Jordan. They want to make a film at all the tourist spots, Petra, Aqaba, the lot. It's to encourage tourism in Jordan—I'd love to do it," she finishes, breathless.

"That sounds great," Rob replies. "We'd have to work out the schedule, of course. When would we leave and for how long?"

"Well, it's in a few weeks," she hesitates. "But you don't have to worry. I'd work with a male model, and I'd be gone just three or four days," she adds. "You don't even have to come if you're too busy."

Stuart splutters into his beer, Keith coughs. In a smooth movement, they both turn to Karam and the girls along the bar.

Embarrassed and not too happy, Rob glances at them, then turns to her.

Karam is alert and listens carefully.

"You sabotaged me," Rob snaps and bangs down his glass, splashing the contents on the bar. "Frankly, I don't like the idea of my wife traipsing around another country, or any country for that matter, with some stranger." His voice is too loud, and heads turn to watch them.

Angry at his proprietorial attitude Genie sucks in her breath and opens her mouth to protest, but Karam is already by her side and squeezes her arm.

"What are you drinking, Rob?" he says.

Rob wipes beer from his hands and empties his glass. "I'll have a pint, thanks."

Skillfully the situation is diffused, and that is that.

"If only for a few days, I would have enjoyed being the center of attention," she says.

He ignores her, and the estrangement grows.

The month ends, they haven't made peace, he takes off overseas, and she falls back into the routine of her life.

9

BEIRUT, NEW YEAR 1975

GENIE SMILES AT HER REFLECTION in the enormous mirror as she walks out of The Marcel and Ibrahim hair salon. They always make her feel like a celebrity, and she loves the new hairstyle.

Rob arrives, on schedule for a change, so they have time to dress for the celebrations.

It doesn't feel like Tuesday, in fact, the whole week she's been out of step with the calendar. Christmas was quiet, many went home for the holidays this year. Now they're all back to work and to welcome in 1975.

The recently opened Holiday Inn Hotel has strung large banners around announcing—1975. *As if anyone is in doubt about the date,* she thinks. Happiness and promise herald the imminent arrival of another year.

A ten piece band plays, couples dance and the halls and corridors fill with laughter, tangible joy at the end of a challenging year barely minutes away.

Like every New Year, hope abounds, a desire that the year to come will be better.

Over stuffed with acquaintances who've arrived, eager to let their collective hair down, optimism floats over the room and, with a dozen of their closest friends they carve out an area to celebrate.

A pocket-sized Lebanese boy, who always wears an ear to ear smile and has the knack of turning up wherever they go, takes Genie to the dance floor. He holds her a little too close, and she separates herself slightly. He rests his head against her hair, and she can feel him breathe her in.

"I'd like to sleep with you," he whispers.

"But you know I'm married."

He pauses for barely a moment and, with a look of deep sincerity, he tells her. "I don't mind."

Genie starts to laugh, un-phased by the rebuff he smiles. "I'm off to Sweden next week. I hear the girls there LOVE guys like me." He is good looking, with dark skin and wild curly hair and Genie can well imagine the Swedish girls will find him appealing. They pull apart as the band stops and is immediately replaced by refrains from mesmerizing middle eastern instruments. They turn and walk off the floor.

Scantily dressed, beautiful veiled girls in sequins and crystals shimmer to the center of the floor, without a pause they dance to the exotic music.

The floor quickly clears, except for Keith and his pretty Canadian girlfriend, Margaret. They slow dance lost to the world, snuggled into each other.

The intensity of the music increases and they change their steps, he begins an odd perhaps New Zealand-Maori version of belly dance, Margaret laughs as he gyrates his tall, slim frame, they haven't yet noticed they are surrounded by exotic dancers.

Keith hears her laugh and opens his eyes, "Shit, are we the only ones on the floor?" He grabs Margaret's hand, drags her to join their crowd, who applaud and laugh at his unselfconscious dance.

Soon every eye is held, hypnotized by the complex movements of the dancers' bodies, the jangle of their ankle bracelets; tiny cymbals periodically clash on their fingers and their coin belts tinkle, a Lebanese blend of Egyptian and Turkish dance, with freedom and zing. Their arms and chests vibrate as they lean back almost to breaking point and transition to an incredible rotation of their hips.

Light and free they float around the dance floor for a couple of sets, enveloped in a fragrance of musk and flowers which fills the air until each girl moves to the edge, circling and shimmying around one sparkling girl draped in turquoise gossamer, who remains lifeless as a statue.

The crowd waits, and Genie gasps into the silence as the woman starts to quiver, relentlessly revealing all of the internal movement of her body. An anatomical magician, she moves her torso like a fakir's snake.

Genie and Rob are entranced, the applause is tremendous.

Before the count down to midnight the distant sound of bagpipes approaches, it grows louder, and conversation stops. In full regalia, Stuart's Scottish colleague enters the room, pumping out 'Auld Lang Syne'.

A loud cheer fills the space followed by more applause, voices join together and sing the two-hundred-year-old lament by Robert Burns:

Should old acquaintance be forgot
and never brought to mind
Should old acquaintance be forgot
for the sake of auld lang syne.
For auld lang syne my dear, For auld lang syne,

we'll tak a cup of kindness then,
For the sake of auld lang syne

Colorful balloons cascade from the ceiling, some pop as they descend. Crystal glasses clink, arms grab, lips kiss whoever is nearest.

"From their mouths to God's ears. A cup of kindness wouldn't go amiss," Stuart toasts her.

"Happy New Year, Stuart and congratulations on your new posting," Genie calls above the din. The flickering lights emphasize the high cheek-boned structure of his face as he smiles back at her.

"It's not until Easter. Amman isn't so far so you'll have a local friend if you two decide to visit."

"We'll miss you," she says as she reaches up to kiss his cheek. Within the hour everyone heads for the exit.

Night encompasses Beirut, and Genie takes a last look down on the city below before taking the elevator. "I'm happy we spent time here, we should come again," she says.

As they leave, just an hour into the New Year, the trouble starts. Celebrations at the turn of midnight have become ugly.

Gunfire is close as they exit the hotel. Hit by one of the shots a pedestrian falls in front of them. A man, perhaps her husband, catches her. His look-alike brother rushes toward the vehicle, driven by a group of shabbily dressed drunks.

Shocked Genie and their friends stop and step back out of the line of fire.

The young man has settled his wife on the ground, he wipes tears from his face and charges over to join his brother.

Genie can see she is not moving.

"Wald il qahbaa," the man yells. "Son of a bitch."

Genie makes a move toward the body, but Rob holds her arm. "It's too late, there's nothing you can do for her," he says.

Perhaps deliberately, the drivers of the car now aim their battered vehicle and drive directly at the men, felling them, before turning into another group of well-dressed revelers, knocking more bodies to the ground.

"Ebn El Sharmouta," they cry back. "Sons of a whore."

One girl in her party dress and a young man with blood covering his face crawl toward motionless bodies that moments ago were filled with life.

Nabil, Keith, Rob and a handful of friends run to the victims on the ground while others flee.

The car runs out of space to maneuver and a group of bystanders circles and pulls the driver and two young male passengers roughly from the vehicle. One of the men has a gun, and as he's dragged from the car, he points and shoots wild.

A cry and Jacqui bends, slowly stumbles like a broken flamingo, blood flows from her wounded leg onto the pavement. With a loud shout, Jacqui's husband kneels and pulls her statuesque frame into his arms.

Without excuses or explanations, amid the chaos, the young men from the car are beaten to the brink of eternity.

On the roadside, Genie and Shana throw their arms around one another, shiver from the cold and from the scene of brutality unfolding in front of them. "What a sorry start to a New Year," Shana cries as they bend beside Jacqui, she makes the sign of the cross and kisses her fingers. Genie puts her coat around Jacqui's slim shoulders, but she cannot stop shivering.

Mary waits as Nabil efficiently finishes a quick examination. "She'll be alright, no serious damage. Bring her to my surgery, and I'll fix her up."

With an adrenaline-fueled surge of strength, Rob carries Jacqui to Nabil's car, Mary climbs in the back with her.

"That was impressive, rather Sir Galahad," Genie says as Rob takes her arm.

"She's tall but hardly weighs anything, bones like a bird," Rob replies. "I think she'll be fine, it may be awkward and uncomfortable to get around for a bit, but Nabil said the bullet missed bone, lots of blood but just a flesh wound."

Mark pats Jacqui's husband on the shoulder, Kat has remained remarkably calm but now Mark takes her arm, and along with Keith and Margaret, they disappear into the dark.

A flashing red light announces officials have arrived, and they immediately construct barricades in the street outside, but respect for the authorities is rapidly declining, and the lack of regard is apparent as people ignore their efforts to bring order.

"This incident may have started as an accident, but the deterioration is because of the economic and religious tensions," Karam says as he joins Rob and Genie.

Adnan puts his arm around Shana. "Everyone's dividing by religion," he says.

Rob turns to him. "I know many Muslims are disenfranchised, but they can't just assume all Christians have everything."

Karam peers at Rob. "Do they not? Palestinian refugees provide slave labor, work for below minimum wage if they wish their families to eat. Economics is the stem of many of the problems."

"Yes, there is inequality, but there are also affluent Muslim families. Christians are such a tiny group in the vast Arab world. No wonder they feel desperate," Rob replies.

"Too weighty for me, I want to snuggle up with my Muslim husband in our bed," Shana says, but Adnan makes no comment, he has his own concerns about the changes taking place. He and Shana blow kisses and head off.

"Happy New Year." Genie waves and turns back to the conversation. "In general Muslims want closer ties with the traditional Arab ways, Christians want a link between the West and the Middle East, how can they reconcile?"

Karam shrugs and smiles, kisses her cheek and shakes Rob's hand.

"A New Year has begun, let us hope there is a resolution for peace." And he too leaves.

Throughout January and into February they move about freely again. In the city, people tout their wares, laugh, smoke and sip coffee. Buses belch out noxious diesel fumes, while slim-hipped, tousle-haired peddlers signal long packets of American cigarettes for sale, running among the cars and Mercedes taxis as if nothing has ever been wrong.

"Lira Lira," hawkers cry, holding out objects for sale.

Life is good. Up in the hills, Rob and Genie are also relaxed. New Year's mishap is forgotten, and the tide has swept on, wiped it from memory.

"It is a beautiful day," Genie says as Rob pours fresh orange juice and plops onto a patio recliner. "How about driving to Saida for lunch?"

They've been closer since the New Year, and Rob is making an effort to maintain it, so he readily agrees.

Just like old times, she thinks as they drive south.

Halfway to the Israeli border, they reach Saida, Lebanon's third largest town. They drive among banana and citrus groves, past the historic port where Jezebel's father was the Sidonian King, a 13th-century sea fortress evidences Crusaders' passage through these verdant lands.

"The town seems busier than usual," Rob says, as clusters of people pass them heading toward the town center. "It is usually more laid back. Saida means fishing village," he says. "Appropriate since apart from glass blowing, fishing is the mainstay of life here."

Lunch is delicious, local fish served with warm bread and a crisp, colorful salad. The traditional hummus and olives are also fresh.

"I didn't realize I was so hungry," she says, as she finishes and orders coffee from the attentive waiter.

A lazy stream of people drifts by, again more numerous than is customary.

Rob's face glows golden as a shaft of sunlight shines on his upturned face. "Delicious coffee," he says. "Almost as good as yours."

He's being sweet these days. Genie smiles.

They finish their coffee and relax among the remnants of their meal, street kids play with a ball and Genie watches and waves.

He closes his eyes and plays distractedly with a sugar spoon.

He never truly relaxes, she notices.

"We haven't spoken about adoption for a while." She realizes with dismay that the words have actually popped out of her mouth.

Rob sighs and opens his eyes. He shakes his head. "We haven't, and we shouldn't."

Ah well, in for a penny.

"It'd be good for us, we could give a home to a child who doesn't have one. There are many kids in need, Rob."

"Absolutely not, Genie. Please, don't start. I'll gladly offer financial help if you find a cause, but I'm not open to actually raising someone else's child. It's not what I want to do. We have a great life just the two of us, can't it be enough?"

"The years are slipping past, I'm not getting younger and I—we have so much to give."

He shuts her out, stares across into the noisy crowd which congregates opposite and is surprised to see Karam watching a column of fishermen as they snake along the road toward them, in what appears to be a protest march. It's led by the town's former Sunni Mayor and now Member of Parliament Maarouf Saad. He is a leftist and that rarest of breed, an elected Palestinian sympathizer.

As Rob watches, Karam senses Rob's eyes on him, he turns and waves. Dodging the crowd, he joins them, shakes Rob's hand and kisses Genie's cheek.

"Hello, there. What are you doing here?" Genie asks.

He ignores the question, sits beside them on the edge of a seat and watches the crowd pass. "Saad has organized a general strike in solidarity with the 'downtrodden poor' of his district. That guy over there with them is the current Member of Parliament, a conservative Sunni. But it is a waste of their time," he says.

Genie glances at him. "Isn't this about Camille Chamoun's company trying to monopolize the fishing?"

Karam nods.

"How are they expected to live if Chamoun and his cronies shut off their fishing rights?" she asks.

"I agree. But injustice no longer evokes the sympathy it once did." Karam lights a cigarette. He nods, toward Maarouf Saad. "As for him, he is wrong if he thinks this will help him politically. The Palestinian Fatah group controls Sidon and the port. He may not realize it, but they funded others against him, he has no political future."

She looks at Karam and wonders how he knows who funds whom. "The rich get richer. To hell with the poor," she says.

A single gunshot interrupts their discussion, it sounds close. Genie involuntarily ducks, her eyes widen, and she looks at Rob and Karam.

"What was that?" she says.

Just a couple of hundred feet away a man has fallen. She holds out a hand to grab Rob.

Across the road, a woman screams in Arabic. "It's the Mayor," Karam says.

The guttural sound of middle eastern grief erupts simultaneously from the throats of several women who gather around the fallen man. A uniquely middle eastern song of sorrow.

Someone yells, and Karam translates. "They say it was an Army sniper that shot him. That is bad."

Rob pulls Genie to her feet and throws a few notes onto the table as chaos erupts.

People yell and run, a passing parade of body odor, traces of garlic and the acrid smell of gunshot. Tables and chairs overturn and land in the street.

Nearby a young man falls over one of the chairs and feet trample him, a crowd runs amok. Rob reaches down and grabs the guy, pulls him from harm, he staggers to his feet and scurries awkwardly away, without a thank you.

People scatter from the potential conflict.

"Come," Karam grabs Genie's arm. Rob clears a passage through the tables, and they run, escaping along a side street.

Horns sound nearby, weapons fire into the air and a sulphuric smell permeates the afternoon air.

"Listen," Karam calls out.

They pause. The sound comes from where they were seated earlier. Tires screech and boots clatter reaching a crescendo. Along the cross streets, uniformed men jump from vehicles.

"Yallah, Yallah,—Hurry, hurry, Get a move on." A commander yells as the military strives to control the crowd.

"If he dies—they will claim him. Martyrs are popular—and useful," Karam whispers as he runs.

"That's pretty cynical," Rob mutters.

But Karam is right.

The sounds of protest grow louder as they reach the car. Gunfire continues into the sky and along the streets of the once sleepy little town.

"I wonder if they'll be able to contain it?" Rob turns to Karam. "Need a lift to town?"

Karam nods, and they wordlessly climb in the car.

Their drive out is hindered by barricades which have now appeared on the highway to prevent access to the town.

"Where did those come from?" Rob asks. "Maybe problems were expected?"

Genie's mind is abuzz, she wonders about the fallout. *Will he survive, how will people react to this attack?* For the entire journey, she remains deep in thought. *In the shifting political landscape is this the lighting of a fuse?*

She has an ominous feeling.

On March 1st their neighbor Victor knocks and enters mid conversation without even a 'hello'. He is holding a decorative bag which he plops on the coffee table.

"The military was ordered to remove roadblocks from the highway at Saida, but they were fired upon. Now fighting has erupted again." He seems unusually irritated.

Rob pours him a glass of scotch and he downs it in one.

"This whole affair is a debacle. The Christian right feels humiliated after the fiasco down there."

Genie listens but makes no comment. It's clear he believes they have a good reason.

"I heard the death toll was three before the Mayor succumbed to his injuries," Rob says.

"That's right. Now, almost a state funeral is planned!"

"Take a seat, Victor," she says. "I'll bring some refreshments."

"What?" he looks at Genie as if noticing her for the first time. "No habibti. I just came to give you these. We were in town and thought you might like them." He picks up the stylish bag and hands it to her as he heads for the door. He shakes Rob's hand and kisses her cheek and is gone.

Rob peers over her shoulder as she opens the bag. Inside is an assortment of large handmade chocolates each wrapped in beautiful, brightly colored foil.

"That was decidedly odd."

For almost a week it is quiet as preparations are made for Saad's funeral.

Rob wakes up late, tempted by the aroma of fresh coffee and the smell of bacon which tickles his nostrils.

"I have a day off." He joins Genie on the patio. "There's a nationwide strike, and apparently we are part of it." He takes bacon and scrambled egg from the covered server and plops down opposite her.

"Everyone is going to watch the media coverage of Malouf Saad's funeral," she says.

"Word is that it will be a big affair."

"Pity we don't have a tv."

He looks at her sideways. "Are you kidding?"

"I'm interested," she says. "We were there, it was significant."

"Mary and Nabil said they'll make a recording on her new 'very expensive' Philips VCR and we can go look," he laughs.

A couple of days later they join Victor and head down to Mary and Nabil's. They are served glasses of iced coca cola, a rarity since it has been banned throughout the middle east.

"How did you get this?" Genie asks.

"Don't see, don't tell," Mary says as she slaps the tv. The screen jumps a little, the picture is not great, but the funeral starts to play in front of them.

"What an incredible display of solidarity with the Palestinians," Rob says.

"Probably the largest ever show of support," Nabil agrees.

Victor pops pistachios into his mouth and drops the shells into an ashtray. He continues to be annoyed and disenchanted with the whole affair.

"It's sweeping the country—huge anti-government protests because of the Army's involvement in Saad's death," Mary says. "Now it's war between Saad supporters and the Lebanese army," she bends in. "Nineteen people dead so far, can you believe it?" She seems excited.

"You know it may have been inconvenient lining for petrol, living with power outages and the like, but at least in England bullets weren't flying around," Genie grumbles. She hasn't been able to go to school in a city rife with fear.

Rob shrugs.

Victor looks at Rob with sympathy, but before he can speak Mary rings for her maid who brings in a tray of tea.

"I made a cake," she says.

Victor stands. "Shall we leave the girls to their tea? We'll have a little something to fortify us chez moi."

Relieved to get away the three men take off up the hill.

Genie finishes her large piece of Simnel cake. "Delicious! I love the marzipan in the middle." She refuses a second slice and sits back "Oh Mary, I'm so fed up, stuck at home with nothing to do. It's great to have someone to talk to. Rob is so defensive when I mention England."

"Well, maybe he should listen. The regular Palestinian people have grown in sympathy with the Palestinian Liberation Organization now they're heavily armed and militant," Mary says. "We're worried, too."

"I've seen them conduct military drills outside the camps. They're not hiding it anymore," Genie says

"You know, I hear a lot of things I shouldn't because they forget I speak Arabic," Mary tells her. "You should just hear Victor! He's furious."

She takes another slice of cake, pours more tea and stirs in two heaped spoons of sugar.

How does she keep her figure? Genie wonders.

Mary ponders before going on. "They largely regard Palestinians as criminals with no respect for authority, to make matters worse their leadership blithely ignores requests to intervene. People have had enough."

"It's true they may exacerbate tensions," Genie agrees "but not all of them want trouble." She thinks about Rob's co-worker Nashad, who has become their friend, and how hard he works for so little money.

Like a small mechanical wind-up toy Mary is full of pent up energy. "Be that as it may, the right wing are busy building their own militias," she says. "The Prime Minister vacillates, the government gets weaker, soon our militia will take matters into their own hands. They're growing in numbers, preparing to fight," she says.

Over the coming weeks they watch developments and Genie remembers Mary's words, she doesn't question how she knows so much, but her predictions prove valid.

None of them yet know, and some may later disagree, but the events that day in Saida will be the beginning of the end.

The St Georges Beach Club sits above the blue water in the bay, minutes from the commercial district, its reputation as an "in"

location plus the string of beauties who flaunt themselves pool-side, make it a highly popular location for bikini watching.

Thank God at least I'm young, tan and firm, Genie thinks, but today she remains inside toying with her food, she chases it around the plate not eating. Behind large, dark glasses she is apart but hears the gossip floating back and forth.

I can only take so much of this rumor mill bar none, she tells herself.

It is hard not to run into people they know, but life seems back on track lately, sort of, and she's learned to grab her outings when she can. Around her, working reporters sit side by side with millionaires, crime lords, maybe royalty and even spies.

Rob joins her and pecks her on the cheek.

"Another shitty day. I've about had it with these people." He takes a long sip of her drink, pushes aside the colorful umbrella and pops the slice of pineapple decoration into his mouth.

Not this again, she thinks.

"I wish I could be more like Mark, he takes it all in his stride."

"Mark's whole life has been easy compared to yours. He had a silver spoon from the beginning, you've had to fight for everything." She signals the waiter and orders Rob a drink. "You don't need to be like him, but you do need to be more understanding. Acceptance is the key to tranquility," she smiles. "That's a great slogan—acceptance is the key to tranquility."

"Don't overwhelm me with moral support," he grumbles. He walks to a nearby chaise on the patio where he flops down fully dressed.

Genie goes to lie beside him on an adjoining chaise. Side by side they ponder Mark and his ease with life here.

"If things keep on like this Mark may very well reach his limit, too," she says. "I don't mean to undermine you, but if you don't learn to let it roll over you it'll break you," she whispers. She takes his hand and squeezes it.

He returns the squeeze but doesn't open his eyes. "I don't think you understand the level of frustration." He thinks about the wasted time he spends trying to pull pigeons out of a hat, or are they rabbits? He shakes his head. "Christ there is no sense of urgency, everything takes forever. Other than Adnan and Nashad not one of them understands what they're doing."

They've been here almost three years, and he wonders if he will ever get used to the lack of motivation and Genie just annoys him when she fails to grasp what each day is like for him. It's alright for her, she's settled in nicely, he thinks. He turns his head and pretends to sleep.

Dressed in pale linen, Karam has paused at the foot of Genie's chaise.

"You know the Lebanese sun and alcohol are a fatal combination." His English is guttural, precise, almost too perfect.

Genie lifts her glasses, but he is silhouetted by the bright sun which hides his face. "There's a certain appeal to fatal combinations, wouldn't you say?"

He bends to kiss her cheek, and she sees him, gives a full smile and takes his hand.

"Karam. Where've you been? We wondered what happened to you?"

"I was in Damascus and also in Aleppo for a few days. Some personal business to take care of. Do you plan to be at the Casino tomorrow?"

"We do." She blows him a kiss.

Genie glances over Karam's shoulder at a man who passes by, his hairy chest covered in gold chains and an arm around a girl with a Texas drawl.

"The husband of your friend?" he notes.

"Yes, Khalil is the biscuit king. Roslyn's English, but he seems to prefer American girls, lots of them."

"Not my cup of tea," he jokes. "They taste of ketchup. It is unavoidable. Their parents, grandparents and great grandparents all ate ketchup, now it is in their genes."

Genie smiles and watches him go. She knows he has dated many American girls.

Rob hasn't spoken, he appears to be asleep.

Most visitors to Beirut come to mix with elegant, even royal patrons and world class entertainers at the glamorous Casino du Liban. It's not their first time here. But tonight is special, it's the big farewell for Stuart.

They park on the hillside above the coast and wander up the velvet carpeted marble stairs to sounds of an orchestra playing softly. An enormous chandelier, one of many, sparkles and reflects over and over in gold-framed mirrors.

Rob smiles at her. "You look beautiful."

It's hard to compete with the plush and lavish surroundings but she does feel sexy and glamorous, her long cerise evening gown slides around her hips as she moves and she wears the necklace Rob gave her when she first arrived.

"I feel good. You look fantastic, too." He has grown a mustache which gives a kind of Omar Sharif quality, and she smiles as a strange girl turns her head to take a second look at him. "You see," she laughs.

Several friends are already chatting against ornate walls of lapis lazuli tiles, and rich ruby and gold scrolled arabesques. Everyone is beautifully dressed, but Jacqui is a knockout, breathtaking and dramatic in head to toe black with rope after rope of pearls twisted around her long neck, African tribeswoman style.

"Wow, you look fabulous," Genie says.

Adnan, like all of the guys, appears Bond-like and dashing in black tie. His elegance reflects in the mirror sheen on his shoes, and in homage to her Catholic roots, Shana wears a small jewel-studded gold cross around her neck.

"We're going in search of a flutter," Rob says. He and Karam leave with Jacqui's husband. Older and more formal than the rest of the group, a highly placed representative of the United Nations Relief Association he is conscious of appearances and is exceedingly diplomatic in all his interactions, but tonight he seems to have relaxed a little as they head off to one of the gaming rooms.

Even with much to admire, Mark's arrival turns heads and starts whispers.

"Who's that?" someone mutters, a hand over the mouth.

It's easy to mistake Mark for a film star with his full head of black hair and Saville Row tux. He's perfect and polished, Kat floats beside him in aqua silk.

I've never been able to get a sense of her, Genie thinks.

Elegant and reserved, Kat never lets down her guard, doesn't engage or share her thoughts. She's highly educated, but her world is built around Mark, James, and her garden, the only place in which she is not ramrod-straight in posture.

Genie threads her arm gently through Jacqui's as they walk to their table in the dark, spectral hued showroom.

"How are you? Does it still hurt?" she asks.

"No, it could have been much worse." Jacqui watches the men walk away. "Rob's looking très Zhivago," she whispers. "Rather dashing, I like it."

Genie laughs. "Me too."

"What about you, my sweet? Your eyes tell me a story. As ever they have a life of their own, constantly moving, searching for something. Want to talk about it?"

"Maybe, another time," Genie says softly.

They reach their seats, bottles of Taittinger beckon in ice buckets on the table, waiters scurry with an array of appetizers. There is a palpable desire and need to relax and escape from the recent troubles.

Stuart is reflective as he looks around. "It's been a great two years, but day by day I become more certain it's a good time to go. I see history repeating itself," he says. "A replay of Jordan's state within a state. Everyone coexisted in peace until militants created conflict."

"Probably two-thirds of Jordan's population was Palestinian," Nashad says wistfully. His fiancée Leila tugs on his arm, she is always nervous about these conversations.

What a pity they always have to be so wary, Genie thinks.

"That's right. After several assassination attempts the King was forced to expel their Liberation Organization along with tens of thousands of ordinary Palestinians," Nabil says. "Not long before you two came here."

Mark leans over and refills glasses. "The year I arrived they tried to dethrone the King and take over Jordan. There was concern at the havoc a stone's throw distant. Kat and I worried about settling and raising a family, but it settled, and the refugees became absorbed."

"Now the ugly head is raised anew and creating chaos here." Nabil sighs. "We were sympathetic after Saida, but they aren't satisfied. Now the Phalangists grow bolder, they won't put up with it. Tension is palpable, and things don't look good."

Rob and the group return, he holds a wad of notes fanned out and waves his winnings, a big grin on his face.

"This is the life," he says.

Genie and Jacqui laugh.

"What?" he asks.

"You had to have been here," Jacqui replies and nibbles a carrot stick.

Out of the loop of the conversation, he takes a seat and a glass, slides in next to Genie, and soon everyone is focused as trained and highly decorated elephants and ornately adorned camels compete with fire eaters, spewing flames into the air.

They watch the spectacular show.

Beautiful, long limbed girls circle their bodies around in an enormous glass sided water tank, like ornate mermaids. Incredible performances in an upscale circus-like atmosphere.

It ends.

It was incredible, the champagne is gone, and no-one speaks for a full minute.

Nashad has held Leila's hand throughout the show as if she might float away and he breaks the silence. "Leila is emigrating to Canada tomorrow."

Rob lifts an eyebrow and catches Genie's eye.

"You didn't mention it. Are you going too?" Shana says.

"No, I can't," he says. "I'm stateless."

Genie looks at him. "Stateless—what does that mean?"

"Poof," he signals like a magician. "You think you see me, but I don't exist, I have no papers!"

Leila puts her hand on his heart as he explains the impossibility of their future.

"Leila has a passport, she's Christian. As a Muslim Palestinian, I belong nowhere, and I can go nowhere."

In the stunned silence no-one can think of a word to say.

"I can't imagine going off to a new life in a new land, not knowing if fate will allow you to marry," Roslyn says to Leila.

"You mustn't give up hope," Shana says. "God never gives us more than we can handle." She almost crosses herself.

The others glance at one another. Shana's faith is not shared by them all. Amid rising animosities, it's difficult to give credence to a benevolent Supreme Being these days, and they all know it is almost impossible for people like Nashad to find a better life.

"For the rest of time I will work, but I will never get ahead!" he declares.

Adnan looks uncomfortable. "You know I have no power to change things, but I am paid five times as much as Nashad."

"The irony is you need success to get papers, but you need papers to achieve success!" Karam says.

Mark is fond of Nashad, his work ethic, the level of education he has fought for and his quiet acceptance of his circumstance. He shakes his head. "God knows, if I could, I would help."

"But you're engaged, doesn't that help?" Genie asks.

Leila turns the engagement ring around on her finger. "We are still praying he may one day join my family."

Mary blows kisses to the group, Nabil pulls his long frame from the seat, he pats Nashad on the shoulder. "If you can sort this out you should follow Leila, soon. Lebanon is in flux, and I'm worried about the future."

The energy disappears with the sad tale, and soon Roslyn, Khalil, and the MECAS students say their farewells to Stuart.

"May I?" Karam doesn't wait for an answer, he takes Genie to the dance floor. Rob is intent, watching them dance. Again he notices their ease with one another. As they laugh a flash bulb pops, captures them. Karam excuses himself and follows the photographer.

Rob joins Genie, abandoned on the dance floor. "What was that about?"

Her eyes follow Karam. "I've no idea."

Karam pursues the photographer outside, he reaches him, holds out his hand and waits. Nervous now the photographer seems to recognize Karam.

He tells him. "Monsieur. It wasn't you I was interested in. I swear."

Karam takes his camera, the young man doesn't resist.

"I am not the Casino photographer. I shoot for the paper, she smiles at me, I watch, her husband pays her no attention and I wait my chance."

Karam pulls the film out. "She smiles at the camera, not you. You misunderstand. Do your job. She is not for you." He returns the camera.

The photographer takes his camera and hurries away. When he feels safe, he calls back. "You pretend to protect her. I am an observer—you want her—for yourself!"

In the shadows Karam waits, watches Genie dance her improvised version of oriental dance with Stuart, she laughs as she shimmies her shoulders and her hips. He is thoughtful. *Damn that photographer, he could not afford to have his photo floating around, and especially not in the daily rag.*

His original thought had been a practical one; get back the snap. But the extraneous comments of the kid have settled into his head.

Is it true? Is something evident to others of which I am not even aware? He never considered them more than friends, but now he wonders. A complication I do not need, he thinks. He must watch out, casual affairs are par for the course, but he has a job to do, has never wanted a serious relationship and cannot afford to start now.

He notices the dance has stopped, retrieves his glass and joins them with apologies.

"What happened?" Stuart asks Karam.

"Let's just say I'm camera shy."

Genie searches Karam's face, but it reveals nothing, "Now what will I have for my scrapbook?"

"Enjoy these days, Genie. I am afraid it will not last," he empties his glass, kisses her cheek and excuses himself.

"Unfortunately, it seems I have been called away."

Stuart and Genie watch him leave, from his back pocket they glimpse the end of a roll of film and exchange glances, Stuart shrugs.

"Come to Jordan, soon. We have to make up for the trip you didn't take." He looks at Rob and laughs.

"You'll come to my birthday party before you leave, won't you?" she says.

"I'll try. I hope so."

Shana watches the crowd leave. "Don't go home! Adnan's brother is staying, we've all night free, we can pretend we're young again."

"Let's go to the Caves du Roy? We can dance all night." Adnan says.

They park in Ain el Mreisseh, a short walk from the Excelsior Hotel, and pile down the stairs to the ritziest and most famous night club in Lebanon, maybe in the entire middle east.

Sounds float up from a German hard rock band, 'Birth Control'. Young and colorful, they perspire as they play in the heat of the club.

Inside is noisy and busy, people drink, dance, smoke hubble-bubbles, unaware if it is night or day. The band takes a break, and three English girls start to perform.

David waves to them from the dance floor. He dances in a group, several of them from the Casino. They circle around David and a group of their gay friends who expertly perform the merengué.

Rob laughs as he watches their antics. "It doesn't compete with the Casino show, but he is entertaining."

"That was a great show, fabulous surroundings but I could feel the tension in the air," Shana says.

Sadly it is true. It is harder and harder to forget and to play like before.

A champagne cork pops, and Adnan begins to pour, too liberally. The sparkling liquid overflows and in less than a second Shana's mouth is over and around the glass, containing all but a few drops.

"Well, that's some skill," Rob says.

She blushes. "I hate waste."

They laugh, Rob takes Genie in his arms and pulls her close, she relaxes into him as they dance, lighthearted for the first time tonight.

By the time they climb out in search of breakfast, it's morning.

"We should do this more often, escape the gloom," Adnan says.

The light is bright, and the warmth of the sun feels good, but Genie shivers as they say their farewells and walk to their car.

"Can we do something for Nashad?" she asks. "Imagine not being free to go where you want? We're so lucky to have been born in England, Rob."

She's right, there's no argument. Rob steps off the curb and almost collides with one of Genie's students who bounds out of a record store clutching a new album by John Lennon. He grins broadly, kisses Genie on both cheeks and with great pride shows her the album.

"I was the first in line—look what I have."

He offers his hand to Rob. "Hello—Mr. Genie. You remember me? I am Mrs. Genie's student." Rob shakes hands and nods. Without a word, he walks on toward the car.

Surprised, the boy watches him go.

"He's really sleepy, we've been up all night celebrating," she apologizes and squeezes his arm then runs after Rob.

"Congratulations on finding the record," she calls back over her shoulder. "See you next week."

Before she even sits in the car, he turns on her.

"What's this Mr. and Mrs. Genie crap?" he snaps. "You worry about Nashad, about your family, even beggars, everyone except me. Mr. Genie. I don't even exist anymore do I?" Angrily he swerves into the traffic.

Where did that come from? She wonders. "You're being silly. Listen to yourself. I don't make a fuss when I'm called Mrs. Rob, do I? What's the difference? They're trying to be respectful in a language which is not their own and which they don't fully have the hang of. What happened? You've suddenly decided to be peeved for some reason."

He mentally acknowledges she's right. He is feeling peeved, but he's no longer sure why. The struggle has been getting to him, and it feels like he's on an emotional see-saw. He takes offense at the slightest thing.

Yesterday he stood forty-five minutes in line for a permit, only to be told it was the wrong line, then another fifty minutes till the next line closed because they were out of forms. "Come back bukra, (tomorrow) or even worse bad bukra, (the day after tomorrow)." An indication there was no guarantee a wait would ever be worthwhile. It isn't her fault he silently concedes.

"Sorry, It's been a rough few days. I know you're fond of your students. I was enjoying having a few moments, just the two of us."

She doesn't answer. *Just the two of them? They were surrounded by people for the last twelve hours, what got into him?*

She stares out of the window at a tall white minaret, and a Mosque comes into view. A series of speakers loudly send out a song of worship, calling the faithful to prayer, but she is faraway, confused by how Rob's moods can change so quickly and speculating what might be possible for Nashad.

Rob clutches the wheel with both hands, he's tense, the lines around his eyes have grown deeper, and creases now run along his cheeks. His lips move but Genie is preoccupied and a little peeved. She's not listening.

A donkey crosses in front of them followed by an old man wielding a stick. He lashes the donkey's rump, misses consistently, and the donkey trots on with a loud and discordant bray. Rob swerves to avoid them.

"Shit! Shit, shit! I've had about enough." He bangs his hand on the steering wheel and the horn. She jumps.

A highly decorated truck spewing out smoke crosses the road and shudders to a halt. It parks half on the pavement, four gunmen immediately surround it and drag the driver from the truck.

"Before I leave this country I'll get a tank and run over every . . ."

"Stop." she interrupts him.

"What?"

"STOP THE CAR," she yells.

He stops abruptly, and Genie jumps out. Dodging traffic, she runs over to the men who poke at the driver with gun muzzles, lifting the edges of his loose trousers, the traditional sirwal. The old man looks fearful and overwhelmed, and furiously works away at his worry beads. They laugh at him, mock his attire.

"Leave him alone. Autrukh liwahdih."

Surprised, the men step back, they stare at her and scowl.

"Kol Khara—eat some shit," one of them mutters under his breath and turns his back.

Rob watches astonished as Genie yells her instructions without thought or fear of reprisal.

"Yallah, ruhah. Go. Go quickly." She tells the driver. He jumps into his truck, and Genie hits the side.

He leans out of the window, spits on the ground and with a dreadful grinding of the gears takes off, smoke belches from the damaged exhaust pipe.

The men glare as Genie runs back across the street, dodges traffic and jumps into the car.

"What the hell are you thinking?" he shouts at her. "You can't do that! It's not your country, and it's not your job to save the world."

She looks out of the window and replies softly. "They're bullies, Rob. How can we ignore it? Didn't someone say if you do nothing evil triumphs?"

"We need to stay out of it, it's not our business." He takes in a deep, frustrated gasp of air. "I damn well mean it."

She can see Rob is upset, but he needs to deal with it.

"I can't help it. We have to take a stand when we see something is wrong or how can we look in the mirror each day and like what we see?"

He is about to respond but reconsiders and reaches for her hand. His earlier harsh words belie his astonishment and grudging admiration at her actions. *Where the hell does that come from?* He asks himself. But he knows it's dangerous to encourage this behavior. Perhaps he should have anticipated it, she has always defended the downtrodden, but this new found desire to protect under such circumstances is a problem.

"We live well here, Genie, IF we keep our noses out of politics and religion. For heaven's sake don't get us involved in internal matters. When we arrived there was a clearer delineation, but now we should get on with our lives and keep clear of trouble."

She looks away.

Unlike Rob, she already senses the changing reality. "It's easy to say stay out of trouble, but how can we just turn a blind eye?" Much of what happens is out of their control, she knows, "I'm sorry Rob, but if injustice is under my nose, try as I might, I won't be able to stay silent."

10

BEIRUT, MARCH 1975

The Party and Aftermath

TWO WAITERS CIRCULATE AMONG THE sixty or so colorful and eclectic friends. Like Noah's Ark they have come two by two; a pair of Americans, two Germans, two Dutch, two pairs of Antipodeans, a cross-section of Lebanese, some Brits, and a smattering of other Europeans. Several spill onto the balconies and dance to "American Pie" which is set to play repeatedly.

David and Marvin have mistakenly come in fancy dress, they arrive late after explaining at a roadblock why they were wearing Dracula costumes with fake teeth.

Throwing his cape around his shoulder, David sashays across the room to join Stuart and the crowd from the Middle East Center for Arabic Studies, (MECAS) who welcome a pilot friend back to Beirut. David holds his cape above his head with both hands and rotates his hips like a striptease artist, laughter spills into the lounge. Arms in the air they all jump up and down to the music.

Noura and her sister wash dishes and occasionally sneak bites off passing trays. They are excited, their mother gave permission for them to be here.

"Foreigners certainly know how to celebrate," she whispers to her sister and giggles as one of the waiters winks at her. She feels pretty tonight, she has put on a dress which Genie bought her and has a magnolia flower in her hair.

Mark is coolly elegant and ex-pat beside Kat, long, languid and elegantly swathed in her preferred kaftan style, the vibrant hues add life to her pallor. They chat awkwardly with the building owners, Kourk and Rubina, whom they have just met.

Kourk intersperses his Armenian tongue with a delightful broken English and Rubina, wide-eyed, smiles as Karam joins them.

"I told my driver he should be to send his son to school, you know for to have a future," Kourk's face crumples. "He took out a long strap of leather, 'This is his future!' he told to me"

Kate and Mark look troubled. "You understand, like donkey?"

Karam interjects.

"Not to whip the boy, you understand? The man plans his son will be like those boys who transport packages tied on their backs. You have seen the people struggle through the streets around the Souks? Their whole life they are bent over with the weight and as they age they can no longer straighten their spines," he turns to Kourk. "But this is not party conversation, let me get you a drink." He signals to a waiter.

The night air is a delicious mix of orange blossoms and magnolias. Laughter and conversation spill over the terrace and, perhaps indiscreetly, across the dark hillside and orange groves beyond.

Genie overhears Kat. ". . . mountains of mail couldn't be delivered, to deal with the backlog they simply tossed it over a wall and burnt it on wasteland in Ashrafieh." She sips her white wine as Kourk raises his shoulders 'til they almost touch his ears.

"What can you be do?"

Genie steps into the group, puts her arm through Kourk's and smiles. "That's how I wrote to Santa Claus as a child, up the chimney."

"Probably worked for you, but we send ours with friends when they fly out. We don't believe in taking a chance." Mark says.

"Chance is a whimsical creature, my horoscope says it's not possible to avoid one's fate," Genie laughs.

A soft New Zealand voice interjects "Well, I for one won't have to worry about these daily challenges anymore, not after tomorrow."

"My God, that's right." Genie turns and throws her arms around Keith. He towers over Margaret, his quiet Canadian girl-friend. He is as golden as ever, this evening he wears a black silk Nehru jacket and an irresistible smile.

"So, tonight is goodbye to you too, Keith?" Genie says.

He smiles, looks uncomfortably at Margaret, who watches and waits for his reply. He puts an arm around her.

"It's a small world, Genie. You never know."

"You want to leave the shortages, the burning garbage and stinging eyes for New Zealand? What are you thinking, my dear fellow?" Mark claps him on the back.

Genie looks Keith in the eye and starts to speak, but he interrupts.

"You seem tall tonight, young lady!" he glances at her extremely high, platform soled sandals and whispers in her ear "I've told you before, you're a beautiful woman, but you wear exceedingly ugly shoes!"

She gently punches his arm, kisses his cheek and turns to see Victor and his wife walk toward Rob, and she joins them, catches snippets of conversation as she passes.

The Colonel holds court. "They say this cease-fire may not last either. Nineteen factions at the last count, and now almost all of the wives are going home. It doesn't affect me, but it'll be hard for many families."

He and Stuart join Karam, Jacqui, and her husband.

"They sell Klashnikovs outside Spinney's supermarket. Can you imagine what it'll lead to? It's not a bad time to leave," Stuart says.

She's seen the weapons on offer, a sign of the troubled times in which they now live. A twinge of sadness nibbles at her as she realizes how many friends plan to leave, soon there may be only a few of their crowd left.

We'll miss Stuart when he goes, she thinks, *we've been through so much together.* He sees her expression and grabs her hand, pulls her out to the patio. The same song still plays, she has lost count of how many times someone has put it on repeat.

"Bye Bye Miss American Pie. I took the chevy to the levy . . ."

They move around laughing and both sing until a blonde girl, whose name she can't remember, steps in between them. Flushed and warm Genie heads inside. She passes Karam, and he catches her hand.

"Happy Birthday, Genie. You look beautiful tonight."

Surprised by his touch, she stops. He drops her hand, and they chat for a while, serious as always he offers his view on the political landscape, then he clutches at his gut. "Are you OK?" she says.

"The doctor said I must abandon my dearest friend, but we have a lifelong, unbreakable bond," he indicates his glass of scotch and takes a slug.

"Well then, I suppose you are beyond my help."

A pretty, slightly drunk American girl sidles over to Karam, she pulls him, asks him to dance and Genie moves away. Karam resists and over the girl's shoulder watches Genie as she joins Rob and Victor. He hears Victor's invitation.

"You should both come for dinner and cards. Next Friday evening, say eight-ish?" Victor seems to be a little tipsy, unusually light and carefree.

"Sure. Should we bring anything?" Rob asks.

"Just your wife."

Annoyed Karam turns to the girl, and they begin to dance.

Rob laughs awkwardly, never sure how to take Victor's humor. He recalls their last visit, Victor was playing pornographic films while his mother in law sat in the corner silently munching on a stack of bananas. He turned it off quickly after they arrived, but they suspect he had played it deliberately, to test their reactions.

Mary passes without a word to anyone and heads outside, Nabil follows, but pauses to explain.

"She's upset. We received a warning. I must choose who I operate on. The Phalangists only want me to help Christians, and preferably members of the party, but removing a bullet from the face is interesting for me, the human body reacts the same way whatever our belief system."

Victor whispers to his wife, and they turn to move away but the lights dim, replaced by dancing candles on an enormous birthday cake carried in by two waiters. Conversations stop.

Heads turn to look, somewhere a few hands clap then there is a loud sploosh and the birthday cake falls to the ground, cream and fruit spread across the marble tiles as heavily armed gunmen crash through the open front door, grenades strapped around their bodies.

The looks turn to cries of horror.

It's difficult at first to see or understand what has happened.

By some miracle, the waiters manage to slide out of the front door unnoticed and unhindered.

The overhead light switch is flipped on and five dark unshaven faces, half-masked by Keffiyehs glare around the room. They appear intoxicated as they point and carelessly wave Kalashnikovs around.

Unaware of the contrariness of the instructions, the tallest gunman announces in heavily accented English, "Nobody move. Everybody sit."

Another one moves to the stereo, Don MacLean's voice sings the final strain, "This'll be the day that I die-e-e," as he scratches the record.

In the kitchen, Noura grabs her sister's hand and pulls her behind the cupboards near the back door. They crouch and Noura holds a finger to her lips.

Like predatory animals the men circle.

One takes Mark's arm, demands his expensive Patek Philippe watch. He moves on to the Colonel whose inclination to refuse dies on his lips when a gun taps the face of his Breitling. He removes it and with a forlorn look watches it circle the skinny wrist of the gunman.

They continue to strut, poking at random as they pass using the tips of their guns. They reach the terrace, surprised to find two dozen dancers huddled together in a corner, fused to the spot in the vain hope they will remain unnoticed.

"Inside," one orders. "Quickly."

The group obeys, no-one feels like dancing any longer.

"Empty your pockets put all valuables on the floor in front of you," the leader demands.

No-one moves.

"DO IT!" He shouts and slaps the side of Roslyn's head. She gives a cry. Khalil's face reddens and fills with fury that his wife was touched, but the men are distracted, watching several girls pull off necklaces and bracelets.

Across the room Jacqui is indignant and cries out as a gunman pulls the pearls from her neck, they scatter noisily across the floor, many are caught in the creamy mess of the birthday cake. Angrily, the man slaps her and bends to salvage some as they roll away. He shakes his fingers to remove the cream, recoiling at the stickiness he casts them aside and grabs a handful of ice from a nearby chiller to clean his fingers, and pulls out an unopened bottle of champagne.

Shana shakes so violently she cannot undo her bracelet, Adnan leans over to help, but his hand is shoved aside. Terror gives her strength, and she breaks the catch, tosses it down.

The rest of the men produce wallets and watches and toss them into piles on the floor with bundles of loose notes.

It's a relatively small cache of money, and after counting it, the men begin to argue. One of them calls their leader by name, "Michel," probably a Christian group, Genie supposes.

All eyes are lowered with occasional peeks at the guns pointed toward them.

From behind an unkempt beard the lead captor scowls and shakes his gun. Mark and Rob look quickly away as Michel approaches. He stops, looks down.

Genie is next to Victor's wife on the floor at the man's feet. He looks at them both, bends and grabs Genie by her hair, perhaps preferring to scare a foreigner. He pulls her halfway to her feet.

Holding a gun against her cheek, he announces to the room. "We want two hundred thousand Lebanese pounds. Somehow you will find it by midnight, or you will be shot, starting with her."

The pop of the champagne cork sounds like a gunshot, and he jumps. Terrified people duck and look around. He lets go of Genie, she falls heavily, sliding on the edge of the mess of creamy cake. She cries out as her wrist gives way.

"Akhrus—shut up," he kicks her and walks over to slap the man who opened the champagne. "Majnoun," he says. "Crazy. Not now."

Tears sting Genie's eyes, and Rob reaches a hand out to touch her, but she keeps her eyes lowered and nurses her wrist. *Stay calm, stay calm, it'll be OK,* she tells herself.

Victor is near Genie, she can almost feel his fury flare, he puts out a hand and pulls his wife back toward him. Across the room Karam watches the men but tries to remain unnoticed, he is a Muslim and a Syrian in Christian Lebanese territory, his fair coloring will protect him only if he doesn't speak.

Michel takes another watch from a pile in front of Karam and Genie holds her breath, hoping there will not be a confrontation. But the man is preoccupied with his booty as he attaches the watch above the other two on his wrist.

She notices he has a tattoo on his arm, a long, ornate tiger. He taps the watch.

"Nine forty. You do not have the luxury of time," Michel addresses the room, raising his gun.

The Middle East Center for Arabic Studies students are wide-eyed, accustomed to the protection of the British government, this is not part of their study and not a situation covered by the rule books.

A few whispers circle the room and heads turn from one to another in despair, but it is hopeless, no-one has so much ready cash. Almost twenty-five thousand pounds sterling, where would they find it and the bigger question of how could they get it so late at night?

Almost enough to buy four houses like the one we left behind in the north of England, Genie thinks. Her brain is turning over the possibilities. *If they don't get the money will the men just leave?*

She doesn't want to think about it. But how will they find it? It's impossible to know if these men are thieves or if they have a political motivation.

She glances at Adnan, he is Muslim too so he could be at risk but, like Karam, he is fair. *Adnan must know of a source of funds to pay people off,* she thinks. *How else can he always get everyone out of trouble?* She tries to make eye contact, needs his agreement before she speaks.

Adnan feels more than sees Genie's attempts to engage him. He sucks in his breath and meets her eyes, he was expecting someone would turn to him. He shrugs his acceptance to her, and she struggles to her knees still holding her wounded wrist.

Across the room, Karam slowly shakes his head at her and Rob pulls her to sit, but she ignores them both and speaks out.

"If you kill us all you'll have nothing. It may be impossible, but the only hope you have of getting anywhere near what you ask is through this man," she points to Adnan.

He takes a deep breath, he knows he may be their only answer. He kisses Shana on her cheek, gets up and touches Genie's arm before Michel can react. She sits down.

One of the thugs moves toward him. Adnan faces him bravely.

"I'll find what I can," he tells them and walks out of the front door accompanied by Michel and a second gunman.

The other three men laugh and squeeze each other. One of them has bad teeth, and they all carry the stench of sweat, but they settle in the doorway, chatter in a mix of broken French, English and Arabic, plan how they will spend the cash. Just an ordinary evening with friends.

"Un voiture Italien, an Italian car, Ferrari," for the first.

"A girl—no two girls for me," the second one jokes. He begins to describe the night he will have.

The third says "That's the only way you'll get a girl. With cash." They all laugh.

Genie's wrist throbs and she attempts not to hear them, she moves carefully, tries to support it. Rob puts out a hand to stroke her arm.

Ten o'clock.

Around the room, people squirm and reposition themselves. She hears an occasional soft whisper from the former patio crowd, now at the back of the room.

Unsupervised, the gunmen now guzzle champagne and imagine spending their rewards. They have grown less attentive.

"If we rush them could some of us survive?" Keith whispers.

"Not from this far back," the Colonel says.

"We have to imagine their goal is to get whatever they can, not cause us harm," Stuart joins in. "What would be the point?"

"That might be logical in Brighton, but this is Beirut," Keith says. "You can never tell what they might do."

After a few more murmurs it falls silent, and the hands on the clock move slowly toward the deadline.

By ten thirty everyone is restless. Kat would like to use the bathroom, Mark shakes his head and mouths the words. "You have to wait."

Victor searches his brain wondering who these idiots might be and what, if anything, he can do about it without revealing himself. If Adnan gets the cash it should end peacefully then he will deal with them.

Although frightened, people cannot sit still, cannot suppress coughs, they clear their throats, there is a constant murmur in the air.

Rubina prays her little ones downstairs are safe. It is after eleven, and she hopes her mother and the children have gone to bed, that they don't open the apartment door. It is terrifying up here, but it is also quiet, so there should be no thought that something is amiss.

So far there has been no violence.

Time to ponder the future and to regret the things that could have been done, Mary tells herself. She was angry at Nabil earlier for putting them in danger by operating on the other side. But now it is clear; danger is all around, it can hit at any moment. She vows to convince Nabil to take their family to Dublin and wait out the fighting.

One question is in every head. Can Adnan find the money, and if he does will he make it in time?

Karam has hardly moved, he watches Genie and Rob, occasionally looks at the Colonel. He overheard the conversation and hopes they have set aside thoughts of resistance. Unless they could get close enough to overcome the men, the guns could casually claim too many victims.

Rob smiles at Genie. He is filled with remorse at the way they've drifted apart, are no longer the young couple who left England a few years ago. He looks at the clock, forty minutes till the deadline. He moves his lips without sound. "I love you," he says.

The wall clock keeps account of the time which remains, half an hour now. One restless gunman starts to pace, and tension gradually increases. All around the room people try to shrink into invisibility.

Genie wonders if they have really thought this through. *Do they really plan to kill us?*

She looks around at her friends here to celebrate her birthday. Mark and Kat, The Colonel and others. And people she has come to love. Stuart, Keith, Jacqui, Shana, and Karam. Is it really possible some of them will die?

Michel and his henchman return to join the others. One points at the clock and they begin to bicker.

Fifteen minutes.

She tries to comfort herself. *What would be the point in shooting us, what would they gain?*

Friends scan the room without moving. They make eye contact and offer weak smiles, of encouragement or farewell.

Ten minutes.

A couple of the girls sniffle, and there is a small sob from somewhere as the moments pass.

Eight minutes.

The men have grown visibly tense. The deadline approaches and they are now faced with a choice.

Six minutes before midnight a car horn sounds, and soon footfalls can be heard on the stairs. The sounds grow louder, red-faced and breathing heavily, Adnan rounds the final flight carrying a briefcase, he almost falls into the room. He holds his chest and scans the waiting faces.

There is a collective, audible sigh of relief and there are a few whispers. People feel safe now, but Genie wonders if this will satisfy them.

Michel grabs the case and peers inside. The others shove one another and elbow to see. One of them reaches over and grabs a handful of notes, Michel slaps his hand, berates him in a mixture of Arabic and French and stuffs the cash back into the case.

Victor's voice rings out, sharp and clear, a guttural insult in Arabic. "Ari bee kellak Fuck everything in you." He stands and adds in English "You have what you came for, now go, ya Kalb, you dog."

He breaks off as he sees Genie shake her head. She hasn't understood what the words mean, but she begs Victor with her eyes. *Please, no. No need to provoke them now it's almost over.*

But he is tall and confident. The gunmen seem surprised at his outburst, one of them raises a gun and Michel turns on Victor in anger.

Who does this 'Putain'—whore, think he is?

Then he stops, recognition crosses his face. Mother of God, he knows who this man is. He puts a hand on the gun and lowers it. "Merde, Shit."

He realizes he may have made a mistake tonight, he has chosen poorly. He looks away and hurries his men toward the door.

"Yaqta' 'omrak—May God kill you," Victor almost spits the words. But Michel and his men have gone, taking the steps down two at a time. Voices whoop in victory as they go, Michel alone remains troubled.

"They are dead men," Victor says.

For a full minute, people stay frozen in place until they hear guns fire outside and the sounds fade as the car disappears down the hill.

A couple of the girls are weeping openly. *Relief probably,* Genie thinks.

One by one friends help each other up, the party is over. No birthday cake or "Happy Birthday" just brief farewells, most people cannot wait to leave.

Kourk and Rubina are the first to escape, followed by most of the MECAS crowd with David and Marvin in tow.

Kat has gone to the powder room, and Mark waits in the hall saying another farewell to Keith who has his arm around Margaret.

Karam approaches and hugs Genie gently. "I am so sorry you were hurt," he says. "And I regret we were helpless to protect you. They spoiled your lovely party," he waves to the Colonel and leaves with him.

"Not the cleverest of thugs letting us see their faces, but of no consequence in this milieu where the order has vanished," Stuart mutters as he comes to see if Genie is OK. She nods and hugs him.

"Goodbye, Stuart, good luck in Amman."

At the stairwell, he joins the Colonel and Karam.

This is the birthday she will always remember, but the one she would prefer to forget.

She hugs Keith and Margaret as they leave, holds him for a long moment, their last goodbye, sadly it was not the happy farewell she had anticipated.

Tonight is over, and she wants the house to be empty, so she no longer has to keep a brave face.

Noura bends to clean the broken cake from the floor, her magnolia falls from her hair. The two girls have emerged from the kitchen pale but alive.

"That's enough Noura, you go home, take some party food with you." She offers the two girls a package.

"We'll all feel better tomorrow, but you should sleep late, take the day off." Genie closes the front door behind them.

In the background the radio announces:

A cease-fire has been agreed upon by all major factions.

She joins Rob on the bedroom balcony. He is shaken from the past few hours and stares out at the city glittering in the distance,

"Did you even know we were fighting? I'm losing track," she says and removes her earrings. "They didn't steal these at least, didn't see them hidden beneath my hair."

He puts an arm around her and pulls her to him.

"I guess it'll be our last party! No-one will come here after tonight!" she says.

He takes her by the hand, turns off the radio, slowly extinguishes the lights and walks her into the bedroom.

Moonlight floods the room as Genie gets onto the bed still in her party dress, a towel around her wrist. She stares at the ceiling lost in thought.

"Are you ok?" he whispers.

"You said I should stay out of it, we should steer clear of trouble, but look what just happened. If our home isn't safe Rob, where is?" she asks.

He pulls her to him, careful not to hurt her injured arm, and holds her close. They are alone and deep inside he knows she is right.

They haven't spoken for the twenty-minute drive, Keith glances across at Margaret assumes her silence is a reaction to the awful evening. He reaches for her hand.

"It's over now, you can relax, but I won't forget the party or my last night here."

Ahead a light flashes in the middle of the road, he pulls over and lowers the window.

"Papers," a deep voice requests.

The light shines in his eyes, he cannot see the man, but he recognizes the accent as Palestinian. He reaches into his pocket for his papers, but that was an excuse. The doors open and four men cram themselves into the back seat.

He begins to protest, but the man at the window walks around and pushes in beside Margaret. She looks at Keith horrified.

"Drive," he says. "To Aramoun."

They climb the mountain road for what seems like an hour, a half moon beckons in front of them. The bushes and undergrowth sway in the headlights, buffeted by the wind. It is a remote landscape.

These are not guys stealing a ride home Keith realizes, and he is worried. They reach a clearing.

"Pull over," the man next to him says.

Before the engine is turned off, they tumble from the car, and the man in front grabs at Margaret, yanks her hair and forces her to the ground. She reaches her arms out to Keith as her party dress is ripped from her.

"No, please," she cries and grabs onto the fabric, vainly tries to cover her body.

The man slaps her, climbs on top of her. He paws at her underwear tries to strip her, she screams.

Keith yells, sprints toward her but the other four circle him, they have knives, quieter than guns. They thrust and stab him, vicious cuts and blows cascade from all sides.

He tries to ignore the stinging pain, but he staggers, weakened by the blood loss and he collapses as the men take turns at Margaret.

"Please don't hurt her. I work for the UN relief association. We're here to help your people . . ."

Genie sleeps in, she cannot face the next day, remembers how close they were to danger. She still has a bandage around her wrist. It's sore but not broken.

Around two Rob brings home warm bread, fresh orange juice, and The Daily Star.

"Hi-i," he calls out

He hears the shower. *I hope she won't be long, I'd love a cup of tea.*

He settles on the sofa, but the newspaper falls from his hands. Almost paralyzed by the headline, he sucks in his breath, moves trancelike along the corridor and knocks on the bathroom door.

"Give me a minute. I won't be long. Put on the kettle, and I'll be right there."

"I think you should come out now," he says quietly.

"Rob, be patient and give me a minute."

"Keith's dead," he blurts out. "He's been murdered."

The toilet flushes and Genie opens the door. "What?" She grabs the paper from his hands and reads for herself.

'U.N. MAN STABBED TO DEATH.
POLICE SEEK 5 PALESTINIANS'

"That's ridiculous." She shoves the paper back at Rob. "He was just here."

Rob watches her face. Her eyes dart from side to side as she searches her brain for explanations.

"They're trying to scare the robbers," she says. "He can't be dead. It's a lie. It can't be true!"

"I'll call his roommate. He should know what's going on."

She follows Rob to the front door while he goes to use the phone, stands at the top of the stairs and waits, eyes closed. *If I refuse to believe it—it won't be true,* she tells herself over and over.

But after a few minutes, Rob returns, his head bowed.

"No!" she cries. "No!"

Rob gently repeats the sad news, word for word. She runs to the bedroom pulls the covers over her and curls into a fetal position. Her loud weeping tears at him as he watches her despair.

Eventually, she falls asleep.

Moonlight floods the bedroom and Rob is still in a chair watching, he has been there for almost three hours.

Genie stirs and stares out of the window. "I don't want to stay here."

Rob climbs beside her on the bed and pulls her to him.

"I won't be able to look another one of them in the face," she says. "Whenever I see a brown face, I'll always wonder, could he have been the one? Who should we trust?"

Rob listens quietly "We can't change anything."

"This has changed me. Keith is the first Westerner they've killed. You said it wouldn't happen, now it has. First, they came into our home Rob, and now this . . ." She opens her hands in surrender and winces at the pain in her wrist.

"We can't stay here. I'll never feel safe again."

"I can't leave, not yet. Give me a little more time. Awful as it is, it's random. It could have happened anywhere."

"For God's sake no, Rob, not anywhere. Are you insane? What will it take for you to see?" She is silent for a long while.

"Why did he try to stop them? She got raped anyway, now she has to live with his loss too."

"Instinct I guess, he probably didn't think."

"Would they have killed him anyway?" she wonders aloud.

"Who can say?"

From outside the moon spills light into the room, the rest of the apartment is in darkness. They haven't eaten since the party, and his stomach lets out a growl. She hears it and with almost robotic movements goes to the kitchen, awkwardly fills the kettle and sits at the kitchen table.

Rob eats leftover party food.

Genie holds a cup of coffee. "I want a Kalashnikov. They're only $40." Rob doesn't reply.

"We could put it there in the doorway next to the powder room, and if anyone tries to get us, we can mow them down."

"You're over-reacting. No-one will get us."

Genie takes a bowl of cherries from the refrigerator and puts them in front of him "What would you have done?"

Rob stops eating. "You know me, I'm a coward."

"Really. What would you have done? I want to know, Rob."

"I don't know, do I? I hope I never have to know."

"Tell me," she insists.

"Will you give it a rest, Genie? Nothing I say can make it better." Rob looks drawn and exhausted.

"What if it were me? Would you defend me?"

Rob bangs his glass angrily. "What are you doing? This is a pointless conversation, you're deliberately provocative. I told you I DON'T BLOODY KNOW."

Genie covers her ears, and silent tears run down her cheeks.

"What do you want me to say? Probably not. There, are you satisfied? As you said, what would be the sense of me getting killed and you being raped anyway?"

"That's what I thought," she says almost to herself.

"For God's sake, I'm not the enemy here."

She looks at him but continues relentlessly. "How will she ever get over it?"

"She'd be better off dead."

"What did you say?"

"I said she'd be better off dead. She'll never be able to forget and who'll want her now?"

Genie stares at Rob and covers her ears again. She rocks back and forth holding her body. A banshee-like wail comes from deep in her throat.

"All I'm saying is . . ."

She cuts him off, "I know what you're saying. What if I were raped?"

Rob puts a forkful of food in his mouth and continues to eat, wounded and attacked.

"What if it were me?"

Rob stares at Genie in frustration. "Stop it. It wasn't."

"Tell me. Tell me." She persists until finally, she explodes. "You're right you are a coward."

He has reached boiling point, he throws down his fork, grabs his glass and takes a long drink.

"Alright. I wouldn't want you again. I couldn't handle it. Is that what you want to hear?"

Genie stands and scrapes her food into the garbage bin. He puts his head in his hands and sighs, he can't win, and he doesn't know what to do to appease her.

"Who are you? I don't even know you."

Curled in a chair, thoughts and fears cascade through her head. She shouldn't have provoked Rob, she knows it wasn't his fault. None of it's his fault, but she's angry, at the world and at him for his denial of the serious danger they face now.

As the sun rises, Rob walks in. "You didn't come to bed."

Genie looks at him. Her eyes are red, her face swollen. "I couldn't sleep. My mind is driving me mad. I keep thinking . . ."

"According to Shakespeare—'that way madness lies'—and it's true. You have to forget it. Shove it out of your mind. Keep busy," he tells her.

It wasn't to be.

11

APRIL 13, 1975

Massacre and Manipulators

IN THE PEACE OF THE early morning, before anything happens, Rob drops Genie and Shana on a corner in Ain el Rammaneh, East Beirut, near the Church of Notre Dame de la Delivrance.

She is quiet, it is only two weeks since their party and Keith's death, and she has not fully recovered.

"I'm amazed you want to do this, given your views on organized religion," he says. Genie doesn't answer right away, her attention has been drawn elsewhere.

A family carrying a swaddled baby enters the church, and she hears uplifting music flow out. A service is underway, she smiles; a baptism.

"I thought she would find it interesting to see a consecration," Shana tells him.

"I'm curious," Genie adds. She realizes it is impossible to satisfy curiosity or understand anything in this part of the world, even when witnessed through one's own eyes, but nevertheless . . .

A commotion at the end of the street attracts them. Amid great fanfare, politician Pierre Gemayel, founder of the Phalangist

Party, arrives with his entourage, he gets out of a large black car and enters the church.

Armed men, probably bodyguards, take positions outside.

She remembers Karam's words to her at the party. "Intrigue is imbibed into the national zeitgeist with the milk of the mother, there is much posturing."

She looks at the overbearing stances of the men, arms crossed over their weapons on the street outside the church and acknowledges Karam's insight. He had also added a caution. "Along with the ancient mistrust of others, nothing is as it seems."

She gets out and closes the car door. "Pomp and ceremony," she blows a kiss to Rob.

"You and Adnan will collect us here in an hour and a half, Rob? Maybe we'll all go for coffee afterward?" Shana says.

Rob nods, unaware of what is about to unfold he drives to his factory.

But, as Genie and Shana walk across the road they see an altercation between half a dozen armed men, who fire automatic guns in the air as they drive by, and the militia who try to divert traffic away from the church.

"Let's get inside, out of harm's way," Shana speeds up.

Genie is not too concerned, by now she knows guns firing in the air is not unusual. But these men refuse to be diverted, so a scuffle begins. As she turns to Shana she hears a shout and sees one of them, the driver, slumped over. The passengers quickly push him aside, take over the seat and drive off.

"Just a typical Sunday in Beirut," Genie remarks, not realizing the guy is dead. To avoid involvement, she grabs Shana's arm and hurries her into the church.

"I think maybe we should leave before anything else occurs," Shana whispers.

"Where will we go? We're kind of stuck 'til Rob comes for us," Genie says. "Let's just get inside."

Quiet returns and the service continues.

As the service ends and people file out Shana and Genie remain behind.

"It's a bit of a circus with the local politician in attendance, shall we wait for the church to clear?" Genie says.

Shana nods. "I'd like to look around, anyway."

The congregation makes its way out of the building, and they wander around the church. The fragrance is divine, it is filled with flowers, the smell of incense fills the air and light pours through the colored windows.

It is not like an English church, but it does have a certain sense of peace, Genie observes.

As the thought of peace enters her mind, the silence is shattered. Shana grabs Genie's arm as a fresh outbreak of gunfire begins. She pulls her back, deep inside the church, but they hear cries and yelling from outside. From their hiding place, they strain to understand what's going on as occasional sentences filter in.

"They say the father of the baptized child is dead," Shana whispers. "Two cars—with Palestinian stickers—gunmen, fired." she stops. "Oh, my God."

"What?" Genie asks.

"Three more dead," Shana says. "It's not safe to leave." She pulls her shawl around her neck, uses it to dab at her eyes as tears begin to fall.

A woman's voice cries out in French, this Genie understands, she whispers to Shana.

"The dead men were bodyguards of Pierre Gemayel. Isn't he the big mucky muck of the Phalangist party?"

Shana nods.

They remain in place, but outside they hear confusion. A voice gives angry directions as the politician is whisked away.

"This is bad, very bad. Gemayal's a big deal," Shana says.

Genie knows she is right. "We'll stay put until Rob comes."

But Shana does not hear, she is on her knees in front of the altar.

Genie walks to her and watches her friend's hands move up and down, side to side in the familiar movement of her faith. She turns as Genie speaks.

"You're wasting your time. God doesn't live here anymore."

Rob and Adnan have heard the news. When they arrive, half an hour later, the street is quieter. They are all convinced revenge will come, but not yet.

With an arm around Shana's shoulder, Adnan hurries her to the car. Rob pulls his stunned wife to him.

"It's not going to end, is it?" Genie is stiff and silent.

"Everything ends—eventually."

"Eventually? This isn't what you promised, Rob, we need to talk."

At the compound, Mark is waiting. "They believed the perpetrators were Palestinians retaliating for the earlier incident. Outraged by the apparent attempt on Gemayel, his son organized a savage response, but he may have been mistaken." Mark says.

He walks with them up to Shana and Adnan's apartment, helps Adnan take his weeping wife to the bedroom where her two little ones climb up beside their mother. She folds them into her arms and Adnan closes the door.

Mark quietly tells them. "A bus filled with Palestinians, many women and children, was ambushed near the Church. You left just in time," he says. "Pierre Gemayel's son and his militiamen took them from the bus, lined them up and machine-gunned them. Twenty-seven are dead and nineteen wounded, including the driver."

Genie stares at him. "How is it possible?" Her tongue feels like sandpaper in her mouth. The horror wraps around her, and she fights her imaginings; little children with their mothers trying to shield them. "We were so close." Genie grabs the arm of a chair and lowers herself, unable to grasp the brutality.

"Things will escalate," Mark says. "This hit the Gemayels, one of the three major power families in Lebanon."

Adnan offers Genie a glass of rosewater lemonade. She takes it and sips, but her hands shake so violently it's hard for her to swallow.

"The Gemayels founded the Phalangist party, and now they're militarized, they won't let it slide" Mark adds.

She grasps the glass with two hands, tries to control the shaking.

"I have to go home," she says.

They reach home before dark without incident.

"You relax, I'll make you a stiff drink," Rob ushers her out to the patio and puts a rug over her lap.

She hears the tinkle of ice followed by a series of glugs as liquid is poured into long glasses. Strains of music come from the radio. Rob brings out a couple of Sea Breeze cocktails. Her hands no longer shake, and the act of drinking calms her.

The music stops and the radio announcer reports:

News report: Palestinian leader Chairman Arafat has tonight called on Arab nations to exert pressure on Lebanon to punish the Phalangists. He has sent a telegram, accuses them of ambushing a civilian bus, killing women and children.

Genie sits stiffly, her back to Rob. He reaches for her, and she pulls away.

"It's no good punishing me."

"I'm not punishing you, Rob. But I can't get it out of my head. Those savages. Who could do this?"

"I understand you're upset, but you're overreacting."

"For God's sake, are you blind? We were right there. It could have been me."

"But it wasn't. It was the wrong place at the wrong time. This area is still safe, try to calm down."

"Safe? A few days ago gunmen came into our home, remember?"

He sits beside her and takes her hands. "One more year and we'll go." He sees she is not convinced. "We'll be more careful," he says. "I'll take time off, we'll get away—soon," he promises.

In the darkness down the hill they don't see the armed Christian militias who have already taken to the streets setting roadblocks, checking the identity papers of all who pass.

"Okay, Rob. I'll stay for now. I'll take the trip with you, but I don't promise I can last out another year."

Anyone who is not Christian is taken, kidnapped, and before too long will be killed. In the west mainly Muslim section they reciprocate measure for measure. Violence has erupted city-wide now no-one is safe.

The message couldn't be more clear: If you want to live, stay among your own. Over the coming days, they huddle in the hills.

"Only a crazy person would venture out in this," Rob says.

The Bus massacre has incited all of the long-standing, deep-rooted, unspoken sectarian hatred and mistrust, and for three days the killing continues. Hundreds of bodies litter the streets.

News of the murders has spread like wildfires. The handful of friends on the hill still seem to get news and Victor arrives with a freshly slaughtered chicken.

Genie recoils, eyes wide, Rob thanks him and hides it in the kitchen.

"The new Lebanese PM sent security forces to defuse the violence, but he didn't persuade Gemayel to hand over the men responsible. He publicly refused, announced he and his Party aren't bound by government authority. He sent Phalangists to release the detainees, claims it was self-defense," Victor says.

Is there a God and what is he thinking? She wonders.

"Stay home for a few days. There'll be a cease-fire soon."

She has calmed a little and wonders briefly how Victor seems to know in advance about the planned attacks and cease-fires, but she doesn't ask.

"Don't even think I'm plucking that!" she says when Victor has gone. "I can't cut off its head, or it's feet. You'll have to do it."

Rob is about to refuse, but sees her face and changes his mind. She hands him a cookery book, a knife, makes a pot of tea and leaves him to it.

She goes into the lounge, stares out of the tall windows at the ocean sparkling into the distance. As always the view moves her, as beautiful as when they arrived, she scans her record collection, puts on Vivaldi and relaxes.

Two hours later, for the first time in his life, Rob has made dinner. The chicken is golden and delicious, he is proud, and she is impressed until she walks into the scene of devastation, which was once her kitchen.

They watch closely to ascertain how safe it is to go to work and, as the fight continues, the leftist Lebanese National Movement, headed by Kamal Jumblatt, joins the fray alongside the Palestinians.

The city is unpredictable.

Over the ensuing weeks, repeated cease-fires are declared and broken, no-one takes them too seriously, with the failure of each they seem more ephemeral and unreliable.

Smoke rises unabated over the city and Rob decides to take a chance and drive to work.

"I stay on the backroads," he reassures her. He doesn't mention how frequently he is passed by vehicles mounted with guns wielded by incredibly young boys who should be in school. They hang off the backs and patrol highways, drive country roads. It is an exciting game, they don't yet realize, death is forever.

After an aborted attempt to go to school in Achrafieh, now a target in one of the three highest parts of the city, Genie decides to stay home till things calm.

"They've promised to call me, but they say students won't venture in any way," she tells Rob when he returns home safely.

From the terrace they gaze out at the ocean which still ebbs and flows, the tranquil beauty pretends life is normal.

"Many of my students have armed themselves, and ride around town as impromptu security forces," she says. "Can you imagine? All those earnest young faces from my classes looking through the barrels of guns and shooting, maybe killing?" she shudders.

Rob feels her sad mood and wraps a blanket around her shoulders. He lights a couple of candles and takes her hand, pulls it to his lips.

"It's terrible, what can I say?"

"They've been robbed of their innocence, their dreams and their futures. I wonder how they will survive such a change in their young lives?" She sniffs and blows her nose.

"A quarter of the country's population lives in Beirut, fifty percent are below twenty, the age when one looks to the future and questions the ways of the past. These youngsters want to play a part in that future," he says.

The recent massacres have left their mark, and people are nervous and suspicious.

She is a virtual, if upscale, prisoner in a Christian enclave while Rob floats between the two worlds, oblivious to the risks he takes.

The next day bombs drop again. Israel has finally retaliated against Palestinian attacks, support for the Palestinians weakens, aggravation increases and the various Lebanese political factions arm themselves, ready to fight.

They have an awareness, a clammy sense that things are off kilter, but as of this moment they aren't yet aware a full-fledged civil war has begun.

12

BEIRUT, JUNE 1975

A View and a Vantage Point

"WHAT NO TOAST OR CROISSANTS?" Rob asks as he walks out to the terrace.

"I'm sorry I can't stand for hours in bread lines, it's like Russia or the Eastern Bloc, nothing much left on the shelves. I bought ingredients, and I'll learn to make it," she tells him. "Have some cornflakes."

They stop and listen to the radio announcer.

News Report: Today, June 1, The capital was calm; however, an explosion wrecked the premises of Marcel and Ibrahim, the fashionable hairdressers. There was no apparent political reason for the attack.

"Jesus!" she says in disgust. "Now there is a cease-fire I scheduled an appointment for Wednesday! It could have happened while I was there! Why would anyone bomb a hairdresser for God's sake?"

"Bad hair day?" Rob replies

"That's not funny." She sprinkles sugar on her cereal and takes a mouthful.

"God where's your sense of humor? Obviously, it's not funny but . . ." he stops. "You OK?"

"You're right," she finishes chewing. "I'm a bit tense. I can hardly wait to be out of here."

He looks at her.

"You promised," she reminds him.

News Report: Today, June 2, The Chief of Militia Forces for Former President Camille Chamoun was ambushed and killed during the conflict between Damour and Saida. Fighting continues between the Christian and Moslem villages.

They turn off the radio and try to get rest, but fresh rocket and artillery fire is constant now, night and day, from fighters perched high in their aeries.

Unable to travel to work Rob's level of frustration is at a peak. "I told you before we leave I'll create a wide trail of bodies. I'll get a tank and drive over the lot of them."

"Listen to you." *This is the first time he has spoken of going home.* "Aren't you supposed to be a pacifist, a humanist, even?"

"How can I be? Humanism involves secular benevolence to others. An enlightened view of freedom. What a joke!" he waves his arms toward the windows and at the world gone mad outside.

She pays attention as he speaks, hears traces of the Rob she used to know.

"There's no enlightened thinking, no thinking at all," he says. "This is the antithesis of humanism."

"They've all bought into the idea that they're incompatible so they only see a world of enemies—one against all."

He looks up from his bowl of cereal with a shocked expression. "Christ, that's heavy before breakfast."

She laughs. "I'm trying to evaluate things, keep a diary. One day we'll look back, and I want to remember accurately without the spin."

"That's excellent, but try to leave time for the baking you promised. I prefer toast or croissants to cereal." He finishes the last of his corn flakes and his spoon clatters in the bowl.

What a simple soul and how easily pleased. She thinks.

"Don't forget, I'll meet you in town later, at the cinema."

He reminds ME not to forget? What a laugh.

She is frightened out of her skin at the ritzy, modern cinema which screens all of the latest international movies. "What a pleasure not to have our feet stick to the floor, like at the Odeon or the Palladium back home," she says.

Rob nods and smiles, and for an hour and a half, they watch an enormous vengeful shark terrorize a seaside community. A young American director named Spielberg thinks Jaws is summer entertainment, but she's not sure why people want to pay to be frightened.

In Beirut, it's harder to avoid the sharks.

They leave the movie and Rob is excited as they head for drinks and dinner at the still new Holiday Inn, in a prime position on the seafront. They were here at New Year, and now he wants a quiet dinner just the two of them.

Tall, skinny and modern, the complex has been three years in the making, and Rob is keen to dine in the much talked about revolving restaurant at the top.

"An eagle would donate its feathers for this vantage point over the city," she says. "What spectacular views." They take a seat by the window, and she orders: "A glass of Champagne, please."

"Make it two," he smiles at her.

"Since when did you start drinking Champagne?" she laughs.

"I thought we should celebrate. It's been a rotten few months. I know you'd wanted to go to Jordan about now. I'm sorry I had a hard time with it. I apologize, and for a lot of other things, too."

The arrival of the champagne interrupts him as the waiter sets down complementary dishes of almonds, tiny smoked salmon blinis each topped with a dollop of cream and a dark green sliver of dill. Large chocolate truffles nestle in a small wooden box, and beside it a small bouquet of brilliantly colored flowers add a touch of nature to the architectural surroundings.

She smiles. "It's OK, Rob. We'll go there together one day." She's distracted by the flowers and lifts the bouquet to her face. "How beautiful." She puts her nose into the spray and breathes in.

The waiter whispers in Rob's ear, and he turns around. Along the room, Victor is at a table by the window in the center of a group that Rob doesn't recognize. They look like businessmen in their summer attire of short-sleeved shirts and light slacks.

Rob lifts his glass and toasts his thanks to Victor. He responds, and one of the men glances in their direction. It is a well-known face, but Rob can't quite place it.

"Victor sent over the food and the flowers." Rob indicates with his head.

Pleased and touched by his gesture, Genie also turns and smiles at Victor, she lifts her glass. "That was sweet of him," she says.

Victor bows his head, and blows a kiss, but does not leave his associates. They haven't seen him since he dropped off the chicken a few weeks ago, but they've heard from Kourk that he's busy with something, no-one know seems to know exactly what.

She looks over again; Victor has already turned back to his group and is engrossed in quiet conversation. All of the tables near the men have Reserved signs on them.

"Did you see that?" she asks. "Something secret is being discussed over there."

Rob glances surreptitiously. "Maybe they're expecting a private party?" he says.

She snorts.

Socially and politically it is a challenging time in Lebanon, and everyone is scrambling to make sense of the new arena.

She feels closer to Rob than she has in a while. He has been hard to reach, distracted lately, so it is revitalizing to break away from the madness and actually talk. She lifts her glass to her lips and looks at him. He's a brilliant guy, so she doesn't understand his refusal to see how things are.

They've lived on the outskirts of the city for close to three years unaware of the poverty hidden from sight. The only clue to the plight of the poor is an increased number of beggars on the streets. Flimsy walls disguise the camps sufficiently to keep them out of consciousness. But tonight, as they pass by, groups of men in uniform carry weapons. They are on patrol.

That's new. What now? She wonders.

Within days, as Genie waits for her promised trip, a fierce and furious fight for possession of the hotels commences, and at the center is the beautiful Holiday Inn. The first major front of the war is near the Corniche, the sophisticated, palm tree-lined boulevard along the seafront, reminiscent of Cannes and Nice, but now abutting this polished and perfumed area, fighters, weaponry and chaos reign.

They listen avidly for news via their neighbors over the next two weeks.

"They call it the Battle of the Hotels," Kourk says as he heads off to his dry cleaning store, dressed in his "business suit" of shorts, white tee shirt, and flip flops.

There is something admirable about the way the Lebanese carry on with life while bombs drop and rockets fire all around, she thinks. *It's an odd sort of optimism, trust in something supreme, that permits life to go on, adjusted to the new norm.*

Genie follows Kourk down the hill, he toots then waves as he turns off to the shops and she heads on into town.

She easily parks, but notices a dramatic increase in the piles of garbage on the street corners.

At Modka Cafe on Hamra Street Genie and David sip coffee, the conversation is subdued. "I can't imagine how much more difficult things can get," David remarks.

"Isn't it insane?" she says. "Look around, the city is abuzz with life, and the energy is palpable, but barely a mile away men are fighting over control of the seafront hotels."

"Only in Beirut," he glances around. "You know darling, it's not good here these days," David is cautious. There are muffled sounds of fighting not far away, but he ignores it.

"Since I arrived Hamra has been my home from home, with intellectuals, avant-garde pundits, the sense of tolerance and freedom to be, think and speak was intoxicating." He checks they are not overheard. "But now, as you see, there's a need to look over your shoulder, curb your tongue. We walk on eggshells."

"I know. Things changed after the Saida attack, but that seems forgotten in the wake of the bus massacre." She waves at a waiter and orders two more coffees. "Do you have any idea who was behind the bombing of the Marcel and Ibrahim Hair Salon? What on earth did that achieve?"

David shrugs. "Most of the attacks beggar belief." He stirs three spoons of sugar into the cup of cappuccino which the sweet waiter places in front of him with lingering fingers. David smiles a full, fluttery smile of thanks.

"I saw that," Genie says. "What a flirt."

David laughs. "Nothing serious, just a little fun. You know Marvin is the only one for me." He sips his drink and makes a face. "It's not even hot! Things are going dowwwwn the bloooodey hillll . . ." He multiplies the syllables. "Marvin isn't as careful as I am and I worry he takes chances."

She agrees his boyfriend Marvin has been provocative lately, wants to take a stand against all of the injustices, but this isn't Hyde Park corner and here has no place for a soapbox.

He continues. "We always met journalist friends along the road at The Strand for a drink, to discuss and argue until the early hours, now we have curfews every few days."

"I was only twenty-four when I came here, an innocent. I must have aged twenty years in thirty-six months. Innocence is lost." She kisses David farewell. "Anyway, we'll be out of here next week, so I don't have to worry for a while."

On the way home, she sees the city through fresh eyes. Piles of rubbish burn on street corners, the smoke and ash in the air is a shock and frequent if sporadic bursts of gunfire have become the norm. The glitter of the early days seems far away. Beirut's beauty is fading, she looks unkempt, unloved.

Continuing divisions have led to a breakdown in infrastructure, and daily it grows more apparent.

For the first time in ages, Rob and Genie risk a trip to the Rose and Crown. Their friends have been subdued since the killing of Keith, many now prefer to meet in one another's home.

The Colonel is at the bar chatting to Karam and looks up expectantly as each new person enters. He seems particularly affected by the now constant violence and has turned the pub into his de facto office.

Karam's face lights up when he sees them. He stands and shakes Rob's hand. Light as a butterfly wing he rests his face against Genie's cheek. She tries to place the faint trace of fragrance. It seems familiar.

The Colonel gets up from his stool and gives Genie his customary kiss on the hand, then goes back to their conversation.

"I'm learning all about Saiqa," he says.

"It has been around for a decade," Karam tells them. "Loose links to the Palestinians and the Syrian Ba'athist Party, now it is the second largest Palestinian group after Fatah."

For a moment the evening proceeds as it has always done, politics and intrigue on tap. Rob orders drinks and settles in to the conversation.

"Didn't they help President al-Assad seize control of Syria?" Rob asks.

"Come to think of it I heard that, too," The Colonel says. "Much of the brutality is attributed to them, it doesn't look good for Syria."

Genie gives an apologetic look to Karam. "Mary told me their ties to Syria limit popularity with Palestinians who don't want to fight against their own people."

"There are widespread defections," Karam says.

On so many levels people are torn and forced to make unpopular choices. Genie thinks. She looks at Karam and wonders how he feels about all of this. A Syrian, proud of his country yet he has lived and worked here for many years. He sees her glance and returns a tender smile. A man lost in the madness. She catches her breath.

The fighting spreads, soon the north of the country is under attack, and they devour the radio news.

News Report: Today, September 7, Tripoli is under fire, bloodletting has begun with exceptionally violent outbreaks between Muslims and Christians. Widespread kidnappings and street fights killed eleven soldiers, part of the buffer force.

Rob is concerned for Adnan's family up north in Tripoli. "It must be dreadful for him, but hopefully as Muslims, Saiqa will leave them alone."

"There's nothing we can do, is there?" she says.

"No. I try to imagine how I would feel if it was my family. It doesn't even have to be intentional, I guess anyone can be caught in the crossfire."

She is touched by a not often revealed side of Rob. *He seems genuinely worried about Adnan.*

News Report: Today, September 10, Saiqa forces attack a northern village killing three priests. The residents have fled.

News Report: Today, September 11, Saiqa forces with guerrillas from the Syrian Baath Party attack another village killing seven and kidnapping ten.

13

ENGLAND, SEPTEMBER 1975

Changes

SHE IS EAGER FOR THEIR annual visit home, a little later this year because she discovered that Johnny Cash will perform in London the third week of September and she gives Rob tickets for his birthday.

"I don't believe it. This is why you wanted to go home later?" Rob says. "So thoughtful." He throws his arms around her and swings her up, a very cowboy gesture.

For some strange reason, Rob is a real country and western fan, an unusual choice for an Englishman. But Johnny Cash is the ultimate, a legend, and Rob has a range of albums by the man in black, which he plays whenever she is out.

Apart from the concert, it is the chance to meet with friends and family, and to breathe—a welcome change of pace.

She looks at Rob. *He always seems tired now although this news has cheered him. So many challenges lately,* she thinks.

At times she's poised for the excitement at others just plain scared. Genie has friends in Beirut, but Rob's frequent travels and work frustrations, present a need when not traveling to escape with his own friends at the pub, often forgetting her and she has become increasingly isolated from him.

The internal scuffles, battles in the city and across the border are a reason for some of the strain. But they haven't been close for some time now, and it's almost entrenched. She wonders if there's any way back to the way they were.

Maybe at home, we will reconnect? She hopes.

The seatbelt sign goes on, and she gazes down at the strip of English channel as they circle and prepare to land. Raindrops streak the window, but it's late autumn in England, so it's to be expected. The green fields and meadows spread out below them, a welcome sight.

Her pretty younger sister Nina is at the airport to meet them with her warm, welcoming, smile and outstretched arms, loving as always.

She feels, more than sees, Nina's smile and she sighs, comforted by the familiar presence. Her sister's hair is swept into a loose blonde chignon, strands of hair form a whisper of a fringe and small diamond earrings sparkle as she turns her head.

She has grown up, too, into an extremely sensual, confident woman who now runs her own business, Genie reminds herself, as her sister leans over to hug her. *Motherhood agrees with her, she's even more beautiful—an archetypal earth mother.*

Lost in her own thoughts, she hasn't noticed the fleeting look of dismay pass over Nina's face at her first glimpse of the sleek, sophisticated, young woman her sister has become, a woman whose sad eyes search the crowd. She notices the secretiveness immediately, it's new, a mask carefully put in place to shield—from who knows what? She feels a gentle pang of regret as she remembers they aren't children anymore and gone is the little girl who used to make her cross her heart and swear every night at bedtime. "If I die before I wake, promise you'll take the rollers out of my hair before you call anyone!"

The woman whose face lights with love when she sees her now has her hair tended by professionals and probably will have forgotten such girlish vanity.

She sees Genie relax, feels the tension flow away as they link arms and she hopes they'll find time alone, to share what's been going on.

"It's great to be home," Rob says.

Home? Of course, this is their home. Sometimes she forgets they once had another life.

Her sister drives them through the damp streets. It looks both familiar and strange. On the car radio, a morning host sounds foreign, and she realizes with a shock that she has changed, grown accustomed to the varied accents of their adopted land.

As they near the coast the highways are unfamiliar and construction is underway.

"They're building a by-pass," Nina says. She seems to know her way around the mess, but it has thrown Genie off kilter. Her home had been fixed in her mind, something safe to hold in her heart. *How could they have just changed it? It was supposed to stay the same.* She is unreasonably disappointed.

Along the seashore, they crunch large pebbles underfoot; the wind blows in their hair, and they slowly reconnect. Rob reaches for her hand.

"Remember when we first came down here," she laughs. "I was wearing high heels, and you suggested a walk on the beach. I was too shy to say no, even though I was not dressed for a stroll on the sand."

He laughs. "You broke the heel of your shoe, and I had to carry you, I remember."

For these brief moments they are connected through their past, their shared experiences. They find time for gentle and quiet lovemaking, Genie's hand over Rob's mouth as they laugh and attempt to be discreet, soundless, just a few steps along the corridor from where the family sleeps. But she wonders if it will be enough to carry them through the months ahead.

Their relatives live close, there are dinner invitations and teas, nights of charades and Trivial Pursuit, a total contrast to the clubs, pubs, parties, and gunfire in Beirut.

Nina takes enormous pleasure in feeding them their favorite dishes and they fall into the flow of local life.

In London they see Rob's show, and as they leave the theatre, he is happy. Outside he dances and sings a Johnny Cash song to her.

> 'Yes, I'll admit that I'm a fool for you
> Because you're mine, I walk the line.'

He does a small shuffle, a slightly disheveled, bearded guy passes and throws a few coins on the pavement in front of Rob. Genie laughs but, suddenly self-conscious, Rob stops.

Other faces, pale, eyes watery in the cold November weather ignore them as they head to the railway station and she is surprised to see piles of garbage on the streets here, too.

The trip is almost over, and she's sad to leave family but feels reinvigorated. For now, they're close; the stress has reduced, virtually disappeared. In fact, it's as if none of the recent events are part of their lives.

Rob is ready, even eager, to return and face the daily challenge. He raises his glass to family and friends at The Arun View, beside the river where her ancestors once built ocean-going ships.

She has given up hope and almost accepted that motherhood is not in her future, she looks out of the tall windows at the murky water and wonders what it must have been like a hundred years before, to sail away into the unknown. In a way it is what they have done, she realizes.

"A toast to Lebanon and to another year without crisis." Rob lifts his glass, his friends laugh, but Genie has a feeling, hard to put her finger on, deep inside she has a premonition of something lurking, something unknown.

They return. And the radio tells them nothing has changed.

News report: Today, Thursday, October 9, The three-day-old cease-fire ended. Heavy fighting resumes in the capital. Twenty-five are reported killed in Beirut with more than one hundred wounded from rocket and mortar fire. In the North, a Saiqa attack has left fifteen dead and many injured. In hopes of further igniting religious strife, they set the local church on fire.

"It didn't improve while we were away," she says, and she wonders if it ever will.

Syria silently and closely monitors events on their border and amid increased concern sends two hundred more Saiqa troops to police the area. A savage attack on Tripoli follows with hundreds of dead.

When Genie knocks at the open door Shana's counter is strewn with mint and parsley leaves, a pestle holds the remains of freshly ground coriander or maybe cumin. She is skillfully preparing zucchini stuffed with a rice and meat mixture studded with succulent pine nuts, her specialty.

She wipes her red eyes and tries to smile. "Onions," she says and tosses the plump, stuffed green tubes into the garlicky tomato sauce she has prepared, they slowly come to a delicious simmer.

Genie can see it's not from peeling onions, Shana has been crying.

"Everything will be fine," Genie says. "Don't cry my sweet, the kids will pick up on it and be upset."

Shana fights a fresh bout of tears. "It's just, I'm . . . I'm thirty years old today," she stammers. "I'm OLD—and look." She lifts the front of her hair to reveal a single, thick grey strand.

"Don't be silly, you're still a baby." Genie opens her arms and hugs her. "With what's going on it's a miracle we're not all grey!"

Shana gives a watery imitation of a smile. "And there's something else," she blurts out. "I don't know what to do about it. When we married Adnan, and I made a pact. I wouldn't raise the children Catholic if he didn't raise them in Islam," she says. "But now with death all around us I think more and more about the end and what comes next. I worry about what I've done. Should I talk to the children about their mortal souls—and mine?"

It's a long time since Genie discarded her religious beliefs and she feels singularly unprepared to alleviate Shana's anguish.

"I guess I'm not the best person to offer advice on this subject," she says. "But I do believe if you make a deal you have to try to live with it. Our word is important. I personally don't believe in all the mumbo jumbo you've been told, and anyway, they're babies, how could they possibly understand? You'll all live to ripe old ages, and the kids can decide what to believe when they grow up."

There are no easy solutions to Shana's dilemma, nor to those questions of faith and conscience so many across the land struggle within these days, Genie thinks as she leaves.

Rob hears the clang on metal as Genie descends the stairs and he turns off the light in the lab below.

He looks up to watch her. She seems preoccupied, he thinks. He sees her turn to wave to the children and Shana who watch from the window.

In the car, Rob tunes to the radio news.

News Report: "Fresh reports of a massacre of passengers on a bus in Tripoli. Local residents accuse the President's militia."

As they drive home the news continues:

News Report: Amid renewed fighting Palestinian Chairman Arafat has issued appeals for peace. The Prime Minister will accompany him to meet Syrian President Assad in Damascus for discussions. In other news, the Al Makassed Hospital is overflowing with wounded and is appealing for blood.

"It's a Muslim hospital isn't it?" Genie asks. "How do they view blood transfusions from non-Muslims?"

"I asked Adnan, and he said since it is anonymously donated they assume the blood is clean, when transplanted it becomes part of the recipient's body. According to Islam, saving a life is a trump card."

"Hmm, It's hard to imagine anyone is aware of that philosophy while participating in all this slaughter."

14

BEIRUT, OCTOBER 1975

Storm Clouds

IN LATE OCTOBER, STORM CLOUDS gather overhead in the skies and also in her heart. She can't put her finger on it, but something nags at her, and it won't go away.

Mary pushes her little girl uphill on a tricycle. She sees Genie's car approach and waves. "Fancy a cuppa?" she calls. "I made some shortbread."

She turns the tricycle toward the house, and the child smiles as Genie gets out of the car, holds out her hand and shakes formally. She's a happy, quiet child, a pretty combination of her Irish and Lebanese genes, pale skin with big dark eyes and a tiny, delicate body, she's dressed in soft, pastel colors and wears small items of jewelry in the Lebanese tradition.

"She looks like Nabil, doesn't she?" Mary says. "Actually, I'm mad at him." She pushes open the door and heads to the kitchen, shoos the maid away and puts on the kettle.

She lowers her voice as Genie follows her. "I don't see why he has to keep operating on those awful people who just want to kill us."

As each week passes, Mary seems to become more partisan. It's strange to notice how she fails to see the one-sidedness of her viewpoint, given the mass killings at the hands of both sides in these recent battles. But people rarely invite friends from the "other" side these days.

While Genie and Mary make tea, the little girl takes out a doll and plays quietly.

"No work for us again, and the shelves are pretty empty at the market," Genie says.

But Mary doesn't comment, she has other things on her mind.

"Yesterday there was a stupid fight in town between a Leftist patrol and a Phalangist waiter. Next thing you know they've burned the entire hotel to the ground. Foreign diplomats and some staff were released, but two waiters have disappeared, one of them is Nabil's second cousin," she tells Genie "I don't imagine either of them will be seen again."

"God, that's dreadful," Genie says.

But, ever matter of fact, Mary has already moved on from the sad story to gossip about the management.

"The guy who ran it was Viennese—ex Hitler youth—disliked Arabs, they say. He spent time at the Khayyam in Damascus—King Faisal's Palace before the '58 revolution. Why come here if you can't stand Arabs?"

Mary keeps her voice low as she sets the table. She glances over at her daughter who is focused on a pretty doll. "We thought it had the protection of some leftist high ups. You'd always find press people there. Oh, they made the best Irish coffee," she leans in. "Of course it was also a useful spot for stashing mistresses."

She takes a nibble of shortbread and pours tea for each of them. The cups are fine china, prettily painted with wild birds and have delicate fluted edges, they must have come with Mary from Ireland.

"Some of the tallest buildings have avoided the conflict, and many of the hotels are still functioning, can you believe it?" Mary says.

"Who in their right mind would come to stay at an hotel in Beirut, these days?" Genie asks.

"Exactly. Just asking for trouble. Now a handful of leftist thugs have dislodged our men and occupy the twenty-eight unfinished stories of the Murr Tower." She almost spits out the word "leftist" like something foul in her mouth.

Genie notices she now refers to the right-wing Phalangists as "ours."

"That fabulous hi-rise building was supposed to breathe life into the area, now look," Mary says.

It's true, Genie thinks. From the upper floors of the Murr Tower building, there is incredible visibility to direct devastating barrages of rockets and mortars into surrounding Christian neighborhoods.

Preoccupied with the capture of Mary's relative she struggles up the stairs loaded with the fruit and vegetables she found at the market. One of the bags splits.

"Damn," she swears softly and abandons the oranges and grapefruit spilled on the landing outside Kourk's. She drops the rest of her goods in her apartment and returns to gather the spilled fruit.

Kourk walks out of his apartment.

How did he do that? She wonders at the coincidental timing.

"You must to buy petrol," he announces without even a hello. "Armed men from Tripoli interfered with the transport of gasoline from Tripoli refinery in Beirut," he pulls a disapproving face which clearly reflects his view on the matter.

But it turns out to be true. In a panic Beirutis rush to fill their cars anticipating gasoline rationing, and in the process they create the feared shortage.

"A rocket fell today at Moslem bakery in Corniche el Mazraa, it killed seven and wounded eleven," Kourk says. "Why bomb baker? In the end, we all must to have bread, and already we have shortage."

"Insane! Rob can't argue about it now. No more bread lines for me," she says.

"The hotel battle will continue. Crazy people." He taps a hand to his head and closes the door.

He is right, before October is out fighting in the hotel district resumes.

She sees Rob pull into the cul de sac and shivers as she puts on the kettle for tea. She's been cold all day, cold and fed up.

Rob walks in, and before he greets her, he turns on the radio. It's become his drug of choice; he has to hear the news.

News Report: October 28, a car filled with Muslim militia approached Parliament House shouting slogans through a loudspeaker against members of the Assembly. Shots followed. Two deputies and a bodyguard of Phalangist Leader Gemayel are reported killed. Leader Gemayel has not been harmed.

"That man has more lives than a cat!" Genie exclaims.

"Yes, and being his bodyguard is not much of a road to promotion!" Rob quips.

The news report stops, and Gemayel's son comes on the radio. He has a soft way of speaking, but his lilting, faintly musical speech, grows strident and harsh when rallying supporters:

> "The Americans and the West have not assimilated the fact that we, the Christians of the Orient, represent their last line of defense against a return to the dark ages, against terror and blind fundamentalism . . . They want to sell us down the river for a barrel of oil!"

His fury is apparent, he is enraged that once again his father has been targeted and the opposing forces continue to attack the fundamentals of Lebanese democracy.

His anger has grown, and fighting has resumed.

News Report: October 29, a cease-fire has been called so tourists trapped in the hotels can be freed. Armored cars and borrowed personnel carriers will be provided for the purpose.

"It only lasted long enough to get them out," Rob tells her when he comes home. "Fighting has already resumed."

"Tell me something new," she says.

"No work tomorrow, that means we'll have a long weekend."

"Yippee, what can we do with it? We're stuck here."

"We could drive up to Jounieh tomorrow, I heard it's quiet up there, and maybe I'll call Victor and Nabil to come over on Saturday?"

"Call them, but I don't want to go out of the hills until it settles down," she says.

News Report: October 31, another cease-fire has been arranged allowing the evacuees to return to collect their belongings if they wish.

"My God. it's like the keystone cops! Why didn't they take their stuff with them? And if they didn't, why risk life and limb to go back for it?" Genie says. She is growing stir crazy. "There may be no immediate danger to us, but these 'skirmishes' as you like to call them mean we are effectively prisoners, too."

"You think I don't understand? Maybe I didn't grasp what I wanted when we left England, but now all I want is to fulfill my obligation, get the hell out and make a fresh start in California. Just nine more months, I promise. Can we just grin and bear it?"

15

BEIRUT, NOVEMBER 1975

A Lawless Land

THE CURFEW IS LIFTED, AND they can finally move about after dusk again.

> News Report: November 3, the Prime Minister announced a new cease-fire in an attempt to demilitarize the Hotel district. The Phalangists refuse to vacate until Muslim militias are replaced by Internal Security Forces Gendarmes.

At work, Mark and Rob listen to the news. "There's a ceasefire. Why not stay for dinner?"

After months of frequent curfews, Genie is eager for company and when Rob calls she agrees to take public taxis to meet them.

In the city it's dark and eerie, the buildings show wear and tear from the conflict, and she is confronted with a real sense of the widespread destruction.

But at Mark and Kat's it is calm. She relaxes on their patio, takes the pear sorbet Kat offers, sips shots from a bottle of Calvados and wonders if they will ever visit France where it is made, see other parts of the world like they used to?

Rob and Mark chat as Kat carries out food.

"It feels remarkably civilized to be out, part of the world after dark," Rob says.

Kat declines the offer of help, so Genie relaxes and inhales the fragrance of the garden. "Fires are burning across the city," she says.

No-one answers.

She stares into the flames leaping from an exotic fire pit at the edge of the patio, visualizes flames in the hearth at her family's home in England, or a bonfire with sausages sizzling, celebrating November 5th. Guy Fawkes night. Unthreatening fireworks, so different from the displays which light their skies these days.

Kat joins them and curls her long legs underneath her. *How does she curl up her legs and still maintain an erect posture?* Genie wonders. Kat never relaxes.

They lean back, look out at the garden. The waxing crescent moon is visible in the sky and reflects over and over in ripples in the pool. A small indistinct animal plops in, shattering the image.

"A new truce was arranged, but no-one takes it seriously. Clashes continued after the 3 o'clock deadline today," Mark says. "Last month Syria mediated a cease-fire, and now a group of leaders wants to discuss the crisis."

An owl flits through the trees, unaware of curfews.

"All mouth and no trousers," Rob complains. "Talk, talk talk and no results. Three thousand dead since April, not to mention the ten thousand wounded."

"The truth is it will never change. Remember just a handful of people run the country, of those, three hold the keys to power and they hand it down from generation to generation," Mark says.

"You remember the Gemayels from the bus massacre? The family founded the Phalangist/Ktaeb party, Maronite Christians active here for 200 years." He sips his cocktail.

"And the Chamouns—behind the Saida problems, also Maronite Christians, they helped gain independence from France."

Rob listens carefully. "I recognize the names of course, but I hadn't realized that power was handed down through the generations. Like royalty," he says.

"Exactly. Except opposing factions want the throne. On the other side, there's Kamal Jumblatt, head of the Druze. Very powerful. Controls probably a dozen left-wing groups, wants an end to sectarianism."

A zap zings out, startles Genie back into the moment, an insect with a death wish self destructs into the illuminated zapper.

"Yesterday Mary told me the Phalangists have ten thousand armed men, they believe the guerrillas have the same," she says.

Across the garden, night creatures perform their nocturnal chorus undeterred by warring factions, and the group falls silent.

"A new dusk-to-dawn curfew for one week." Kourk shakes his head, his hair now shows traces of grey, and although he remains outwardly cheerful, Genie can see he worries for the future of his family, too. "The PM got the leftists to withdraw but the Phalangist right changed minds and fighting continues."

"It's an insane place," Genie says. "It affects us because Rob needs to move between the two worlds, but as a local, it seems your life goes on around the fighting."

He grunts. "Yes, life goes on."

Once again they are stuck at home.

> News Report: Saturday, November 8, another cease-fire has
> been announced.

"Nothing significant on the news?" she says, as she sips the remains of her hot chocolate.

Rob stares into space. Untouched his drink grows cold, and he remains silent.

Battle spotting has become their occupation, but tonight, from their terrace, they see little activity.

It's incredible how we've settled in, to this odd existence. She watches Rob, *It's getting to him,* she thinks. The radio has become a crutch for him, without the constant news reports he cannot relax, it is the only way he can decide if it is safe to venture out.

Their life has a rhythm, a somewhat discordant beat, but nevertheless, she has again agreed to try to hang in for the time Rob needs.

They watch cautiously through the weekend. Tensions remain high and although there is technically peace, wondering and waiting is the new norm.

The Hotel district seems quiet since the cease-fire. Things are still quiet on Monday, and against Genie's wishes, he insists on going to the factory, he mollifies her with a promise.

"If I can work for one whole week we'll go to Cyprus. I have business to do, you can relax, you'll love it."

She feels listless, and the promise of a getaway is tempting. Watching from the terrace, she sees Rob drive past Mary, out walking her dog and her child. He slows to say hi, and Mary looks up, calls Genie to come down.

Genie grabs a jacket and runs to join her.

"A month till the New Year, let's see what that brings!" Mary says.

"We're off to Cyprus for a few days soon, I can hardly wait."

"Well, I hope it calms down, or you may not be going anywhere. Thirty Israeli Phantom & Skyhawk jets flew in from the sea this morning. They attacked camps in the north and south, dozens killed, more than a hundred wounded south of Saida, that's the second attack after they almost leveled a camp in May."

She sees Genie's face and stops, looks around to make sure her little one is out of earshot.

"They hit a nerve center and training camp for guerillas near Tripoli. The oil refinery caught fire, and Lebanese anti-aircraft fought back. Israel says it's in response to attacks against Jerusalem and a settlement, say it's preventive, not punitive. They haven't responded measure for measure to attacks by Palestinians out of concern for us and the internal conflicts, but they say this can't continue."

"They do have a point," Genie says "But I pray nothing stops our trip."

Cautious about his movements Rob keeps his fingers crossed for a peaceful existence, but at the factory, Adnan takes him aside.

"I've begun to worry about Shana and the kids, it's being whispered she isn't Muslim."

"But you're a respected figure out here and even in parts of the city."

Adnan shakes his head. "Nothing is predictable anymore. We're in a Muslim area, for survival people divide along secular lines."

He has a point, it has become a lawless land. Later in the day, sporadic and heavy fighting is reported across the country, and Rob turns his focus back to the daily problems of getting around and finding sufficient food.

He hopes the weeks will pass without more severe conflict, perhaps Genie will grow calm and forget his recent promise to take her with him to Cyprus.

But she doesn't forget, peace is restored, and before the month is over Genie collects on her promise, they fly out to Nicosia.

16

DECEMBER 6, 1975

Black Saturday

IN NICOSIA, SHE CAN RELAX.

She bites into a slice of chilled watermelon, the juice runs down her chin, and she accepts a tissue from a pool attendant who passes with a spray bottle of suntan lotion. He holds up the bottle,. She nods. He sprays her in a cloud of coconut smelling oil and walks on.

Exactly what I need. No explosions, no bread lines, just the chance to be pampered. She smiles a thank you to the young man, finishes the melon and dips her red-nailed toe in the pool to test the water.

As Rob walks from the hotel into the blinding sun, he blinks and scans the poolside. It is unusually warm, his meetings are done, and he'd love to join her in the pool, but soon they have to head back.

He spots her, without difficulty, she performs an odd but effective side stroke, keeping her hair and her sunglasses dry, the only person who wears sunglasses in the water. She reaches the end, kicks the edge and turns swiftly, still managing to maintain her make-up and hair intact.

That's my girl, he smiles and remembers last night, How natural and passionate she can be away from the mood of gloom and doom which overwhelms them in Beirut these days. *She has a facility for overcoming trauma once the triggers are gone, thank God.*

Unaware he's in the shadows, she dries off, combs out her hair and removes the cap on her lipstick. Molten red liquid slides from the container onto the tiles. She stares at the pool of red and gasps. His footsteps are familiar, and she glances up.

He kisses her damp cheek. "We have to get going, the flight home is tonight."

She points at the pool of red. "It looks like blood!" she says and bends to clean the mess.

"Leave it, they'll take care of it."

"I wish we didn't have to go back."

"I know. Me too, but the cease-fire seems to be holding, and I must think of the work waiting."

An abandoned second edition newspaper on a table catches Genie's eye as she passes. She picks it up and hands it to Rob.

```
'Black Saturday–Beirut Streets Flow with Blood'
'On Saturday, 6 December 1975, four young men,
reportedly Phalangists, were assassinated in
Beirut.'
```

"You know they have to sell papers, so they bloody well create drama."

He takes the paper, throws it down and dismisses it. "We only left a couple of days ago, you saw how things had improved." He sounds frustrated, impatient.

"You think so?" she sees his face and says no more.

While they are in Nicosia, the discovery of four young bodies has led to a violent outcry. Revenge is swift and bloody. Nothing satisfies the thirst for retribution. In retaliation for the deaths of their men, outraged rightwing Phalangists take hostages. Some leaders attempt to stop the massacre, but the fury and madness once unleashed cannot be stopped.

Night falls early in December, and they land in the dark to an almost deserted Beirut Airport. A taxi driver approaches them. They walk past, but he follows, undeterred.

"Not safe alone. Ees dangerous. They killing anyone."

A man from the only other car at the airport gets out and adds. "You do not know? The capital shudders. Militias spread tentacles, seek vengeance. Street battles and mountains of bodies, they pile up."

The taxi driver warms to the theme. "It is fury, like wild forest fire, consumes all. Cannot be contained."

Rob sees her face and takes Genie's hand.

"But who?" she asks.

"The Phalangists. Hundreds upon hundreds—Palestinians and Lebanese Muslims murdered in streets, insatiable the lust for blood."

"There are checkpoints round city." The other man interrupts, eager to tell the story.

"Dozens of militiamen spread to central market, shoppers panicked from violence, they abandon purchases in streets—flee for their lives."

"Il y a un couvre-feu de vingt quatre heures," A man on a bench nearby calls out as he sits and waits—for something—next to an oversized suitcase.

"Merci," Rob nods.

"A twenty-four-hour curfew on the streets?" She holds tight to Rob as they continue to their parked car and pull out of the airport.

Genie is at the wheel. Not one car is on the road. "Do you think the taxi driver may have been right?" she asks.

They reach the coast and still no other car is to be seen, Rob doesn't reply as he fumbles for the radio.

"This feels spooky. Maybe we should have gone the back way," he mutters.

She hisses at him. "Shush!" And they concentrate on the funereal tones of the announcer on the radio.

News Report: Estimates indicate up to six hundred dead, three hundred hostages still missing. Authorities urge you to remain in your homes. Unless you are a doctor or have a life-threatening emergency—stay in your homes. We repeat, do not leave your homes.

"Shit," Rob mutters.

Tense and quiet they drive along the deserted street, cautiously, as if lack of speed will shelter them from harm.

Just a mile before their turn off a barricade is manned by a lone and extremely young boy with round frightened eyes and camouflage clothes that are too large. He waves a flashlight and a large weapon which appears heavy for him.

They stop.

"Christ, he looks ten years old. He should be in school," Rob whispers.

The frightened boy appears tired and overwhelmed at the job he's been given. His eyes lock on to Genie, like a scared rabbit she can't look away. She sucks in air, a loud rasp and holds on to her breath, maybe the last she will ever take.

The boy doesn't break eye contact, her fingers grip the wheel so tight a sharp pain shoots up her arms, she feels a vibration shake her body.

We'll die here on this deserted road, by mistake, not because of what we've done or who we are, but because we're in the wrong place at the wrong moment, she thinks.

Her lungs ache, and her eyes water as the boy eventually breaks eye contact and turns away. Miraculously a ramshackle car has come from nowhere. He walks to it, she watches through the overhead mirror as he demands identification papers.

They listen. There is a loud exchange of voices. Rob turns to look over his shoulder and gasps.

"I think the driver pulled a gun, Jeez!"

Gunfire crashes into the vehicle from the boy's weapon.

Rob yells as he is jolted headfirst into the dashboard. Tires screech and he flails as their car lurches forward. "What the hell are you doing?"

Without a word, she charges ahead, a trail of smoke behind them. The boy refocuses his target, and gunfire crashes into the trunk, Rob ducks, furious at Genie.

"What the bloody hell are you thinking? You must be off your rocker!"

Her knuckles are white on the wheel, but she drives fast, her foot pressed hard to the floor.

"To hell with you, I'm not waiting to get killed when there's the remotest chance of escape. That boy was petrified, who knows what he would have done?"

They speed north on the highway, don't slow until they turn into the hills. The wheels skid and screech as she careens around the bend.

The danger has passed, and she lets herself cry with relief.

"You may be right, it was your choice. I should keep quiet," Rob puts a hand over hers, she relaxes her grip on the wheel and eases her foot off the pedal.

But as they climb the stairs past Rubina's, Genie's shoulders slump. Their Armenian landlady has left her apartment door open. Spider-like she waits to catch them as they return.

Oh God, not now, Genie thinks. *Can't I get a moment to recover?*

Rubina walks awkwardly and lopsidedly out of her apartment, her child clings to her skirt.

"They came by today. We must to pay. For bandages and medicine. You, too," Rubina informs them.

"Medicine, bandages? They're lying. They want bullets so they can terrorize, kill and steal," Genie explodes.

Rubina recoils, shocked by the vehemence of Genie's reply. She shrugs. "You may be right, but we don't have choice."

"I have a choice. I'll donate bandages and medicine. Not money." Rubina looks to Rob, but he says nothing.

"It is wise to pay, to protect us," she says.

"Protect us? Protect us from what? They're the ones we need protection from! Tell them. I won't buy bullets to kill people we don't even know, or worse still people we love. I'll give medicine if they want it."

"I will tell, but I think they will want cash."

And Rubina is right. By now the fighting requires vast amounts of money, and they need to find it, somewhere.

In newspapers and in play by play reports at work, when Rob makes it across town, they learn of increased hostilities.

Fate has decreed they find themselves living in a heavily Christian, and by definition Phalangist, enclave while Rob's factory is in the heart of Muslim territory.

He hears the lunch siren, puts down the paper and walks out to meet Mark who has invited him for lunch.

Rob pauses to admire the flowers between the factory and the lushly planted oasis surrounding Mark's villa, the sweet scent of the seemingly innocent, pink and red oleander bushes teases his nostrils.

They round the corner to see Kat and James swimming, she waves and climbs out, slips on a kaftan, wraps a towel around her head and disappears into the house.

Rob feels a twinge as he watches the warm family life.

Mark and Rob sit pool-side with a couple of drinks watching James as he dives into the pool, Rob casually observes Mark, noting his mannerisms. For the umpteenth time, he wishes he could be more like Mark, who is always so bloody relaxed, at home in every situation.

"It's getting overgrown. Kat tries, but the gardener doesn't come anymore, and it's a big garden," Mark says.

Rob looks around. "It's still a beautiful garden. I rather like what nature is doing, it's almost startling to discover this oasis so close to the factory."

"Mmm. We feel far from whatever's going on around, we've always loved it." Mark sips his drink and leans back lazily. "I was born in the tropics, so England, although the 'motherland' has never actually felt like home to me. My only time there was at Oxford where I met Kat, and she couldn't wait to leave the cold."

Kat effortlessly carries out an oversized tray laden with Arabic bread, raw vegetables and Haloumi, a sizzling fried goat cheese. She places it in front of them and takes a seat.

"Delicious," Rob says, scooping up cheese with the bread.

She watches James swim.

"Come along darling, come and eat," Kat calls. James reluctantly climbs out and joins them, she wraps him in a brightly colored towel.

"He'll have to go to England soon, to boarding school. He's ten already. It'll be hard, but given the situation . . ." Mark says.

"Do you never think of leaving?" Rob asks.

"Never. We love it, despite the occasional flare-ups. We're isolated from it here, as you see."

"I love the lifestyle, but work is a daily nightmare. I don't know how you do it."

Mark shares a look with Kat and smiles at Rob. "We were raised to it, dear boy." There's a small plop as two baby frogs jump into the pool.

"Genie would leave tomorrow if we could." He makes no mention of how bad their personal situation has become. "But the American partners won't consider causing a problem with the Licensing Agreement, they say it's a go when my contract is over."

Unnoticed Kat has magically disappeared and reappeared with dessert and coffee.

Light of foot, Rob observes, *she'd make a great burglar.*

Insects flit around, and James jumps up in excitement. "Tabsoun!" he cries as a pretty, plump little brown creature with short legs stops, smiles at them, speeds over a large rock and disappears into a nearby tree.

"Is it a guinea pig?" Rob asks.

"Actually they're related to elephants. It's a hyrax," Kat says matter of factly. "They sing; tweets, squeaks, whistles, and wails."

"She's a fount of facts. Knows all about the flowers and fauna of these parts." Mark squeezes her hand, pulls it to his lips.

They're still like newlyweds, Rob sighs. He sips from his small cup of Arabic coffee, wonders if maybe they could have been happier in a place like this, resort style, rather than isolated out in the hills.

As Rob starts his car, Mark calls an invitation through the window.

"Come over tomorrow, around seven thirty? We haven't seen Genie for a while."

"I'll ask her," Rob says.

But despite the nominal cease-fire, hostilities resume, and there is no get together, they go nowhere.

December 1975

Victor passes below and whistles up to them. "Are you receiving?" he laughs as Rob peers over the balcony, and his head disappears into the front entrance.

"Those stairs are a nightmare," he says as he pants toward a seat.

"It's good to see you," Rob says. "We never see anyone lately."

Genie puts out a selection of nibbles, pours glasses of chilled white wine and joins them.

"Better to stay home and stay safe," he says.

"True, it's safe if we never, ever go out, but we have jobs and friends, we're not yet thirty, too young for home and hearth," Genie says.

"But it's such a beautiful home." He sips the wine and switches topics. "The Army is covering Parliament House and the Post Office, they've delayed leftist advances, but there's new fighting for the Hotels. They have Anti-tank rocket launchers, RPG-7's and vehicle-mounted recoilless rifles," he exclaims. "Stay home, enjoy the view and the rest."

She rolls her eyes at Rob, Victor sees her and laughs. "If you venture forth, risk is inevitable, but I suspect you like a little danger?"

"Nonsense."

The Phalangists hold on to the Holiday Inn, but a close-quarter battle continues for the Phoenicia Hotel. The St Georges Hotel falls, and the Lebanese Army launches a successful attack on the hotels.

Her worry for Shana and the children and for Mark and his family are second only to the fears she has for herself and Rob.

News Report: On December 10, the Muslims called the Palestinians for help, and for two days the Phoenicia and St Georges Hotels repeatedly changed hands. Now fighting has temporarily halted.

"After all the bloodshed I bet both sides realized they've not improved their original positions," she says.

Rob opens the fridge looking for something to cheer him up. "I don't think it's getting better. They announced another truce, but it's ignored. You're right nothing's gained, except more and more killing."

For fresh air, she is huddled in blankets on a chaise on their terrace. Rob plops beside her. Mugs of hot chocolate liberally dosed with brandy offer little cheer during another home detention, but from out here they at least see some of what is unfolding—their window on the world.

A plume of smoke billows up, a long grey funnel curling into the sky from the top of the Holiday Inn on the peninsula.

"I wonder if it's severely damaged?" she thinks aloud.

"If it wasn't before it is now. Honestly, after all this I can't imagine what state it's in."

Sure enough, fighting goes back and forth, taking and retaking until mid-December.

News Report: December 18. A Syrian delegation has arrived to mediate peace. Lebanese Gendarmerie detachments have replaced Muslim and Christian militiamen in each of the hotel sites . . .

"Too little too late," Genie says.

> . . . In other breaking news, some forty or fifty bodies have
> been recovered from the Phoenicia Hotel.

"My God," Genie shakes her head. "Remember the celebrations at the Phoenicia? Can you imagine it blackened and
strewn with dead bodies?"

Rob is silent. *What is there to say—and next week is Christmas. How does the carol go? Silent night Holy night, all is calm
all is bright.* He doesn't want to admit it, but he's losing faith.
Christ Almighty, he wonders what he is supposed to do now?

They schedule their lives according to the radio, their lifeline to the world, answering an omnipresent question—will
today be safe to venture forth?

For the first time, they sit without chatter, both ponder the
same question. The future. For the country, for Genie and Rob
and for their friends.

And after Christmas, the unthinkable happens.

The day after Christmas Mark puts down his cup of coffee and
finishes writing New Year cards to friends in Europe. He glances
at his watch, walks out to his car and waves to Adnan who is
coming down the stairs from his apartment.

"Shana is making Irish coffee," Adnan calls.

"I have to get going. Friends are going home and taking our
letters. I said we'd be at the airport by 3."

James runs out of the house. "Can I come? I can be dressed
in two minutes, Daddy."

Mark ruffles James' hair. "Alright, but be quick."

The boy runs inside, slips on shoes and in his room he grabs a sweater. They jump in the car, wave again to Adnan and leave.

Darkness has fallen, Genie and Rob listen to music and eat the remains of yesterday's turkey when there is a knock on the door. They are surprised, no-one is expected, but Rob gets up and answers.

"I don't know what happened, it sounds important," Rubina says as Rob follows her downstairs, she looks serious and waits while he takes the call, she asks no questions but has overheard the news.

Rob thanks her and goes back to Genie.

"That was Adnan, Mark hasn't made it back from the airport. He saw him leave with James just after two and no-one has heard a word since."

Without speaking Genie grabs her coat and they head to Kat's.

Shana and Adnan are already there.

"It doesn't take five hours to go to the airport and back. Something's wrong. They must have had an accident or Mark would've called," Kat says.

There is a combined sense of helplessness.

Kat paces, cannot settle. Genie tries to put an arm around her, but she slips away to the window, attempting to contain the emotions which seem all engulfing.

Shana looks at Adnan, her eyes ask the unspoken question on all their minds. He leaves. No-one needs to ask where he has gone.

Half an hour later he returns and sits heavily on the couch.

"It's not good news, I'm afraid. Six people were kidnapped at the airport this afternoon. Two Swiss, two French Jews, also an unnamed man and a boy, perhaps Mark and James. His car is still parked at the airport."

A strange cry snags in Kat's throat, and she grasps the table.

Adnan looks exhausted. "We don't know where they are. I have questions being asked . . ."

"What do you mean questions? Do you know these people?" Genie interrupts,

Rob tries to shush her.

"No. I won't be quiet," Genie says.

Adnan looks sadly at her. "No, Genie I don't know these people, but money opens mouths. For enough money, someone can always find out. It takes time and great care." He exaggerates the last word looking hard at Genie. "I know it's not easy, but we must go through channels. Interference could be fatal."

Genie turns to Rob. "You said we'd have a better life. You agreed if I were unhappy we'd leave. Well, now I'm unhappy."

She bites her lip, wishes she hadn't said that right now. At this moment they need to focus on Mark and James.

Hours pass, but no word comes.

Out in the night somewhere, Adnan talks to whomever and searches for news of Mark and James.

Shana leaves to put the children to bed, and Rob turns on Genie "You do realize he's putting himself in danger over and over by trying to help all of us?"

"I know."

She feels ashamed she challenged Adnan. He has always been there for everyone. But she no longer trusts, not even what she sees. Everything has a spin, and with so much deception she feels out of control.

Rob and Kat are preoccupied.

"They've been my life," she says. "I can't imagine being without them."

"Jesus, we shouldn't be thinking like this, Kat. You can't give up hope," Rob says. "Adnan won't. He's experienced at this. It may seem like a lifetime, but it's only been a few hours."

"I hope you're right. In any event, it seems unlikely there will be news tonight. Go home, I'll call if we hear anything," Kat says.

Sensing she would prefer to be alone, Rob and Genie reluctantly leave her.

He hopes his words of encouragement are not misplaced. It's unusual no word has been received if they've been kidnapped for ransom, but the alternative, in which Mark and James have already been killed, is unthinkable.

As they leave, Adnan returns home. He looks tired.

"Mark and James best hope is to spread the word that someone wants them back, someone who's willing to pay," he tells them. "I'll continue to ask questions, but I need Abbad and his uncle to come up with an attractive offer."

"I'm sorry I was awful, earlier," Genie says. "I know you do so much for us all."

"We are all under pressure. Tomorrow I'll call more of the groups which the company pays to stay protected."

As they leave him, she can see he's frustrated at the lack of information.

"He's probably worried about Shana and the kids, too. This kidnapping brings things too close to home," Rob says.

All of the men Adnan contacts promise to get back to him, but hours and soon days, tick by and the phone remains silent. No ransom is demanded and, if they're still alive, he suspects this may be some as yet unknown splinter group.

These days anyone can get weapons and go into business for themselves, he thinks. No-one challenges them because it's assumed there's a connection to a more powerful faction. A perfect scenario for entrepreneurial thugs.

On New Year's day 1976, in a dank warehouse piled high with bananas, a large grim spider clambers over a foot, along a body and disappears under a hood. The body squirms violently letting out a muffled cry.

At the far end, separated by several large stacks of green bananas, a young body is also tied hand and foot, so small the hood over his head reaches almost to his waist. Women and children prod and flick at him with sticks and loud gurgles come from the backs of their tongues, an alien and terrifying sound, especially while hooded and in darkness.

In the absence of contact with reality James' small body twists and twitches, he is covered in red welts.

A man in a Keffiyeh puts a gun in his small hand and whispers. "We will take off this blindfold, you will see your father and you will shoot him—or you will die." He takes away the gun. "He is a pig." He spits.

From his end of the warehouse, Mark hears James small voice. "He's not. He's good and kind." The man slaps James' face leaving an unseen handprint. The boy cries out.

"Be strong, I love you, James," Mark calls. He struggles to get to his feet, but a brutal punch knocks him down. Invisible hands wield sticks, stinging him into submission. Prodded and hit, he curls over, his hooded face on the ground. The anger and spasm of helplessness when he hears his son's cries are crushing, but nothing compared to the anguish and desperation when he hears nothing.

What are we going to do? He shudders at the answer. *Nothing.* He knows their only hope must come from outside.

He tries to overcome the daily whispers in his ear. "When we remove this blindfold you will kill your son, or watch us kill him—slowly."

The ululating sound grinds on his nerves, the mental torture is worse than the constant sting of the sticks. With the hood over his head, he can't tell how much time has passed. They release his hands to eat a few morsels of food, which he pushes awkwardly under the hood. He hasn't seen James since they were taken, but occasional sounds give some small reassurance.

If we eat once a day we must have been captive for a week or more, he thinks. *Maybe it's a good sign. They could have killed us right away, unless they were after a ransom. They must be negotiating,* he decides.

Genie and Rob go each day to Kat's to offer moral support, they tell themselves, but there is little anyone can say to ease her distress.

"She won't eat. Hardly had anything since they were taken," Genie tells Rob as they leave the factory. "She tries to maintain her stiff upper lip and composure, but she is barely holding on."

With the Syrian mediation efforts, fighting in the Hotel district subsides, the main participants move elsewhere, but no word of Mark or James.

"Any news of your friend?" Kourk asks. "Now the New Year is here, anger is spreading over sniping and kidnappings of civilians in Christian areas," he tells them. "It's almost a siege, now we have food and fuel shortages, anger rises." He pulls a stern face, nods his head up and down and returns to digging in his garden.

He seems to be a haphazard gardener, but the grounds cover an acre, and he has carved out a small area to plant across the front. Colorful flowers add a moment of beauty.

"It looks good, Kourk," Rob tells him as they head inside.

News report: On January 4th, in a tit for tat response, four hundred right-wing forces blockaded the Tel al-Zaatar Palestinian camp and cut off supply routes. One road is open for the possibility of escape, but occupants refuse discussions. At this time, a stalemate exists, and inhabitants remain trapped. The blockade may extend to other slum districts nearby.

"Jesus."

News Report: January 5, the Lebanese National Movement
has retaliated against the south-east of the capital.

"That's your area," Genie tells Rob "You shouldn't go in
today. It is not safe, they took Mark from over there."

"They took him from the airport. And at a holiday when it
was desolate. I'll be fine."

"Rob, tomorrow's Friday why not take a long weekend.
We could drive up to Jounieh, it's quiet up there we could clear
our heads."

But he insists. Genie worries for Kat and of course Mark
and their son, so like every day since the capture, she again goes
across the city with him.

It's insanity, she thinks, *and it won't help anyone if we are
hurt, too.* But they feel the need to show solidarity

"There is no word," Adnan tells them. "I have turned over
every lead I have. Abbad and the big boss have now offered a
substantial reward."

"Someone is sure to find them for that much money," Rob
says.

Genie has her doubts but keeps them to herself. "I hope
you're right."

In Mark's cellar, another night is over, but it is impossible for him
to tell night from day. *It must be two weeks or more,* he thinks.
Food is less frequent, judging by the weakness in his body.

He calculates time by the brief periods of silence which occur
when he imagines the men are sleeping. He rolls his sandpaper

tongue around his mouth. His teeth hurt, his mouth feels foul, and he aches all over, but they're still alive.

The fighters, bored now the holidays are over and with little to do, move back to the Hotel district.

When they return home, Genie stands on the terrace and watches the city. "We should move our beds and the stove out here," she says. "There's an entire planet out there, and I stand on the corner of this terrace in a watered-down attempt at living my life."

In the distance a cloud of smoke rises from some unrecognized building, she turns to listen as Rob turns up the radio and is lost to her.

And then Adnan calls. "We've found them," he cries, his voice ecstatic.

At last some good news. They are elated.

Rob feels the need to hurry to the factory. They park, and he runs like a schoolboy through the gardens to Kat's house, he can't wait to tell her.

She weeps, and together they help her to Adnan, who waits with the car.

Rob sees how frail she is, bent over from the strain, her already thin frame is now skeletal. Through her dress, he notices the bumps on her shoulders where her bones protrude.

The old gatekeeper grins, he has the gate open, ready. Word has spread. He and a small group of workers wave as they speed out of the compound. Mark and his family are respected, maybe even loved.

There is an increasingly pungent smell which Mark has recognized. Rotten bananas. *They must've been unable to sell or move them because now they are rotting.*

As he ponders this a man's voice intrudes. "It's almost time. Are you prepared? He's begging us to do it . . ."

Mark and James can't see the men enter wearing Keffiyahs, but they hear more than the usual number of footsteps approach. There are no longer women's or children's voices.

Mark welcomes the cessation of the constant sticks hitting at him, *Something has changed. Something is happening.*

One of the men grabs hold of James' arm.

He is blindfolded and cries out "I won't do it. I won't."

Hearing James' cries Mark tries to call to his son, he gets to his feet, but his voice has gone, and his legs buckle. A brutal kick takes him by surprise, and he crumples. A man on each side of his body drags him, he can hardly walk.

He is aware of James' small sounds of pain as he struggles as well. In a futile effort, he gropes for James' hand. The hoods remain on their heads as they are dragged and roughly shoved into two separate cars.

It is hard to think clearly. Mark is concerned James isn't with him, but his mind gropes for answers, switches tracks as he imagines this must be a good sign. Why put them in cars otherwise? They could have been left to die and rot in the dank place they've been in for weeks.

After a seemingly unending journey, the car stops and Mark is dragged out. He hears James whimper and sags with relief to have his son close by.

"Don't worry, my boy. Be brave, it'll be OK."

The butt of a gun smashes into his head. He staggers and falls.

"Get up."

But Mark doesn't move. The man turns and leaves him on the gravel. Dust and pebbles cover Mark and James as the cars speed off.

Face hidden by the keffiyeh around his head, one man peers from a car window and aims his gun, he cocks it. Then he shoots into the air. A Lebanese expression of satisfaction.

Hands tied behind them the two hooded bodies remain where they are, unmoving.

The engine sounds fade but James doesn't dare to move or even speak, he waits to hear his father's voice.

A couple of minutes pass, and he hears another car approach.

The sound is different, quieter, no grinding gears, James notices. He stifles a groan and wonders if they have come back. *And then what?*

He has heard his father and Adnan speaking about groups who trade prisoners like monopoly pieces? His father is silent and doesn't move.

Help me, Daddy, he silently prays.

A car skids to a halt, footsteps approach and almost unbelievably, there are familiar voices and a fragrance.

Rob and Adnan call—but he knows his mother is near.

James' voice is weak, but he calls out. "Help us, please."

Adnan and Rob rush to Mark. Kat runs to James. She kneels beside her young son, pulls him into her lap.

"It's alright, my darling. Mummy's here," she bends over and cradles his small body. Kat is devastated, she can hardly bear to see him so thin, so vulnerable.

"Mark, keep your eyes closed and open them gradually." Rob removes the hood, but Mark doesn't hear them. He's unconscious.

Kat holds tight to James and turns to look at Mark, she stifles a gasp, her hand over her mouth. Mark's face is gaunt, a beard has started to grow in, it is white, and his dark hair has thinned, that too has turned to white. He is still, there is no movement at all.

Between her husband and her son, this elegant, restrained Englishwoman breaks down and sobs.

It's the first time Rob has seen the boy since their release, and he pats James' back. James clings to him in a long hug. The lump in Rob's throat threatens to spill over into tears.

"Let's go to the hospital and get your Father," he says and helps James into the car beside a subdued Kat.

She has at last allowed Genie to put an arm around her. *Perhaps she needs the comfort, or maybe she is unaware I'm even here,* Genie thinks.

They pick up Mark and head to the airport. He has aged, not surprisingly. She wonders vaguely if this is a permanent change; certainly, the mental scars will be near impossible to slough off.

At the departure desk, there are tears. Goodbyes are tough, they don't banter, those carefree days are in the past. The flight is called, and the small family leaves.

"He's been my mentor as well as a friend, helped keep me sane here," Rob says. She reaches out and takes his hand.

News Report: January 10, Today Phalangists occupied the Holiday Inn while leftists took the Phoenicia. No other significant changes have occurred, and all parties maintain their positions.

"My God, This is unbelievable!" she says. "It could go on forever, we'll be sitting here old, wrinkled and grey and our lives will have simply passed us by."

"I told you before, nothing lasts forever."

"That's actually not true," she tells him, but she hardly expects a serious response. She recognizes it is only a few months until his tenure is up and then the promise of a new American life.

17

"HOW CAN YOU LEAVE ME here now? There's hardly been a day of peace in weeks. Mark has only just been freed, and there are break-ins all over, women assaulted."

Months filled with almost daily conflict have left her reeling. She barely eats or sleeps, one drama has barely ended, and Rob is about to take off alone on a trip.

She looks at him as he folds shirts into an open bag. He finishes, zips the bag and picks up his briefcase but doesn't respond. He is smarting over what he perceives as her unwarranted complaints and lack of support, lately.

"Why don't we both go and not come back until it gets calm?" she asks.

"Syria called a cease-fire. It's all back to normal."

"Normal? There's nothing normal about any of this," her voice shakes, and she bites her bottom lip. "I don't feel safe, and you don't seem to care."

"Oh Genie, don't. Please stop. You know you'll be fine. I'm not going on holiday, I have a damn job to do." He grabs a coat from the hall closet, for half a moment he wonders if he should take her too, but everything's booked, it's too late.

He looks back at her. "You'd be sitting around all day in the hotel just twiddling your thumbs, waiting, and I'd be under pressure worrying about you. At least here you can see friends or relax in your own space. Just keep the doors locked." He pats her head.

She has lost the argument, nothing will dissuade him. Reluctantly she grabs the car keys and follows him out,

"You're bloody insane," she mutters.

"Try to make sure the tank is always full, you should buy a gas can to keep in the car. They're rationing here now. Deja bloody vu," he laughs as he briefly remembers one of his reasons for leaving England, but he shakes the memory away.

Along the airport road, sentries check cars at a military barricade. The line is long, and Rob grows anxious as the moments tick by.

"I'll miss my flight if they don't get a move on."

Their turn comes, the swarthy sentry has no spark of life in his eyes, he stops the shell shot car, observes the damage and raps on the driver's window.

"Do you fly?" he asks her.

Genie lowers the window. "No, I'm driving my husband."

"Passengers only," he growls.

Rob turns to Genie and reaches for his bags. "It's OK. I can make it from here."

She shakes her head. "No, it's a long walk."

The sentry grows visibly impatient. He taps the car with the tip of his gun "Only passengers. No private autos. Turn!" His English is heavily accented, perhaps Egyptian.

Genie puts the car in gear and turns her face up to him. "That's ridiculous. I'm only . . ." she stops mid-sentence as the sentry lifts his gun.

He puts it casually to the side of her head. She feels the click as he primes it. Recent events flash through her consciousness, her heart falls, and she gasps. "Ok."

Rob glares at her. "For once why can you not argue and do as your told. I'm so tired of your constant resistance to the way things are." He gets out and hails a cab without saying goodbye.

She notices lately he creates an argument before he leaves, and she wonders if it's from some sense of guilt at leaving her, maybe he feels better if she's the bad guy.

Ah, well no point in trying to get inside Rob's head. She cringes at what an impossible task it would be to navigate his mind and understand what motivates him.

On the drive home, she passes a makeshift wall which has been patchily constructed to hide the refugee camp from the view of people who come and go to the airport.

Beyond it, shanty-style buildings are supplemented by corrugated metal structures and lean together in disarray. Strung overhead a schizophrenic mass of wires and electric cables carry essential services from structure to structure. No-one has chosen to live in this place, it is a matter of fate—destiny some might say.

She shudders. Lebanese authorities put up the high graffiti-daubed walls to try and disguise what exists beyond, but through the asphalt of the cracked roads weeds and bushes force their way up, seeking light and life. They add to the overall sense of abandonment. An absence of hope.

Whether to contain the people inside or to hide the shameful reality of their existence and allow the wealthy to sleep at night is not clear, but one thing unites many of the people here, they encourage the education of their children, a hope it could mean escape, even if it takes decades.

There but for the grace of God . . . she thinks

Her attention is drawn toward groups of armed men who march along what had once been a quiet roadside. She stares, surprised at this new militancy. Her bright green car catches the eye of one man. He stops, holds up his hand, aims an imaginary gun at her and 'pulls the trigger'.

An involuntary cry escapes her, and she speeds away.

Walking distance from Taksim Square the large Hilton Hotel in Istanbul is set amid beautiful gardens, a welcome escape for Rob who needs this time to relax and recover from all of the recent drama.

He is reflective, he loves Genie, but her constant nagging for them to go home is tiresome.

Why won't she give it a rest? They have just to wait it out.

Although he is in the city on business, he makes time to explore the numerous places he visits, a little break amid the demanding work. Since Friday is the day of prayer in the middle east and weekends are part of the work week, he leaves home on Friday and gains a guilt-free way to immerse in local features, food, and fragrances.

He booked his hotel for the accessibility to the Topkapi Palace, the Hagia Sophia as well as the Sultan Ahmed Mosque, above all to one of the world's most beautiful coastlines, the Bosphorus.

"I recommend Rejans," The concierge tells him. "It originated as a meeting place for White Russian emigrés escaping the Revolution, and caught on with the intelligentsia."

Rob smiles and thanks him, but he already knows Rejans. He loves the unique mix of Russia and the old Ottoman Empire, and the food: a mezze, stroganoff, and dessert.

In the middle of each table sits a bottle of lemon vodka, charged according to the amount consumed. This evening Rob's stress levels lower as he drinks freely from the bottle in front of him.

By the time he finishes night has fallen, and Rob signals his pleasure to the concierge upon his return.

He heads to the bar in the hotel. A Filipino folkloric troupe finishes a performance, and a dancer approaches. Rob gives her his stool, she smiles and orders a drink. Gallantly Rob pays for it, downs his own and leaves.

He gives an involuntary jump at the soft ding of the elevator. The doors slide open, Rob presses 14 and searches his pocket for his key.

The door almost closes but a hand holding a half-full glass reaches through the gap, and it slides open for the pretty brown-skinned dancer to slip in. She holds out her free hand.

"Isabella."

Rob takes her hand. "You dance beautifully."

Another ding as the elevator arrives at the fourteenth floor and she laughs and waits for the doors to open. Rob gets out, holds the door ajar, and with a flourish and a half bow he passes her his business card. She leans into him, and kisses both cheeks, she looks down at his name.

"So nice to meet you, Rob Miller," she laughs as he gets out. The doors close and she turns the business card over in her hands.

I just made a complete idiot of myself, he thinks

In total darkness, Rob stands at the window of his room high above the Bosphorus. Istanbul twinkles below.

Why didn't he bring Genie with him? He asks himself. He could easily have done so, but lately, it has all begun to grow so hard. She seemed to have adjusted well until Keith's death, but the recent killings have set her off again. He thought they'd long since overcome her dependence on him, now it seems to be back.

No, he needs some time to himself. When she has to, Genie always rises to the challenge and manages. *She isn't a child after all.*

A sharp knock at the door shakes him from his reflections. Rob looks at his watch. Who could it be at this hour? He opens the door and Isabella, the tiny dancer, brushes past him into the room, she clasps a bottle and two glasses.

He steps aside, astonished. Isabella passes him and smiles over her shoulder at his expression.

"Close your mouth you'll catch flies," she says in a sing-song voice and laughs, a light, girlish, tinkling sound. Her coat falls, under it she wears high heels which accentuate her lean muscular legs, and a long string of pearls which drape down the center of her back, swaying as she moves.

Her bare skin shines golden from the moon which softly illuminates the room. She is tiny and beautiful and watches his reaction through her long sloping eyes which glow catlike as she turns in the moonlight.

Rob dares not move.

For Genie in Beirut a different nighttime falls.

The usual nocturnal performance of tracer bullets fly back and forth over the city and light the sky outside. She tosses, turns and without success longs for rest. Even with a pillow over her head, she can hear the muffled noise, but after a while, she drifts into a light sleep.

A louder than usual explosion bursts outside, she flings off the pillow and sits up. It felt like it was in the room. She reaches for the glass of water beside her bed. It's empty.

Sleepily she pulls herself up and pads in the semi-darkness along the corridor. The kitchen patio door is open and in the trees on the hillside beyond cicadas keep up their nightly call.

From the ocean side of the building, bombs continue to burst as she takes out a fresh bottle of water. She hears a sound. She's petrified.

It seems to be inside the apartment. Genie holds her breath, strains to hear, steps from the fridge's circle of light and closes it. Her heart pounds and she also closes the kitchen patio door, tiptoes across the room and peers along the hallway.

Rocket bursts fill the night sky and illuminate the ocean side of the apartment. From the open door of the living room, light falls across the entry hall.

She watches in horror as the handle on the front door turns slowly. The door is locked and doesn't open but fear washes over her and she drops her water bottle. It splatters. She jumps.

"I have a gun. Ana dhahib liqatlik—I'll kill you," she screams out. Her panic rises, she picks up one of the shoes Rob has left abandoned at the door and bangs furiously, scratching the surface of the wooden door.

She hears whispers outside on the landing, soft footsteps recede on the stairs.

The taste of terror is familiar. She throws aside the shoe and leans her ear to the door. *Perhaps they gave up?*

She waits, no sound or movement. She peers through the peephole. Nothing.

Breathing deeply she scurries back to her bedroom, to safety, slowing to glance out the corridor windows. She peers into the darkness, and she freezes, like a block of ice.

A pair of trouser-clad legs dangle at eye level.

Oh, my God, they went to the roof.

Her mind is not processing, but adrenalin fills her, and as the body lowers itself she opens the door. A man reaches eye level, still holding on as his feet scramble for a foothold.

She recognizes him. She saw this face before, weeks ago. At her party, he grabbed her hair, pointed a weapon at her head. His eyes widen as he sees her and one foot finds the railing.

Without pausing for a second, she charges, with all her strength she butts her head into his torso. The sudden unexpected assault dislodges his hands and foot, and he is pushed outward. She briefly notices the tiger tattoo as he falls three floors to the ground below. A cry. Muffled shouts. Footsteps. Silence.

The hammer that knocks inside her heart signals her to move. She locks the balcony, runs into the bedroom and locks that door also. The pounding has spread to her head, and the rapid banging won't stop inside her chest.

She waits. Waits for them to come.

But it's silent. Genie's eyes search for a solution, for escape, help. But her mind focuses on the unavoidable fact—she has been recognized.

Am I a target? Could they know Rob is away and how? What can I do?

She sinks to the floor, pulls her knees to her chest and buries her head. *Like a damned ostrich*, she accuses herself. Her spine feels like jello, and there is a weakness in her legs, but she knows she needs to think, and an idea creeps into her confusion.

Make them believe I'm not alone.

She pulls herself up, clambers onto her bed, turns on the lamp and starts to talk—to herself. She picks up the newspaper, rattles the pages. Converses with the empty space beside her, words fall out, she comments on articles, occasionally she climbs out and bangs the wardrobe door.

As the night deepens, she keeps up a constant stream of chatter—until she doesn't.

The Blue Mosque calls the faithful to prayer.

"British Airways, how may I help you?" the voice asks.

"I am booked to Beirut today. I need to delay," Rob says.

Tilted drunkenly against the wall, she wakes to sunlight on her face, amazed and thankful she is still alive. She doesn't understand. There's been total silence since Rob left almost a week ago and last night has left her defenseless and afraid.

What will happen today? Will they come back or have they been to the police about me? Did he survive the fall?

Her brain drives her mad. She scrapes up the little courage which remains, opens the back patio door and looks down. Nothing. No sign of anyone. All trace is gone as if it never happened. For two hours she does nothing, waits as her mind does battle.

Should I tell Rubina or Mary? No, she decides. *What if they don't understand, want to go to the authorities? Things are crazy here now, no proper law and order. No, I'll just wait and see. And if no-one knows, maybe that's the end of it.*

She needs to stay busy, a project to fill the day to stop her from going mad.

On a large chopping board she chops and chops and chops. An enormous knife expels her frustration as she attacks oranges, lemons and a variety of vegetables. It feels therapeutic. By the end of the day vast quantities of marmalade, lemon curd and mustard pickles are lined up in sterilized jars. She writes neat labels and stores the bottles and jars in ordered lines in the cupboard.

At least there's something I can control.

She washes the large knife, dries it, carries it to her bedroom and places it under the pillow, but when darkness comes, she feels vulnerable again. Vulnerable and isolated in the desolate hills. A mass of nerves, the smallest of sounds makes her jump.

What would it take for Rob to pick up a phone to Rubina or Kourk and ask for me? But she accepts he doesn't give a second thought to her or her safety from the moment he steps on a plane.

In the morning an unfamiliar ringing sound startles her from sleep, her hands curl around the handle of the knife, and she glances at the clock. How did she sleep so late?

"Made it to another day," she mumbles.

The persistent sound from the entrance door below piques her curiosity. No-one ever has rung the bell in three years.

She throws on a shift dress and hurries across the corridor, she peers out over the balcony, still holding the knife. The metal and glass door squeaks open.

"Let me in," Mary looks up and waves. "I have half an hour to myself. Put on the kettle."

A little red-faced and sucking in deep breaths she reaches the top landing holding a raffia basket filled with fresh artichokes and pomegranates.

"For you." She holds out the basket. "Eat the artichokes with a little lemon and garlic butter, they're good for the liver and the heart," she smiles. "We brought them with us from the Bekaa valley."

She notices the knife in Genie's hand. "What's that about?"

Genie tells her an edited version of events, confesses she recognized the man from the party.

In a matter of fact manner, Mary announces, "You need a gun! I'll tell Victor, he knows weapons, maybe he can help?"

"No don't say anything, please. I don't want problems."

Mary takes a seat in the kitchen and watches while Genie busies herself with the tea.

"Did you know pomegranates are often put beneath houses here to bring prosperity?" She picks one up, turns it around in her hand and tosses it lightly into the air. "But I like another idea that it represents hope and the immortality of the soul. Mohammed supposedly encouraged pregnant women to eat them if they wanted beautiful children. Islam believes there was a pomegranate tree in the Garden of Eden."

"The immortality of the soul. I rather like that," Genie says as she pours their tea. "Do you suppose if I eat lots I'll get beautiful children?"

Mary looks hard at her. "There's still time. You're not thirty yet."

"It seems unlikely, Rob's never here, and it takes two to make a baby," she says. She puts out two jars of her lemon curd alongside the scones and cream she has served. "Anyway, take one of these with you, it's the least I can offer. You know I'm annoyed and hurt Rob left me alone here under these current circumstances," she complains.

Mary studies her. "I don't like to say it, but I'm surprised, too. It seems cavalier to say the least. But Nabil and I always found Rob a bit casual about the whole situation here," she pauses and glances up. "Don't misunderstand me, I know he's a great guy, life and soul and all that, but when the parties stop he does seem a bit disconnected."

She takes a sip of her tea. "Word is an actual civil war may well be underway now. If Syria sets up home here who knows what's going to happen, they promote a total power share between Muslim and Christian." She takes a breath and another scone. "It's a good thing we're not right in the city," she declares. "Actually I'm trying to convince Nabil to go to Dublin, might not be bad for a while, 'til it all calms down."

"Really, you want to go too?"

"He hasn't agreed yet, but I'm working on him," she slathers a large dollop of cream and lemon curd on her remaining half scone and somehow manages to pop the entire thing into her mouth. Her cheeks bulge, she resembles a chipmunk as she nods her head.

"Rob won't even consider leaving," Genie tops up the tea. "He seems to have tied his entire future, and even his sense of self-worth, to success here followed by a move to the USA, anything else is a distraction."

She offers Mary another scone and refills the kettle.

"Fundamentally Rob's a non-political, peace-loving guy. I suspect he's so taken up with the daily hassles he can't even countenance the bigger nightmare we're in the middle of." She pauses. "He doesn't consider, if it keeps going down the tubes, his efforts won't even matter."

"I'd have words with him if I were you, he should be here to protect you not running off to one or another foreign country all the time. At least Nabil and I are in this together."

"I used to think we were, too," Genie replies.

Unable to face another sleepless night in fear Genie decides to take matters into her own hands and she heeds Mary's advice. Taking a quick shower, she throws on yesterday's outfit, grabs her purse and goes to find a solution, one that doesn't depend on Rob being home.

Two hours later, flushed in the face but with great determination, she struggles up the stairs dragging an awkward and resisting box to the apartment.

Half an hour later she drags the empty packaging back down and gets into the car.

There was no big celebration for the end of 1975, everyone was too worried about Mark, but so far this cease-fire has lasted, and she can get across the city. Rob has a belief and hopes that 1976 will see improvements and she waits to see if he is correct.

Many of the wives have gone home, and Jacqui may relocate any day, so Genie calls hoping to meet up.

She parks and looks around, there is indeed a change in the way Hamra feels. Although not in disarray like other parts of the city it lacks energy.

She catches sight of Jacqui who has arrived ahead of her. *Even a war can't stop her punctuality,* Genie smiles, and waves. *And how is she able to look as calm and put together as ever?* She kisses her cheek and sits heavily in her seat.

Huddled at another table Karam and a couple of men are drinking coffee. One of the men wears a uniform Genie doesn't recognize. When he sees her, Karam waves but does not smile.

Jacqui regards her friend from behind large square sunglasses and looks over at the other table. It is January, but her glasses afford a sense of safety when she hides behind them.

"That's Karam, isn't it? Who are those guys, with him? Look like heavy hitters."

Genie shrugs.

"I always thought he had a thing for you . . ." She leaves the thought hanging and watches Genie's face. She laughs. "Ha, you should play poker."

In a softer voice, nervous of whose ears might hear, she says. "We're off soon, probably no more than two months, we're not sure where yet. Like everyone we're keeping a low profile, just trying to stay out of trouble," she stops.

She orders two glasses of champagne and smiles at Genie's raised eyebrow.

Genie seems tightly wound, no longer so light-hearted, she notices. *Still searching for something.*

"It's early, I know, but we have to celebrate the arrival of another New Year after all," she chuckles.

Karam's colleagues leave, and he heads in their direction.

"Incoming," Jacqui whispers and turns. "Why don't you join us?" she smiles at Karam.

"I would like nothing more, but sadly I have a commitment. I came only to say hello. Next time, perhaps?"

He turns to face Genie. "You look very beautiful, as always," he says. "But your eyes are sad." He reaches over and brushes hair away from her eyes. "I think you are wise, sadness is for those who understand."

Jacqui looks at him, then at Genie.

"We must not stand in a place of danger, trusting in miracles," he says now encompassing Jacqui, whose mouth is slightly open. "Take great care, both of you."

When he leaves they look at one another. Jacqui starts to speak then waits as the waiter sets the glasses on the table.

"Just who is that man?" she says. "He meets with who knows who, shows up everywhere and speaks like a cross between the Dalai Lama and Albert Einstein." She looks around to make sure no-one can hear. "But he is absolutely gorgeous, and no-one would blame you."

Genie taps her hand and laughs. "Stop it."

"Okay my darling, now tell me about you. Your eyes still scan the world I see. Are you as unhappy as your 'windows on the soul' seem to indicate?"

Genie smiles and waits for the waiter to leave before she answers. Once she starts, she cannot stop.

Jacqui listens attentively and patiently without a word. When Genie finally finishes her tale, she raises her glass.

"To us all and to a better future. At this point you still have a future," Jacqui reaches out a cool, long-fingered hand and touches Genies' face. "I've loved having you as my friend but I'm not blind, and my advice for whatever value it may have— get out while you can. Out of the country, and if Rob won't go, probably out of the marriage, too," she pauses then with a little laugh she says. "Remember, don't stand in a place of danger expecting miracles."

Genie thinks about Jacqui's words as they say a final fare-well. She decides to drive on to the factory where somebody must surely know something about Rob.

On the telephone, no-one has told her anything, and she is too embarrassed to call again. With some trepidation about her safety, she takes the road from Hamra to the "other side" to find out what happened to her husband. Lost in her reflections Genie turns into the factory driveway, she has driven the whole journey in a fog. Maybe she should put her concerns aside for now, but Jacqui's words run around in her head.

The gatekeeper looks unusually down, he hardly waves as she drives in.

Shana opens the door, and Genie senses something is up, some-thing unspoken. She goes directly to the kitchen sink, moves aside a bottle of bleach and removes two anonymous bottles without labels.

"Irish Whisky or sherry?"

She pours herself a teacupful from one of the bottles. "I keep a supply on hand for stressful occasions," she says. "An

Irish tonic, and of course I have to keep it hidden. Adnan says we must be cautious now. Alcohol is frowned upon this side of town. Adnan's worried all the time."

Atop the factory in big armchairs in Shana's sitting room, they toast with their teacups. "You know I'm growing frightened, too," she confesses.

Although Genie's not hungry, she politely nibbles one of the formidable looking rock cakes Shana has made, hoping to avoid a broken tooth, but it is surprisingly moist and delicious.

Genie sips her "tonic," probably how Shana has managed to last so long up here. "I expected Rob days ago," she says.

Shana shakes her head. "I've not heard a word, perhaps things got complicated. I'm sure he's fine," she hugs Genie. "No news is the best, don't they say? But I could ask Adnan when he gets back from Damascus, if you'd like?"

As she climbs back into the battered car, Genie recalls Rob's words from long ago. "You'll have to make a life for yourself." She hadn't imagined how true it would prove to be. Under other circumstances, she wouldn't mind, but these days she can't get a grasp of the fluctuations in their life. She feels vulnerable, alone in the hills and is surprised to know Shana is scared, too.

She puts the key in the ignition and shakes her head.

Get it together she tells herself. *Go and find supplies—I need yeast.* She flatly refuses to stand in bread lines at the bakery, so now she bakes her own, with increasing degrees of success. The first debacle she discovered holding open the front door.

'A doorstop,' Rob had announced. 'Waste not, want not.'

The frequency of supermarket closures has increased, and she's building a store cupboard. Rice, flour, tinned fish, dried yeast and powdered milk to add to her homemade produce. With these basics and some spices they can survive for a few days, even weeks, if fighting increases and it becomes necessary.

But today she wants to be normal, fresh fruit and a joint of meat, maybe a bottle of wine. *Who knows, someday soon I may even dine with my husband again?*

When Rob's plane lands at Beirut airport, he looks around to see if the curfew has lifted, wonders if the office contacted Genie and if she might be here to meet him. He feels some guilt over the way he left but reminds himself, if she was a little less difficult, a little more willing to flow with the changes, he wouldn't have been so frustrated and maybe nothing would have happened in Istanbul. Anyway, it wasn't such a big deal, after all, no-one is any the wiser and the stress has reduced, undoubtedly a good thing.

He realizes she isn't there and grabs a taxi.

Across town, in the supermarket, Victor spots Genie. He watches as she puts fruit to her nose, selects ripe ones and adds them to her basket. It's the first fresh produce she's had in weeks, and she's unaware of Victor's scrutiny as she grabs a head of lettuce and palms a couple of large tomatoes.

His voice in her ear makes her jump. "What are you doing here? Where's Rob?"

Startled, she faces Victor but doesn't answer. *Who does Victor think he is and since when did she need Rob to go grocery shopping with her?*

"You must know it's dangerous now, you shouldn't be out without your husband; actually you shouldn't be out at all."

She opens her mouth to argue.

"Genie, I insist on accompanying you home."

She tries to refuse, but Victor forcefully takes her by the elbow and maneuvers her through the store to the cash register. Locals watch their exchange, embarrassing her, so she pays for her shopping and allows him to guide her by the arm outside.

"Leave your car you can get it later."

They've known Victor for three years, and he has always been charming and polite, a little suggestive at times but she has never regarded him as domineering. Dumbfounded by his behavior Genie gets into his car and they drive up the hill in silence as she tries to make sense of what on earth is up.

His voice interrupts her speculation, the tone penetrates and pulls her back to the present.

"Close your eyes."

"What?" She immediately looks out of the window—a knee jerk reaction.

By the roadside is a dead body and beside it another; a torso with no head, no legs. Flies buzz over the corpses. She's horrified but can't look away.

"Oh, God no."

They pass close, and she sees a long, Tiger tattoo. It covers one arm.

"I told you not to look," he snaps at her, but gently reaches to put a hand over hers.

"One of them is that gunmen from the party, isn't it? They cut off his . . ." she breaks off, tears flood her eyes.

"Why cry for them? You know they would have killed us all without a single thought. They were out of control, followed no cause, used the conflict to steal, rape and kill, you of all people must know that." Victor drives on. They don't speak.

He knows! Her head is swirling, *Did Mary tell him he was at my house? At the party Victor said he'd kill them,* she thinks. *But it's crazy, impossible, isn't it?*

She tries to push away the questions which engulf her. Not Victor. He couldn't do something like this, he's their friend. And anyway how would he even find them?

As they pull into the cul de sac a taxi exits and passes them headed down the hill, she doesn't notice it.

Rob is only steps ahead of them, he struggles through the door with a briefcase, a garment bag, flowers, and a jewelry box. The apartment is empty. He pushes the door with his foot and stops in his tracks, stares down the barrel of a Kalashnikov, apparently fully loaded, set up in the kitchen doorway pointing at the front door. It is positioned to prevent unwanted visitors, and the ominous presence startles him.

"What the . . ." Before he has time to process what he sees, footsteps sound on the stairs. Still shocked, he turns as an ashen-faced Genie walks past him without a word.

Close behind, Victor walks in and stares without speaking at the Kalashnikov, he turns to Rob.

"I guess it's hers," Rob shrugs.

Sounds of retching come from the bathroom. Rob looks at Victor and raises an eyebrow.

"She's a little upset," he doesn't explain further.

Rob walks quickly to the bathroom door. "Genie? What on earth's the matter? Are you alright?"

She doesn't reply.

He turns back to Victor. "What's going on?"

"You should not under any circumstances leave the building until Monday, or at least not before midnight on Sunday." Victor holds up a hand as Rob opens his mouth. "No questions, Rob, trust me." He glances again at the machine gun and leaves.

When the voices stop and the front door closes Genie opens the bathroom door, hoping they are alone. She approaches Rob's outstretched arms.

"You can't imagine what it's been like," she says. Rob waits patiently for her story, but when she trips over his suitcase on the hall floor, she recalls his extended absence.

"Why haven't you called?" she asks. "It's been a week and not a word. How can you be so bloody uncaring? I'm up to here," she lifts her hand to her chin. "I don't ask for much, but you should call me. This isn't life, it's a life sentence, and I'm not getting time off for good behavior."

What a welcome, he thinks. But he wants peace, so he counts to three. "You're right. I should have called."

And her anger flows away.

"That gunman from the party, Michel, is lying by the roadside down the hill, or at least parts of him are," her voice trembles. "He came here to the apartment the other night."

Rob is all ears now, he reaches out and pulls her to him, sees tears in her eyes. "What? Sweetheart, that's dreadful."

"It's been terrible, Rob. I've been terrified, without you."

"Let me get you a drink, I want to hear all about it." He takes her to the couch, grabs a chilled bottle and a couple of glasses and settles beside her. *Shit, now I feel bad. I should have been here,* he chastises himself.

Genie takes a glass of wine and sips. She's almost ashamed to have considered her fleeting suspicion of Victor. *I won't mention it. He's our friend, and Rob would be shocked, or worse he would laugh at the notion of Victor's potential involvement.*

18

JANUARY 18, 1976

Qarantina-Karantina

LATE INTO THE NIGHT THEY discuss her trauma and toss around speculations as to why Victor told them to remain closeted at home.

They are still tired when the quiet, mild January morning comes—too soon. It's just warm enough to sit outside, and they write letters home, read and hide away, out of respect for Victor's advice.

When the noise begins they instantly realize it comes from the Qarantina refugee camp on the coast below them.

She goes inside to the bookcase and retrieves a book on the history of the area.

"Do you know how it got its name?" she asks.

He looks up.

She paraphrases. "For a century and a half it was a quarantine area 'til the railway came in 1895, creating a link on the pilgrimage route via Damascus to Saudi Arabia," she says. "The local Mosque offered vaccinations from plague and cholera."

"Sounds like even then it wasn't a great place to be," he says.

"The railway helped Christians flee Damascus, and sixty years later Armenians came, escaping genocide in Turkey, later the Kurds. A revolving venue for refugees."

Genie stops reading and strains to hear the sounds filtering up the hill. She goes on, tries to ignore the gunfire.

"The tent city became today's rickety tin and wood, shanty buildings. At the turn of the century they planned to demolish it, but fire almost resolved the problem."

She stops.

They are both listening now, every fiber focused on the sounds from below, which grow louder.

Sound magnifies as it rolls up the hill, she thinks.

Genie looks across at Rob, but he doesn't speak. Gunfire goes on and on.

Rob has his head in his hands.

It's rare to see him display emotion, he tries to keep it tightly under control, she thinks. *Some idea he was once sold, about men and stiff upper lips.*

And then it is quiet.

She waits, then reads aloud again from the book in her lap. "Despite deplorable conditions, vulnerable people survived. Overcrowded and disease-ridden, waves of peoples in desperate need found refuge from famine, wars, and massacres, in this safe 'haven'," she stops.

Neither of them speaks for several minutes. The air is dusty below, but they are too far away to see clearly.

"Now it has extended onto private land." She puts down the book and stares ahead. "I heard they wanted the land for development and the proposed highway up to Tripoli, do you suppose that's what this is about?" She stops as rockets, and insistent gunfire comes from across the hillside below. Eager to display their prowess others join the fracas.

"I don't know," he lifts his shoulders and opens his arms in a gesture of helplessness. "In two decades Beirut has grown from three hundred thousand to more than a million. A quarter is non-Lebanese, and two-thirds of those are Palestinian." His voice lacks energy. "I guess Christians see a gradual erosion, a takeover," he says.

His words are lost as another closer volley of gunfire echoes. "Sounds like other camps are joining in."

He goes in to turn on the radio. The day wears on, and they hear reports that Qarantina has been overrun by Maronite Christian right-wing militias.

More than a thousand have been massacred.

A thousand people.

Of all the camps and slums of Beirut, Qarantina will be remembered for what has happened below.

She thinks of the two bodies on the hillside yesterday and shivers, she cannot imagine that multiplied to a thousand. *When government splinters, monsters take over,* she thinks. More radical factions have appeared on the scene, and it is impossible to track who, if any, are the good guys.

Her body trembles and she holds the sides of her seat trying to control her reaction.

Rob picks up his camera and adjusts the telephoto lens, tries to look down at the camp as the bombardment continues, but he sees nothing but smoke. He wonders if Genie could be right, should they go from this place where life no longer has value? This beautiful country which the Lebanese say they love, but each waking moment they destroy.

The day continues, and the news confirms two other camps have joined the battle.

They abandon the watch and move inside. Behind them the night sky is filled with tracer bullets and unceasing rocket fire.

Flashes reflect on the Kalashnikov—on duty in their doorway. An occasional red glow from Rob's cigarette lights the darkness, he is silent and pensive.

The ratt tatt tatt seems to go on forever but, like all things, it eventually stops. The area of squalor and misery which for many was their only home has been razed to the ground.

Genie sits on the floor, her head in her hands. "Those poor, poor people. What on earth are we doing here, Rob?"

It's a good question, he thinks. He blows a long, slow stream of smoke into the air. "I don't know anymore," he shakes his head. "We need to survive for just a few more months if we can."

"Survive," she snorts. "People are dying all around us because they can't leave. We have the ability to go, but we don't. It's insanity. We should pack up and take our chances with the future. At least we'd be together—and alive."

He makes no comment, the day has taken a toll on them both.

Explosions and the distant sound of gunfire perform their nightly concerto. The bedroom is illuminated by moonlight, and from the flares of tracer bullets, dozens of mosquitoes fly around, buzzing interminably in Genie's ear.

Rob turns over in bed, from between the crisp, clean sheets he stares at the moon outside. "I love you, Genie," he whispers.

She doesn't answer. She's still upset that Rob left her alone for a week and the destruction today is another reminder of why they should pack up and go.

Distracted by the buzz in her ear she brushes at it, but the noise doesn't stop, she feels a sting, and she angrily waves the creature away. But the buzzing continues.

Sleepily she climbs out of bed and hunts the mosquitoes. She smashes them on the walls, on the windows, her hands start to hurt, but she has become obsessed. Grabbing a pillow, she climbs on the chair and squashes more against the wall. As they fly higher, mock her, she throws the pillow at the ceiling, kills them to stop the stinging bites on her arms and face and the interminable buzz in her ear.

Rob sighs, turns over and drifts into sleep. He mutters to her. "Stop. Go to sleep, for God's sake."

She climbs on the bed. "I can't."

When she does go to bed one hundred, and eighty-two blood splatters and squashed creatures decorate the walls and ceiling. Hunting and smashing the infernal insects has helped get her through at least one bomb filled night.

The ineffective pyrethrum candle has almost burned itself out, just a small green piece with a trail of smoke remains by the time she falls into a restless sleep. The light of dawn filters across the silent room.

"I can't get them off!"

She sits ramrod straight, brushes furiously at her body and her legs.

"No-oh," she cries and scurries to the bottom of the bed, she brushes away dozens of spiders which crawl all over her.

"Help, help me." Her cries of distress wake Rob.

"What is it? What's going on?" Rob jumps.

"They won't get off."

"What? What won't get off?" He moves to calm her.

She continues to frantically brush, but slowly she looks at Rob and at herself and realizes—there are no spiders.

"Come on, try to sleep. You were dreaming."

He gently guides her back to her bed. It's getting to her, he tells himself. He lays beside her and holds her, but before the next thought comes, he has fallen back to sleep.

Genie stares at the ceiling spattered with bugs and murmurs to the emptiness.

"It seemed so real."

The following day there are whispers in cafes and at school that the Palestinian Liberation Organization who controlled Qarantina may have prevented many of the women and children from escape, thus making it more newsworthy. A horrendous possibility she thinks. Other voices counter, blaming the attackers.

Horrified, but no longer surprised by the lengths the militants will go to further their individual aims, they listen to the whispers but stay silent.

The days are unpredictable. Life in the morning—death by nightfall.

Ignoring all that has happened Rob goes off to work in the hope roads are open. But she can't stop the images her mind conjures, it leaves her empty, powerless. Out of the blue, she has an idea, maybe she can help, offer supplies, blankets, dried food, even matches to survivors?

When she finishes work, she grabs a taxi and rushes to the shops.

At Spinneys supermarket she finds everything she wants. For once the shelves are well stocked, and she fills a cart with canned vegetables, fruit, and soups. She grabs jars of honey and boxes of crackers.

When the cart is loaded she goes to the front and takes another. This she fills with half a dozen flashlights and boxes of matches. "Damn," she mutters and turns to grab can openers. She stops a curious employee who escorts her to aisle 13b to find blankets, and she loads in every one they have.

The cashier gives her a strange look but says only. "Would you like help to your car, Madame?"

She accepts help to a taxi outside and, with the aid of the driver loads the goods into the trunk.

She instructs him to pass by the Qarantina camp.

He looks at her as if she has gone mad, but doesn't argue.

When they pull up there is nothing. Nothing to be seen. Nothing to be done. It's spookily desolate. She opens the car door disregarding the driver's protest.

How is it possible that it has all gone? All those people and the entire camp obliterated? Every structure. She recoils, there is no indication that it ever was. *Where are the survivors or the bodies?*

She shivers, nothing remains but confetti-like rubble and scattered among it, like crushed and macabre party favors, tiny flashes of color, torn pieces of fabric, fragments of broken toys covering the ground.

She recognizes the undeniable reality: there can have been no survivors. Along with the people who once lived and played there, the camp has disappeared from this world.

Deflated she gets back into the taxi.

He is grumpy now, doesn't understand what this woman is doing. She returns home, and the man takes payment, dumps the goods inside the downstairs lobby of the building and leaves. She hears him mutter. "Majnoun." And she wonders if he's right, maybe she is crazy.

She trudges up and down the stairs before unpacking the supplies. As she enters the second guest room to store the blankets, she sees a small pair of brown feet on the bed. Noura is curled up fast asleep. The door opens with a soft creak, and the young girl wakes with a start, lets out a cry and scrambles from the bed full of apologies. She helps Genie carry up the remaining supplies.

An hour later Rob and Victor pass Noura and a young man as they struggle with an unwieldy mattress and several blankets on their heads, the men exchange glances, but they don't speak. Noura lowers her eyes, as they continue on their respective journeys.

At home Rob finds Genie struggling to store the remaining blankets in the closet. The guest room bed frame has no mattress.

Still the same girl, he smiles. *Trying to make things better.*

"I ran into Victor. We're having a drink on the terrace, fancy one?"

She nods and tidies the last blanket then looks at the cans of food and jars of honey. *What will I ever do with all this stuff?* She wonders. She shoves them, still in their shopping bags, into the closet.

Victor is tired, she notices, *looks like he hasn't been sleeping. Well, who can sleep these days?*

"We passed Noura on the hill. Has she gone into the removal business?" Victor asks.

"No, she hasn't. Do you know she'd never slept in a bed before today, can you imagine? Never felt a mattress under her body. Since the day she was born, she has slept on the ground."

Rob shakes his head and rolls his eyes. Victor gives a distracted smile, frequently glances downhill. He puts a magazine on the table, on the cover is an image of a fighter standing on the Qarantina rubble. She ignores it and plops onto a chaise her back to the view.

Rob pours a glass of Arak for himself and one for Victor, he adds water, and she watches as the fine droplets scatter the light, turning the liquid translucent. He walks through the sliding door and offers a bowl of pistachio nuts.

"They boasted no-one could crack the British Bank of the Middle East, but now with the war, they've demolished the place and stolen the vault," he tells her.

"Who did?"

"No-one's sure, maybe the Palestinian Liberation Organization. After they captured the Holiday Inn maybe they realized, 'Oh we've got control of Bank Street, what an opportunity.' When the looting was finished, they decided to dynamite the vaults, but they blew it," he laughs, pleased with his joke. "Get it? Blew it! They seriously injured themselves."

Victor chips in. "There's such speculation, it's hard to make sense of it. Some say they hired professional Sicilian or Corsican Robbers, probably mafia, and hit eleven banks. Or another story—Muslims and Christians cut a deal to share the loot or maybe Russian Mafia in tandem with Israel's Mossad or possibly even the IRA did it."

Rob chuckles. "Whoever it was they got over 50 million pounds sterling in currency, gold bars and jewels from the British Bank and more from the Banca di Roma. They say the different factions doing the looting then decided to rob each other. What a hoot!"

It doesn't sound like a hoot to Genie, but now she notices Victor. Clearly preoccupied he paces the terrace then walks inside, he lifts the Arak bottle, looks through the doorway at Rob who nods and he replenishes both their glasses, comes out and sits again.

"It's impossible to know the truth," he says. "There's even a version being whispered of soldiers, possibly British, heavily armed with state-of-the-art weaponry, blasting their way in, quickly securing the bank, but the thick steel poses a problem so they use plastic explosives, after several hours they finally blast a hole through. So much money!"

Rob grabs a handful of nuts and tosses them one by one into the air and skillfully catches them in his open mouth. "And poof they are gone." He emphasizes the explosive "pooffff."

Victor smiles, still apparently on edge.

"Are you OK, Victor?" she asks. "You seem tense. Are you thinking about Qarantina?"

"No, Just tense times, habibti," he says.

Before the words have time to settle an explosion shatters the quiet afternoon and rocks the building. It's nearby this time. Genie is the closest, and she jumps.

"Jesus!" Rob runs to her, together they peer over the edge of the terrace.

The air is filled with dust; rubble and large pieces of metal fly about below.

"What now? We're not in the battle zone," Rob says

Her ears feel strange, a wooziness inside her head, concussion-like. Just like the bombing at the airport, she remembers. The world seems to move in slow motion. She looks at Rob, he shakes his head and blinks.

"I think it's near Nabil and Mary's," Genie says. She sprints for the door, shaking her head to clear it, too.

Victor jumps up, runs into the house and blocks her path. "Wait."

She stops, astonished, turns to Rob who lifts an eyebrow in question.

Victor quickly stands aside. "Of course you must go, but just be careful. I'll follow shortly," he leaves. He has grown fond of this innocent young couple and wishes them to remain outside of this, but of course, he cannot stop them.

They take the stairs so fast when she turns to the second flight Genie slips down the first three steps, sending a sharp jolt up her back. She grabs for the railing and steadies herself, stops herself from falling farther.

Strange I never noticed before how slippery the marble is. She makes a mental note to be more careful in the future and immediately ignores her advice, desperate to find out if her friends are safe.

Her head has cleared but her back aches. Rob has sprinted ahead, already out of the building. There's a sense of desperation in how he is reacting, but on the hillside, he slows and takes her hand.

Outside Nabil's the dust has almost settled, a gate hangs on a hinge beside the bombed-out remnants of his car. Genie and Rob tread cautiously over the debris, through the gate, then stop. Nabil is kneeling on the ground, his arms flopped at his side staring ahead into nothing, a supplicant in front of an invisible altar.

Beside him the maid is draping a large white sheet over a tiny body A little arm with a bracelet on the wrist rests nearby, the maid's eyes are filled with tears. Next to her is a dead puppy, lifeless like a toy.

Rob shudders.

From inside the house come sounds of Mary's agony, a gut-wrenching, barely human howl, and more faintly another female voice gently tries to calm her.

Nabil blinks his eyes trying to focus as they bend beside him. He sees their mouths move, hears words being spoken but can't comprehend, as if an unknown unrecognizable language is being spoken. All understanding is gone, nothing makes sense. His face is drawn and pale, and Rob watches as the shock starts to surface, it creeps through his body until it finally registers in his eyes.

"They bombed the car," Nabil whispers. "They bombed it to punish me, and my baby was playing nearby, she was hit by the flying metal. Our beautiful little girl, not even three, outside with her little puppy." He looks up at Rob. "Who would do this?"

He shakes his head and catches sight of the little arm. Without willing them to his hands lift over his head, slender fingers tear at his hair. Rob gently puts the child's arm under the sheet and puts a hand over Nabil's. He turns his face away, his mouth is pinched closed as a strangled wail comes from deep inside, in the back of his head. It grows until his frame is racked with the effort of containing it.

Genie stifles a sob at the raw anguish playing out in front of her. Rob gently lifts Nabil from the ground, helps him inside.

"They warned me. Said I could not operate on the enemy. I never imagined . . ."

"They?" Rob asks.

"The Phalangists." The words rip out of him, and he says no more.

After what seems like hours, but is, in fact, thirty minutes, an ambulance arrives with noise and blaring sirens. Moved by the tragedy greeting them, the men quietly remove the body and with muffled footsteps leave slowly, drive away in silence.

Victor joins them, and they move inside.

Three bright-eyed dolls with a staring white teddy bear sit on the couch beside Mary, unchanged by events. But the room is a witness that just one hour ago a little girl also lived here.

Selflessly Nabil puts aside his own grief to focus on Mary. She is unrecognizing and unrecognizable, her polish stripped away to the ragged core, almost mad with grief. He sits beside her, his arms encircle her, and he pulls her head onto his chest. She grasps the soft white bear, clings to it as if he will give her back what they have lost.

Genie sits beside Mary, reaches out but there is not a flicker in her eyes as she rests against Nabil and stares straight ahead, tears unconsciously streaming down her face.

Words easily wound but they have limited powers to heal. What can I possibly say? Genie wonders.

"Pass me that medical bag, Rob," Nabil says, and on auto mode, he takes a needle in one hand and administers a sedative.

Rob marvels at Nabil's strength and composure. *I can see what makes him such a formidable doctor*, he thinks.

Soon Mary's shoulders slump as the sedative begins to do its work and Nabil gently slides her head onto a cushion lifts her legs onto the couch and places a light cover over her. He draws the drapes, and he lays beside her. It is a room of mourning

There is no sanity in this insane world. We are intruders in this raw and private scene. Genie thinks, and with Victor, she and Rob take their leave.

Subdued and quiet for a moment they stand on the hillside until Victor breaks the silence.

"It was supposed to be a warning. No-one wanted to hurt the child," he murmurs, almost to himself.

But Genie hears, and she turns on him. "Why would you suppose that?" she snaps at him.

Victor looks uncomfortable, wonders how he could have said that out loud. Recovering quickly he shrugs his shoulders.

"They named me Godfather, for Christ's sake, and now look what these imbeciles have done." He really is angry now. "I can remember her little face when I gave her the bicycle for her birthday and her sweet voice. 'Merci, Oncle Nabil," he pinches the top of his nose. "Merde—Shit! I'm just supposing . . ."

Rob squeezes his shoulder.

"This was stupid, and I have an enormous, obsessive hatred of stupidity," Victor says.

But Genie cuts him off, she's not listening.

"They ride around with guns and destroy whatever displeases them. But a child is innocent, like all the daughters, sons, mothers and fathers these idiots harm because they'd rather kill than work."

Victor keeps his head bent, breathes rhythmically and clenches his hands.

"You are not from here Genie, you will never understand."

"Understand? How can any sane person understand? What changed? Friends are now enemies because of their religion? Yesterday they were brothers, their families played together, ate together, laughed together," she starts to weep. "Now some stupid affiliation to an archaic and ancient set of beliefs tears their world apart? All religions destroy." She sinks onto a large boulder at the side of the road. Rob kneels and puts his arms around her.

Victor looks uncomfortable, reaches out and touches her cheek.

"It is not so simple, habibti. I wish it were. Our differences run deep and have formed over centuries." He bends to kiss her cheek, slowly walks away and continues up the hill to his home.

A bleating sound distracts her and Genie stops, looks up to see the butcher further downhill outside his little shop, the only store in the hills. He holds a resisting sheep and raises a knife to slay it.

"Stop." Genie sprints down to the surprised butcher. He looks at them as he holds the sheep with one hand and a large knife in the other.

"How much?"

"What are you doing?" Rob tries to grab her.

She pulls away. "How much? For the sheep? Kharoof—the sheep—kharoof—Combien? How much?" Her voice is on the edge of hysteria.

"Genie, stop it. He's a butcher. He sells meat, not animals."

She starts to sob, shakes her head. "La. No. Staap. Batal. Please . . ." She falls dramatically to her knees, throws her arms around the sheep and prevents the butcher from slaying him.

"No more slaughter—not today." She buries her face in the grubby fur.

Rob is thoroughly embarrassed at this un-English performance. He doesn't know what to do, but the man seems willing to sell the sheep to these strange foreigners and with a makeshift leash, a rope around his neck, they slowly lead him home.

Victor glances over his shoulder as Rob and Genie barter with the local butcher. *What is she doing?* He wonders as he sees her kneel and put her arms around the sheep. *Chelou, crazy woman. Cute though, challenging and intriguing.*

He is Lebanese to his core. This land is his mother, the teet which suckled him, he sprang from her womb and would gladly give his life to keep her a haven, a homeland for his brothers and sisters, the outnumbered Christians in the middle of the vast Pan Arabic wasteland.

Never drawn to weapons or to violence, Rob had once joked about himself that he was a lover, not a fighter, and Victor feels the same way, he likes beautiful things and an untroubled life. He shrugs his shoulders. Needs must, and he now has the responsibility for dealing with these morons.

The attack on the child has devastated him. They were instructed to bomb the car—the car—a warning—a nudge to Nabil, to do as he was told and stop fixing the enemy. But no, now Nabil and his wife are lost to their own personal tragedy, and he won't be helpful to either side. What idiots he has been given to work with.

These fucking fools have taken the life of an innocent little one riding about on her fucking bicycle. She was a Christian, God dammit. Couldn't they fucking see her? The stupid fucks.

His stomach growls. He pushes aside the anger. Another growl. God, he could do with something to eat and a cold drink.

His thoughts turn to his pretty young wife at home with the fresh Labneh she prepared this morning.

A little olive oil, some za'atar and a few slices of Arabic bread; he can take off his shoes and forget about all this nonsense while he decides what to do.

19

JANUARY 20, 1976

Damour, Lebanon

FROM THE TERRACE, GENIE CAN still see the debris and damage downhill at Mary and Nabil's, and a fresh wave of sadness strikes her. She plays with her breakfast.

She cannot imagine what Mary and Nabil must be feeling today, but they will need time and space to comfort each other without the strain of visitors. *In a few days, we'll reach out.*

She has yearned for a child for so long, only recently accepting the emptiness inside as a permanent absence, she cannot conceive of the pain in having a child, loving it and losing it in this way. Every mother's nightmare, worse than never having a child at all, she imagines.

The last three days have been unendingly horrendous.

She finishes her strong black coffee and with an effort pushes aside her thoughts. So far today is peaceful. She thanks the universe and she remembers downstairs she has a sheep to tend to.

With Noura, she washes the beautiful, fluffy animal. He would be happy to remain dirty and refuses to stand still as they scramble to clean him. The struggle and the work, the bubbles and his gentleness take her away from the dark beast which has flown in to sit on her shoulder, threatening to swallow her.

She names the sheep, Baahleb. Childish but she likes the innocent sound.

He steps back, knocks into the bucket and the suds fly, soaking them. Noura laughs in delight as Genie rubs suds from her hair and begins to feed him flowering plants. She ties a bell on a long red ribbon around his substantial neck, it tinkles as he chews, blissfully unaware of his narrow escape with destiny.

"He seems happy in his new home," she tells Noura, as they rinse him off.

Genie buries her head in his damp fur and snuggles him, proud of the sweet-smelling woolly coat, thankful that at least he is alive.

"I'll take this stuff up Noura, you go on home," she tells the girl, and picks up the soap, wet towels and bucket.

Noura is happy to run off. She loves her job. Working for this woman gives her pleasure; actually, it gives her joy. Madame is quiet, generous and she never beats her. With the money she earns, her family now eats a little meat with the vegetables her twin brother grows on their small plot of land up the mountain. And they can buy honey to drizzle over the delicious ashta cream she helps her mother make on Sundays.

It was difficult when their father died, but now life is good again. She loves to sleep with her three smaller sisters on the soft bed she was given, so different from the earth smell which came through the straw and thin cloth she was used to. How different is their life from the lives of the ajnabi—the foreigners—she thinks with a deep sigh. She is proud of her heritage, but if only God had chosen that life for her.

—✕——✕——✕——✕—

Genie struggles upstairs with the bucket and cloths. Before she has the chance to close the door, Rob calls out to her.

"The right-wing Christian militias have blocked the coastal road down south. The PLO and cronies say it's a threat," he announces.

She drops the cleaning materials in the kitchen and joins him on the patio.

"Always something," he adds.

She points over his shoulder at the ocean below jammed with a flotilla of boats. "What's all that? It's like the Henley Regatta." It is unusual to see so much activity on the water.

Rob turns, and sure enough, hundreds of small craft scurry northward.

Their door is still open and Kourk their landlord raps and enters with a platter of vine leaves.

"That's lovely. Thank Rubina for me." Genie takes them from him, kisses his cheek, and they walk together to the kitchen.

"Have you been watching all those boats out there? Do you know what's going on?" she asks.

"They are survivors, they escape Damour."

"Survivors? Of what?"

"Another massacre, hundreds decapitated. Nuns raped and murdered, they say."

"No!"

"Unborn babies cut out from mother's wombs and pinned to tables."

"Stop" Genie screams, she can't contain herself, puts her arms over her ears and turns to Kourk, "Don't tell me any more, I can't know these things." She shakes her head from side to side.

Kourk reaches out to put an arm around her, but she trembles and pulls away. Rob runs in.

"How will I tear these horrific images from my mind? I can see it all," she gasps for air. "In my mind, I see it, Rob." She sinks to the floor, her head in her arms, the earlier wail has been replaced by rapid gasping and panting sounds as she fights for breath.

Kourk looks at Rob "You should to go back to England. We have no other place, but you could to go. Look, look at her."

Rob pats Kourk's shoulder and walks with him to the front door making it clear he should leave.

"Genie will be fine, she needs time, the shock will pass, she's a survivor."

Kourk shakes his head and calls out. "Goodbye, habibti."

Hunched over, hyperventilating she cannot answer.

Rubina has heard the scream and is halfway up the stairs as Kourk descends. "What happened?"

They chatter back and forth in their Armenian tongue as they go back to their apartment.

"I've never seen someone upset like this. Genie feels the pain. Rob makes a big mistake if they do not leave. But he doesn't listen, what can you be do?"

"Will she recover?" she asks.

He shrugs, picks up his son and nuzzles his tummy. The little boy giggles.

Rubina closes their front door, but she takes the worried expression on her face inside with her. She has always liked their young tenants, they've even become friends, but these days it seems Genie has her heart and one foot out of Lebanon and its conflicts. She can sense the couple is a continent apart from one another, the estrangement is apparent.

Rob puts on her favorite music, a sweet counter-tenor sings and centuries slip away as the beautiful strains of medieval music and Alfred Deller's voice sound out, in stark contrast to the terror outside. He puts his arm around her and gently leads her to the fresh air.

The sun sets over the ocean, pink, blue and grey clouds, heartbreaking and beautiful. Most of the boats are already out of sight, farther along the coast, seeking refuge who knows where.

The music engulfs her. *How can such beautiful sounds exist in this ugly world?* Her tears roll silently onto her chest.

It grows dark. *"Men loved darkness rather than light because their deeds were evil,"* the New Testament quote from long ago pops into her head. *Is this the evil the disciple John spoke of?* She doubts that he could have imagined this level of brutality.

"Tell me you understand. Soon we can go, spend the rest of our lives in California."

She doesn't respond.

Tracer bullets resume, like noisy comets over the city.

"Adnan and Shana invited us to dinner tomorrow. It may help get your mind off things."

She stares at him. Tears stain her cheeks. *Get my mind off things? He must inhabit another world. How will I scrub my mind clean? It feels like rape and Rob is so immersed in a world of plastics he has lost touch with what is real.*

He stays beside her until she falls asleep, then he slips out to find Victor, to discover what has actually happened.

Victor always seems to be in the know, but Rob is unprepared for the shock when he sees him, wild-haired and uncharacteristically distraught.

Maybe I shouldn't have come. Rob thinks. *What if he has lost someone today?*

He welcomes Rob in but continues to pace the room, frequently excuses himself to walk to his front door. Rob hears him barking out what sound like orders in Arabic to a series of men who continually knock. Eventually, the knocks cease, and Victor gets them each a beer, they sit at his dining table, and he tells Rob a terrible tale.

"Apparently the local priest desperately tried to get help. He called politicians on both sides, all were full of regrets, but not one of them helped. Jumblatt their local parliamentarian said he could do nothing because it depended on Yasser Arafat, can you imagine?" Victor's lips curl in disgust. "Their lives depended on a Palestinian leader?"

Rob is taken aback, he has never seen Victor like this.

"Anyway," he continues. "He supplied Arafat's phone number and wiped his hands of the matter, safe on Rue Clemenceau, not worried that so many are about to be massacred! The idiot who answered the phone wouldn't put the call through to Arafat. When the priest told him the villagers didn't want violence or war, his cavalier reply was: 'Father don't worry, we don't want to harm you. If we are destroying you, it is for strategic reasons.'"

"Strategic reasons?" Rob puts his head in his hands unable to understand this madness, the lack of value given to human life and the deep-rooted hatred which grows with each new barbarity.

"We signed a pact with the Palestinians in 1969, allowed them their own army and to use Lebanon for attacks against Israel, but they've turned against the hand that feeds them. The dogs now refuse our help, they fight US, destroy OUR villages. We have to find homes for five thousand—five thousand can you imagine? All those who fled by boat."

"I heard many of the local Lebanese fighters are kids who know no better, regard it as a part-time job or war game? They shoot a few people then go for a swim or a game of football." Rob says.

"That's true, but this new breed of killers are imported from outside, monsters trained in hatred, without heart or humanity. They derive pleasure from humiliation and destruction."

Victor's wife comes to offer food, he breaks off, lost in his thoughts for a moment, he waves her away, gets up and closes the door.

"I don't want to distress her," he explains. "Tomorrow the Red Cross is permitted to bury the bodies. Because of dismemberment casualties had to be calculated by counting heads," he tells him. "The family of Elie Hobeika and his fiancée were also killed, it seems she was raped."

The name means little to Rob but seems significant to Victor. And Rob will hear more of Hobeika, from today he will become a manipulator and murderer, aligning initially with Israel, later Syria and for a final act of betrayal will pay with his life.

"They will all pay. We'll make them all pay," Victor says with such conviction Rob glimpses again the level of hatred being brought to the surface. He shudders.

Nothing was handed to Victor, everything he has was hard-won, and he will fight tooth and nail to maintain his life and lifestyle.

Rob hasn't noticed Victor's use of the word "we" and imagines his anger to be justifiable.

Two days ago one thousand were massacred, today 582 more. Rob realizes the fighting has left few families unaffected,

Shoulders slumped he heads home. He kicks a stone, watches it roll down the hill, it comes to rest. It doesn't fight back. But people are not like stones, he knows. Every kick, every attack continues the momentum. More and greater revenge. Awareness of the awful atrocities demoralizes him. He acknowledges the physical danger they've tried so hard to avoid may not be the only thing to fear.

Events change people.

Another day of tragedy is over but sleep no longer promises rest, the horrors linger into the dark.

That night in their bed Genie dreams:

She stands on a battlefield. Bullets whistles around her and she ducks, looks at her arms, then at her body, nothing hit her!

Machine-guns rattle and she turns, sees villagers lined against a wall, one by one their bodies crumple to the ground, shot. She tries to cry out, but no sound comes.

To her right, a Maronite priest sprinkles holy water on a house. He finishes, stumbles past her to a burnt-out church, skeletons and bodies are scattered, the coffins and vaults broken open.

She follows.

On the ground, a dead woman still hugs her children's bodies.

"God, No." Genie cries out.

She spins around as cries fill the air. "Allahu Akbar!"

They charge from the hills, a multinational mixture of faces slaughtering men, women, children, and animals.

"It is the apocalypse," the priest cries, his eyes turned to heaven. He runs into a nearby house and begins to drag out corpses.

"Why?" Genie screams out.

She sits up in bed yelling, her nightgown drenched, her hair clings to her face, and she rubs at her body tearing the skin from her arms. Rob reaches over, stilling her hands.

She hits at him, but he wraps his arms around her, holding her tight. She continues to struggle, but he holds on, and she grows calm and opens her eyes.

"There, there," Rob croons. His voice is gentle, like her grandmother who held her through her nightmares as a child. She leans into him.

"I thought I was there," she says. "These visions in my head. I feel complicit, just knowing about it."

Eventually, she falls into a troubled sleep, and he watches as she tosses, pale and drawn, the frequent spasms tell him once again she is dreaming.

Kourk may be right, Genie is taking it to heart. In the dark, Rob tries to reevaluate. He keeps his arm around her through the night, strokes her when she whimpers and holds tight as she shudders.

But while they are asleep between five and eight thousand People's Liberation Army regular troops covertly enter Lebanon from Syria. The game is changing.

The radio crackles to life, and Rob shakes his head.

> News Report: January 21st, A high powered delegation of Syrians arrived to help impose a cease-fire. Chamoun says it is a Syrian invasion that threatens world security.

He wonders if it will make a difference. Undoubtedly Syrian President Assad will ignore the posturing.

Rob turns off the radio and wakes her gently as he leaves for work. "You know I can't leave right now, but maybe you could get away for a bit. Take an official leave from school. Home to your mother, maybe? Give it some thought."

She does think about it, but recent events have left her exhausted. She doesn't want to travel or leave Rob to face things alone. For better or worse she made a promise when they married.

She washes her face, puts on mascara and dresses, hopes that looking better will make her feel better. This is the only home they have, so she stays.

Perhaps now the Syrians are here the worst is behind us? She hopes.

The next day on 22 January 1976, Syrian President Al-Assad brokers a truce between the two sides.

When Rob comes home, he tells her. "Assad has moved thousands of secret troops into Lebanon. He's determined to prevent the destabilizing effect disintegration in Lebanon would create for him."

"If they're secret how do we know?"

"You know how it is, word of mouth is more efficient than the media. They say he has plans to bring the Palestinian Liberation Organization back within Syrian control where he thinks it belongs. Now things should improve," he says.

News Report: January 22, A Syrian-sponsored cease-fire and political resolution has been agreed. Equal representation of Christians and Muslims in parliament, the abolition of religious quotas, except for the highest positions, and a Prime Minister elected by Parliament, not appointed by the President.

"A significant development," he says.

After the past several days she is fragile, but she sighs with relief. "I wonder how it will work? It does seem hopeful."

But later, when they are almost ready for bed, Victor knocks on the door. He has a bottle of good red wine and seems to have already enjoyed a fair helping of a previous one.

Rob welcomes him but signals to Genie that coffee might be a better idea.

Weaving unsteadily to the sofa Victor plonks the bottle loudly on the table.

"Little known secret items have been agreed to in exchange for government acceptance of the change in distributing senior posts."

His words are slightly slurred, they have never seen Victor out of complete control before. He holds up a finger.

"Number one." He pauses, searching his memory. "Removal of heavy arms from Palestinian camps in Christian areas. That's good," he says. "Second, Palestinian Liberation Organization's acceptance of the deal," he looks up, tries to focus on his audience. "Not that you can trust a promise from Arafat and his lot."

Genie pours Arabic coffee, and Victor accepts a cup.

I should have used the old china, she thinks, as the cup rattles precariously in the saucer on its journey to the coffee table.

Victor sees her worried expression and smiles. "Sit, sit. I was just telling Rob, the last most significant secret agreement. Syria will accept responsibility for ending the fighting in Lebanon!"

"So President Assad and Syria will now play a major role way into the future?" Rob says.

"Exactly! Syria's President will control OUR fate! Syria's President! I can tell you this, the Phalangists are not happy," Victor says.

He finishes the coffee, leans back against the soft cushions and closes his eyes.

In a sign of helplessness, Genie opens her hands and mouths silently, "I think he's asleep."

Rob looks at Victor but doesn't reply.

"I'm going to bed," she whispers. She gets up to leave, kisses the top of Rob's head.

A soft snore comes from Victor and his head droops, as Rob gets comfortable in the armchair.

"Thanks a lot," Rob grins. "I guess it's gonna be a long night."

In spite of Victor's concern a month slips by without incident, and by late February she feels herself recover a little.

She struggles in from the supermarket laden with goodies.

"It arrived," she says. "The stuff for my sheep. Timothy grass, Alice white clover," she reads the packets as she unpacks. "Sweet clover, buttercup. Kourk says I can plant half of the acre downstairs, across the back near the orange groves."

"I never took you for much of a gardener," he says and picks up a magazine.

"Bird's-foot trefoil legumes and lespedeza," she reads. "Don't they sound exotic? They stop stomach worms so she won't get bloated,"

"My God, stop. It sounds disgusting."

Genie laughs. "Well, she loves dandelions and forbs." She is certain he'll ask about forbs, but he ignores her. "They're non-grass, non-woody flowering plants."

"Now I won't have to die wondering," he says.

20

BEIRUT, MARCH 1976

The Pink Envelope

IN THE MOSTLY CHRISTIAN NEIGHBORHOOD of Ashrafi-yeh, around Genie's school, more than 100 rockets crash down, and the school is no longer recognizable.

"The school called," she tells Rob. "I am not to come back. I'm not required to teach."

He stares at her.

"There is no longer a school."

He sees she is upset and he reaches out, touches her hair.

"Guess I'll have lots of time for tending the sheep and the clovers," she says.

He sees her sadness. Although she hasn't been able to teach on a regular basis during the troubles, it was a lifeline to normalcy and a connection to friends. Now many of them have already gone, and this is the final break.

"I'm so fed up, and I ache in places I never knew existed!" She tries to stretch, but the tension from sleeping rigid and in suspense through gunfire which continued all night takes its toll. "I don't remember when I last had a good night's sleep."

"News of the latest cease-fire hasn't permeated to all factions, so there's still random shooting, but I'm sure it'll get better once they're all informed."

Rob remains hopeful and goes to work, accepting things are great now Syria is taking an interest, but she lives in a permanent state of wariness, a readiness to flee if needed.

Astonishingly, a care package from Genie's sister makes it through to the factory and Rob is happy as he munches on Licorice Allsorts, which she included for him.

Relaxing at his desk perusing The Daily Star Rob glances up, in the corner Nashad is quietly isolated. His nationality puts him more at risk each day, and both he and Adnan are serious now, there's little banter without Mark. He misses the camaraderie they all shared, it's an ache that doesn't go away, and at times he wonders how Mark and his family are faring in their new life in France.

The lab is quiet, they haven't been producing much for a while, so there is nothing to color match or quality control. The overseas plants are working but, for now, the big bosses seem to have lost interest in this location; there's even been a whisper that Rob and Genie might be relocated to Tehran. He doesn't think for a moment he can sell that idea to Genie.

Only one shift operates, the remainder of the men garner more by joining one of the growing groups of militants, paid either in cash or by taking conquered goods.

Strangely life is more comfortable with nothing to do. Rob looks in the packet in front of him, incongruous and colorful among the austere laboratory paraphernalia, and he chooses a roll of black licorice with a white center, his favorite. He no longer has to feel frustrated at the indifference and incompetence of the workforce, but the days are long even though he comes in late and they work reduced hours.

Soon after five, Rob heads out of the compound. The gatekeeper grins and hands him mail as he passes, he tosses it onto the passenger seat. A pink envelope falls and as he accelerates it slides unseen under the seat.

The sun is about to set, and this letter in its pink envelope will change the course of their lives.

His mood is reflective as he drives along the coast to meet Genie for dinner. Streaks of gold and red, slash across the heavens and reflect in the repeating arch and curl of the waves as they ripple onto the shoreline.

The ocean seems tinged with blood, he broods, enveloped in the glow from the early evening sky. He has begun to notice more things lately. The deterioration all around saddens him, but he still finds traces of beauty.

What a glorious place this was, he thinks, slowing as he spots his destination ahead

The Sultan Ibrahim restaurant is surprisingly busy, it usually manages to stay open from lunchtime until late at night and continues to be popular.

Rob is starving, he's only eaten from the packet of licorice all day, he realizes.

He spots Genie, seated in front of the usual array of crudités. She scoops hummus onto a piece of Arabic bread, looks up as the door opens and waves to him.

He greets a couple of foreign journalists as he passes. Surprisingly Karam is with them.

"I thought they'd all gone home," Genie says as Rob sits opposite her.

"The last and the toughest," he jokes. "But your Syrian will be here to the very end, I suspect."

She ignores his sarcastic remark. "This was a good idea. It's been a long time. I saw a lot of military vehicles in town when I changed taxis, but there was no problem getting here."

She speaks in a subdued voice these days, he notices, like a shadow. He relaxes.

"Good, this is how it should be."

They eat well and talk a little. Genie is still raw, and he tries to be gentle. As they order coffee, the group of reporters leaves and Karam heads in their direction.

Rob gives an inward sigh. He didn't want company tonight, he's trying to get Genie back on track and worries Karam might say something, tell her things he would rather she didn't hear.

"It has been a while, I saw you last in January, with your friend Jacqui, I believe," Karam says to Genie. "Almost two months ago. Where have you both been?"

He notices tell-tale signs of suffering in Genie's face, small frown lines have appeared between her eyes, and below them her once beautiful eyes are dull. Concerned, he takes a seat and orders a drink. He watches her.

"A lot has happened," Rob says.

"I know you live not far above the Qarantina camp, I wondered how that would affect you."

"Yes, first that and then Damour," Rob reminds him. He glances sideways at Genie.

She seems calm, takes a sip of her coffee and slowly recites the recent events; the closure of her school, the capture of Mark and the tragic bombing at Nabil's.

Karam reaches a hand across the table and rests it on top of hers.

"I am sorry for your friends," he says. "And for all that you have had to suffer." With his thumb, he delicately wipes away a tear that escapes down her cheek.

He notices Rob's surprised expression and pulls his hand away, takes a napkin and offers it to her.

"It has been a terrible time for many," he says. "But I believe now it may show improvement."

Of course, he thinks it will improve, his lot is in charge. Rob is annoyed with Karam's gesture of familiarity toward Genie and wonders again why he seems to be ever-present. *Maybe the gesture was a cultural thing*, he thinks. *Bloody foreigners!*

But Karam is very proper and polite as they finish and when they say farewell he says.

"There is an Arabic proverb: 'Listen if you would learn; be silent, if you would be safe,'" he pauses. "Be very careful what you say and to whom you say it in these days," he tells them.

They speed along the darkened road each lost in thought. A short distance ahead three soldiers loom in the headlights, they flag them down. Rob brakes hard, and the pink envelope slides out from under the passenger's seat. It touches Genie's foot.

A soldier comes to the window. "Papers," he demands.

Genie shows him her passport.

Rob pats his pocket. "I must have left it at home."

"Get out of the car."

"We've been for dinner at."

"Out of car." He waves his rifle at Rob who silently gets out.

"And you," he nods to Genie.

"I showed you my papers."

"Get out of car." His English is limited.

She is annoyed at his rudeness and frustrated at Rob. "You asked for my papers. I showed you my papers."

Another soldier watching the interaction shoots out a headlight. Genie jumps and glares at Rob as she climbs out and is shoved at gunpoint into a hut. *God, how things have changed from the days when we were treated like royalty.* She pulls her coat around her as a strong wind blows from the ocean, buffeting them.

Inside no-one looks at the papers. Confused they look at each other as the men turn and walk outside.

"I don't think they want to hurt us, I think it's a shakedown," she whispers to Rob. She places a 100 Lebanese pound note with one corner protruding from her passport on the desk.

One of the soldiers glances through the window, and another walks in, takes the money, leaves the passport and stands aside.

She tries to push down her irritation. "It's stupid to go out without papers with all the problems around now," she says. As they get in the car, she sees the pink envelope and retrieves it.

The wind has worsened, and oversized tufts of tumbleweed fly around, sand and debris limit visibility and pound the car as they drive. Rob grabs the wheel tightly, to keep from veering off the road. He stops at a traffic light.

Why does he bother to stop when the road is deserted? She wonders.

She opens her purse to put away her passport and notices she is still holding the pink envelope. As she opens it a perfumed photo flutters onto her lap. An exotic, maybe Chinese, girl smiles up at her.

The light changes and she grasps the photo as they drive on. Her mouth is dry, and she can feel her heart start to race. They pass under street lights, and she stares, glimpsing odd phrases.

"I still feel you, the scent of you." At the bottom the signature, Isabella, with a little hand-drawn, red heart. "PS: We will be in Cairo next month." She feels her hands perspiring from clutching tightly to the letter.

The car swerves to avoid the carcass of a donkey spread across the road, and she is jolted into the dashboard. Rob puts out a hand to save her and hears the sound of guns firing close by. He veers off, turning into an unknown dark street.

Genie stares ahead, the road grows narrower until it becomes an alleyway but she can't focus, can't make sense of what she read. She grips the note; a drowning woman clutching at her last hope. There must be an explanation? If she accepts it is real, she will drown.

Deeper in they attract curiosity, people hang from ramshackle buildings ululating loudly in the darkness, a jungle telegraph.

For no apparent reason, it falls silent and the alleys grow narrower. They're in a ghetto, perhaps one of the camps? This isn't an area they would customarily visit.

"I don't like this," Rob gasps looking in the rear view mirror. As the words are spoken a truck appears behind them filled with men, grenades draped across their bodies. It follows, gets closer, pushes, almost riding on the bumper.

"What the hell do they want?" he mutters.

Before he can say another word, the car hits them and hits them again, pushing. He has lost control of the vehicle. "Shit!" He tries to speed up.

From a tiny side alley ahead another vehicle screams out turning the corner on two wheels, dust flies into the air clouding his vision, it almost grazes the front panel as it cuts them off.

They are caught front and back. The rear vehicle again pushes, and Rob has no choice but to follow.

A mile, maybe less and they are corralled under a bridge, the front vehicle halts, the other pulls in close behind. They're trapped. Above their heads, they hear the faint sound of cars, people going to their homes, but no-one can see them hidden from view and completely vulnerable.

She should be frightened, but Genie can't get the image of Rob with the girl out of her head.

His voice interrupts her thoughts. "Christ, now we've had it."

The trucks extinguish their lights. A man in the front vehicle turns around, he strikes a match and lights a cigarette, his eyes watch them as he puts the flame near his face and blows it out.

Rob's nerves are jangling, he can't see anything. He groans and looks around desperately into the blackness.

"Can you see them? Where are they?" he twists in his seat, sees Genie's stony face and reaches for her hand. She pulls it away.

"What the hell!" he says. "We're not far from the airport, do you suppose they're the ones who took Mark?"

"Don't speak to me," she tells him.

I can't believe she's blaming me. Alright, I forgot my papers and I took a wrong turn, but it was a freaking accident. She's such a bitch lately.

They sit and wait, but nothing happens. Waiting—not knowing—is terrifying. Rob grows more anxious as the time passes. He notices Genie is strangely calm, but he doesn't want to upset her further, so he makes no comment.

What a mess, she thinks. *Like Mark and James, no-one will know what happened, and we'll disappear as if we've never been.* She feels numb, unconnected to the fear. *So much suffering and for what? It's hard to continue caring.*

"I need to pee," he whispers "Badly. I had too much to drink." He moves the seat back and crosses his legs, frowning.

They wait. Genie leans against the seat, closes her eyes. *I'm not going to fight,* she decides. *I'll wait for it to be over.* As a child, when her father beat her, she had learned to slip out of her body, float above, look down, removed, safe. *Should I try it now?* She wonders.

"Oh, God," Rob groans and recrosses his legs.

He sits upright as lights come from the opening doors of the vehicle in front. Men get out and bang the doors, immediately darkness resumes—then silence.

Dreadful, deafening, mind-numbing silence.

She can hear Rob's breathing, a few whimpers of discomfort and perhaps fear. It's excruciating to wait, and by now Rob's bladder is causing severe discomfort.

"If I don't do something soon I'm going to . . ." he breaks off noticing the spare gas can behind Genie's seat. It's only half full he remembers, and in desperation, he yanks off the cap and squeezes himself over the opening, he awkwardly lets the water flow. "I'm sorry," he says.

It smells of asparagus and salmon, she notices, surprised she is aware of such things, and she cranks the window a few inches for air.

Outside is silent. *Are the men still there, what do they plan?* She shivers, recognizes she's cold. Fear has left her skin and clothing damp, it clings clammily to her.

They come. Four, with guns, two on each side pull them from the car and push them in front of the vehicle.

Her heart races and her head pounds. Rob has fallen awkwardly against the car, leaning close beside her at an awkward angle, their hips touching. She tries to move away.

"La—No." One of the men pushes at her shoes indicating she should take them off. He turns and takes Rob's. Carrying the footwear, he moves into the shadows. Slowly one by one the others disappear into the dark.

They wait.

"What are they playing at?" he whispers. "Should we try to run for it?"

"Run where, on these rocks and without shoes? We don't know where we are, worse we don't know where they are." Her quiet tears fall.

Rob reaches for her, but she turns away.

"Don't touch me, Rob," she says and slides to the ground.

A little before six the first light filters under the bridge. They have been propped against the car for hours without sleep and are stiff and chilled. In the early light the front truck slowly becomes visible, it appears empty, but they are still caught between two vehicles and can't drive away.

A set of old stone steps beside the bridge ahead seems to lead to the road above.

Should we leave the car and make a run for it? He wonders. He looks around at other ways of escape. *We're still in unknown territory even if we get to the top. Will we be able to make it?*

Too anxious to move, not knowing where they are, he turns to Genie. He points to the steps, mentally readies himself to run, but as he watches, feet descend those same steps, bit by bit the four armed men appear, weapons raised.

Too late he realizes: *They did leave last night.*

The men form a line facing them. One walks over, pulls Rob to his feet. In unison, the other three raise their weapons and point at him.

Genie reaches out, clutches at Rob's leg. "No! Don't hurt him," she cries, holding on to him.

Rob feels the warmth flow between his legs.

"Christ."

They both close their eyes.

Gunfire fills the air, a high pitched rhythmic sound. She can smell the gunpowder and a faintly uric smell from the saltpeter. The smoke tickles her nostrils.

Rob lets out a breath, looks first at Genie then at himself. Unbelievably they have not been hit.

"Arseholes. The bastards, they're playing with us," Rob whispers between clenched teeth.

"Four hundred lira." The man who is holding Rob's shoulder smiles a snaggle-toothed grin and opens his palms. He behaves like he's bartering over apples, not demanding a ransom.

Confused Rob fumbles for his wallet. *Is this it? Is this all they want? Is it over?* The questions stumble through his brain.

The gunman spots the stain on Rob's trousers. His grin widens, and he winks, turns to call out to his friends. They laugh. He takes the wallet, counts four hundred Lebanese pounds and hands the wallet back. He doesn't take a penny more.

Waving the notes in the air, the man saunters back to his buddies. One of them slaps him on the back, they divide the money, jump into their trucks and drive off in two opposite direction, hands honking the horns.

"I knew it. I knew it wasn't serious. They didn't plan to touch us," Rob crows.

"Shut up. I don't want to hear your voice," Genie snaps.

He glares. "Jesus, what's your problem? It's over now."

She doesn't respond.

He does not suspect how right he is. Life as he has known it is over, invisibly their lives have changed—forever.

She is silent on the journey home, they park, and she notices Kourk's children under the building playing with the sheep. Laughing, they drape him in a pretty scarf and feed him treats, he bleats in pleasure as she approaches, but turns away to chew on a handful of the flowers they offer.

The stairs seem unending as, exhausted, they climb to the safety of their apartment and walk into the kitchen.

"I'm dying for a cup of tea," he says.

Genie stares at Rob for a moment.

He glares back.

"Tell me about your girlfriend."

"What? Who are you talking about?" He is taken aback. Where did this come from?

"How many are there? There's no point in lying." She takes out the letter and waves it at him, puts it inside her blouse.

"Who's it from?"

"You tell me, Rob. Make me understand," she cries.

He reaches out to her.

She slaps his hand away, growing angry. "Don't. My God, either there IS more than one, or you plan to go on lying to me," she pauses. "Istanbul—ring a bell?"

He turns pale and searches for an adequate answer. "What did she say?" he whispers.

She starts to pummel him. "Just tell me the truth."

He stares calmly and doesn't reply, considers his response. Shit! So that's what's been eating her.

He brushes a hand over his eyes, his brain searches for some explanation. How much does Genie know? What did the girl write? He wonders. Will Genie believe it was a mild flirtation? Perhaps a business lunch or dinner? *God, I've already forgotten all about it.*

She can see his mind consider all of his excuses, she paces the kitchen.

"Answer me!"

Her frustration builds, she feels her emotions take over. She grasps a nearby vase and smashes it to the floor. Water and flowers carpet the tile.

Rob jumps but remains silent.

Her eyes scan the room, zero in on a block of knives, she descends on them, sweeps them from the counter. One knife sticks in the toe of Rob's shoe.

"Hey, watch out!" he jumps, pulled out of his reverie.

"Why am I here?" she cries.

Stunned, he watches as she turns to the metal Venetian blinds. She grabs, tries to pull them down then ineffectively attacks the metal slats.

Blood runs up her arms, and she is sobbing. Droplets fall on the floor from the cuts on her hands and arms. All the while she hurls words at him.

"I came for you. I stayed to be with you, to support your dreams. The other wives left . . ."

He stares fascinated. *What is she doing?*

She pushes the hair from her eyes, smearing her face Apache like. She never imagined she possessed this level of—what? Anger, fury, pain? It has her in its grip, owns her completely, she can't control the depth of her agony, how to make it stop.

"You left me alone, terrified I'd be raped, and you wouldn't want me."

Her hysteria mounts further. She searches for ways to harm herself, wants to take the pain out from her head, and she moves quickly to the gas stove. She turns it on, lifts her hand to the flame.

Shocked into reacting, Rob lunges for her and grabs her away. He puts his arms around her, but she wrenches herself from him, slapping him.

He watches open-mouthed, astonished. He can't imagine this level of emotion.

As fast as it came her fury evaporates, soft tears fall as she stops and looks at Rob, seeing him with new eyes.

"You weren't even thinking about me, were you? You never think of me! You were too busy fucking her," she whispers. "Didn't you ever once think how frightened I was, here alone?"

"Genie, I'm sorry." A lump forms in his throat, tears prick his eyes, and he tries again to hold her, but she wrenches herself away and walks purposefully to their bedroom.

He goes to the fridge and grabs ice, then follows—helpless he watches her tear apart the two beds.

Her face is bloody, her hand burns and is blistered but she doesn't care, she throws bedding to the floor and pulls the two frames apart. She remakes them into two separate beds.

"How could you be so stupid?" she asks, so quietly he has to strain to hear. He holds out the towel containing ice.

She ignores him and shakes her head.

"You gave her our address? I didn't need to know. I HATE you. You're stupid, you can't even do this without getting it wrong."

She rushes out grabbing the car keys, drops of blood follow her along the hallway, marking her path.

"Death or departure," a voice whispers. "It's a choice."

The car moves with her body behind the wheel, but her brain is in a faraway place.

"Just drive," the voice in her head tells her.

Weeks filled with loss and death. Now the final betrayal. She blinks her eyes, but the monster is still there. She feels him.

Infidelity hurts, but the immense pain is the awful awareness that Rob cared nothing for her. She is in Beirut for him. He asked her to remain in this disintegrating world with him then abandoned her, scared and in danger. Just took off, found a lover and stayed, not one call.

How easy it would have been. 'Are you ok, I'll be home . . .'

What an unconscious idiot to give her our address.

But it doesn't matter anymore. The emptiness worms its way into her psyche, and she can no longer fight the invisible, congenitally malformed creature which resides in the vacuum which once held her self.

She stares at the barren road ahead. She fought to recover from the pain of Keith's murder, from the slaughter all around, Rob's words if she were raped, "I wouldn't want you again." But slowly she crawled back.

The violent massacres at Qarantina and Damour peeled back her eyelids, forced inescapable insights into the hatred surrounding them, a violation of her brain as powerful as a physical assault. She wasn't there, but she can't scrub the images from her head, feels the screams at night in the darkness, as she waits, wills herself to escape in sleep.

I could have left him, gone to safety like most of the other wives. Why didn't I leave when I had the chance? But I didn't. Out of what? Love? A sense of duty? What a joke. Now I don't care. Our marriage has been murdered, one more victim of the war, and I just need oblivion.

Tears fall, blur her vision, but she doesn't wipe them away. She feels like a creature void of life. Disconnected from herself. An Automaton. Her mind is a mess, she can't think . . .

Is this how it will always be? she wonders.

The car drives on. Dust. She notices dust in the headlights. The paved road has run out.

I've lost touch with friends in England. The years have passed, and I've gradually been swept into this new life. Lost contact. Life is like that. You step out of your place in it, and those left behind simply close the space as though you were never there, she thinks. *And here? Here it's madness, hatred, pain, and emptiness.*

A silent thought creeps back in, wraps her in its warmth and slowly shoots spidery webs into her head.

There is a solution, it whispers. End it. Do it. Go on. It will all stop. You want silence? Happiness? For God's sake—do it. Find a tree—a wall, over the edge of the hill. Anything will work. Foot on the pedal, shut your eyes and drive!

She shakes her head, tries to push this gauze over her brain aside, but it's insistent, encompasses her, alluring and finally irresistible.

She stamps her foot to the floor.

The speedometer registers the maximum and the engine howls, her muscles cramp as she presses and presses—her foot will go no further. Smoke billows from under the hood and she smells it, tastes the dust.

"Aargh." An ugly, harsh scream tears from her throat, fills the space.

Through the squall of dust and pebbles she spins, a silent fairground ride, out of control the car screeches in a 360-degree turn.

She hears her own sobs as she rams on the brakes, the car skids and shudders to a noisy stop on the unmade mountain road.

She smashes her hands on the wheels and surrenders to ugly, wrenching wails until she's dry and empty, a piece of chaff, a husk to simply blow away.

The dust settles, and the tears subside. Genie stops shaking, feels cleansed. She has embraced the truth. She may be surrounded by desolation and despair, they may have hit rock bottom, but she has value, she doesn't need anyone to fulfill her. She is determined to live.

Rob's eyes widen as she returns covered in dust and heads straight to the bedroom. Her appearance is wretched, her hair and clothes hang filthily about her. He has never seen her like this before, in all of their marriage he has never caught her without her makeup, her hair in place. When he wakes each day, she's already "done."

He takes a step back and stares, she has the look of a convert from a religious retreat—transformed.

Almost a week passes without conversation. Although filled with questions, Rob makes no comment.

The familiar pull between work and home life, to take a risk or opt for safety in their retreat in the hills, still tears at him.

Genie doesn't understand or agree, she doesn't actually speak to him anymore, but he needs to go to work if only to get some space, Rob decides.

She has been so unhappy since the Damour massacre and now with that stupid letter she's unreachable. He is genuinely sorry, never intended she'd be hurt, but it's too late now, like everything else it seems it's all in the hands of the Gods.

Adnan hands him a coffee and pats him on the back.

"Cheer up, Rob," he says. "Nothing is as bad as it seems. We are still living, so we have hope, no?"

He sips coffee then sighs, little does Adnan know. He remembers seeing a woven mat somewhere, *"Abandon all hope, ye who enter here,"* where was that? Probably a pub with a twisted sense of humor, in England, no doubt.

But Adnan hasn't finished. "Look at Nashad, he has received permission to go to Canada to marry his Leila."

"Really? When did that happen?" Rob asks.

"I received the visa yesterday," Nashad smiles and holds it out for inspection. The joy is back in his eyes. "I will leave at the end of the month," he says. "After I have finished the work outstanding."

"Congratulations, Nashad. I am so happy for you. Genie will be thrilled, too."

"Thank you, I can hardly believe it." He goes back to his work.

Rob nods, thinks of the enduring love of this responsible young man and Leila and the challenge they have overcome, his thoughts return to Genie. At home, there are no signs of improvement, and he has no idea how to fix it, feels exhausted all the time, and he hates it.

Before the letter, he was briefly optimistic, hoped the involvement of Syrian President Assad would make a difference here, but in spite of this new Syrian presence the violence has escalated and another refugee camp, Tel al-Zaatar in East Beirut, continues under siege by Maronite Christian militias.

None of it seems to matter. *Should I just pack it all in? Would that appease her?* He wonders.

He opens the front door and almost falls over a suitcase in the hallway. He sighs, drags himself to the bedroom and sits on his bed facing her back as she sorts through her belongings.

"Nashad got a visa and permission to join Leila," he says.

He is surprised when she turns from the open wardrobe and answers him. "That's wonderful, I can't imagine how thrilled they must be."

They fall silent.

"And the case?" he asks.

"With or without you, tomorrow I'm leaving, too."

She hopes it remains peaceful for her to get to the airport and that fate, a quixotic unwelcome guest, has no other plans for her.

21
THE AFFAIR

THE MORNING GENIE HAS CHOSEN for her departure is a beautiful, clear day. She hasn't called anyone, told anyone, hasn't even booked a ticket yet, but that shouldn't be a problem. If she leaves for the airport in an hour, she can get a ticket home today. She plans to disappear and start over.

With the decision made, she feels lighter. Since the school was bombed, Genie has been stuck at home and has taken care of the house, Noura no longer comes and, for probably the last time, she spoons coffee grounds into the pot.

Now she's ready to leave she feels less anger toward Rob. Actually, she feels nothing, there's nothing to be gained in feeling hurt and vengeful.

She takes a cup to him as he watches from the balcony. He points below to an overloaded red Morgan screeching to a standstill.

Damn, she thinks. *I'll never make today's flight now!* But she is happy to see friendly faces. *Oh well, today, tomorrow, what's the difference really? The rest of life is ahead.*

Karam is squashed into the car, sharing his seat with a giant world globe and a trombone. The globe spins as the car parks. She smiles. *He always appears comfortable in his skin, no matter how odd the circumstance.*

Rob quickly hides Genie's suitcase in the hall cupboard and calls to her as he runs downstairs to greet a red-faced and slightly breathless Colonel and a fresh and relaxed Karam.

"I've come to bid adieu. Can't stay in a place that'd shoot my car. My work of art." He points to two bullet holes in the body and strokes the chassis as he would a lover.

"Can you believe it?" He seems genuinely shocked and saddened by this affront.

Rob shakes his head. "Hard to imagine!" He claps him on the shoulder and tries not to smile. "Come on in and have one for the road."

"OK. Perhaps a farewell dram?"

Their voices approach the top of the stairs and Genie comes to greet them. She hasn't slept, is unusually pale, but she kisses them warmly.

The guys head to the living room, and Rob sets a bottle and glasses on the coffee table. Genie glances around for her luggage, notes he must have put it away.

She brings in nibbles and curls her legs under her on one end of the couch, far from Rob. Bandages from the attack on the metal blinds are only slightly visible below her sweater, but eagle-eyed Karam spots them. She sees him look, pulls on her sleeves and tries to listen as they chat, speculate and revisit never ending intrigues.

The Colonel is excited about his trip and says he has almost no regrets about leaving.

"It's a long journey, you should eat before you go," she says and goes to prepare a meal.

After a few minutes, Karam follows her to the kitchen. He gently lifts her arm, revealing the bandaged wrists. He looks at her, without speaking.

She pulls them away from him. "It's not what it seems."

"Oh, Genie," he says and tilts her face to look at him. He sees a flicker of her unhappiness, but she turns from his penetrating stare and picks up a tray loaded with cold ham, scotch eggs, and hummus. She adds warm homemade bread and a salad.

"Truly."

Conversation slows as they eat, a local Arabic music station plays softly in the background.

"I like the music," the Colonel says. "You've rather embraced the local culture haven't you, my sweet?" he observes, as she gathers plates and heads back to the kitchen.

She has embraced many of their ways she realizes, as she spoons coffee into the water and stirs. She lights the flame and holds the long-handled pot over it, waits for it to come almost to a boil. Like boiling milk, there is a split second to grab it and slowly bring it to the edge of the flame, prevent the contents from overflowing. She holds one side of the pot over the flame allowing a rolling boil.

"A true expert," Karam says leaning in the doorway. She puts a plate of baklava in his hands and pushes past him.

"Maybe your last Turkish coffee," she says to the Colonel, and they watch as she pours the thick sweet liquid into demitasse cups.

"You've mastered this art, too," he compliments her, sipping the dark fragrant drink. "As I said, almost the native by now."

But not for much longer, she thinks.

The Colonel glances at his watch and puts down his cup "Better get a move on," he sighs, and a subdued procession treks down to his car, each one conscious that the numbers dwindle as more friends give in and leave.

One last check everything is secure, and he climbs in, blows extravagant kisses, carefully puts his beloved car in gear and waves, the trio watches.

"To home and to Mother England," he calls. The Colonel and his car disappear into the distance and into their history.

"We should've left, too, long ago," Genie speaks to the air. "I'm stupid to let you decide on my future."

"Home? To power cuts and poverty, strikes, and unemployment? You'll never live like this again."

"You think this is better?" She laughs.

"A skirmish followed by a cease-fire. We've seen it all before."

Karam watches without comment.

"You live in total denial," she says and turns to see Rubina approach, tucking in wisps of recently grey hair which escape from her loose chignon.

"They've been again to collect money," she says. She sounds resigned. "They are not happy."

"None of us are happy," Genie says.

Karam turns to Rob. "What time is the taxi service from here?"

Genie looks over her shoulder to Karam as she takes Rubina's arm and walks with her back to the building. "I'll get the keys and drive you home. I could do with some fresh air."

"You are sure?" he replies.

Rob opens his mouth, stops and turns to Karam. "How was the road? Was it safe?"

"It doesn't matter," she calls back.

Karam turns as he hears the loud, insistent bleats from the sheep grazing under the building. He raises an eyebrow. "Nice red collar. Decorative bell. An unusual choice of pet!"

"Genie bought it to protect it from slaughter. She has a need to save, to shield the helpless." Rob replies. "It's both her strength and her fatal flaw."

They fly down the mountain. She takes the turns too fast, makes a left at the coast road and joins the flow of traffic into Beirut.

Karam says nothing.

At the red traffic light, cars jostle for position, as usual, some climb the curb, others cross lanes or mount the grassy median divider until the light turns green. Then, with a screech of tires, they race off, eager to be first. A display of speed for a few yards until they fall back to a dawdling donkey pace.

He glances at her. "What is wrong Genie?"

"Nothing."

"You seem distant and sad, unlike yourself. I always found you magical. A Genie who reflects sunshine."

"My grandfather used to call me his sunshine." She sniffs. "For a man who hates women you've certainly mastered flattery."

"You should not laugh at me. It is true I have little regard for silly girls, but you must surely know after all this time that I am in love with you."

"Love? It's a four-letter illusion. What could YOU of all people know of love, Karam? I've watched you." she derides.

He raises his hand, deflects, hits his own head. "Stop the car." He makes to open the door while it is still in motion.

She swerves, brakes and stops the car, glares at him, shocked and furious.

"What do you think you're doing? Wait for me to stop, do you want to kill yourself?" she shouts.

"Why would you mock me? You must surely have understood my feelings?" he says. "Why do you think I hang around all those superficial people who mean nothing to me? Haunt the places you might be?"

He stops, sees the tears which slide silently down her cheek, and he reaches over to hold her. "I am sorry I tried to slap you. It is not my way, but you really wounded me."

"It's not the slap," she says. "It's—it's—everything."

Her shoulders shake, she loosens the scarf from her head and buries her face in it. Karam keeps his arm around her until the weeping subsides.

She stops and looks up, he has tears in his eyes, too. His look of profound distress moves her, she knows his words are true. How could she not have seen? *What a total mess!* She thinks.

Pulling herself away she throws the car into gear, and they drive on in silence to Karam's building in Ramlet el Baida.

She pulls up and turns off the engine.

He touches the side of her face. "I am sorry, Genie, it was unforgivable," he reaches again and lifts up her wrist, he strokes it. "But remember, habibti, life is all we have."

His eyes look into her, and she doesn't want to look away, wants him to stay, suspects he can make her pain go away.

But he gets out and leans back before closing the car door. "Never lose hope, Genie. It may be hard to recognize right now, but she who has hope has everything."

She watches him walk away, climb the steps and is swept up in an enormous emptiness. *Don't let the door close. Make him come back.*

He has offered comfort for months, has been a constant, asking for nothing, just being there and caring.

Her head says she's crazy, but she ignores it, takes a deep breath, turns off the ignition, grabs her purse and reaches for the door.

The slam of the car door surprises Karam, he turns to see her lock the car and follow him.

He says nothing.

She stands in the doorway and looks around. The studio apartment is large and high ceilinged, sparsely furnished with an enormous, beautiful, oriental carpet covering almost the entire room. A small bed and several tables with hundreds of books are on one side and on a mosaic, obviously handcrafted, Syrian games table two elaborate chess sets are "in play."

Karam pulls her gently inside and turns on a transistor radio, scratchy music fills the room, and the sound transports her to another place, another era.

In one corner on a narrow counter, she sees a stove top and a blue Turkish coffee pot, beside it a frying pan, a selection of plates, cups and some beautiful Persian, hand blown glasses. A tiny fridge whirs relentlessly.

Half a dozen candles in wax-covered Chianti bottles cover the flat surfaces and another pile of books stacked on the floor tilt dangerously to one side against an antique, undoubtedly expensive desk.

He takes two of the Persian glasses and pours in red wine, hands one to her.

She puts her nose to the glass, breathes in and drinks deeply.

"The wine is delicious." She walks across the room, slips out of her shoes and loosens her hair with one hand.

He watches each movement. "Are you sure you know what you are doing?"

She sips some more, nods. "Hold me."

He walks toward her and touches her hair, cups her face in his hands.

"My Genie is ready to escape her lamp?"

She empties her glass, places it beside the bed and sits. "I want to escape the pain."

He kneels beside her, gently bends her toward him and she feels herself relax as his lips brush over hers, she responds. The dreamlike sensation which began at the car hasn't lifted.

His eyes don't move from hers as he strokes her hair, her shoulders. He sits next to her, lowers his gaze. His kisses move to the back of her neck.

Shudders move up her spine. "Oh God, yes," she breathes.

The passionate intensity of their lovemaking shocks them both. The bottled up anguish pours from her mind through her limbs, she feels possessed as it flows away.

He envelops her, they move in absolute unison to unknown, unexplored places, touching and feeling. Tears fall. Skin on skin—like silk; stroking and sliding, and breathing in. Tongues and fingertips, toes linked and grasped tight, pushing and pushing and finally letting go—in a shuddering, pulsating climax—together.

Not a word is spoken but the euphoric release from months of tension exhausts itself, and they fall asleep in a tangle of damp limbs and sheets.

She sought a brief respite from pain, but in his tenderness, in this unexpected coupling, she finds absolution, and she sleeps.

Unnoticed the sun sets and occasional car headlights throw shadows across them, illuminating the ceiling. They sleep on.

She stirs to the wonderful smell of cooking, her nose wrinkles, and she is back in the present. Disorientated she glances around and pulls the sheets about her.

In the glow of candlelight, the slightly under-loved room is transformed, it could be a romantic artist's attic faraway from the strife. Karam has lit every one of the candles and is busy at the stove.

He places a tray on the bed. Arabic bread, hummus, olives, salt and two glasses of red wine. He carries four fried eggs in the frying pan from the stove.

She's amazed at how relaxed and unselfconscious she feels. There is no awkwardness as they sit cross-legged on the bed and eat from the pan. Her mouth is half full. "I didn't realize I was so hungry."

He takes a long swallow of his Chianti and leans his back against the wall. "Tell me your story."

She looks at him and wipes her mouth. "Long story."

"We have time."

She fastens the sheet toga style. "At eighteen I vowed I'd never again let my father beat me, so I left home. That same day, my mother left. My leaving broke up the family and changed all their lives. I thought only of myself, didn't consider them. I haven't forgiven myself."

She tilts back her head, closes her eyes and breathes deeply.

Karam pulls her gently into his arms. "There is an Arabic proverb: 'Never a mistake, always a lesson' I believe this."

"I like that idea. But I don't think I had learned my lesson. After my parents separated and my father was gone; I moved home until my mother met a new man. He was awful. None of the children could stand him or his myriad rules."

She falls silent.

"Go on," he urges.

"I met Rob. He was smart, funny and ambitious. We didn't understand anything of love, but we wanted to change our lives, so we married. My brothers and sisters were scattered to the wind. Coming here was his dream. I eventually embraced it, too. But in this new world we've reacted in different ways, slowly become strangers."

They fall silent, watch the patterns of light on the ceiling.

"Rob is a chemist, an engineer. You are an enigma. He may try, but he will never understand you."

She considers this for a while. *Maybe it's true,* she thinks. *Perhaps that's the real problem, we are friends, but neither of us understands the other.* Genie stirs. This is hardly the time or place for soul searching.

"So tell me why you live so frugally? Your family lives well, a butler, a chauffeur, maids."

"Precisely. I find it abhorrent that so many have so little, while a few . . ."

"Sound communist philosophy," she teases.

"You laugh Genie, but I am a communist."

"No Karam, you're an idealist."

"Once, perhaps. But disillusionment has turned me into a grumpy cynic."

He pulls a face and sets the tray and pan on the floor, she laughs and curls into his arms. Slowly they stretch their bodies beside one another. She kisses his eyelids, he reaches behind her head to stroke her hair, coils it around his hand as he pulls her to him. Slowly and rhythmically they exorcize their demons.

Sated, still breathless, their bodies tingling and damp, they fall back on the pillows, arms flung over each other.

From the radio the voice of Diana Ross scratchily sings:

'Wasn't it me who said nothin' good's gonna last forever?'

Genie hums with the song:

'And wasn't it me who said, let's just be glad for the time together?'

"Are you OK?" he whispers.

She murmurs softly in his ear and rolls away from him.

"I'm fine, Karam, but you know I have to go."

"If you promise to come tomorrow, I want to take you to a special place. Meet me at noon, here?"

"I will."

And suddenly all thoughts of fleeing from Lebanon, take flight. She has not felt this way before, not even in the beginning with Rob. She's giddy and girlish and feels like hugging herself or hugging the man selling ice cream or the falafel vendor. She wants to hug the world.

She wakes in the lounge, stiff and achy from the recent lovemaking, followed by a night spent on the couch. Morning sunlight fills the apartment. There is no sign of Rob, who was asleep when she got back in the early hours and left without turning off the radio this morning. The news permeates her consciousness.

> News Report: March 11, 1976, The Brigadier General commanding the Beirut barracks, reportedly without an army, has occupied local tv and radio stations and has declared himself provisional military governor of Lebanon until a legitimate election can be held. He has called for the resignation of the President in a de facto military coup. Opposition Leader Kamal Jumblatt stated: 'If he does not resign, the revolution will continue for our complete control of power.'

Provisional Military Governor, God, what next?

She is fuzzy headed, still tired, but has sufficient awareness to admire the chutzpah of the man. She wonders if she's caught in some dark, Monty Pythonesque comedy. Even she understands what the Brigadier attempts is futile. What on earth does he hope to achieve?

As for Jumblatt—if it weren't for his underhanded dealing, we wouldn't have this President now!

She glances at the clock. *Eleven fifteen. How's that possible?* She holds it to her ear, shakes it, but it is ticking just fine. She makes herself tea, but with the first sip, she remembers her noon appointment.

Like a banshee, she whirls around the apartment getting ready and sees Rob's note.

"Took the shuttle taxi and left you the car, please pick me up later."

Thoughtful, she thinks.

She takes the keys and peers into the hall mirror. *Do I look different? Does it show?*

Too late now anyway!

Outside his home Karam waves, as she approaches he almost smiles.

"No questions—drive north," he instructs. "I believe we have time, I have an appointment at five thirty. I tried, but I could not reschedule," he says.

A dozen miles north of Beirut the Jeita Grotto is hidden from the outside world. Two separate but connected caves were inhabited in prehistoric times. Now wonders nestle in the uppermost galleries including the world's largest known stalactite.

Karam holds his hands over her eyes as they enter the cavern. When he removes them, she gasps at the beautifully lit, almost empty chamber, cranes her head hard to take in the extraordinary and complex compositions.

Why have we never thought to visit in the years we have lived along the road?

Then she remembers. After the first few months, Rob's work took over.

"My God it's incredible," she whispers.

Karam turns and pauses, about to say something, unsure. He kisses her and gives a self-conscious smile.

Genie sees his dilemma. "What?" she says.

"It occurs to me—this place is a metaphor of the love I have for you. Even before it was revealed, it existed, growing slowly, unseen."

Her turn to be speechless, drawn in by the imagery and the words. *Is this from Karam, or in his culture are sentiments more poetically expressed? I need to be careful*, she thinks, *this is powerful and seductive.*

"What a beautiful thing to say." She slowly moves on to explore deeper into the cavern.

They are quiet on the drive back, aware that confusion looms. Along the coast road foamy white clouds obscure the afternoon sun, and soon they reach the Corniche, pass Raouche, the Riviera club and into the narrow streets of Ras Beirut where she stops outside Karam's.

He turns to her and kisses her lightly, climbs out and leans over to close the door.

"Call me—soon," he says. "Ya Ayuni, ya albe."

"What . . ."

He motions with his hands. "My eyes and my heart."

She blows a kiss, puts the car in gear and escapes. Filled with excitement like a little girl, she wants to laugh out loud and speak his name. "Karam, Karam."

She doesn't feel like fetching Rob who will finish work soon. Not yet. She needs to take her mind off the emotions which chase around, bump into one another. Needs space to think and review what is happening.

A week ago she was ready to leave, to fly home like a migratory bird at the end of its journey. Now she's poised on one leg not sure where to put her foot.

Is this a fling or could it be more? What will people think? Ours is a small tight community, and no-one will forgive this apparent betrayal. Could I face the censure, and does Karam even want more than this? Do I? How would we live? His small garret is elegant and romantic for illicit meetings, but to live there? Impossible.

A car horn startles her. The light has turned green, and she's not moving. Cars swirl around her and through the intersection.

She takes her foot off the brake and heads to Roslyn who is always willing for retail therapy, but a maid answers the front door.

"Pas ici. Coiffeur," she says in broken French, touching her hair which is hidden away in a scarf.

"Damn!"

Back in the traffic she quickly does a U-turn and goes to find Roslyn at the hair salon.

※———※———※———※

A pile of hair, like a sleeping Pekingese, covers the ground at her feet. Genie sucks in her breath.

"Do you like it?" Roslyn glances in the mirror. It's a massive, dramatic change. She looks fantastic, but almost unrecognizable, with a Vidal Sassoon style box cut and Genie wonders how Khalil will react. Not well, she imagines.

They stroll along Hamra Street. Shopkeepers materialize in doorways, beckon them in, recite their wares and the bargains on offer. In the more exclusive boutiques, well polished and beautifully dressed salespeople chat and occasionally glance from the windows. In a couple of hours, they will finish for the day and get back to their real lives.

"I wanted to get my hair done before my big debut," Roslyn says. "Don't they do amazing work?" She admires her reflection in the shop window.

She scrutinizes Genie's face. "But you look radiant today, too. What's your secret? Rob must be doing something right," she jokes.

Genie smiles and touches her face. "Well, he leaves me the car every day, wants to be nice I suppose." She hasn't mentioned Rob's affair, and she won't, nor hers, probably.

Roslyn has spotted Jacqui at a curbside table at Movenpick unselfconsciously spooning out an ice cream sundae. She wipes whipped cream from her sophisticated nose but retains a smile of pleasure on her lips.

She's grateful for the interruption as Genie and Roslyn slide in beside her.

Jacqui looks sad. "It's confirmed. We've been posted to Jakarta, we go next week. I know things are coming unraveled here, but I'll be sad to leave. I'll miss you."

Genie considers for a moment. "I thought I'd leave, too. But now I'm not sure what to do."

"We're staying of course." Roslyn lifts her head from the menu she has been inspecting. "Khalil and his family would never go anywhere else, with over a thousand employees, and after a century in business, well . . ." she lifts her hands, and her eyebrows raise, too. Looking around, Roslyn leans in. "More importantly, finally, I'm going to be a teacher," she smiles. "Tomorrow's my first class, say you'll be there?"

Jacqui shakes her head. "Sorry, too much to do. Today was my last class, you'll be fine."

"But I'm a mess. Khalil doesn't want me to do it. Please, please be there, if I get into trouble you could step in," she pleads. "I'm sick just thinking about it."

"What a queen of drama! It's beginner's nerves," Genie says.

Jacqui and Genie laugh but Roslyn senses she has almost convinced Genie and rests her head on her shoulder. "Pretty please?"

"Alright, I'll be there, I promise."

A couple of Syrian armored cars drive by followed by two T-54's. The friends look at the military vehicles and turn to each other.

"You know our President formally asked Syria to intervene." Jacqui leans in conspiratorially. "I heard Assad asked the US not to interfere if he sends Syrian troops into Lebanon."

Another Syrian vehicle passes by.

"Looks like they agreed!" Roslyn laughs. "Khalil told me the Palestinian Chairman, Yasir Arafat, was involved in breaking apart the Army. Now there's no independent army and Syria is the only hope for peace and stability." She sees David approach and drops her voice. "Anyway, right now most of the country is controlled by Palestinian forces. PLO, PFLP, tra la-la-la-la, who can keep track of them all?"

David's blonde hair falls over his eyes and today with no classes to teach he looks slightly hippy. Along with many gay people he has found Beirut more accepting of their lifestyle.

He stops when he sees them and pulls out a book from the woven bag he carries over his shoulder.

"Here's the Fowles' book I told you about, The Magus. Read it, it's thought-provoking." He passes it to Genie and turns to Roslyn before he walks on. "Don't you look fabulous? Totally modern. Ready for tomorrow, my cherub?"

Her face reddens, she nods and turns back to her friends as David blows kisses and moves on.

Genie's attention has been pulled across the street. Karam and another man climb out of a chauffeured MBZ. She cranes her neck as she sees him enter a building, he strides through the tall doors without noticing her and is gone from sight.

Roslyn follows her gaze. "Sometimes I hate this place, everyone knows everything. It's impossible to have a secret," she says.

Genie scans Roslyn's face. *Does she suspect?* But she reads nothing in Roslyn's expression, and she dare not ask.

22

FLAMES, SMOKE, AND DIVORCE

THE SUITCASE REMAINS IN THE hall closet, and they seem to have reached a tacit understanding. "Least said, soonest mended" is the best policy. This new disconnected state ironically appears to work, and they remain polite and civil with one another.

The week has been relatively quiet. Nothing has been discussed about the future, Genie walks through and joins him on the terrace. The radio, Rob's constant companion, plays soft music as he looks out to the smoke rising in the distance.

"All of these failures have given Syria time to get the OK from Israel and the US to install a stronger presence here. There are riots in town again. But I imagine it'll quieten with some strong arm law and order!" he observes.

She leans on the handrail beside him. "I have to go in tonight," she pauses. "This is Roslyn's first class I promised her moral support," she emphasizes the word promise.

He continues facing the city. "It's too dangerous. Three people were killed at lunchtime when shells fell near Shaker's pharmacy on Hamra. One of the guys from work was nearby, he said there was nothing left but the dead men's shoes, and pools of blood," he turns to her. "His apartment was shelled, too. A bullet hit the wall above their daughter's crib, he's taking his family back to Alexandria. You shouldn't go in, 'phone her and explain."

He sees the resistance in Genie's expression. "OK, I'll do it," he says and goes to telephone from Kourk's apartment below.

She watches the smoke spiral in the distance. After a few minutes, Rob returns. He opens his palms. "The lines are down."

"So I have to go. I won't let Roslyn down, I gave my word."

"You're impossible. You'll risk your life for this? No-one keeps their word all of the time." Rob shrugs as Genie takes the car keys.

"So that's your world view?" she shoots at him as she leaves.

The barb finds its mark. Wounded, he turns away. *To hell with her, why care if she gets hurt? It'd be her own fault.* He has been feeling guilty for the recent events. *It's true the timing was terrible, leaving her home scared and maybe in danger.* But he hasn't made a habit of it. At some point, they have to work it out. Staying out half the night and sleeping apart isn't going to make it easier.

He pours a drink and wonders if it's only for Roslyn she takes this risk. What an impossible woman, sometimes he wonders if maybe it'd be better if she did leave.

Flames and smoke leap into the air from burning truck tires littered along the road to Achrafieh.

Like Guy Fawkes night, she thinks. But it isn't—it's a war zone. Genie swerves as thick smoke reduces visibility. The air is acrid, her eyes sting, and she blinks tears away.

A mangy dog appears from the smoke in front of the car. Her foot smashes down on the brakes, and she skids, hydroplanes over the wet surface out of control toward a group of men in bloody hand to hand combat.

She braces herself, icicles of fear crawl up her spine but, intent on their fight, the men ignore her. As her vehicle spins she slaloms sideways across a bridge and into a burned-out bus. She hears the crack of her head against the side window, her neck jerks violently and her eyes close.

Around her, the fighting continues unabated. Seconds tick by and her eyes open to a sharp ache in her shoulders and neck. A thin line of blood trickles from the side of her head. She blinks, tries to focus.

Fumbling in her purse for something to blot away the blood, she rubs her eyes and holds the bloodied remains of the tissue over her nose.

"You're so, so stupid, Genie," she mutters to herself as she fights to ignore the pain.

The stalled car refuses to start.

"Damn it. Come on, come on," Genie pleads. She assumes the impact may have flooded the engine, what does she know? She waits, the seconds drag, she tries again, it comes to life.

At the Language Center, Roslyn is a hit. A natural teacher, she had no need for help. Her beam could light the city as she walks arm in arm with Genie to the car.

"I feel GREAT. Thanks for the moral support. I'm so jazzed," Roslyn turns on the car radio loudly as they drive through the

back streets to her home. Her smile widens when Helen Reddy
sings out her hit:

'I am woman let me roar,
in numbers too big to ignore.'

"That's perfect for me," she laughs and breaks into song.
She's too excited to notice the damage to the car or the bruise
on Genie's cheek.

"I should have done this years ago," she says. "I feel light as
a cloud, I'm my own person for the first time."

They pull up outside her house "See you in the morning,"
Genie laughs. "I'll drop Rob off then I'll collect you. We can go
in together, maybe grab a coffee and croissant on the way."

"It's a date."

Genie sits for a moment. Roslyn does a small dance, curt-
sies to the empty street, shakes her short tresses, enters her house
and closes the door.

She laughs out loud, Roslyn's happiness is contagious.

Inside her home, Roslyn does not immediately sense how dark
the mood is.

Khalil nurses a bottle of scotch. He glares at her as she
walks in, she is beaming, and her eyes sparkle.

"My brother was here tonight," his speech is slightly slurred.

Roslyn pays little attention. "That's nice." She kisses him on
top of his head and slips off her shoes. "You know I'd been so
scared of tonight," she tells him as she kicks off her high heels
and rubs her feet.

Khalil bangs down the bottle. "Listen to me woman, I don't even know you anymore. 'What do you need with a woman who works against a husband's wishes?' he asked me. 'We have money, a large company. What kind of man are you?'"

She picks up her shoes and handbag and walks to the door "Khalil, you're drunk. I'm going to bed. You'll feel better in the morning. We can talk tomorrow. I'm exhausted but happy, and I want to stay that way."

Inside Roslyn's bedroom, the morning sunshine falls across her eyes. She keeps them closed and slowly stretches as the memory of last night's success curls out tentacles and wraps them around her. Thick locks of her cropped hair fall over her forehead and a smile comes to her face, remembering her recent victory.

How wonderful to see all those faces focused on me, eager to learn. Roslyn brushes the hair aside, recalls the light in her student's eyes as they grasped the concepts. She is startled by loud voices in the room and opens her eyes, fully awake.

Across the room, her husband and his brother argue and throw things into suitcases.

In the doorway a maid cries softly, she twists her apron in her hands.

Roslyn is confused, tries to make sense of the scene which unfolds in front of her. From below she hears her children's voices call:

"Mumma?"

She puts a long bare leg out of the bed.

Her brother in law scowls across and throws a robe at her. "Cover yourself. Get dressed."

"Get out of my bedroom, who do you think you are?" she yells at him. She pulls the flimsy robe around her and turns to Khalil. "What's going on? I don't understand."

Khalil won't make eye contact, and his brother nudges him.

Head bent he intones. "I divorce you, I divorce you, I divorce you." He quickly turns and leaves. Scurrying down the stairs, he almost slips as he heads out of the front door. *Well, that's it—done—now perhaps they'll all leave me alone.*

He didn't plan on going this far, but his family, especially his brother, were so incensed by Roslyn's behavior and independence that he's grown sick of the constant complaints. He's a little concerned for his children, but his mother said kids are resilient. Anyway, it's been seven years, and the excitement has long gone, if he's honest, he's looked around a little lately, and he wouldn't mind a change, even a little bachelor time.

Roslyn stares in shocked disbelief. What on earth just happened? She wonders.

She screams, attempts to grasp more clothing around her body and tries to run after Khalil. "No o o! You don't mean it. I don't understand. Khalil, come back."

But he's gone.

Her brother in law glares at her, blocks her way out of the bedroom and with a rough push thrusts her back inside.

Conscious of his leer she puts her arms around her half-dressed body.

"I said get dressed, Sharmouta," he snaps. "Whore!" He slaps her brutally around the face.

She sobs and throws on clothes. This can't be happening.

In heavy Beirut traffic, Genie drives cautiously. She approaches Roslyn's house and searches for a place to park. This morning she avoided the coast and so far has not seen any further sign of Syrian intervention.

"What's going on over there?" she wonders aloud. She sits up straight as she sees Roslyn being dragged from her house. She double parks and runs over.

Roslyn reaches for her. "He's divorced me, he's keeping my children. It's insane. It was his brother."

In the doorway a man watches the events play out, a smile on his lips.

Probably Khalil's brother, Genie imagines. *But where is Khalil?*

"I think they're sending me back to England . . ." Roslyn is crying now, loud awful sounds.

She tries to fight but is no match for the two burly men who hold on to her. Quickly and roughly the swarthy guys with guns in their belts shove her toward a waiting car. One of them pushes Genie out of the way, and she falls back against the wall.

Noise, madness and Roslyn's weeping fill the air, and a few onlookers have gathered in the street to watch.

In less than a minute Roslyn and her expensive bags have been thrown into the vehicle. She scrambles to look out of the rear window, sees her two children banging on the glass in the house behind her and tries to call out, but the door slams, and it speeds away, shooting through a red light.

Genie stares after the car. *It happened so quickly, and without warning,* she thinks, but almost immediately she remembers Khalil with his parade of foreign girls at the clubs.

Warning or not, Roslyn is gone. She is divorced—from her husband, her home, her children and her friends.

Surrounded by crumpled bed sheets and scattered clothing Genie rests against Karam. A tray perches on the corner of the bed, the remains of Arabic bread, hummus and cheese with a fragrant magnolia in a glass. She picks up the flower and puts her head to the bloom. She vaguely remembers mentioning her love of the fragrance, and he took note.

She stares into space and mulls over Roslyn's summary expulsion and wonders if they will ever meet again, it's unlikely, she knows. This morning was a shock, and she worries for the little children who now have no mother.

They sip red wine and lazily stroke the length of each other's bodies.

"Khalil divorced Roslyn. They sent her away. Back to England, I imagine," she says.

"Aah."

"He only had to repeat 'I divorce you' and it was done." She waits for a response, but it never comes. *A man of few words.*

The stubs of candles flicker in his Chianti bottles, cast a glow in the room and shadows across the ceiling. Karam continues to stare at the patterns above him. "I questioned whether you would come."

"I wasn't sure either. It's a bit complicated." Genie kisses her finger and puts it to his lips. "I feel like I've woken from a long sleep. More of a coma, in fact!" She turns to look at his face, should she ask why he was in the chauffeur driven car? It's none of her business, but he seems to appear all around town, and she's curious. She plunges in. "I saw you on Monday on Hamra getting out of a big, shiny, bourgeois car."

Karam continues to look at the ceiling. Seconds pass, and slowly he looks at her. "I did not see you."

Leaning on an elbow, he scoops hummus onto a finger and places it in her mouth. She swallows the mouthful, takes another sip of wine and realizes he has no intention of explaining.

He lazily walks to the bathroom. Genie watches his firm legs and tight body, the strength in his shoulders.

"It's peaceful here," she says.

"Peaceful?" he calls out.

"Calm. No friction or lies. No barriers between us."

He wraps a towel around his waist and walks back to bed. "Just the biggest barrier of all."

She raises an eyebrow.

"Our cultures . . ."

"Do you think that's important?"

"My sweet, naive girl. Do you not see it? We fight. For survival, for land, for the right to be."

Genie sits up. "What are you saying, who's 'we'?"

He kisses her and pulls her onto him, encircles her, so she loses the ability to move.

She struggles halfheartedly, tries to escape him. "Why would you be fighting?" She struggles more. "Are you with Syrian Intelligence, like they say?"

He releases her, leans back on his elbow and looks her in the eye. "THEY? They also say 'believe nothing of what you hear and half of what you see,' the Middle East is full of rumor and intrigue." He gently cups her cheek with his palm, pushes her hair aside, kisses her neck, moves slowly toward her ears.

"Seriously Karam, what's going on?" she breathes heavily and struggles to continue. "Are you involved in any of this chaos?"

"We are involved, all of us. If we live on the earth we cannot avoid involvement simply because we are here," he kisses her eyes and mouth, buries his face into her hair and breathes heat onto her scalp. She resists for only a moment, it's impossible to focus.

"Did you know not so long ago all of this land belonged to Syria?"

She pulls the sheet around herself and over her head, Arabic style. *Many Lebanese wouldn't agree with you,* she thinks, but she remains silent.

"When I was at University in Turkey, the Syrian students protested about the 6-day war, so I hired a bus. We were young, believed we should fight for our country. I rose early the next morning for our departure, I waited and waited. Not one student appeared. Most people are full of talk, but when it comes to it . . ." he stops and sets the chessboard on the bed. He has Genie's full attention, he is rarely this forthcoming. He leans toward the pieces. "Tactics change but not strategies."

What do you mean? She asks.

"Cash. Lots of it, supposedly to help the Palestinians, comes from overseas and goes to the pockets of the leaders. They live well but sacrifice their people who never see a penny of it. The people are pawns. You see how they continue to live?"

He takes a black Queen and looks at Genie. "It is whispered they bribed the leader of the Lebanese Army with twenty-five million dollars, they took over the army barracks and expelled the Christian soldiers."

He holds the Queen and knocks white knights across the board.

"Lebanese once welcomed fleeing Palestinians with open arms, gave them several refugee camps outside the city. Now the city has grown, the camps have a stranglehold, and the Palestinians grow militant. They are no longer welcome."

He circles the black pawns around the White Queen.

"After a quarter century as refugees, they have finally lost patience and hope. They have armed and joined dissidents worldwide. It is hard to see the real players, it will not end soon, and it remains to be seen who will be left standing. Like Jordan, a state within a state, and the Lebanese are not happy."

She has heard much of this before from others. *Everyone knows the problem but no-one sees a solution,* she thinks

He pulls her down beside him, abandons the lesson.

She breathes in his aroma, a blend of soap and sweet musk that is Karam, deliberately and willingly she loses herself. After the weeks of solitariness and detachment, she embraces the human contact, their physical compatibility; remarkable, instantaneous and satiating.

Afterward, they come—the words—tumbling out. Words of love and longing, of hopefulness, betrayal and dreams and possibilities, and so many, many maybes.

"I love you," he whispers.

Can it be? She closes her eyes and drifts into sleep.

An explosion shakes the windows, and she wakes with a start, gradually realizes where she is.

"Oh my God. It's almost morning."

Karam reaches out for her. "Stay. Don't leave."

"I can't stay. If we're serious, I have to talk to Rob. I don't want to be cruel and let him wonder what is going on."

"OK, tell him, but try to tell him soon."

She plants a kiss on his high forehead, throws on her clothes and runs home.

On the journey, her head is filled with questions. *What is happening and what just happened with the board game?* She realizes she's not sufficiently experienced to evaluate this affair, nor worldly enough to comprehend the larger picture at play in Lebanon. But she knows it's an increasingly dangerous place and this may be a dangerous game she has placed herself in.

Why is Karam so damned mysterious, why not be straightforward? she wonders.

As she tiptoes into their bedroom a last thin trickle of smoke rises from a pyrethrum candle in the doorway, a fan whirs quietly back and forth. In the half-light, Genie undresses, and in the pale glow of the moon, Rob watches her.

"You were a long time. I was worried."

Genie doesn't reply. He turns to the window, sees the moon struggle to escape from behind a cloud. Explosions, distant gunfire and tracer bullets light the sky.

"Genie. I know I've hurt you, I don't show my feelings, but I do miss you—a lot."

23

BEIRUT, LATE SPRING 1976

Final Battle for the Hotels and Pax Syriana

ON MARCH 17 HISTORY REPEATS itself with another back and forth battle for the hotel district. An all-out offensive in Beirut. They can do little but listen and watch as the beautiful city is torn apart.

They rarely see friends now, many have left. Stuart to Jordan, Jacqui is long gone to Jakarta, no further word of Roslyn. Without proper goodbyes, they have lost contact with so many.

Kourk remains his usual happy self, from time to time Genie and Rob are invited to eat with the family. Kourk's eyes sparkle when he plays with his two little ones, and Rubina watches calmly always with a doting smile on her face. They stay calm through all of this. *Trauma is nothing new to the Armenian people,* Rob supposes.

"On March 21 the Palestinian Liberation Organization, and other leftists beat the Phalangists in the Holiday Inn. They were intoxicated with success and began to celebrate. Then the Phalangists recaptured it," Kourk says.

Rob laughs, but Genie can't find humor in any of the stories these days.

The Holiday Inn! She thinks of the restaurant and bar, the fabulous view across the city which now makes it so desirable to the warring factions.

Over the next two days, they listen.

News Report: One hundred and fifty more are dead, three hundred wounded as Palestinians mount a counter-attack downtown, hoping to remove all Phalangists west of Martyr's Square. The Holiday Inn is recaptured. According to sources 65 militiamen escaped through passages, with seven dead bodies, including three young girls.

"It hardly seems any time since we sipped champagne there and enjoyed those treats from Victor," he says.

"The passing of an era," Genie says. "When I said it was an amazing vantage point I never imagined how it would be used. Now the view is of destruction and devastation," she sighs. "It was only open for a year, now enchantment has fled leaving a ghost to haunt the seafront of Beirut."

Still beautiful, the Mediterranean reminds of past days of privilege and peace, but no-one looks or remembers.

Rob hardly goes to work, and when he takes the risk, he stays no more than a few hours. The city must be avoided at all costs, and the back roads are often impassable.

"Lebanese National Movement, (LNM) leftist militias, control strategic points around the center and now focus on the port area," Rob tells her. "The St Georges Hotel, the Phoenicia Hotel, and all other high rise buildings are under attack."

She is only half listening. *How will I see Karam?*

"With the loss of the Hotel district the Christians risk losing the war," Rob's voice cuts in.

And what will that mean for us? she wonders. Their former playground is a bloody battleground.

In the city, the fighting continues but at home, a quasi-truce between them remains in effect and to stop themselves going crazy they drive north to the town of Jounieh, which so far has remained stable and quiet. Here they can breathe without fear and shop for a few basics.

When they return from the moment of sanity Victor catches them. He looks surprisingly well, they have seen little of him lately, and he had been looking drawn since Damour.

"Pierre Gemayel appealed to supporters and now heads a force of more than eighteen thousand Phalange," he tells them happily.

The number surprises Genie. "They're growing, almost doubled since Mary first mentioned them to me."

"Come in, have a drink," Rob says.

Victor opens the car door for Genie. He kisses her cheek, grabs a bag of their shopping and walks with them, opens the downstairs door for her.

He continues. "They've seized The Hilton and Normandy Hotels, created a concrete barricade to keep control of the port." He relaxes and tries to make a couple of jokes.

Shades of how light and charming he used to be, Genie thinks. *Sad how things have changed.*

He empties his glass. "You realize control of the port is vital and strategic?" he asks. "It's a big deal."

Rob offers to replenish the drink, but he declines.

"I have to go, I have much to do."

Rob fills his own glass.

At the door Victor pauses. "Gemayel's men stopped the Lebanese National Militia and Palestinian advance, at Rue Allenby, and Syria threatens to cut arms shipments to the Muslim factions. Both sides now agree to a cease-fire."

"Great," Genie says. "Let's hope this one lasts."

"From your mouth to the ears of the Gods," Victor smiles and he's gone.

"How does he know so much?" Genie asks as they look out at the city. In spite of the cease-fire Victor mentioned, the smoke hasn't ceased. It should be quiet, but they still hear shelling, intense shelling.

Rob takes a long pull at his lager and shrugs. "Who knows and frankly who cares? But I do like hearing what's going on. Victor said Jumblatt protested, of course. The shelling you hear is between his lot and the Phalangist forces."

Victor's optimism pays off, and the Battle of the Hotels is essentially over. A new front line exists, Syria quickly seals the borders, blockades the ports and the Palestinians no longer receive armaments. With the backing of both America and Russia, the Syrians move men and weapons across the border and slowly a semblance of order returns.

The following day Rob tosses a copy of a newspaper onto the kitchen table.

"The Financial Times writes that the US and Israel have realized having Syria in Lebanon is preferable to an unstable potentially radical state. 'For the logic of a Pax-Syriana . . . is they will seek to control the activities of the Palestinians'" he reads. "Looks like they're here to stay."

"Maybe that's not so bad," she replies. "At least the fighting has stopped, and we can get out and about."

Maybe I can see Karam?

In continual flux, the port has become a means of generating private wealth and goods remain scarce, difficult to obtain. Beirut is now divided by what is known as the Green Line.

Rob takes his life in his hands by traveling into the heavily Muslim area to work, and she hasn't had the heart to leave or to talk to him while things remain such a challenge.

They have no political or religious affiliations yet looking as they do Rob and Genie would undoubtedly be regarded as partisan. Everyone is armed and skittish, and there's no way to know who is crazy enough to pull the trigger just because . . .

He struggles to continue production in spite of the varied things stacked against him, the challenge of an unskilled, disinterested labor force, reduced in size due to recruitment into one or another of the Muslim militias. Now, there's a new challenge—access to raw materials.

It's risky to traverse the Green Line dividing the city, the shuttle taxi avoids the area, and without her job, she has no justification for needing the car; thus she still has little access to Karam.

But gradually the Syrian influence is felt.

At work, Rob relaxes, feels a measure of control, and at home, they settle into an easy way of being friends. He doesn't push, the stress around them makes it easier to accept, even welcome, the lack of emotion at home.

"It remains subdued without Mark, but Adnan runs the factory and life plods on," he tells her. "Shana's very Irish, always with a story, and she brings down sweetmeats frequently. The kids no longer attend school, I guess she needs periodic escapes."

She smiles and pours tea. "I made a lemon cake," she cuts a slice. "You could take some with you."

"I have a meeting at the Commodore Hotel after work on Wednesday. We could have a drink there afterward if you like?"

It's almost three weeks since Genie saw Karam and she jumps at the opportunity. She can go in a little early and meet him for coffee on Hamra.

A smile forms when he sees her and widens as he watches her walk toward him. She sits opposite and runs her eyes over his face.

"You look beautiful," she says.

He laughs. "That should be my line. Have you told him?" Karam asks as he adds honey to his tea.

She shakes her head.

"I understand it must be difficult."

She feels his disappointment. She reaches across the table, touches his fingers, he curls them around her own.

"We take our lives in our hands every day now, Genie, and I just want to spend time together, before it is too late."

It is a salutary notion, the time could come when it will be too late.

"I long for you, Karam, I do, but this is so hard."

"I want to reach out and touch you when I wake and at night. I never thought I would feel these things."

"Just a little longer," she says.

The Commodore has become the rendezvous for most of the remaining expats and journalists who now launch themselves from this watering hole. When they get to the bar they bump into David, he has aged and is no longer dapper and trendy. He adorns a bar stool drowning his sorrows.

They heard his beloved Marvin was killed during the recent battles, not while protesting, merely caught in random crossfire.

"I've been offered a position in the far east," David says. "But I can't bring myself to go. So far I haven't had the heart to accept he's gone forever, can't get around to saying goodbye."

Genie can see David's heart is broken. She hugs him, he is thinner now, and she fears he may never recover.

"How are you surviving?"

"Now the school is gone I manage on a few odd teaching jobs. There are still some private students whose families want to start a new life elsewhere and will need English. Even so, I have to choose my students carefully."

"We're always around for you, David, if you can make it over to us," she says. But she knows it probably won't happen, and this could be another final farewell.

8 May 1976 "Happy Birthday to you, Happy Birthday to you," Genie sings into Rubina's telephone. "Happy birthday to you," she finishes. "No, Mumma, of course, I couldn't forget? It's the same date every year, isn't it?" she laughs. "I wish I could be there."

At the other end of the telephone in England, she can hear as her family celebrates her mother's forty-eighth birthday, a sharp pain stabs through her. I miss them, she realizes.

"Send her birthday greetings from us," Kourk mouths. She passes on the message and puts down the phone.

"Did you see Syria got their candidate elected?" Kourk asks. "He lost by just one vote in 1970, because Kamal Jumblatt switched sides at the last minute, but he's now our President-elect," he tells her. "What can you be do?" he shrugs. "Patience pays off."

"Perhaps this will bring calm? An end to the conflict."

His thunderous expression in his usually cheerful face tells her more than his words could convey. He has no illusions and almost no hope of an end to the conflict.

Tired of Waiting

Finally, after two more weeks and tired of waiting, Karam comes to call. She is not thrilled he took such a risk, either personally as a Muslim in this area, or because Rob still does not know of the affair and she wants to tell him in her own way.

Karam has borrowed a car and, as it happens, today Rob has gone to work. Karam won't take no for an answer, and he agrees to drive down the hill to Antelias to wait if she will take the next taxi and meet him within an hour.

They grab the opportunity to get out of town and head into the hills away from the mess to the Bekaa valley, ignoring the trucks and dated cars making headway through the dirt and chaos on the main highway.

"Maybe we should make a run for the border?" he half-jokes.

But they both know this is impossible. There has been no talk about the future. There's a keen, shared awareness that Genie or Karam could be gone tomorrow. For the moment there is a silent recognition that living in this moment is all they have, maybe all they will ever have.

A wrong step, the wrong place, a sniper, a rocket, even a crumbling piece of masonry. Their existence has a fragility and a fatality to it, a thousand ways to die.

She sometimes thinks about going home, but, like Rob, Karam won't leave, and she won't leave him, not now. Their mood lifts with each mile between them and Beirut, and he points out a sign for a small remote restaurant.

"It's my treat today! Let me order?" she says.

He smiles and opens his hand to allow her entry. "By all means," he says and follows her into the rustic interior.

"Grenouille?" she reads. Neither of them knows what it is.

Genie signs with her hands "Is it fish?" She places two hands together and "swims" them through the air. Their waiter nods then shakes his head. She looks at Karam who is highly amused and continues to observe without comment. Another waiter makes a quacking sound. "Oh. duck!" She flaps her hands like wings. "I love duck, yes, oui, Sukran," she says and turns to Karam. "Would you like duck, too?"

"No." He shakes his head. "I would prefer steak."

She orders and sits back.

He pours glasses of Arak. "I could have asked them in Arabic, but it would not have been nearly as amusing," he says.

"Well, you see I managed. I'm a great mime! Do you think we could get Lebanese wine? Chateau Musar, maybe?"

He laughs. "We're lucky to get Arak or even water in these times."

They're the only customers in this small family affair and conversation is self-conscious as their waiter hovers. The chef, however, does a speedy job and soon Karam tucks into his steak. He pauses. Genie stares at her plate.

"What is it?" he asks.

"My thoughts exactly." A plate filled with large limbs in sauce has been put in front of her. "Quack?" she asks the waiter.

A young girl comes out of the kitchen and looks at the plate. "Non, Madame," she says "Ribbet, ribbet!"

Karam bursts out laughing. "Frogs legs."

She smiles, the staff leave and she leans across the table. "The frogs would be enormous, with legs this size I'd be able to ride them!"

As they wait for coffee he takes a slightly crumpled newspaper from the next table. "It says the US recognizes the constructive role of the Syrians," he says. "You see. We have become useful."

"That's true. Syria seems like a parent trying to control naughty children," she agrees. "Without their intervention, we'd still be trapped in our homes."

"I thought this, too. It has not been easy to achieve."

She looks at him, about to speak.

"Enjoy your Grenouille," he smiles. His face has that closed off look again. He wants no questions. No more will be said.

On Thursday, May 27 Rob comes home with worrying news.

"Kamal Jumblatt's sister has been assassinated. Armed men broke in, shot and killed her and injured her two daughters."

"That means trouble," Genie says. "Their family is no stranger to violence. They assassinated the father when Kamal was four."

"You're right, this is bad," Rob agrees. "Hard to imagine but Jumblatt controls over 70% of Lebanon now, between his own and twelve other leftist groups. He's merged them into the Lebanese National Movement (LNM)."

He sighs with pleasure as he sits down to dinner. Genie has prepared a Shepherd's Pie and a variety of vegetables, but his eye has already caught sight of a Lemon Meringue Pie on the counter. THE dessert, his favorite, which she makes only rarely. She says her fingers bleed as she grates the fresh lemons, and he is surprised she wants to give him such a treat these days.

He finishes a second helping of pie, scoops all of the potato from the edge of the dish, and takes the last of the vegetables.

"Last August he was in favor of significant reforms, abolishing the quota system which favors Christians. Now he challenges the government's legitimacy."

His appetite hasn't suffered through all of these difficult and often dark days, she notices, and she smiles. She is hoping to create a nice mood so she can amicably discuss the future with him. Karam has convinced her they need to be together, soon.

"Two months ago he swore if the President didn't resign they'd continue the revolution till they seized power." He pushes his empty plate aside. "How the worm turns. It was his single vote that put the guy back in office."

"That was six years ago, meantime we've regressed a cen-tury or more." Genie makes coffee and puts a slice of the dessert on Rob's plate.

"They're a major ally of the Palestinian Liberation Orga-nization, and Syria doesn't like him or his Communist ideas," he says, his mouth full of meringue. "The guys at work reckon Syria doesn't want a collapse of Christian Lebanon with that lot on their border fomenting trouble."

"You don't think they had anything to do with it?"

He shrugs, finishes eating and turns to her. "That was so wonderful, Genie. I had the most dreadful day today, you can't know how much better you've made it. Thank you."

And so she says nothing,

Three days later an avalanche of missiles and shells again lands on Beirut. Bombings reach the airport and runways close to traffic.

News report: June 1, 1976, Approximately two thousand Syrian soldiers and six hundred supporters have intervened in the north against the Army of Arab Lebanon.

"I can't listen anymore. I'm going down to the market."

The tanks come, an endless column weaving and threading through the Bekaa Valley to the east. Man and machine deter-mined to quell the chaos.

She finds mangoes, grapes, broccoli and other treats for her sheep Baahleb. *He has become my confidante*, she thinks, *a little one-sided, but he always listens.*

As she and Rob leave the next morning, she takes down a mango and some zucchini. Baahleb knows her now and walks over to greet her, or maybe to get the gifts she brings. Either way, she is happy to pat him and briefly tell him of her problems. He nuzzles and bleats in response. Responding to Rob's toot, she runs to the waiting vehicle.

Along the road to Rob's work, a thundering noise shakes the car, open-mouthed Rob looks over at Genie.

The Syrians are here.

Along the coast road, an unending convoy of Syrian tanks trundles relentlessly from the north toward Beirut. Genie and Rob are living out the daily news.

The procession pays no attention to the small green car, but they are witness to twelve thousand regular Syrian troops on the move, focused on their mission—occupying Lebanon.

Now they have the opportunity to deal with Palestinians, leftist militias, Sunni extremists as well as any anti-Ba'athists sheltering in the country.

Silently Genie and Rob observe the advance of the soldiers as they turn the car off the coast road to drop Rob at work.

The smell of Polyethylene being processed tells him today the factory is operational. He's thankful.

"Look, do you want me to take you home?" he asks. "Maybe it's not wise to go to town today?"

She shakes her head. "Actually, perhaps this will make it safer."

"Well, be careful. I don't know what all this is going to mean to us. I'll only work till two."

For the first time in weeks, he reaches over to peck her cheek. Shocked, she doesn't react. He gets out, and she heads back to town.

I should have told him, she thinks. *He seems to feel things are on the mend. But it's hard to find the right moment. You're an emotional coward,* she tells herself.

When Rob walks through the door, it's mayhem, abuzz with news of the Syrian arrivals.

"They're driving along the coast now," Rob says "Genie, and I just passed them. Thousands of them."

Adnan turns his glum face to him. "In fact, a contingent has already stopped at Abbad's mother's hotel, they've billeted there."

Rob struggles to imagine the beautiful beachside residence, a semi-private oasis, now being taken over and inhabited by soldiers like the rough ones he has just passed.

"They've poured out all the bottles of liquor. Poured them onto the floor because it is against their religion. What a waste," Shana says.

"What about Abbad and his mother?" Rob asks.

Adnan shakes his head sadly. "She has left to Paris. Says she will never come back . . ."

"Abbad has also abandoned the beachside home," Shana says,

Shana's voice cuts in. "They're burning mattresses. Why would they do such a thing?" She is disturbed by the unnecessary waste and destruction.

Discussion of the foreign invasion leads seamlessly to the recent confusing political developments. A former banker was elected President a month ago, but the current leader refuses to leave office, an insane stalemate.

"It's almost certain Syria's Al Assad has chosen the new man," Adnan says. "In fact, it was so dangerous the Assembly couldn't vote at the traditional place."

He turns on the photo-spectrometer and shoves in a small piece of plastic material.

"Imagine terrified lawmakers dragged through barrages of mortar and machine-gun fire to some polling place they don't recognize." Adnan puts his eye to the machine "Twenty-nine of them vetoed the proceedings," he adds with a smile.

Rob finds it hard to keep track of it all. "I thought Damascus supported the Palestinians?"

"They did, but now Assad's broken away from them," Adnan says quietly. "I hear they're more concerned about keeping goods flowing from the port. They don't like having enemies so close, plus there's always their belief this was once their land. Who can know the future?" He leaves the thought in the air.

Rob puts on his white Lab coat and sits at his desk. *It's exhausting trying to follow the myriad changes and to hold onto each vanishing hope for things to improve.*

"It's whispered Israel has supplied advisers, weapons, and tanks since early May, so it could be argued they are on the same side. Insanity! Mark talked about La Vie Libanese, it's never dull," Adnan chuckles to himself as he breaks for coffee and together they sip the hot sweet liquid and enjoy Shana's pastries.

Adnan turns to Rob "They whisper there are mercenaries in the trees behind your home" he says. "Libyans I hear, and perhaps others. They're training up there."

"Oh My God, that's all I need! Genie will have a fit. She already thinks it's time to go."

Foolishly, he doesn't tell her.

Karam's happiness is obvious. He won't explain, pretends he doesn't understand when she questions him. But she can feel his energy. He opens his arms wide and takes her face between his hands as he kisses her.

Their meetings are brief now, and they are never sure when the next will be, but it adds a "frisson," a layer of excitement. Karam agreed he will no longer encourage her to tell Rob, will trust her judgment and wait till things calm down.

"I only have three or four hours, we drove in together, and it's safer to pass with a man these days near the Museum. We have to go the back way."

"Voila!" He turns her around and like a magician pulls a cloth off the table to reveal a remarkable variety of Syrian specialties. A whole fish smells sensational covered with caramelized onions and fragrant spices. Lamb kebabs speckled with parsley and garlic sizzle beside a platter of rice and a Mediterranean salad.

"I bring you—a taste of Syria," he says displaying the array of dishes.

Eyes wide, she stammers "Where—How?"

"Eat." He pulls her to a chair and loads food onto a plate.

"I'm impressed."

He offers a fork laden with kebab, and she is silenced. "I could hardly wait for you to get here. These fragrances were almost too tempting," he says, as he joins in the feast. "My cousin came from Aleppo and brought so many treats," he beams.

This is a serious man who is unaccustomed to smiling, but now he almost purrs.

After weeks of deprivation, the taste and memories stirred by these foods make them aware, for a fleeting moment, that another parallel but entirely different life exists beyond the borders.

He no longer bends over holding his abdomen, there's been a dramatic reduction in his use of alcohol. Around them, the world falls apart, but he looks great. He confesses that since he cannot get to work every day, he is writing a novel. He's secretive about it, but she has no doubt this is a great decision.

They finish their repast and lazily make love, both of them too full to expend much energy.

"Maybe we should have tried this first?" he laughs "But I confess the food was even more tantalizing than you!"

She throws a small punch at him and laughs. "It was delicious, but now it's gone, and I'm still here. I will tantalize you long after this meal is just a memory!"

24

BEIRUT, EARLY SUMMER 1976

Secrets and Lies

ROB STILL DOESN'T TELL HER, not even on June 6 when he gets confirmation that Syrian, Algerian, Palestinian and Libyan commandos have arrived via Damascus into their area.

He thinks she has lost her source of information now Mary has gone.

After the loss of their child, Mary and Nabil's house has been abandoned, the bombed-out car stands outside, witness to the catastrophe. They have asked around, but Victor retains a mysterious silence on the subject, no-one knows where they've gone.

A few days later, a leading Russian delegate visits Damascus, confirms Russian support to Syrian President Assad, wishes him success, and any initial hesitation evaporates. Syria now feels free to attack.

Syrian forces apply a blockade of largely Muslim West Beirut, including the Palestinian HQ.

If she wants to see Karam, she must travel with Rob to the factory then via back streets into the part of town where he lives. It is increasingly dangerous and makes for limited excursions and a blight of information.

News report: Kamal Jumblatt's Progressive Arab Front has fought fiercely repelling Syrian tanks.

Rob turns down the radio. "Forty thousand Syrian soldiers are in Lebanon, and it looks like they'll quash Kamal Jumblatt's forces."

"Forty thousand?" she tries to visualize the number as uniformed men.

He finishes eating breakfast. *Nothing gets between the man and his stomach*, she thinks.

"Stay home, violent clashes are reported in the mountains, dozens of attackers have been killed," Genie says.

"I'll be fine," he says, but he shows no sign of leaving. "It's unsafe for you to go out alone, though," he looks at her, holds her gaze and for a moment she wonders. *Does he suspect something?*

She holds her breath, should she speak, confess?

He looks away. "There are too many checkpoints. I can hardly keep up."

She takes a breath. It's true, in town the Green Line is like Berlin's Checkpoint Charlie. More than a year from the start of the conflict and they can't move freely.

He flicks through the English language paper. "What a week," he says. "Protests in Poland, they've almost doubled the price of food. Protests in South Africa, the government has attacked thousands of demonstrating students. So, it's not just here," he says.

"No, it's not just here. But we," Genie emphasizes we, "are not in those other places."

He pours another coffee and turns up the news, but the radio isn't encouraging:

News Report: Syria has called for a joint Arab peacekeeping force. In the past twenty-four hours more than two hundred have been killed and three hundred wounded. One of the worst periods of the entire civil war.

"How can they say that?" she asks. "Have they forgotten how many died on Black Saturday?"

"I guess they figured it wasn't officially a civil war at that point," he says and picks up his keys.

"You're not going?" she asks.

"I've become an expert at the secret turnings, when to hide and wait, how to avoid trouble."

He leaves.

He's mad, I'm telling him tonight, and that's that.

At work there is no guard at the gate, it's silent. This is unheard of, and he's apprehensive.

"What now?" he mutters. He parks and looks around. No workers, no sound of machinery. He sniffs, no smell of hot plastic in the air. He looks through the lab window.

Shana is inside with Adnan, and he has his arms around her, they both look upset. Shana has red eyes and a puffy nose. Rob is surprised to see her without her cheerful smile and greeting.

She sees him and bursts out. "Gunmen have broken into the boss's summer home in the mountains." She stops, takes a deep breath and continues in a small voice. "They've killed all of the cousins, even the maid, and the dog." Her sad eyes turn toward Rob amid a fresh batch of tears. "The little children were the same ages as ours, used to play together when we went there," Shana blows her nose.

"It's the middle of the week, and both bosses are in Paris, Allah be praised," Adnan says. It is unusual to hear him use the religious term. Adnan rarely shows his emotions making him a good negotiator, but today he's visibly upset as he recounts the events.

"His cousin's entire family were there—you met him at the Phoenicia, the happy young guy with the silver Aston Martin," Adnan says. "All dead now, even the little babes!"

First Keith, then Mark and James, now the family I work for. It sinks into his consciousness. *Violence is getting closer. The city is crumbling, there are occupation forces to keep the peace, nameless faces wander the streets with heavy weapons, and I take my life in my hands by coming here. What am I waiting for?*

Rob frantically evaluates this latest event, useless, pointless deaths, he struggles with the inability to understand why.

"I think we may have to consider leaving," he says. "You guys should think about it, too." He turns to Adnan who has an arm on Shana's shoulder.

"I'm sorry, maybe the Syrian's will improve things, but for us, for Shana and the kids, this area is a poison chalice, and we're all targets."

Even while he speaks the words, he knows he may not tell Genie—not yet.

When Genie calls Shana the following day with birthday greetings for her little boy, she is shocked to hear the news that Rob decided not to share.

"Thank you, Shana." She puts down Rubina's phone.

Why didn't he tell me? It is inexcusable. How dare he decide what I should or shouldn't know. Her head reels. The beachside hotel is occupied, mercenaries in the woods behind their home, now a massacre of the family at their home.

She glances out of Rubina's doorway, peers uphill through the tall windows in the stairwell.

Are they there? Are they staring at me from between the trees? Her skin crawls. She sees nothing but feels a presence, something malevolent, watching and waiting. Probably her imagination. She remembers the carnage of the past year and her knowledge of what men can do in times of war.

So it's come to this? she thinks. Rubina watches her.

"Are you ok, would you like water?" Rubina says.

He thinks he has the right to decide for me in matters of life and death. She feels a dark cloud roll down the hillside, it encompasses her. It's inconceivable he would NEVER mention these events to her. If she had any doubts, they are gone, this is the final straw.

"Water would be nice, Rubina. Could I just make one more call."

June 16, 1976, The Decision

"Welcome, Ambassador," the driver says as he ushers him into an Embassy car, he opens another door and the Economic Adviser, climbs in.

He buckles into the driver's seat and glances into the rear view mirror as he speaks.

"To reach the President it will be necessary for us to cross the Green Line today, so please don't be concerned if we are stopped at a roadblock in town," he says. "No danger is expected."

The US Ambassador looks at his associate, this last remark seems unusual but as they leave the Embassy compound an escort vehicle accompanies them, and this is Beirut, not some far-flung outpost.

The two Americans settle back for the short journey, they do not see the driver wave away the second car, effectively dismissing him, leaving them alone, abandoned.

In the opposite direction, a few miles along the coast, the journey home gives Rob time to consider the choices facing them. He's not in a hurry to get there, prefers time to evaluate things fully before he discusses them with Genie. He knows what her answer will be.

He has to collect a jacket from Kourk's dry cleaning store in Antelias and decides to stop off for a pint afterward, to gain some perspective.

The days of swinging into town to join buddies at the bar after their respective work day has long gone. He's wise enough to steer clear of the city now.

Chores finished he finds a seat at a pavement cafe, relaxes and raises the glass of golden liquid to his lips. Puffy white clouds float in the afternoon sky overhead and drift out over the Mediterranean. In one of the clouds he makes out the shape of a dove, it's soft, white wings spread wide. He marvels again at the beauty of the coastline.

"Shit," he says aloud. He realizes no matter how much his head tells him he should go, he doesn't want to leave yet. He wants to follow an orderly path. Finish his obligation here then on to his California dream. All in good time.

A few minutes drive away, before the formation of the Green Line made passage impossible, almost visible around the beautiful bay, three bodies are unceremoniously dumped onto a beach in Ramlet al Baida; coincidentally not far from Karam's home.

Karam puts away papers in a desk drawer, sets out a few wildflowers, opens another drawer to take candles from a large pile. Placing them in the Chianti bottles, which have re-formed wax stalactites into impressive works of art, he rests matches beside them, arranges food and pours two glasses of red wine.

As an afterthought, he changes the sheets on the bed and takes out two fresh towels.

And he waits.

As the late afternoon creeps into the evening, he fears she has been delayed or is perhaps not coming after all. It has been more than two weeks since they have been together, but she sounded so confident when she telephoned this morning. "One way or the other I'll be there this afternoon," she promised. "And this time I'm staying . . ."

He knows above all things she fulfills her promises, never takes a commitment lightly, so he tries to remain optimistic.

There's still time. He wonders what could have triggered this decision, nothing too dreadful he hopes, but he's encouraged. Now they can plan for the future.

It's impossible to predict when something will prevent a rendezvous these days, he knows, but he is reassured now Syria has finally stepped in.

In his neighborhood kids roam around taking pot shots. There's a hole in the wall of his apartment, luckily high enough to have missed him. *It will take time to control the lawlessness which has reached insane heights,* he thinks.

He goes to the window, there is little activity outside. No sign of Genie's green car.

In the rubble-strewn streets a lone courageous, or maybe desperate, cart holder sells lemons and oranges. It no longer looks familiar out there, gone is the elegance, it resembles a village in some blighted country.

A young boy rounds the corner. "Cigarettes. Rrrothmans, Maalborouh, Kent," he yells.

Karam runs down the stairs and chases the boy who has almost reached the end of the desolate street. He purchases a couple of packs and gives him a tip. The boy smiles and scurries on.

"Cigarettes Americain," he calls out as he disappears.

It's growing darker. Karam lights the candles, wondering why she has been delayed, he eventually eats.

The candles burn down, he stares till they almost disappear, he remains at the table, lights a cigarette and blows smoke circles up to the ceiling. Thoughts of what might be, fill his mind and he wonders how they will ever manage to resolve their problems, admittedly insignificant when viewed against the chaos which currently reigns, and the decisions which he needs to make.

The minutes tick by, and soon it's dark. Karam lets out a sigh, he scrapes leftover food into a bin and blows on the candles. Glancing one more time out of the window, he is sure something is different. It's silent outside. He finishes his cigarette—goes back into the street to discover what is happening.

"A cease-fire has been imposed," someone calls out.

Syrian tanks have taken strategic positions around the area, and the PLO seems to be out in full force. As he reaches the Corniche people wander about with a new alertness. There is still no light in most of the buildings, and the Lighthouse remains in darkness, but he can sense something from the people he passes.

Hope, or acceptance?

He briefly thinks things will return to normal. So why is she not here? he wonders, now concerned she is ok.

Refreshed, Rob gently rests his dry cleaning in the back of the car and heads into the hills to Naqqash. The music on the car radio stops, and he hears the broadcaster's serious tones as he announces:

President Gerald Ford spoke at 4:05 p.m. to reporters at the White House, the following is a recording of that speech

The Assassination of our Ambassador in Beirut, and of our Counselor for Economic Affairs, and their driver is an act of senseless, outrageous brutality. The United States will not be deterred in its search for peace by these murders. I have instructed Secretary Kissinger to continue our intensive efforts in this direction, to get in touch with all of the governments in the area and with Lebanese leaders to help identify the murderers and to see they are brought to justice. That is the way we can best honor the brave men who gave their lives for this country and for the cause of peace.

It's impossible to imagine they'd kill such a high ranking American diplomat!

Nausea creeps over him as Rob is forced to accept that if he wants to live, there is no way to justify staying here. The truth crushes him, fate has made the decision.

Genie hums to the soft sounds of Alfred Deller's "If music be the Food of Love."

It is the first thing he hears, the melancholic strains compliment Rob's mood. He stares at her suitcase again in the hallway and walks out toward the terrace, collapses into a seat and looks off to the ocean.

The view never gets old but there's a new dreadful and palpable sadness about him, he is a lost soul. *Why did I wait?*

Genie approaches quietly, she heard him come home, and now she senses his despair. She pours tea for each of them and offers him a cup. "Rob, we need to talk."

"I've been blind."

She sucks in her breath. *So this is it. He knows.*

"Look I'm sorry but . . ." she says.

"No. I'm the one who's sorry," he interrupts. "It's taken me all this time. I've been so fixated on my career, on what it would mean if I failed. I thought you were disloyal always wanting me to leave, but you've been right all along," he holds out his hands. "Let's leave. Go home."

"What?" Did she hear it correctly? Something mammoth must have taken place for this switch. In shock, she considers her reply. "What's happened?"

He pauses, tries to gather his thoughts. After all the secrets what can he say? He begins to speak but is drowned out by the squeal of tires.

Gunshots echo.

In unison, they rush to the rear window. Below, in the cul de sac, a heavily armed, gun-truck screeches to a halt. Manned by four men in military gear, a flag flutters on the front, a series of geometric shapes, suggesting a green cedar tree on snowy white, the flag of the Lebanese Phalangist party.

Genie peers through the window as a swarthy man points up at their apartment.

"I think you may have blown it. It may be too little, too late."

It's too late for me, too, she realizes.

25

Captivity Begins

FOR MORE THAN HALF AN hour the truck struggles to find a satisfactory parking place. Voices shout opposing directions, and the vehicle goes back and forth.

Even this they fight over, she thinks.

Fumes belch as each new voice offers a fresh option. Finally, they stop.

"Either the driver is fed up, it's time for a coffee, or they agree this is the best spot to be had," she says.

"How can you be so cavalier?" he asks.

"If they'd wanted to kill us they'd have come in, guns ablaze."

The driver and his co-pilot clamber to join the others and between them valiantly maneuver the rocket launcher to point upward, after more intense discussion the back of their apartment is in the line of fire. Two men jump off and head into the building.

"Shh!" Rob grabs Genie—pulls her out of view.

She pulls her arm away. Strangely she is more curious than frightened.

Hidden, they silently watch the men enter. One holds the tip of his nose, blows its contents onto the ground as he passes.

"Ugh, how disgusting," she mutters and heads to the front door. Unconsciously she lifts a hand to tidy her hair, faces the closed double doors and waits. But no-one comes.

"What are they doing?" she whispers.

Like the wait for a delayed flight—minutes drag. Rob maintains vigil at the window, but the men have settled and are concerned with lighting a fire, a small, open-hearth affair in a clearing below, near the trees.

"What do you suppose is going on?" he whispers. The words leave his mouth at the same instant the doorbell rings.

Genie jumps, and they glance at each other, fear grips her and concern connects them for the briefest of moments.

"Don't answer it," he whispers.

It rings again. Genie notices, for the first time, it is a startling sound. On tiptoes, she peers through the peephole. Rob grabs for her, but again she pulls free. She expects to see an ugly man holding a gun but instead a distorted image of Rubina looks up at the spy hole in the door. With no reply, she turns to leave.

"It's Rubina. She's alone," Genie whispers and slowly cracks open the door to peer out.

Rubina glances back, stops on the stairs. "You're in bad trouble." She looks at Genie and Rob silhouetted in the doorway.

"They say you should have paid, now they will take you if you try to leave. Everyone MUST pay, like all of us."

She turns, comes back to them, seems overwhelmed and breathes a loud sigh of defeat.

"They're serious now. Look what happened to your doctor friend." She shakes her head sadly takes Genie's hand in hers. "I'm so sorry, but there is nothing we can be do for you. We want no trouble. They forbid us to help, we have children, we must to think of them."

She walks away and again stops, her eyes glisten. "You must not come to our door. They watch, come to us without warning—on many days."

Genie softly closes the door, she feels the warm breath from Rob's loud sigh of relief.

"Well, we're still alive, no guns firing, maybe there's space to make a plan." He ambles inside, pours a brandy, swallows it, pours another and sits with the bottle open in front of him. His mood darkens as the bottle empties, and his optimism disappears.

The apartment fills with loud Arabic music from below. A few months ago Genie would have welcomed it, now it's a reminder they are strangers in this land, and potential danger waits, a few floors away.

They don't turn on lights, and gradually deep darkness permeates the apartment, it matches the dark dread in their hearts.

Genie shivers. "Now what?" she wonders aloud.

"You tell me. You refused to pay. This is your doing."

Is he right? Is this my fault? She doesn't think so. *They are thugs and how could we possibly collude with them after the dreadful things they've been doing?* She ignores him.

The night deepens, and haunting music continues to waft up from the gun truck, softer now. The men smoke, occasionally one glances upward, but they have made a camp, and there is no indication this will be a short siege.

They are trapped.

Genie looks toward the city and imagines Karam in the far distance. *How will he know what has happened, why I haven't gone to him as promised?* Instead of resting tonight in loving arms she will stay here with Rob, nursing her secret until who knows when?

Rob knows he reached his decision too late, but in his frustration, he blames Genie for the mess they are in. To understand what's going on around them and what choices, if any, there are, he listens to the radio continuously, it's a lifeline.

It crackles:

US President Ford's Personal Representative will go to Damascus to accompany the bodies of the slain American officials to the United States. Chairman Arafat, the Palestinian leader, has arrested eight individuals. He offers to hand them to the Arab League but will not hand them over to the USA.

No word passes between them for two days. They search the "what ifs" of the past months, and alone re-evaluate their lives and how it came to this.

In a daily ritual, Genie makes morning coffee and in the afternoon dinner, but she places Rob's on a tray, takes it to the coffee table, and she sits alone at the kitchen table. They avoid one another, delaying open hostility, but it permeates the air.

He feels helpless, on some level wants to reach out, hold her like he used to. *But she's been such a bitch for so many weeks now and has resisted all attempts to make things right,* he thinks. *All right I hurt her, but for how long is she going to hold on to her anger over Istanbul? I can't un-ring the damned bell, for Christ's sake, and she's done her fair share of flirting.*

The seventh day. She marks a circle on the calendar.

In this time God created the world and was ready for a Sabbath day of rest. In contrast, we passed six days of idleness, six days of life we will never get back.

She wonders how soon someone will notice they are missing, asks questions, perhaps attempt a rescue?

Rob faces the ocean, she passes the lounge where he sits, zombie-like. The week has been hard on him, she thinks. His escape is the radio and the bottle. The latter used to be a social pastime, a pint or two with friends and on special occasions green chartreuse, a pretty, but in her view unpleasant, herbal drink. Now she worries at the quantity he consumes regularly.

Another week and she attempts tentative communication, tries to draw him into a discussion of their plight, but he isn't interested in conversation, prefers a liquid escape.

In the first few fuzzy moments after waking, she indulges the fantasy that she'll open her eyes and find herself elsewhere. It's a game she plays. Each morning she imagines a different, far away place. Sometimes sand and sunshine, sometimes umbrellas and rain, but always, always, there's peace and freedom.

Slowly she opens her eyes, but like all the other days, she's still here.

The days, weeks, maybe months, stretch in front of them, and she wonders how they will cope.

Asleep in the other bed Rob snores softly. *Well, no point dwelling on things that can't be changed,* she tells herself.

"It's been two weeks. Someone must notice soon and send help." She reaches over and lowers the retractable lamp, which he has pushed high into the ceiling.

He glares at her. "Put on some bloody clothes."

He pours the remaining wine into his glass, takes a long swallow, turns away and switches on the radio.

News Report: Sunday, June 27, 1976. Beirut International Airport was heavily bombed. A Howitzer blasted a 30-foot hole in the roof of the crowded terminal building where hundreds were trying to flee the civil war. A Middle East Airlines Boeing 707 was hit, killing the pilot. There were no further casualties.

They eat little, and the week passes. Alcohol is Rob's sustenance, and she has no appetite, can't face food. *The food supplies will last longer like this,* she thinks.

A diary helps her stay sane, sometimes she glues cuttings from happier times into her scrapbook, but the sound of the radio is ever present, fills the apartment, and she wishes she could avoid hearing the news.

News Report: Right-wing Christian forces warn they will close the airport by 'whatever means they judge appropriate' unless guaranteed leftist armaments won't come in. In Damascus three planeloads of Sudanese troops, in Saudi planes, join peacekeeping units.

They call the invading armies peacekeepers. What a joke, They're certainly not here for peace.

"The British Consulate has shut up shop," he says.

"Like it or not we're in this together and alone—until the end." She looks at him, but he has already turned away.

She sighs. They are stuck with each other, two people who would rather be with anyone else in the world.

> News Report: The airport briefly opened under the protection of Libyan and Syrian forces, long enough for the US envoy to arrive. Middle East Airlines is the only carrier serving Beirut but now all incoming flights have been diverted after the recent terminal hit, it has closed indefinitely.

The announcer seems to take a breath before continuing:

> All forms of telecommunication are gone, and a dangerous trip by road to Damascus remains the only possible escape. Beirut is cut off from the outside world.

"My God!" She glances across at Rob to gauge his reaction, but there isn't one.

"Cut off from the outside world! That's devastating. No-one will know whether we're alive or dead."

No response.

They flinch, sometimes actually jump from the fierce battle which rages for six straight days outside, and Rob no longer relishes the news, but he cannot resist listening.

In the distance, heavy artillery, rockets, and machine guns fire, near the Palestinian refugee camps and along what she imagines is the two-mile Green line.

She looks out over the hillsides and streets that separate her from Karam. *How are you, my love? Are you even alive?*

The broadcaster's voice breaks in:

News Report: The refugee camp of Tel al-Zaatar, home to 20,000 Palestinian refugees continues under siege. The situation is considered dire.

She knows this once well-defended stronghold is in enemy territory and the weeks' old blockade prevents the supply of water and food.

She shudders. "Imagine those parents and children facing starvation. They're in worse shape than we are."

He ignores her.

News Report: Today, July 5, 1976, The PLO and their allies launched an offensive against the north. The Iraqi news agency reports Syria strengthened forces in Lebanon with an infantry regiment and an armored brigade to the Bekaa Valley. Rightist militias have resisted an attempt to take Beirut's harbor and Martyrs' Square.

She sits cross-legged on the couch, from lowered eyes she watches him. He's so full of resentment, he has swallowed the smiling, handsome boy she married.

What did I ever see in him? She wonders. *Whatever it was is long gone.*

"This is a nightmare Rob, but if we could face it together, it would be much easier. If we could talk, encourage each other."

"You created the nightmare, talking won't fix it." He refills his glass.

Well, that told me! He won't discuss it, but if the men come through the door, if we have to face an attack, I'm going to use the machine gun. I won't go out begging and crying. I'll fight. I'll be shot—and it'll be over.

On some level, she can't imagine death, but when she tries to consider it, she knows it is better for her than being hurt or sexually attacked. *The machine gun was a smart purchase,* she thinks. She feels a small measure of control in this out of control situation.

Mid-July—Slow—slow weeks. It's hard to read, to concentrate, but she has kept her diary and found a handful of crosswords in old papers, even tried to invent a couple. Rob works at reducing the stock in his "cellar" and listens to the radio, but mostly they wait.

Another night falls, and she sits on the floor, dusts the Kalashnikov, it's become a routine. Illogically she finds this comforting, the knowledge that she has this and won't go willingly. She'd seen Margaret once after Keith's death, the ordeal changed her. The light was gone from her eyes, her hands permanently balled into fists, difficulty making eye contact, there probably wouldn't be enough years of living for her to be healed.

The apartment is plunged into darkness. Genie stops the rhythmic cleaning of the weapon, gets up, flicks the light switch on and off.

Nothing.

Without a word, Rob walks over and slowly, without optimism, tries the hall light. Nothing. He turns and noisily collides with the machine gun.

"Jesus. If they don't get me your bloody contraption will." He lights a cigarette and sits, silhouetted against the sky.

"Could it be a fuse?" she asks.

"No. It's another bloody mind game."

She replaces the gun in position, between the kitchen door and the powder room, lights a large fat candle and takes it with her to the bedroom. At the French windows, she hides the flame from an outside view, but she can't resist glancing out. The gun truck, black and ominous in the night, waits outside but the men are not to be seen.

The magnolia bends its head in the hall, wilted from lack of water, she misses the fragrance. Another massive explosion rattles the windows, and she jumps, the candle flickers, she licks her fingers, snuffs it out and shelters in her bedroom behind a closed door.

Alone in the dark room, she lets her thoughts run amok.

What innocents we've been, what fools. We came at life like small children, accepted it at face value but out in the world master manipulators stopped at nothing to achieve their goals. No-one and nothing was precious, they'd sacrifice friends, families and the community to create doubt and destruction over their opponents.

Mortar fire and tracer bullets zing across the distant skyline like a New Year celebration.

Some celebration! She floats back in time; can almost hear the bagpipes, the oriental dancers, the laughter. Another lifetime.

New Year—only one year ago—when they danced with their friends. Now they're all gone to the corners of the earth.

It's impossible to believe anything, to know anything, she thinks. *In comfortable hotels or apartments, men sit with mistresses, drinking, fornicating and never thinking about the carnage they create.*

She shudders, blows breath onto the window and slowly traces her initials on the misty glass. From the past, she almost hears her grandmother's voice. "Too much thinking tires the brain." Maybe she was right, dwelling on things could drive her crazy and anyway she can't do anything.

She thinks of Karam, whispers his name softly, "Karam." *How will he have reacted to the lack of contact, of news?* She remembers the chess game when he tried to explain things to her. She thought him cynical, but God is she wiser now, and for all the world she wishes she were not.

And what of him? Is the powerful attraction enough to cast aside her less than satisfactory marriage? Beyond that, is he actively involved politically as some suggested, and if so, on whose side? Is he an idealist? What a mess! She tells herself. *What Innocents—What Fools. I should never have stayed here.*

The announcer continues:

News Report: July 30, 1976, At this time all remaining US nationals are encouraged to leave. Many US citizens have gone to Damascus, the road has grown increasingly unsafe, and the PLO has offered protection, so far escorting 300 to a beach in Beirut. An American ship has arrived to take the last remaining citizens home. On July 27 all embassy staff and another 300 Americans were evacuated by sea. The embassy is now closed.

Rob is angry.

"Unlike our bloody Embassy." He goes to the French window. "Keep your heads down, they advised. Leave the windows open so the glass won't explode. Some help they were! Now it's too late. No-one even knows we're here." Rob turns away from the window and reaches for a bottle. "The Yanks regard every citizen as significant. More than you can say about our bloody lot."

There is nothing to see from the balcony, the city is quiet, but two more weeks of their lives have quietly slipped away, in two days it will be August.

One day at the end of my life I'll regret losing this time.

She has never been good at waiting, but now there is little else to do. But for what? For rescue? For the men below to grow tired and then . . . ?

Would they come inside to get us? Surely they wouldn't shoot at the building, Kourk and Rubina have paid their protection money.

She paces the length of the veranda, wonders why they are only being guarded on one side. From the ocean side, the hills fall away through the orange groves, and no-one seems to pay attention. *Perhaps they realize it is too high to escape? Maybe they're sending a message with the truck outside? Was the bombing at Nabil and Mary's a warning?* she wonders. *A lesson to the family, and to the whole region, that to refuse Phalangist demands was potentially fatal?*

The tantalizing smell of meat roasting at Kourk's floats up.

"God, I'm hungry." She closes the patio doors and heads to the room they call their "store," glances at the shelves lining one wall and regrets there is still a substantial supply of alcohol, set up when they happily accepted donations from friends returning home.

I wonder if we could handle things differently, pull together if he wasn't able to self medicate? she wonders.

She turns to the supplies of canned food purchased after the Qarantina disaster. She had tried to help the refugees, but now it is a Godsend for them.

Crackers and honey for breakfast with coffee or tea, and soup every day. Far from homemade but warm and filling and the crackers also work with her homemade pickles.

She opens the cupboard wide and looks in. Just ten cans of soup left. Five of tomato and five of mushroom.

Rob can have the mushroom, I never liked it, she thinks, as she takes two.

Six more cans of Mandarin oranges, six niblets of corn and ten cans of spaghetti, she takes out two of spaghetti, as well.

"Thank you Chef Boyardee," she kisses the can.

Rob hates this food, she understands his reaction, but she appreciates the feeling of a full stomach.

They eat dinner and by nine pm darkness has fallen.

Surprisingly she has been dozing, but a beautiful voice permeates the night, draws her to the window. Such beauty amid so much rage, hidden from view, a single female voice commands attention as she sings a melismatic tune. It briefly suspends Genie's consciousness of where they are. Fascinated she looks down and sees a couple of the men dance, others clap their hands. For a moment they seem more human, less threatening, and in spite of herself, she smiles.

A minute after the girl concludes her hypnotic song a radio blares out a fresh round of Arabic music. The men start to eat and spit. One goes across to Genie's car, unzips his pants and urinates on it. The other men laugh.

"Pigs." She mutters, all thoughts of their humanity gone.

Time drags, she is alone but prefers the solitude. It's hard to tolerate Rob's growing animus, his drinking helps lull him into long periods of sleep and so the weeks pass.

She misses Karam every day, wishes she could explain.

Sleep is elusive. Nights are not quiet, the sounds taunt Genie, refuse her escape. But eventually tonight, as always, she drifts into a restless sleep.

The French doors to the bedroom balcony shudder as another colossal explosion shakes them. There is no need for electricity as tracer bullets and rocket fire light the room. Crawling from the bed, Genie cannot resist peering out at the men below, like touching an aching tooth. One strikes a match, lights a cigarette.

Don't they ever sleep, she wonders.

He looks up.

She gasps, scurries out of sight and back to the safety of her metal bed.

In the morning when she goes through with coffee and crackers, the large couch in the lounge is vacant. Her once beautiful white settee carries an indentation from Rob's permanent residence. It waits for him to crawl back and curl up. Here he passes his days, and when tired he stretches out and goes to sleep.

For days and nights, he doesn't move from this spot, except to grab an occasional fresh bottle from the ersatz "cellar" he once was so proud of, and to occasionally use the bathroom. He attempts a liquid escape, but no matter how he might wish, he can't climb into any of the bottles.

There is no electricity, but Rob found an old transistor radio, it gives lousy reception, but at least he maintains contact with the world.

He sighs. Genie doesn't want to hear any more. She reaches over yet again to lower the lamp which he has pushed back high into the ceiling. He snorts. She grabs her diary and silently walks away.

She goes to the shower.

Sunlight pours through the high window and for an instant it's an ordinary day, anywhere. Water washes over her, sluices away the aches in her shoulders. She lifts her face to the warmth and feels more human as she lathers her hair, breathes in the fragrance of the shampoo, an earlier extravagance from her hairdressers before their business was bombed into oblivion.

The familiar perfume drifts her back to earlier times when it had all seemed perfect, and for this one moment her bathroom becomes a spa, she imagines the fingers of water is a firm hand massaging her, the aromatic steam fills her lungs, she relaxes. "So good."

A sputtering sound—and the water stops.

She shivers, dragged from her reverie back into the present. She's not in a spa, she's trapped in her apartment, covered in soap.

Shampoo runs into her eyes, and they sting as she fiddles uselessly with the taps, turns them on and off, praying that water will flow again. No luck.

With a deep sigh, she mops at her face, wiping the remaining shampoo from her eyes. With towels wrapped around her head and her body, she walks along the corridor to Rob who is in his usual position on the couch, guarding the bar.

"They've turned off our water."

Rob continues to sip at his drink. He ignores her.

The frustration rises in her voice. "Did you hear? We have no water," she pauses. "Remember last year the Sohat water company wanted increased sales, so a relative in government turned the city water off for a few days, do you think that's what's happening?"

In front of him the brandy bottle is balanced on its head— empty, and he nurses an almost empty glass of red wine from a half consumed bottle. He doesn't look at her. Through a line of empty bottles in varying colors and sizes the sun casts kaleidoscopic shades onto the marble floor. She glances down at the unusual design.

"Water? Who cares about water? You're going to get us killed so what does water matter?" he laughs, an ugly distorted sound as he stares into the space between them. "You always have to take a bloody stand, don't you? It'll be wooden overcoats for us."

"Don't you dare judge me. You wanted to come here, to stay here." Tears well up in her sore eyes. "If you could have lived with our money buying bullets to shoot our friends you should've said so. But no, you said nothing. You never say anything. It's your passive-aggressive way, so you don't have to take responsibility."

He finally looks at her. "What we need is gas to make a run for it."

"How could we run with those monsters down there? What we need is a plan of action."

They have become great consumers of time. Like money, it just goes, more than two months now. She pores over the selection in the bookcase. Rob looks up, he has calmed down since the recent outburst and has taken to sketching in the mornings, he looks out of the window and draws. They are pretty good, and it seems to bring him a measure of peace. The recent anger has subsided, they are too tired to fight.

"You must have read them all by now," he says.

"I have, and I read For Whom the Bell Tolls and The Magus twice, now believe it or not I'm reading the Bible."

"I didn't even know we had one."

When she carries in a tray of food in the afternoon, Rob is standing on the terrace shrouded in a blanket. She glances at him briefly, for the most part, they've stopped seeing one another, like fixtures which are necessary but not sufficiently attractive to garner attention.

It is late summer and has been hot and humid lately, so she wonders why he seems to feel the cold. He goes back to the couch, and she imagines it giving a sigh.

"After this, the only cheese left is a wedge of Parmesan and a half stilton," she says.

He takes a slice of pumpernickel bread, a gift which had lurked unopened for months, and a sliver of the stilton cheese he always enjoyed. He notices the reduced offerings on the tray and liberally adds rum to his coffee.

He signals Genie to listen to a static-filled BBC news broadcast on the old transistor radio. She doesn't want to be near him, but obediently she waits.

26
AUGUST 1976
Deprivation

ROB HAS MORE THAN A month's growth of stubble, almost a beard, and Genie's hair is lank and untidy. They look drawn, their faces are thinner. In spite of their best efforts, they feel unclean. The water hasn't come back on, and they collect drips from the taps, keeping the small supply in the bottles for drinking.

> News Report: August 12, 1976, the Tal al Zaatar camp has finally fallen.

They make it to another morning, She scavenges through the kitchen cupboard, hopes to find some lost or forgotten scrap of food hidden in the back, but without success.

> News Report: After fifty-two days of siege men entered through the sewers to explode the ammunition dump inside the camp. This lethal blow ended the siege, leading to heavy criticism of Syria from around the Arab world.

When he walks in the next morning, she has the radio on and has her faced buried in a tissue.

"During the evacuation of Tal al Zataar militia forces gunned down two thousand people. Many women were raped," she says.

He sits down beside her. Today for some reason he's polite as he listens to the news.

> News Report: August 13, 1976. Following a several month siege, the militias yesterday expelled the inhabitants and destroyed the Tal al Zaatar camp preventing any possibility of return. Many survivors have been resettled to the emptied Christian village of Damour, site of the January massacre.

"Waste not, want not," he says. "And so the world turns, sandcastles against the flood tide."

Shocked by his apparent detachment, she turns it off. "What's the point in torturing ourselves? We can't do anything."

He has grudgingly accepted that her plan to flush the toilets only in extremis makes sense, urine is not harmful so it can wait and they have three toilets luckily. The guest bathroom is reserved for more serious requirements and they load disinfectant when necessary. Noura had been a great proponent of disinfectant, luckily Genie kept her well supplied.

Their bodily function has greatly reduced, only once a week or so, a surprising benefit from the limited consumption of food.

Nevertheless, parts of the shining, white apartment Genie was once so proud of now smell faintly like a hospital ward.

No-one is coming to their aid.

'Sshhwh' the odd sound of air in hollow pipes gushes out from the tap. From habit and in hope, she turns it on each morning, day after day, again and again. Occasional drips collect overnight in a saucepan, enough to brush their teeth and dampen a cloth to clean their faces. They have long since abandoned trying to stay clean.

Deodorant on dirty bodies, she thinks. *Not pleasant.* She wonders what her mother would say. *What must they all be thinking without news?*

August is over. *Hard to imagine they could be like this until the food has gone.* They've used all the cans stored in the guest room. They hadn't helped survivors of Qarantina because there were none, but they had been vital for them in these past weeks.

Again she wonders what they will do? Surrender or starve? And what would surrender look like?

She opens the kitchen cupboard. A few jars of piccalilli, marmalade and three of lemon curd remain from her earlier endeavors. She'd never imagined they would become such essential sustenance when she was making them. An almost full box of powdered milk, hardly used because of the limited water available. Several boxes of crackers, three cans of sardines, two of tuna, a jar of black olives and two slightly wrinkled potatoes complete their supply.

Emergency salad Nicoise, she thinks and spots two bottles of Grenadine at the back of the cupboard alongside boxes of

Turkish Delight, gift wrapped for family back home, now co-opted to complement their emergency supplies.

The last dribble from a bottle of drinking water fills the kettle. Three full five-gallon bottles remain.

Maybe we need to start rationing. Two cups of tea each per day and a glass of pink grenadine milk, crackers and preserves? There's a pop as she lights the stove, she wonders how long the two bottles of gas will last as she opens one of the boxes of her mother's favorite treats. Powdered sugar spills on her chin as she chews the soft sweet candy.

"Baaaah." She drops the box and sprints to the rear kitchen window. A loud distressed bleat echoes up from below. The tiny sheep's bell rings out loudly.

Rob has heard and follows her.

"Baaaah." Her bleating sheep digs its front paws into the ground as two men vainly try to drag it to the truck. In the struggle the bell falls off, tinkling it rolls into the dust at the side of the road.

"No-oh." She pulls the handle to open the kitchen balcony door. Rob grabs her and holds her back.

"They must've learned it belongs to us," he says. Genie struggles, but his grip is firm.

"Don't be crazy," he says through clenched teeth.

"Yallah, hurry up." Another of the men yells. He pushes the other two aside orders them to help him. Resistance overcome, the sheep is lifted and loaded onto a truck.

"They'll kill him," she cries and runs to her gun in the kitchen doorway.

"Are you mad?" He clutches her, she struggles, and they fall to the ground. She crawls on.

"They'll kill him, they'll eat him."

The gun loses its balance and crashes to the floor between them. Rob's arms are firmly around her but she fights, they roll on the floor, she continues to grasp for the edge of the butt.

The slap on her face stings, and she recoils, stops, holds on to her cheek. Enraged she glares at him.

"What're you going to do. Shoot? Don't be stupid. If you do, they'll kill us!" he says.

The truck's engine starts, and she scrambles away from Rob to the door, peers through the glass and over the edge of the balcony. She watches, helpless as her sheep is driven off.

Rob pulls her back in, she doesn't resist. "We can't do anything, Georgina. Come away."

"I loved him. He was so gentle, demanded nothing just to be fed and protected, and we couldn't even do that." Tears fill her eyes. "They say if you save a life you're responsible for it."

"You did the best you could."

"I did nothing, they have all the power, now. The men are showing us they can take us whenever they want."

Her tears fall, and for a moment she lets herself be held as she weeps. "How could we end up like this?"

Neither of them speaks, but soon she pulls away and with robotic movements walks to the bathroom.

She scoops a little water from the saucepan, pats her face and gags as she dry brushes her teeth. Holding on to the basin she stares at the gaunt face in the mirror. *Who is that? Where did she go that innocent girl who came for a better life?* Her haunted face stares back, without answer. Brushing hair from her eyes her wedding ring catches the light, she holds out her hand, touches the ring and abandons herself to an uncontrollable sense of futility and loss.

Her weeping carries along the corridor.

Rob puts his hands over his ears. *She's not the only one who senses the desperate situation,* he thinks. A man is supposed to protect, and yet he's out of his mind wondering what waits for them, so scared in fact drink seems the only escape. He feels useless. He walks toward her, stops for a moment. *What good will it do? She'll only push me away, it's pointless,* he decides, and turns away.

Genie interrupts the broadcast Rob is tuned to.

"We should try to leave."

"You're bloody mad."

"No, I've watched them. In the evening about an hour after sunset, around nine, the girls arrive with food. They've set the table under the trees. I think we could get out while they eat, without being seen."

Rob turns to her "Listen to me. They'll catch us, and they'll kill us. Forget it."

She opens her mouth to protest, but he cuts her off.

"You think you're special, don't you? Full of bright ideas, parading around like Lady Muck! Well, let me tell you, you're not special, you're nothing. The days when being a foreigner brought respect and deference are long gone. So wake up and smell the magnolias!" He nods his head at her dying plant and smirks.

A shudder envelops her, she walks away and says. "What have you done with my husband. You're not Rob. You're some horrible stranger who occupies the place he used to be."

On the bedroom balcony, she waits for another day to end as the sun sets over the ocean. *Beautiful, as always. The sun continues every Godforsaken day on its ordained journey with no knowledge of the chaos below.*

She scans the coastline but can't relax, her idea won't go away. They have to try and help themselves. Soon she is back again at the window watching the men below, it's become an obsession. She steps quickly into the shadows to avoid being seen.

As expected the girls soon arrive. And she marches into Rob. "Come and take a look."

Resentfully he throws aside the blanket he wears around his shoulders and follows. He sees the men move almost out of sight of the building to eat.

"We should try. I know we could do it. We don't have much food left, and when that runs out, we'll be forced to choose: make a run for it, starve, or face those monsters."

Without a word, he walks away.

At noon the following day, a burst of rocket fire shakes the windows. It startles them both. Genie drops her book and runs to the open French windows. Shells fly back and forth across the valley below, presumably bombardment of another refugee camp below. It is close enough to hear but the curve of the hill blocks the view, and they can see very little.

"It's never going to end. We sit here day after day, no light, no water and soon the food will be gone," she yells. "To hell with you, you're an idiot. I'm going—tonight. You can stay and wait if you want, but you'll do it alone."

Night falls on the horizon, but way out over the ocean a series of funnel type clouds perform a dangerous dance into the overcast, grey clouded skies and approach shore.

Is this a sign? She wonders as the waterspouts grow in intensity. She is mesmerized by the spectacle and wonders if fish or sea creatures are swept into the vortex. The light fades, and rain creeps in from the ocean toward them.

She jumps. Rob's passport drops onto the bedside next to the small bag she is loading with a few essential items. She looks at him.

"I still think you're mad, but ok we'll give it a try." An enormous flash of lightning illuminates a half smile on his face. Tendrils shoot out across the night sky followed seconds later by a deafening thunderclap. Torrential rain buckets onto the terrace splashes against the windows. A full-fledged thunderstorm.

Rob sits down slowly and exhales. "So that's that. Summer is hardly over, and tonight we get a freak thunderstorm? Seems like the Gods are against us—again."

"No," she replies. "It may be perfect. Look, they won't expect us to do anything, especially not in this."

She points, below men run for cover and zip inside a temporary tent structure on the truck. It's dark and silent for the first night in weeks.

Clutching small bags, they edge their way down the stairs. She hopes no-one hears her heart pound. To be out of the apartment feels strange, vaguely overwhelming. Rob hides his emotions well, but he must also be terrified, she imagines, as he cautiously and precisely follows in her footsteps down the stairs.

They wait in the hallway. "It's not too late to turn back," Rob whispers.

But it was surprisingly easy. The storm has left the way clear.

"I'm going," she says and pulls the door open slightly. She slips through and holds the door. Rob throws his bag over his shoulder and slides through, gently closing it behind him.

They run under the house, pause, then over the low back fence into the orange groves. Out of sight, they stop for a moment.

In the heavy rain it is hard to see far ahead, but Rob signals and runs across the uneven ground, down through the trees, she follows.

"I don't remember a stream here. Bugger," Rob swears softly as his foot disappears. Covered with water, he steps back. Rain fills his mouth as he opens it to splurt out. "We have no idea where we're going."

"Let's keep moving," she calls. "Keep heading downward."

On the dark hillside, they stumble through unending orange groves. Branches claw at them and blinding rain limits visibility. Genie wipes water from her eyes and continues.

Rob clambers awkwardly onto a large rock. The sudden volume of water destabilizes the powdery hillside, and the weight of his body on the boulder dislodges it. It turns sideways and slides, washes away the ground below and takes him with it.

Genie reaches out to grab for him, but her footing is no more secure than his. As they clasp hands, she is carried downhill, too. Muddied and bruised, they come to a stop in a ditch, the boulder hits Rob in the face, rolls a little, then stops.

He cries out, she covers his mouth to muffle the sound, but a dog begins to bark not far away, then a voice. Someone has heard them. They glance at each other, across the way is Nabil's darkened house, almost halfway down the first hill. The area has been patrolled since the bombing.

Someone, presumably on patrol and suspecting looters calls out, "Khallas, stop."

They hear the dog bark approach, it must have been unleashed, and it dashes in their direction. A shot rings out, smashes into a tree close to Rob's ear. He bends to hold his arm over his head, almost deafened. They stop. Rocks slide as the dog slithers ineffectively to gain a foothold, still barking savagely, but it doesn't get a firm footing. There is a painful yelp as the owner kicks it to encourage it to try again.

Rob yanks at her arm, and they scramble desperately, grab onto roots and trees, slip, slide and climb away from the barking creature. Blood pours from an enormous gash on Rob's face and trickles into his eye, his clothes are torn, one bloodied knee pokes through his pant leg. He looks around but cannot see Genie.

What the hell are we doing? he wonders.

They abandon the chase and, aside from the hailstones which now sting their arms and heads, it is quiet. Below them the road has washed away, off to the side a barbed wire fence is a recent installation, they search for a way through, it cannot be scaled. They're lost with no passage forward, no way to escape except past the security patrol.

Rob shakes his head as he sees her clamber nearby. Making eye contact and without a word, they turn and begin the long climb through the groves, back to their apartment.

Drenched and filthy they stagger in. The rain still pounds on the windows and balconies. Covered in mud, they collapse on the floor.

Another Day—Another Dollar

An umbrella pokes out, and Rubina follows it through her open apartment door. She's covered in what looks like an enormous plastic bag. Her laundry was out overnight, and now she has to try to retrieve it from the roof before it blows away. She could not imagine such a storm at this time of year.

She stops in shock as she steps outside. The stairs and landing are covered with muddy footprints.

She can't tear her eyes away, stares at them for almost a minute and frantically turns to look through the stairwell window at the men huddled below. Her heart pounds in her chest as she runs inside, grabs a bucket of soapy water and throws it onto the telltale signs. She mops furiously, tries to scrub away all of the woes of the insane world she now inhabits.

After a few minutes of frantic scrubbing, all evidence that Rob and Genie left their home has gone. She looks toward the apartment above. She has been ordered to stay away and is too frightened to ring the doorbell and disobey.

She passes, filled with remorse, and heads to the roof.

Unaware that Rubina passes so close Genie peers despondently through the rear windows at the wet world outside. Torrential rain continues, and she is devastated that their attempt at escape was futile.

She goes over it again in her mind and wonders if they could have made it but for the rain.

The rain! It hits her, and she laughs that the realization has taken so long.

This is water! Water that's running away, precious life-giving water we've collected in tiny drips for weeks and now it pours from the sky and runs down drain holes.

Rushing from the kitchen, laden with bowls and buckets, some of which she drops as she runs to the terrace, she calls to Rob.

"Help me."

Nursing a drink, not the first of the day, understandably given the large bandage almost covering his face and one eye, Rob watches but doesn't move.

She turns, saturated. "If we're stuck here you'll need water too." Reluctantly he takes some pots, places them in line beside hers. Rain sheets across the patio and collects in the receptacles.

Back inside he dries his wet head and stares through the windows.

Clad in a bikini, Genie returns to the terrace, staying close to the wall she slowly lathers her hair with fragrant shampoo. The pounding rain cascades like a waterfall over the edge of the building from the roof, and she steps into the fast flow, leans her head back and lets the soap wash away, rubs the foam from her face. It slides down cleansing her body and a bar of soap skitters across the marble ground, she bends to retrieve it. She lathers her arms and her torso, luxuriates in the purifying sensation she has missed for weeks, She props her legs one by one onto a dining chair and smooths away all of the accumulated dust and dirt.

Rob watches each movement. He can't believe she is smiling. *What powers of recovery,* he thinks. *Just a little water and she springs right back.* He both envies and resents her resilience.

A smile on her face she raises her arms and looks at the heavens, stretches upwards. Her body is covered in bruises and deep scratches, but after so long without water this is like heaven. She feels revitalized.

The momentary joy in her face moves him, but she catches his glance, and he looks away.

With towels around her, she steps inside, closes the door and breathes in deeply. "That's the best I've felt in weeks."

He avoids eye contact, and she follows his gaze toward the rain falling into the containers and splashing across the patio.

"My grandmother called them white horses." She indicates the white spume where the rain continues. "On rainy days we'd sit at the window and watch, imagine them charging into battle or running across prairies."

He glares at her. "You think I care what your grandmother called them, or what you did as a child?"

The light goes out of her eyes. She looks at Rob's face and remembers—she no longer loves this man. No, more profound than that. She no longer likes this man.

He turns to listen to the radio.

She won't let him get to her. She feels the best she has in weeks.

The evening turns to night and Genie brings in tea. She smells sweet, clean, her hair shines, and there is a presence he hasn't seen for a long time. Thinner, but still pretty. As she pours a cup for each of them, Rob notices she has painted her nails. He continues to watch her, regrets he didn't take advantage of the rainfall earlier; nevertheless he looks neat, coordinated, has made an effort. Since the argument Rob hasn't taken another drink, a half-finished glass sits on the table. He reaches over and turns off the radio.

"We've got to talk, work it out, Genie. I've been thinking. I've written her a letter." He holds it out to her. "I should've told her I was married, that I liked being married, but things seemed so bleak here."

"It's too late now, Rob. How can you post a letter? And anyway too much has happened that can't be changed."

"I don't believe that. I'm not good at emotional stuff, you know my background. Worker bees, we never talk touch or share feelings. I have no formula to resolve this. What I do know is that you used to make me feel like a king and I miss it." He reaches out a hand. "Look at the life we've shared. I'm sorry about the anguish, I'm sorry for the affair, I'm sorry about everything, Genie. But when all's said and done, I still love you."

She picks up her cup and moves to look out of the window, avoids eye contact. "You don't even know me anymore. Being here has changed us both."

"I know I've been impossible lately, I've blamed you, but I felt shut out, lonely. I miss you."

He gets up and moves toward her, reaches for her, she flinches.

"What's that about? You think I'm going to hurt you, for God's sake?"

She just can't do this anymore. Can't pretend and hide.

"It's not that. I think we have at least to be honest with each other."

He waits.

"How can you possibly love me? Just this afternoon you were vile to me again."

She turns to face him, knows this will be the end.

"At that moment I realized, I don't know you, don't even like you anymore." She screws up her courage and goes on. "I don't want to hurt you, Rob. I just want all this to be over, I want to be free. I've fallen . . ."

"Stop! I don't want to know."

"I've fallen in love. I've made love . . ."

Rob grabs her elbows. He shakes her violently, the hot tea spills, the cup falls from her hand, crashing on the floor. She doesn't react.

"With Karam?" he spits it out, lets her go, grabs the half-drunk glass of scotch he had avoided all day and downs it in one gulp.

"Yes, with Karam. He looks at me and actually sees me, the flesh and blood human being with a beating heart and needs. He listens when I speak of my fears and doesn't brush them aside because they're inconvenient. He takes time to reassure me. He says he loves me."

"You stupid bloody woman, did you think I didn't guess when you came home in the middle of the night?" He smashes the glass, cuts his hand on the shards and wraps a tissue around it. "So why tell me now?"

"It seems you knew!"

"I suspected. That's totally different. Now what? I'm stuck here with you, and you choose to put this in my head! You did it on purpose, didn't you? For revenge?"

"What?"

"You know what. You wanted to hurt me, to punish me," Rob accuses.

"No, Rob. I did it for me, not against you. I felt betrayed, abandoned, unlovable."

"Unlovable, UNLOVABLE!" he yells. "The whole of bloody Beirut fauns all over you and I never complain. What a fucking idiot I am."

"You're not an idiot, I was in pain. So much death and destruction. With Karam I found sweetness and hope," she stops, blows her nose.

"Sniveling won't fix it."

Worn-out she leans again on the window stares at Beirut.

Karam is so close, but he could be in another solar system for how remote he seems. She turns to face Rob. "This is crazy. It's been almost ten weeks, and we could be here forever, we'll soon be out of food."

She starts to pace, straightens a picture and pulls down the lamp over the coffee table. Rob looks at the lamp but says nothing.

"We must get a message to Adnan. I can't believe the company has done nothing," she says.

"What exactly would you suggest? There's a slight fucking problem out there, or have you forgotten?" He picks up a book, ignores her. Why doesn't she just shut up and go away?

Genie stands over him.

"Oh, I know. I'll wait till dark, blacken my face, swing nimbly over the terrace under cover of night and get reinforcements. How's that?"

"Yes," she says.

He looks at her. She has finally gone insane. "I was being facetious. I'm not James fucking Bond."

"No you aren't, but you thought you were in Istanbul, didn't you?"

"Jesus Christ! I'm not going anywhere. You go!" he snaps.

"Not you. A note. My God, you're useless."

Rob springs from his seat, pushes her back against the wall, hands around her throat.

"Useless? I'm tired of being cooped up, tired of the food, of that damned lamp you keep fiddling with and most of all tired of you and your relentless optimism." He drops his hands and punches the wall.

Genie holds her throat, tries to control a cough. "I know what you feel about me. You've made it abundantly clear."

As well as his head, Rob's hand is now bandaged, too. He struggles to take wrappers from his dry cleaning then opens Genie's side of the closet and throws in the debris, it lodges on the shelf. He sees her diary in which she constantly scribbles, recording who knows what or why, and he takes it, carefully closing the door.

How much longer, before things get more violent? she wonders.

Rob's gentleness and sense of humor have left him, under extreme conditions people change.

She searches for a scarf to put around her sore throat and opens her wardrobe door, piles of garbage cascade onto her. She steps back, grabs a handful and storms along the corridor.

"Why did you throw this in my wardrobe?"

"I didn't think you'd notice," he smirks.

"You arrogant, opinionated, judgmental sod."

He smiles—enjoys her irritation. *Good, let her see what it feels like.*

She throws the rubbish at him, walks out of the lounge and bangs the door behind her, it slams so hard the glass insets shatter. He smiles to himself and turns the news back on:

New Report: Intense fighting has destroyed the most important public buildings.

"Hmm. I see how intense fighting can do that," Rob chuckles and looks at the glass which now covers the floor.

Without opening it Genie steps back in through the frame of the broken door, avoiding the glass shards which stick up, she switches off the radio.

"Have you seen my diary?"

No answer. Genie turns to leave and glimpses his smirk. "I know you have it, you ghastly human being."

He ignores her, pretends to read his magazine.

"If we ever make it out of here, I never, never want to see you again."

Another night creeps in on them, but while Genie sleeps, Rob rummages quietly in a cupboard. Slowly he takes out a toolbox, opens it and reaches in.

27

BEIRUT, EARLY FALL 1976

Disintegration

SHE CONSIDERS IGNORING HIM AND just taking care of herself, but that would be adolescent, she decides. She'll be civilized.

"Beef Wellington." On the plate Genie hands him, rice and mustard pickles nestle.

He looks at the plate. *She's finally lost the plot.*

She ignores his reaction. "I think you're right, we need to call a truce. We should ask Kourk and Rubina for help."

"She said we mustn't go to their door. They have kids, we can't put them in danger."

"I know. We should write a note, tie it to a piece of string and lower it down to Kourk's patio."

"For what? They know we're here. They can't do anything."

"In the note put the factory number and ask them to phone them. Adnan got Mark freed. He may not even know what's going on with us. He fixes things—for Abbad—the gunmen at our party. Maybe he can help to get us out?"

"Mm. Perhaps it's worth a try. We should have tried before."

The idea gives them hope. Together they search out materials. An old ball of string in the drawer, a blank page from the front of a book to write on. After back and forth discussion, Genie carefully pens the words.

Rob looks out onto the cul de sac. The men on that side busily pick their toes and various other body parts. He signals to Genie. On the corner of the opposite terrace, she lowers the note on a long string, slowly drops it down the back of the building, against the wall, almost invisible. At the top is a small bell to signal when there's a reply.

The fragrance is strong from the orange groves below, and the dark green leaves are shiny from their recent shower. It's hard to reconcile such beauty with the fighting and death across the land.

They watch the string make its descent.

Below at his door, Kourk is handing over money to a gunman, behind him the note sways unseen outside the window. The man leaves and Rubina turns, throws a hand over her mouth, she stifles a squeal as she realizes their narrow escape.

"What if he'd seen?" she cries and rips the note from the string. She glances around.

Kourk reads the note twice and lifts the telephone. "Abbad El Hassan. Sukran, Merci, thank you."

Adnan walks into the office as the Receptionist ends the phone call.

"What was that about?"

"Mr. and Mrs. Rob are alive. They can't get out of their home. They want help. I told them . . ."

"It's OK, I heard." He cuts her off and goes back to the lab. He dials and speaks quietly into a phone. He pauses, waits for the voice at the other end to recognize him.

"Last month you called and asked for news. Well, both Genie and Rob are alive—but trapped by the Phalangists." He holds the phone tight to his ear and listens to the reply. "You should think carefully. It's dangerous for a Muslim to go there. I don't even know what can be done."

Inside his apartment, Karam puts down his telephone.

So there it is, he thinks. *She could not come. But they are still here.*

A taxi climbs into the hills. As it enters the cul-de-sac, Karam immediately spots the gun truck and taps the driver on the shoulder.

"Turn around. Make it look natural."

One of the gunmen notices and walks toward them, his machine gun over his shoulder, poised and raised.

The driver waves, gives a toothy grin, completes his turn and leaves.

"Majnun. These crazy taxi drivers." The gunman relaxes and returns to his position.

Genie wears makeup again, for the second time this week, for some inexplicable reason, she feels optimistic. The broken glass from the door has been swept to one side. Rob's bandages are gone, but he still has an angry gash on his face.

"Lunch is served. Chateaubriand, fresh asparagus and new potatoes."

She sets down the tray with two plates of white rice, two glasses of pink powdered milk and a few of the remaining pickles.

"Let's make an effort. I'm sure once there is a word from us someone will help." She reaches to lower the lamp, but it doesn't move. Rob ignores her. He looks secretly pleased.

She tugs again. "What have you done? You've cut the cable, haven't you? I loved it, that's why you've ruined it."

Rob takes a mouthful, he looks smug.

"You had no right. What if I destroyed your things?"

"Go to hell."

She walks to the much-reduced bar, takes a cigar box. "Do you like this?"

She hurls it out of the window into the orange groves. She pulls off her wedding ring and holds it out for him to see.

"Or maybe this?"

The ring flies out, catching the glint of the sun as it falls into the waiting trees.

A little way down the hill the taxi pulls over and parks. The driver is nervous about this area.

"Lahtha. A minute," Karam asks.

"La, No," he responds.

"Bee Kam? How much?" They agree on a price and Karam passes over a handful of notes. It's risky here in Phalange territory, but he trusts his light coloring will make him less noticeable, unless he opens his mouth, of course. Then they'll know him for a Syrian. From the taxi, he watches the apartment building.

What on earth is going on up there? he wonders. He spots Genie spin around, hold up an unrecognizable liquor shaped bottle, watches it fly out in a wide arc and crash against a tree. There is a sound of splintering glass.

Inside she frantically searches for things to throw, Rob's eyes grow wide in dismay and he tries to grab for it, but fails.

He yells out, chases her to the patio and grabs her. He is shaking, furious, he lifts her by the throat off the ground, walks a few steps with her and pushes her hard against the wall, her feet dangle and scrape for footing. The movement pushes the air from her body, and she tries to cough, stares into his furious face.

The look of fear in her eyes astonishes him, and his fury dissipates. He drops her and without a word walks back inside. He can't believe what they have become.

From the taxi, Karam watches the attack, he is horrified and instructs the driver to flash the headlights on the car. They flash again. He was confused as the objects flew out, but seeing Rob hurt her makes him want to jump out and grab her right now.

She moves away from the window, he sucks in his breath, it seems she is not seriously hurt. He knows it would be madness to react in daylight, he watches for several more minutes then taps the driver on his shoulder, vowing to return.

"Khalas, Yalla. That is enough, go." The taxi leaves.

Outside their apartment the string jerks wildly. The bell tinkles softly and stops. With weightier matters on their minds, they neither see nor hear it.

But downstairs Kourk's arm is aching and he eyes the food Rubina has prepared, waiting on the table. He grows impatient, and he stops shaking the string.

Night falls Genie is pale and quiet, she bends over, holds her tummy and almost crawls to the bathroom. Along the corridor, she can hear Rob fiddle with a static-filled radio. The battery is too weak, and they cannot hear a thing, but she hears his anger and frustration

"Now we'll never know what's happening," he shouts out as he throws it down.

She comes out of the bathroom and calls to him. "The only possibility is to go to the car radio."

"You're a raving lunatic."

I can't go on like this, she thinks. *I feel so weak and I sure as hell won't get help from Rob.*

She thinks she probably needs a doctor. *Maybe the water from the drips has made me sick, or the meager food supplies were too old?* She doesn't know—but she is sure of one thing— they need to know what's going on out there so they can see if there's a way out. They must try something to help themselves.

Outside in the night, a darkly clad figure moves cautiously between pillars under the building, through the garden. A few feet away at the gun truck, the men eat, drink and talk to two local girls. Music plays. A fire burns.

In the reflected light she recognizes her maid's brother, he takes a stick full of roasting meat from the flames.

She crouches, runs behind a tree. Waits. Runs to another tree. She is at once exhilarated and terrified to be outside alone in the dark. Except for the failed attempt at escape in the rainstorm the other night, this is the first time she has left the building in months, and she feels vulnerable, exposed, particularly on this side of the property. The darkness may be her friend, but she doesn't trust it. Hidden from sight behind the tree Genie stays still and watches the men, one of the girls sitting with them turns. Surprised and saddened, she sees it is Noura.

They had been close, but times have changed, and she can no longer trust old connections.

Only a few steps to the car she thinks, but she would feel no more intimidated trying to cross the Berlin Wall. She senses danger all around, and her feet try to fight her, feel frozen to the earth.

The orange blossom and the olive trees smell heady. *How is it possible to notice at a time like this?* She accepts all her senses are in overdrive.

A musician starts to play nearby, startling her and bringing her back to the moment. The worst danger is standing still and doing nothing, she realizes.

She has practiced this in her mind. Bending low she creeps to the car and cautiously gets in, quickly removes the overhead bulb and holds her breath. Her heart pounds for several seconds, but no-one comes for her. Crouching low in the seat she first turns the radio volume down low then puts in the ignition key; slowly, she sucks in her breath, her brain repeats the mantra, *be careful not to switch on the engine.* As the faint sounds of the BBC news comes on the radio, she lets out her breath.

It ends, she turns it off and waits.

Across the way, outside the window, the noisy group still eats and laughs.

She opens the door and runs. A black ghost between the trees. Her breathing is heavy, her heart as loud as a snare drum. She looks back, the men still joke with the girls—no-one heard her. She got away with it!

A hand covers her mouth, and she freezes. Held from behind, hand over her face, she is slowly turned around. Her eyes grow wide, and she whispers.

"Karam. Is it possible? How?" Her backbone turns to jelly, and her knees almost give way.

He holds onto her, stops her falling, signals silence and beckons her to follow. He pulls her behind him, back into her garden on the other side of the grounds, where he pulls her into his arms. She breathes him in and raises her face to his. Their kiss is almost rough as they cling to one other.

In a soft whisper, he tells her. "I thought you had changed your mind when you did not come and made no contact. Adnan told me you were still here and no-one had seen you for weeks. Yesterday I tried to come by taxi, then tonight with no moon I thought to try again."

"They've had us trapped for nearly three months."

"Aah. That long?" He holds her away from him, searches her face, now he understands why she has been unable to contact him.

"You look pale. Are you sick?" He feels her brow. "You are hot." The music stops, and he stiffens. "Life here has become impossible, you must leave," he whispers.

"But how? You've seen them." She nods toward the men. "We can't even get near the windows on this side. They say they'll take us. How did you get here?"

"A friend with a car. He waits below. Come." He pulls her.

She puts her arms around him, holds him and rests her head into his neck, but doesn't move.

"Karam, I can't."

He holds her at arm's length and looks at her. "What are you saying? Your feelings have changed?"

"Not at all, but I can't just leave without a word to Rob."

"Genie, I saw him attack you." He pulls back to look at her. "You appear to be ill, we should find a doctor."

She shakes her head.

"Perhaps you no longer wish to leave him?"

"Karam, I do, but once he was a good husband. This place changed us. I must tell him. I have to live with myself."

A stick breaks nearby. Karam folds her in his arms, turns her away to shield her with his body. They crouch in the foliage, she feels his heart pound against her.

He searches her face as they wait, hoping not to be found. "'To thyself be true, and not be false to any'. I read your English poet, but now I think it is a mistake." He remembers Rob's words. "She has a need to save."

He tries again. "Please, please come," he urges.

More foliage breaks and they tense as a man approaches. Relief floods over her as he squats in the bushes close by to relieve himself. She lowers her face to Karam's shoulder, and they wait. Eventually, the man adjusts his trousers and walks back.

Karam pulls Genie to her feet. "You know this is insane. More attempts, more danger, but I will try to come again, with a car. In five days, on Friday. I hope we will not regret the delay. Same time. Be ready." He takes her in his arms, strokes her hair, kisses her mouth and her hands. "We must leave Lebanon. I hope loyalty will not be your fatal flaw."

She bites her lip, tears threaten. *How can I let him go and leave me behind?* But, for who they once were, she owes it to Rob to help him, too.

He brushes her tears away, holds her face in his hands and kisses her eyelids. "Go. I will watch until you are safe." He gives her a push.

When she is under the building, she turns, but Karam has disappeared.

Inside the apartment, Genie hesitates, doesn't look at Rob. *How can I explain this? He's sure to make a big deal of it.* She takes a deep breath, "David was executed last week."

"David from school? That was on the BBC?" He looks at her, incredulous.

"Karam told me," she says. "He was down there."
"What?"
"He came yesterday and saw the gun truck. He was below, watching. He came to help us."

"Us?" he says. "Do you think I'm stupid?"

"For God's sake, Rob I just told you David's dead, and you fixate on this? The point is he'll try to help us both get out at the end of the week."

But in the morning Genie writhes in her bed, soaked in sweat. When she tries to get up, she collapses on the floor. Too weak to climb in, she curls into a ball on the floor.

In the lounge Rob stirs, his tummy growls, he is hungry, Genie has been missing all day, and he hasn't eaten.

He finds Genie on the floor, lifts her onto the bed, brushes aside her damp hair and notices the yellow color of her eyes.

For the first time in months, she doesn't resist.

"I think it could be hepatitis. That's pretty serious."

Throughout the night he keeps an eye on her, Genie groans in her sleep. They have no medicine, and he knows it can be fatal, but there is little he can do. He waits, bathes her head with a cold cloth from time to time, finally, he shakes her awake.

He offers sweet tea. "You've been out of it for four days. Karam's supposed to come tonight. Can you make it?"

Dressed in black, she rests against the door and holds her tummy, two bags wait at her feet. She looks at her watch: eight fifty pm.

Rob sees she is unquestionably sick. "Are you sure you can do this?"

"I can't carry the bags, but I'll meet him."

He peeps through the spy hole in the door.

"Watch the back garden. I'll signal, then you can come with the bags."

And she is gone.

Karam drives slowly and cautiously into the hills. Excited that at last, the long wait will be over, he is nervous about seeing Rob under these circumstances. He stops his rumination, his pulse races, two half masked, heavily armed men block his way. They ask for his papers.

He fumbles. He is in trouble.

"Limadha 'ant huna? Why are you here?"

Even without papers as soon as he speaks they know him for a Syrian, they pull him from the car and drag him to a ditch at gunpoint. He doesn't resist, what would be the point? Another gunman joins them and drives the car into the bushes, he turns off the engine and puts the keys in his pocket.

Inside the dark building, Genie moves slowly. Like a wounded cat she rounds the stairwell and comes almost eye to eye with the men outside, she slips under the stairs and out of the back door.

She has never felt so weak, the tether dangles where her sheep used to graze, and she pauses for a moment to remember him, climbing slowly over the low fence she finds a place to wait and watch the orange groves below. A sharp pain hits her, and for several moments she can't breathe. No sign of Karam.

Night animals hoot, scurry and slink but she is unafraid of this danger around her. There was talk a few months ago of a jaguar in the hills and certainly foxes, wolves and even hyena could be near her in the bushes. She trembles, but she knows the real danger walks on two legs.

Loud gunshot echoes in the hills below, followed by another, startling her.

Upstairs, Rob hears the shots. He glances at the clock and heads to the terrace. Peering over he sees Beirut in the distance, but he can't see Genie.

She must have gone! "Lying bitch," he says into the air.

Toward the edge of the patio, near his feet, he notices a dirty piece of string. The bell has rusted and no longer rings, but there's a dull clunk as he pulls at it and finds a crumpled note in a plastic bag.

Deflated, he picks it up, walks inside and throws the bags in the closet. He reads the note.

When the front door opens, he is astonished. Genie walks in, doubled over and downcast. She leans on the wall and sinks to the floor.

He quietly closes the door.

"I thought . . ."

"He didn't come." She is motionless, spent.

Rob holds out the note. "Abbad's gone to Paris. Call in a month. They can't help us. No-one from that side wants to risk this area," he says and sits opposite her. They've lost their energy. "Looks like we're on our own again," he sighs.

"Paris. Living the good life at the Georges Cinq and to hell with us. We could starve to death or worse," she complains.

"It's no good having a go at me."

But she continues. "They only understand self-gratification."

"He probably didn't even think."

"Precisely. Did you know the accountant washes after shaking hands with us because we're unclean? How can we be friends when that's how they feel about us?"

"This is pointless."

"I don't want to be killed for being in the wrong place at the wrong time."

"For Christ's sake Genie, give it a rest. No-one cares what you want. I am so, so sick of you. I wish you had left me. It seems I won't have a moment's peace until you're bloody well dead and gone. I wish they'd caught you and fucking shot you," he stops, horrified as the words come from his mouth. But they cannot be unsaid.

They stare at one another in shocked silence.

28
THE GRAND FINALE

SHE RUNS OUT, STAGGERS DOWN the hill, through the trees.

How can I stay with him? At this point I don't even care what happens, I have to get away. It crosses her mind to wonder how he'll feel if they do catch her and kill her. *Who cares how he feels—guilty I hope!*

Tears stream down her face as she proceeds through the orange groves, stepping slowly. She didn't realize how incredibly weak she is but her desperation fuels her ability to press on, she couldn't stay one minute longer in the same house as Rob.

What fools we all are. I trusted Rob and I trusted Karam, now, if I want to survive I must find a way to take care of myself.

The moon disappears behind a cloud over the ocean below. The mud of last week has dried, now the path is more accessible. Nabil's house is still dark, and she wonders where they are, Dublin perhaps?

Pretty much everyone has gone now. A daily, flotilla of Lebanese sets sail from Jounieh, up the coast, to Cyprus. A column of the world's best-dressed refugees.

Now the rain has stopped she can see where the temporarily erected barbed wire fence across the hillside ends, and she slips around.

If the weather had been better last week we could have seen it, then he wouldn't have spoken those vile words today.

A stab of pain and a wave of lightheadedness hit her. *But what do the words matter, if it was already in his head?*

She leans against a tree, perspiration drips down her back, she removes her jacket, drops it on the ground. She's forced to acknowledge something serious is wrong, and she tilts her head to the sky, utters a prayer for strength and energy to whatever universal power might listen.

Her feet say she has staggered for miles, but she knows they are lying. She stumbles on through the final field dragging her jacket and is rewarded with her first glimpse of car headlights as they drive along the main coast road below.

In five minutes she reaches the junction between the highway and their small tributary road into the hills and almost falls the last few steps into a ditch at the side of the main road.

An approaching car heads south on the main highway at breakneck speed, almost hitting her.

She steps back. In the bushes, half hidden, she bumps into the edge of an empty vehicle. *An odd place to park.* She knows there are no homes in the immediate vicinity.

A faint whisper disturbs her, and she forgets the pain in her body as fingers of fear claw at her. Who could be here? The only people who pass by this corner are residents heading into the hills above, they wouldn't be out on foot. *Could it be a neighbor? Did something happen to the car?*

She steps back, looks around carefully in the dark. She covers her mouth to prevent a gasp escaping. The leg of a man protrudes, half hidden by the foliage. She steps back. It sticks out at an odd angle from his knee, probably broken. She recoils further, remembers the torso by the roadside last January.

She has come this far, she needs to keep on, she tells herself.

But this is not a dead body, it moves, and she hears a soft groan. The sound is weak, but she can't mistake the voice.

"Is this a mirage?" he says.

"How is it possible? You came."

He tries to reach a hand out to her but has no strength, it falls to the ground. "Of course I came," he whispers.

Spread out in the ditch, weak and washed in blood, Karam can barely move.

"I think my ribs may be cracked. They shot my leg, and I am a little worried about my lung." He holds one arm across his body and tries to laugh. It hurts, and he stops.

"Look at us. Perhaps this was always our destiny, the rest was a bewitching and bewildering dream."

She tilts her head back, chokes on her tears. "I'll get help," she says. He is too weak to stop her and with a spurt of strength she runs to the main road.

A couple of military vehicles trundle by but don't stop, she coughs as the dust flies in her face. A car passes, guns poke through open windows. Young men's voices shout and loud Arabic music screams out from the car radio. She ducks out of sight.

Cars pass on the other side, heading north, but few come in her direction. She grows desperate, but finally, a large vehicle approaches and slows, prepares to turn into the hills.

She stands on the edge of the road. "At last," she says. "I stopped a car."

The lights momentarily blind her, and she shades her eyes, waves frantically. It slows to a stop.

Karam tries to speak. But groans at a pain in his chest.

"Hold on for a moment, help is here," she calls over her shoulder to Karam and wipes dusty tears from her face.

The car passes her, then slows and pulls over, the engine stops. She hears the clip of hard shoes on the tarmac, her view is blurred by the incandescence of a flashlight as a man gets out and slowly approaches. She turns, shields her eyes. As he gets close, she sees the brown-shirted uniform of the Christian militia, with two words she cannot read in this light, inscribed on the breast pocket. She knows it indicates Lebanese Phalange.

Oh, God, she thinks. *What now?* She scurries back to Karam as the man approaches, then stares in horror and absolute shock.

"My God, Victor, not you? You're one of them?"

"Not just one of them, Genie. I am the head of this area."

"Look what they've done."

Victor nods at Karam whose eyes are closed. "It's too late. I'm afraid I can't help him." He takes one of her arms. "Come."

"No, we can't leave him. Please, help him," Genie begs, and turns to cradle Karam. He groans.

She is also weak, and Victor easily pulls her away. She tries to resist, pummels him, but she has little strength, her strikes are those of a small child, he smiles.

This new weak creature is so changed from the woman who wanted to defend the world.

"How could you let them do this? We were all friends. How could you?"

His driver walks over and grabs her harshly, holds her as she rants.

"Make no mistake. I am your friend. Without my special regard for you, you'd be dead. I protected you, didn't let them come and take you. I hoped you'd capitulate. Now your friend, probably a Syrian spy, comes to rescue you and I am forced to act." Victor speaks matter of factly, without emotion.

Genie glances at his face, but it reveals nothing. "He's not only my friend, but he was also yours!"

"Friendships have altered. This is a fight for our existence. Now. Get in the car."

She recalls those same words uttered, what seems like years ago, by Karam. "We fight for our existence."

She shudders as the driver releases her.

"I won't leave him."

Victor reaches for her, but she pulls away.

"Enough of this. You are not a child. You see how it is. If you come now," he pauses. "You have my word; we will not kill him. It will be in the hands of the Gods."

Genie bends to Karam. "Tell me what to do," she begs. "If I go with them maybe it'll give you a chance?"

He squeezes her hand. "You must go," he whispers. "Always remember, you were my eyes, my heart, and my life. Ya Ayuni, ya albe, ya hayati."

She covers him with her shawl and tries to reach for his face, but the driver picks her up like she's no more than a bag of cotton balls. He half carries, half drags her and throws her into the car, enjoys the control he exercises. She tries to look out of the window, the last look, unable to control the tears. As soon as the door closes they drive off in silence, she rocks back and forth, ignores Victor, a man she believed she knew.

God, what a place. Who can you trust?

His voice breaks through. "I'll come for you in the morning. I'll help you to leave Beirut. If you remain after that, it will be out of my hands, I fear you will both die." Slowly he helps her out of the car. She tries to avoid eye contact and walks painfully and slowly back to the apartment.

The driver glances conspiratorially as the men watch from the gun truck.

In the darkness of the bedroom, she painfully revisits the past few weeks. Tomorrow it will all be over, one way or the other.

Outside, in the distance, bombs explode, interspersed with sporadic bursts of machine gun fire. Inconsolable, Genie puts her face in the pillows to mask her sobs. Pale and red-eyed, she continues to weep quietly for what seems like hours. *For so long I've wished for the chance to leave and put it behind me. Now my head is in such a state of turmoil I can't process the idea.*

Finally, she drifts into a fitful sleep.

Rob packs the last of the few things they can take with them. He retrieves her diary, a wedding photo falls out. His tears come, and he doesn't wipe them away. Big, silent sobs rack his body. Unshaven and thin, he has a crisis of conscience, *What a mess we've made.* He lights the candle beside her and watches over her.

Outside the gunmen crouch around an open fire wrapped in blankets. One glances up when he sees a faint light flicker above.

"Look. Look there. We sleep on the ground, and those two have soft beds to rest in. It's time we ended this."

Angrily a murmur of agreement spreads. One grabs a gun and strides toward the building.

Noura drops her bag of food, chases after him and bars his way.

"Stop. You think Monsieur Victor will not punish you? He guards this woman. This is not wise," she turns around to face her brother. "Do you forget, brother, she has often been good to me—to us?"

She reaches out, smiles at him and persuades him back to the fire. The other men watch, away from the flames they have lost interest and slowly return to seek warmth at the fire. One picks up a mijwiz, another a lute. Noura hums with the music, her voice grows stronger, and they relax.

From inside Rob hears the music which Genie had always loved. Tonight it holds nothing but sadness.

Outside the bathroom the morning sun lights the magnolia, it is bent over, brown and dead. Genie leans against the basin, she has no strength.

Rob pulls a bag from the closet, and the radio falls out. The jolt gives it a burst of life, static sounds give way to the voice of a radio announcer:

Karam Sulman, son of the Syrian writer and intellectual, was found today on the coast road outside Beirut severely beaten and with two bullet wounds. He remains in critical condition in the American University Hospital. In further developments . . .

Rob switches off the radio and folds her in his arms. "I'm sorry about Karam, about all of it. I didn't mean the things I said, Genie. I lost sight of what's important."

Her body shakes. "I hate them. God, how I hate them."

"But he's alive!" he reminds her.

A sharp rap startles them. Victor is flanked by two unsmiling men. He is in uniform, a pistol on his hip, He moves to kiss Genie, she recoils, and he glances at the Kalashnikov still resting in the doorway.

"This letter will take you through most of the barricades. There are now 22 factions so be careful to whom you show it. Do NOT show it to any Muslim group or they will surely kill you on the spot."

He produces a map for Rob which keeps them to the mostly Christian side of the Green Line, with a crossing marked at the Museum.

Genie avoids eye contact as he escorts them to their car.

"Whatever you may now think, you were special to me, Genie," he tells her. "Long ago I said you'd never understand. Someday in the future when you reflect, I hope you will remember I have been your friend. I wish this could have ended differently, for us and for Lebanon."

"Thank you, Victor," Rob says and shakes his hand. "We appreciate you looking out for us."

He climbs in beside Genie.

The fighters do not bother them as they walk to their car, Rob carries two small suitcases. They have left behind almost all they possess in the world, mementos, treasures, books, family photos, everything from their life here. He is convinced they will soon be back.

Before they are out of the cul de sac, the men have climbed into their vehicle and are packing.

Rubina and Kourk are on the balcony weeping silently. Genie looks up at them from the car window and waves as they disappear from view—forever.

The road down the mountain is quiet, as they turn onto the main road, she sees the car Karam had been driving, still half hidden in the bushes.

Further along the coast are inescapable signs of the conflict. The road takes them into town, and they approach the first barricade, Rob holds Victor's permit.

They wait, two cars in front of them a man is dragged from his vehicle, two grubby men in uniform lift full gas cans from his trunk. They shake the cans, open them and douse him with the contents.

One takes a box of matches from his pocket and strikes. The man's eyes widen, and he begs. "La, no."

The flame flickers, and he is set on fire, a human candle. His screams are unbearable, from an unimaginable agony.

Genie whimpers and Rob shoots out a hand to cover her mouth. He pulls her head to him, shields her ears.

"They don't allow smuggling. Don't do or say anything, please. We could die." Rob whispers.

She nods.

The guard walks to the window, points at a tall, shell pitted edifice. "There's a sniper in that building. Y'allah, Ruhah, get going. But not in straight line."

They slalom between unrecognizable buildings, avoiding sniper fire. Bullets whistle past and narrowly miss them.

In a building in front, unseen by Genie and Rob, they are lined up in the crosshairs of a rifle scope. A bullet is released smashing into the windshield, and they swerve violently.

Genie screams, Rob fights to recover control of the car, peers through the hole in the windshield and accelerates.

"Are you OK, have you been hit?" he asks. He swerves and drives on, without time to look at Genie.

She shakes her head. "I'm OK, you?"

"Yes."

They race through a blackened, burnt out city.

The once beautiful buildings and glamorous hotels are no more, many are merely blackened shells. Water runs from broken pipes and sputters down the sides of shell shattered edifices, it splashes to the ground into rotten piles of indeterminate origin.

In the distance a fierce battle rages, massive shelling gets louder. They drive fast and don't speak.

An occasional piece of vegetation pokes through the broken asphalt, and mangey dogs scavenge amongst the rubble and rubbish, some fight over the scraps they find. Smoke fills the air, the road is strewn with carcasses; a cow and a couple of donkeys. Dark feathered birds screech as they claim their lunch.

A few lumpy piles of clothing dotted around are probably bodies. Here and there, in pools of mud, they glimpse a foot or an arm attached to the rotting fabric, almost molded into the earth.

The smell permeates the car. It is awful, overpowering—stinks like rotten meat, probably from the dead bodies still inside the abandoned buildings.

Genie coughs, covers her nose. "Be careful which way you go."

With Victor's documents, they get to Hamra in one piece.

Hamra was her first exposure to Beirut. The area which seduced her, made her fall deeply in love, more than four years ago.

Now she looks around at the familiar landmarks. It has been damaged less than many other areas. They find sanctuary at The Commodore Hotel until recently filled with the buzz of activity from international journalists. It is quieter here now, only a few diehards remain.

With only Lebanese money, now worth pennies on the pound, they are just able to place a call to the factory and Adnan is at the other end of the line. Rob gets a lump in his throat as they speak.

"We've shifted the main production to Tehran," he tells Rob. "Only a few are left here, it's a ghost town, but I still haunt the place and report to Abbad in Paris. It's good to hear your voice."

Rob is silent for a moment, fights to stop the quake in his voice. "We're at The Commodore. We need to get out. Can you help us?"

Adnan in his usual understated, uncomplicated way assures Rob.

"I will fix it."

Genie is doubled over on the bed, asleep. Rob has found morphine for her through the hotel manager, who introduced someone who may have once been a doctor, but who no longer has a home, a surgery or a hospital, and now spends his last few lire at the bar below. The doctor assures them she does indeed have hepatitis.

"All we can do is help you rest," Rob tells her. "He says we have to wait for it to pass." He doesn't add the doctor's other news, thirteen people have died from the outbreak. Against the number of deaths from other causes, it seems insignificant.

The following day, true to his word, Adnan collects them. Shana and the children are with him. Their car is loaded with bags.

"The only airline operational is MEA, they can fly you to Amman. I called Stuart, and he will meet you, help you find flights on from there as soon as he can."

Shana puts an arm around Genie.

"Adnan agrees with you, we will be safer in London," Shana says in her familiar Irish lilt. "I don't want to leave him, but for the children . . ." She doesn't finish.

The drive to the airport is a blur for Genie. The morphine has helped reduce the pain, but she is in a less than aware state as she goes through all of the motions and, happily for Rob, she merely follows instructions.

The farewells at the airport are tearful. Shana and the kids cling to Adnan, they don't want to let him go.

"We'll be back in a few weeks when it's calm," Rob assures him.

Genie stays silent, she will never return. She has made her own pact with whatever Supreme Being is out there, to allow her to live, and in return, she promises she will never, ever come back.

Inside the plane a stewardess offers Rob a newspaper. He points at a headline.

"Lucky we made it. No airport access for months from our area after last night's explosion at the Museum."

Genie closes her eyes and tunes to a radio channel. The pain is almost too much as the voice of Diana Ross sweetly sings, tears at her heart and whisks her back to a small studio apartment filled with candlelight:

Touch me in the morning then just walk away.
We don't have tomorrow, but we had yesterday.

He sees her tears and takes her hand. His lips move, and she tears herself away from the memories, pulls the pneumatic headset from her ear to listen.

"It's all behind us now. We made it out whole," Rob says.

"Did we?"

The plane takes off, and the strain has already started to lift from Rob's face.

It may be behind him, she thinks. But for the rest of her life, she knows she will look over her shoulder. Every clap of thunder, each bang of a door or the backfire of an engine will take her back. Back to these days of passion and pain. The days when her world disintegrated.

The End

POST SCRIPT

THIS IS INSPIRED BY ACTUAL events and in some cases by real people, but the stories woven are from my imagination. The individuals acted only as an inspiration and added some authenticity.

I loved Lebanon. But with the benefit of a rearview mirror, I can see my story amounts to "no more than a hill of beans," to use a famous quote, when set against the wider canvas of the crumbling middle east.

I found the people to be hospitable, charming and generous. I am neither a politician nor an historian, but even I, as a stranger in a foreign land, recognized the same names recurred over and over when mentions were made of power. The feudal nature of a land where the sons are groomed by the fathers to take their place leaves little possibility or hope of real substantive change.

To have experienced the warmth extended to me, juxtaposed against the awful things that were done, is schizophrenic. Injustice, poverty, loss, and fear are monstrous motivators to conflict. There is little doubt, although the people have a history of tribalism, they do not relish the yoke which keeps them in poverty, no matter who is the ruler, no matter what his or her religion.

When I look and see the destruction the middle east conflict has spawned, the ruin of the lives of millions of Syrians, Iraqis, Lebanese, Libyans and on and on; as well as the terror we all now face every day in the west, I remember those times when it was all beginning.

My characters I have named Rob and Genie, and I have written them as we were—innocents. We thought ourselves sophisticated as we escaped the UK, land of strikes and shortages in the early 1970s, and as we found a life in the upper echelons of the new land. But we were young, caught in a circumstance of which we could have no real understanding.

ACKNOWLEDGMENTS

THANKS GO TO MY SUPPORTIVE and wonderful husband, Tom Lanny, my first reader, my partner, and my biggest supporter in all things. Thanks also to Shaun Jefford, for convincing me to convert this story from a script to a novel, and to Roger Perry for continually spurring me forward. I am grateful for the encouragement of Eva Garcia Mendoza, and Erin Servais my editor, who encouraged me by loving the story, and to Martyn Ravenhill for his technical tips.

The staff at Scribe made it possible to craft my manuscript into more than I had imagined. My thanks go to them all. To Steve Ushioda, who was always available and generous with unstinting advice and support. Bethany Luckenbach and Jeff DeBlasio for their patience, help, and attention to detail. Also to Tim Durning for his evocative designs and exceptional skill, and the uncanny ability to fulfill his commitments.

CPSIA information can be obtained
at www.ICGtesting.com
Printed in the USA
BVHW031135020719
552377BV00008BA/900/P